THIRTEEN FANTASTICAL TALES FOR THE END OF DAYS

Featuring authors:

Keith R.A. DeCandido
John L. French
Roy Mauritsen
Edward J. McFadden III
Samantha Mills & Briana Vandenbroek
Terri Osborne
Jordan Petti
KT Pinto
Matt Schiariti
Hildy Silverman
David Lee Summers
Patrick Thomas
Robert E. Waters

Edited by Diane Raetz

www.padwolf.com

Other books by Diane Raetz:
New Blood edited by Diane Raetz & Patrick Thomas.
Once More Upon A Time, a Mystic Investigators book
by Patrick Thomas & Diane Raetz.

Apocalypse 13
Anthology published by Padwolf Publishing, Inc.
Padwolf Publishing & logo are registered trademarks of Padwolf Publishing, Inc.

Padwolf Publishing Inc.
PO Box 117 Yulan, NY 12719
www.padwolf.com

Edited by Diane Raetz
Padwolf 13 Series Managing Editor: Patrick Thomas
Art Director for Padwolf Publishing & Padwolf 13 series: Roy Mauritsen
Cover art "Uh-Oh" by Roy Mauritsen. Used with permission
First Printing, October 2012
Copyright © 2012
Printed in the United States of America

ISBN 978-1-890096-49-6

Ragnarok and Roll by Keith R.A. DeCandido, copyright © 2011
Many Hands And Other Parts by Patrick Thomas, copyright © 2012
A Plague On The Land by John L. French, copyright © 2012*
Counting Sheep Among The Stars by Edward J. McFadden III, copyright © 2012
Mirror, Mirror by Samantha Mills & Briana Vandenbroek, copyright © 2012
Hollow (Be Careful What You Wish For) by Matt Schiariti, copyright © 2012
A Garden Resurrected by David Lee Summers, copyright © 2012
A Djinn, A Werewolf, and Grey Walk Into a Bar by Terri Osborne, copyright © 2012
Black Market Magic byHildy Silverman, copyright © 2012
Indeh by Robert E. Waters, copyright © 2012
Norman's Ark by Roy A. Mauritsen, copyright © 2012
There's Something In The Earth by Jordan Pettit, copyright © 2012
By Invitation Only by KT Pinto, copyright © 2012

*Characters & locations used in this story- Nemesis, Paddy Moran and Bulfinche's Pub are copyright © and Trademark ™ by Patrick Thomas and used with Permission.
All stories contained in this volume have been used with the permission from the authors who retain the ownership to their works. All rights reserved. This book or any portion thereof may not be reproduced or used in any manner whatsoever without the express written permission of the publisher. No part of this publication may be reproduced, distributed, or transmitted in any form or by any means, including photocopying, recording, or other electronic or mechanical methods, without the prior written permission of the publisher, except in the case of brief quotations embodied in critical reviews and certain other noncommercial uses permitted by copyright law. For permission requests, write to the publisher at the address above. This is a work of fiction. Names, characters, businesses, organizations, places, events and incidents either are the product of the author's imagination or are used fictitiously. Any resemblance to actual persons, living or dead, events, or locales is entirely coincidental.

To Lilith
Because your texts brighten my day

Acknowledgements:
There are many people who helped make this anthology happen-but two in particular must be thanked. Patrick Thomas who nagged me to 'make it happen' when I was distracted by the joys and horrors of buying a house and Roy Mauritsen; an extremely talented writer and artist who designed a front and back cover that far exceeded my dreams.
Thanks guys. I couldn't have done it without you!

Table Of Contents

INTRODUCTION
page 5

RAGNAROK AND ROLL by Keith R.A. DeCandido
page 6

MANY HANDS AND OTHER PARTS by Patrick Thomas
page 31

A PLAGUE ON THE LAND by John L. French
page 40

COUNTING SHEEP AMONG THE STARS by Edward J. McFadden III
page 60

MIRROR, MIRROR by Samantha Mills & Briana Vandenbroek
page 73

HOLLOW (BE CAREFUL WHAT YOU WISH FOR) by Matt Schiariti
page 90

A GARDEN RESURRECTED by David Lee Summers
page 103

A DJINN, A WEREWOLF, AND GREY WALK INTO A BAR by Terri Osborne
page 114

BLACK MARKET MAGIC by Hildy Silverman
page 127

INDEH by Robert E. Waters
page 145

NORMAN'S ARK by Roy A. Mauritsen
page 163

THERE'S SOMETHING IN THE EARTH by Jordan Petti
page 176

BY INVITATION ONLY by KT Pinto
page 197

AUTHOR BIOGRAPHIES
Page 205

Introduction

The large screen television blared unthinkable news. Libya had launched "The Bomb." Other nations, including the one that was nominally his own, were preparing to retaliate. The Apocalypse was upon them.

Hands shaking he pulled down his suit jacket and straightened his tie. Even though he'd been trained for this moment since childhood he wasn't able to approach it without fear, without horror, without pain. What he was about to do was irrevocable. It would change the past and present of every creature on earth from the smallest amoeba to the largest kraken that resided in the oceans depths.

The bottom desk drawer sprung open in response to his fingerprint. The lead lined box creaked open after scanning his eyeball. His great grandmother had been the last one to open the box. She'd used a wand. One of the billion changes that had occurred since the last use was the planet's reliance on technology. He wondered what would hold sway next time.

From the box he took computer-one unlike any other in the world. This one, appearing to have been made of an iridescent crystal, had a holographic screen filled with a countdown, currently showing 45 seconds. Now that the decision had been made and the moment was upon him he moved with assurance. His fingers flew across the keys and as he inputted the critical code. The world stood still as the countdown froze; its decline paused at 3 seconds.

Up came the critical question. "Are you sure you want to delete this file."

There was no hesitation as he hit "Yes." The television went black, the world outside of the luxurious bunker no longer in existence. Moving surely he inserted a disc into the computer and waited. Moments later he typed in "Install."

The computer changed into a small altar. "Ah," the man thought to himself, "The gods would rule this creation. It could be worse." He placed the small altar into the lead box that had stretched to fit the new shape and secured it in the base of the desk. Then he strolled over to the book shelf, took down a very specific leather bound book and carried it to the desk. Mourning the small loss of simple luxuries like pens in this incarnation he took and quill and dipped it into the inkstand beside him. Opening the book to the title page he crossed out the 13 under Apocalypse and wrote in 14. He then flipped to the first empty page and began to enter his story, wondering how it would stand against the master works of his predecessors: Keith R A DeCandido, Patrick Thomas, John French, Edward McFadden, Samantha Mills, Briana Vandenbroek, Matt Shiariti, David Lee Summers, Terri Osborne, Hildy Silverman, Robert Waters, Roy Mauritsen, Jordan Pettit and KT Pinto.

Outside waves crashed against the shore. The wind rustled leaves in the world tree. A rooster crowed marking the dawning of a new day and creatures small and large began to stir.

Author, musician, gamester and all around Renaissance man, Keith DeCandido gives us this very unusual tale of a subpar cover band that nearly brings about Ragnarok and the scuba diver that fights the inevitable.

Ragnarok and Roll
by Keith R.A. DeCandido

It was Thursday night in Key West. Thursday, Friday, Saturday, and Sunday nights always meant the same thing for me: head to Mayor Fred's Saloon, order a pint of beer, and sit down to watch 1812 play.

So I was kinda surprised to walk in and see a different band on stage tuning up.

"What the *fuck*?"

Mira, the Goth waitress (not to be confused with Adina, the mousy student waitress, or Lainie, the beach bunny waitress), was walking past me as I entered the open-air saloon and asked that very loud question. She stopped in mid-delivery of two glasses of some kind of froofy pink concoction—yes, I'm female, but I don't do girly drinks—to say, "Hey, Cassie. Yeah, 1812's kinda takin' a break."

I frowned. "Hey, Mira. What does that mean, exactly?"

Mira tilted her raven-haired head to the side in a manner she probably thought was meaningful. "Well, they *still* can't find a drummer after—you know."

I nodded. Zeke Bremlinger, their drummer, was killed by a nixie in the Gulf of Mexico last month. "This island's *full* of musicians, they can't find a drummer?"

"Not a permanent one. C'mon, Cassie, you *know* what drummers are like." Mira shuddered.

"I *told* you that Terry was a bad idea," I said with a grin. Terry was a drummer Mira had dated for all of two weeks before he flaked out on her, which was a week-and-a-half longer than I thought it would take him.

"Yeah, yeah." She rolled her eyes. "I'm surprised Bobbi didn't tell you."

"She didn't dive this week." I worked part-time as a dive-master at Seaclipse, a dive shop on Stock Island, and 1812's guitarist Bobbi Milewski was one of my regulars. "In fact, she cancelled Tuesday. Now I know why, I guess."

"Uh huh. The usual pint?"

I nodded. "When you get a chance."

She moved on to serve her customers. I looked around for an empty table, of which there were many. When 1812 was playing, I usually sat to the left—as far away from the pool tables as possible, as that would only get me in trouble—but near the

6

front. That gave me a nice view, but allowed other people to get closer. Or I'd sit by the big ficus tree that Mayor Fred's had been built around. (Back in the 19th century, it was Key West's hanging tree.)

This time, though, I thought maybe it'd be best to take a table near the back, by the big glass table where they sold Mayor Fred's merchandise: T-shirts (I was wearing one tonight, as it happened), shot glasses, postcards, mouse pads, keychains, and so on, all with Mayor Fred's logo. The merch table was conveniently located near the exit, the ideal place to be in case this new band sucked.

Which, let's face it, they probably would.

All right, it was only fair that 1812 needed a break. Having your drummer get killed by a mythical creature really took the zing out of your motivation to play music four times a week. But dammit, they were *good*.

I made a mental note to give Bobbi a call tomorrow. Wasn't sure what more I could do—I already killed the damn nixie—but what're friends for, right?

Still, it was weird not seeing them on a Thursday night.

Upon achieving my hard-won Masters Degree in English Literature from the University of California-San Diego last spring, I'd decided to spend a few months driving across the bottom of the country in Rocinante, my battered old 1985 Ford F-150 pickup truck: Grand Canyon, Albuquerque, Austin, New Orleans, Biloxi, the Everglades, and finally Key West. I figured I'd stay for a week or so, spend my days scuba diving, my nights at the bars on Duval Street, and then head back home to start on my PhD.

After two nights of karaoke, mediocre cover bands, old farts with acoustic guitars, silly dance halls, and more covers of "Brown-Eyed Girl" than I ever expected to hear in a 48-hour time period in the places on Duval, I finally turned the corner onto Greene and found this open-air bar with a huge fish over the entrance, a big tree in the center, and a four-piece band on the stage that was plowing through "Sunshine of Your Love."

Two were up front: On left-handed guitar, a short blonde white woman in a white T-shirt and blue sweat pants; on bass, a tall black man with dreadlocks, wearing sunglasses, an open button-down T-shirt, and drawstring pants. Behind them were another short blonde on the keyboards—she came up front to play a second guitar or mandolin every once in a while—and a short, round white guy with a shaved head, and the world's longest chin-beard behind the drumkit. That last was the late Zeke Bremingler.

Bobbi's the lead guitarist, and she was like a buzzsaw on Clapton's riff. They followed that with "Love Reign O'er Me," where the keyboardist—Jane Ann Naharodney, who insisted on the stage name "Jana Naha"—made the piano sound like a waterfall. But what won me over was when they did Paul Simon's "You Can Call Me Al." Not only did Chet Smith nail the bass line, but Jana whipped out a tin whistle for that solo. Even Simon used a keyboard for that when he played it live.

Best of all, they didn't play "Brown-Eyed Girl" once. Or "Freebird," for that matter.

After my week-long trip entered its second month, I started talking to the band. By then I'd spent enough time at Seaclipse that they were thinking about hiring me, especially since I was a certified dive-master *and* I knew how to steer a boat. Luring not only Zeke, Bobbi, and Jana, but all six of Bobbi's dive-nut brothers to take their business to Seaclipse did the trick. I'd become good friends with Bobbi, Jana, and Zeke, and Chet tolerated my being in his presence. (He's a bass player, what do you want?)

Nine months later, it was a rare 1812 gig I didn't show up for. Sometimes there were odd circumstances—I was sick, they needed me to run a night dive at Seaclipse, having to get that dragon out of the garden of the B&B I was living in—but I'd tried very hard never to miss a gig.

This was the first one *they'd* missed.

I looked at the new band. They were setting up, plugging in, tuning, and so on. Well, most of them were. There was this one guy, not too tall, with flowing blond hair, a red-blond goatée, ice-blue eyes, and one of those physiques that men probably thought impressed women, but which bitter experience has told me usually meant the guy was compensating for anatomical deficiencies elsewhere. He was standing off to the side, trying to look important while not actually doing anything.

He just *had* to be the lead singer.

Mira came over with my beer. "So who are these guys?" I asked as I grabbed it and gulped down a quarter of it at once.

"They're called Jötunheim."

Running the back of my wrist across my mouth, I asked, "Seriously?"

Nodding, Mira said, "Yeah, with those two dots over the O."

"An umlaut? Geez." I shook my head and looked over at the lead singer, who was now chatting with a woman in a tank top and shorts who'd just come out of the rest room. "How Nordic. And short, blond, and sinewy over there looks like a Viking who wandered into the wrong century anyhow, so the name kinda fits."

"Actually, he's kinda cute."

I whirled and stared at Mira. That drummer, Terry, that she dated? She went out with him because he was very tall, extremely skinny, and had dark hair, which put him in company with every other guy Mira had dated in the nine months I'd been living in Key West. Jötunheim's lead singer was the exact opposite of her type.

She also had this goofy smile on her face. Mira had dark hair, pale skin, wore all-black even in the hot sun of Key West, had black nail and toe polish, and smoked like a chimney. I think I've seen her smile once, maybe.

So why the hell was she getting moony-eyed over *that* guy?

A signal from another table got her attention and she went off to help them, so I didn't get the chance to ask her about it. Reaching into the pocket of my shorts, I pulled out my smartphone and looked up Jötunheim. Unfortunately, all the references I could find online were either to Norse mythology, Marvel Comics, or World of Warcraft, so not much help there.

By the time my beer was down to almost nothing, the band was ready to start. Ihor, the bartender, grabbed the PA microphone and said, "Okay, everyone, let's have a big Mayor Fred's welcome for Jötunheim!"

The applause that followed was a mix of excited and reluctant. I went for a good old-fashioned golf-clap, myself—just enough to be polite.

"Good evening, Key West!" the singer said into the microphone up front. Next to him, the two guitarists—one acoustic, one electric—and the bass player were doing some last-minute tuning. I noticed a violin on a stand on the floor next to the acoustic guitarist, and I shuddered. A good fiddler was a noble thing, but a bad fiddler could absolutely and irrevocably destroy a band's entire sound forever.

"My name's Gunnar Rikardsen, and we are Jötunheim."

I shook my head and chuckled. With a name like that, he almost *had* to call the band Jötunheim, didn't he?

The electric guitar broke into the eleven-note riff from the Beatles' "Day Tripper." As openers went, it wasn't a bad choice. Everyone knew the song, and it bounced, so it might get a few feet onto the dance floor—which at Mayor Fred's was just the bit of floor between the stage and the bar.

Having said that, the rendition wasn't anything special. I mean, the notes matched what Lennon and McCartney did, but there wasn't any oomph.

So imagine my surprise when the song ended and the applause practically shook the beer glasses off the tables, it was so raucous.

I'd only heard applause like that in Mayor Fred's once before, about two months back. That night, 1812 was particularly *on*. It was Saturday, the place was packed, including about a dozen college students there for somebody's birthday, and they'd just *killed* with everything they did. The birthday boy asked for a Bob Dylan song, and they decided to do "Like a Rolling Stone." Jana's keyboards pierced the crowd, filling the room with the five-note organ bit during the chorus, Bobbi did a buzzsaw of a guitar solo, and Chet, Jana, and Bobbi all sang "How does it feel" in three-part harmony with so much energy that I got goosebumps just listening to them. I still get them, thinking about it.

The Thursday night crowd at Mayor Fred's, which was about half the size, responded with the same enthusiasm to this mediocre version of "Day Tripper" that Saturday night crowd two months ago to the most transcendent version of "Like a Rolling Stone" I've ever heard in my life.

And it only got worse. Don't get me wrong, they were a perfectly adequate cover band, but that just made them like everybody else on the island. None of the musicians screwed up anything—which actually put them one up on some of the guys on Duval Street—and Gunnar had a nice little tenor that he didn't strain too much.

But the crowd just ate it the hell up. It was like they'd gotten into a time machine to see the Rolling Stones in 1971 or something.

There was only one other person who didn't seem impressed: an older guy with a shock of white hair, sitting up front near the speakers. He nursed an amber drink of some kind—bourbon? Scotch?—and seemed to be very much not enjoying himself. I wondered why he didn't just leave.

I wondered the same thing about myself. After the crowd went batshit for the most uninteresting version of "House of the Rising Sun" ever, I noticed the second guitarist picking up the violin, at which point I finally gave up. No way was I subjecting myself to that.

I finished off my second pint of beer, got up, and headed out. I didn't pay my tab before I left. Normally that wasn't an issue, especially on a Thursday, because I'd be back the next three nights. Now, though, I wasn't so sure.

Still, everyone who worked there knew where I lived and where I worked. Hell, Mira, Lainie, and Adina probably all had my debit card number memorized...

I walked out onto Greene Street, the evening breeze blowing through the rat's nest of blond curls that I laughingly refer to as my hair. It wasn't even midnight yet, so there were plenty of folks on the street, and I found my mood—already soured by what just happened in Mayor Fred's—worsened by having to landshark through throngs of drunken tourists, drunken college students, and drunken locals.

(The way you told them apart, in case you were wondering, was simple. The tourists crashed into you and then apologized; the students crashed into you and *didn't* apologize; and the locals were able to avoid crashing into you.)

Luckily, after I made the right onto Duval, it was only a couple of blocks to Eaton Street. Cover bands, drunken shouting, and wretched karaoke all competed for my ears' attention. I was so used to closing Mayor Fred's down at four in the morning that I forgot what a zoo Duval turned into between the hours of ten p.m. and two a.m.

Just as I was about to cross Caroline Street, walking past the Bull and Whistle, a shit-faced white guy walked up to me, beer dripping from his five-o'clock shadow—which was getting into prime time at this point—and asked, "Where'za strip clubs at?" Then he squinted. "You're fuckin' tall, lady."

"I'm also tall when I'm celibate," I said with a smirk. At 5'11", I got that a lot. Then I gave him directions to the Mel Fisher Maritime Museum, which closed over six hours ago.

"Nicely done," came a voice from behind me. I turned to see Lio, the six-seven, no-necked bouncer for the Bull. "Shoulda known you could handle his drunken ass on your own, but I was here for backup just in case."

"'Preciate that, Lio," I said with a smile. I'd never actually encountered Lio anywhere but in the doorway to the Bull, but since that bar was a block from where I lived, and halfway between it and my primary night-time destination, we saw each other a lot. I was fairly certain I'd never told him my name, and I had no recollection of how I learned his.

With a nod to Lio, I continued to Eaton, turned left, and walked the two hundred feet to a white house with a big blue porch, on top of which was a sign that read BOTTROFF HOUSE BED & BREAKFAST. For the first month, this was where I'd stayed. After that, with my cash reserves starting to run out, I offered to update the B&B's web site. The owner, Debbie Dellamonica, had web skills that were probably cutting-edge in 1996 when she created the site, and as far as I could tell, she hadn't updated it since. I brought it into the 21st century, and she let me stay there *gratis* as long as I maintained the web site and did whatever other work around the B&B needed doing.

I walked around the main house, wandered through the garden's palm trees, past bushes and our parrot Harry S (who was asleep, thank goodness), before arriving at one of the rear cottages. I trudged up the wooden stairs to my second-story place, using my key to open the sliding glass door.

"My goodness, are you ill?"

I sighed. Somehow, I just *knew* that the captain was gonna give me shit. "No, I'm not ill, I just decided to call it an early night."

"The only time in the past you have returned from your drunken perambulations before the witching hour was when you were suffering an illness."

I pulled off my cream-colored Mayor Fred's T-shirt, which I knew would get the old bastard's blood boiling.

Sure enough: "Must you do that?"

"It's my damn house, I can undress if I want to." I had on my one-piece bathing suit under the shirt and my shorts anyhow.

"In fact, it is *my* residence, bought and paid for by the fruits of my own labors, thank you very much."

"Cap, I'm really not in the mood for the usual banter tonight, so can we just skip to the part where I take my clothes off, you disappear in a huff, and I go to sleep?"

Now he sounded concerned. "You *are* ill."

"No, just cranky."

"Oh dear. It's not your moon time, is it?"

I stopped in mid-shorts-removal. "'Moon time'? Okay, now you're just making stuff up. They didn't really call it that in the nineteenth century, did they?"

"My wife did, on those rare occasions when she spoke of such things before me."

"Which was never?"

There was a brief, semi-awkward pause. The captain and I had those periodically.

Look, I don't know why no one else who stays at the Bottroff House can see or hear the ghost of Captain Jeremiah Bottroff, the wrecker captain who built this place in the 1840s, but I can. He's been my *de facto* roommate since I first started staying here, and he's also far from the weirdest thing that's happened to me. I didn't talk to Debbie about it—or anyone else, for that matter—but I'd kinda gotten used to being his Mrs. Muir over the past nine months.

There was a sudden breeze in the room, which meant he was gone and I could strip in peace. I'd long since stopped being self-conscious around the captain, but I didn't always want to fuck with his head, either. It wasn't his fault I was his first (and so far only) source of conversation the past 150 years.

Since it was still spring, I didn't need to turn on the AC. Keeping the windows open and the wooden ceiling fan over the bed going did the trick. So I just fell onto the bed without even bothering to pull the covers down. My head hit the pillow, and then I proceeded to stare at the ceiling fan for a very long time.

You ever try going to bed five hours earlier than usual? I know people who can do it, no problem. Me, I tend to settle into a rhythm, and it's a bitch to get out of it. In college, I got up every morning at the time of whatever my earliest class of the week was, even if I didn't have that class that day. Drove me nuts.

I tried everything, from trying to let the oscillations of the ceiling fan hypnotize me to getting up to check my e-mail to taking a quick shower to tossing and turning. For all that, I didn't actually fall asleep until almost five.

Like clockwork, I woke up at 11, crawled out of bed, guzzled some of Debbie's amazing coffee—she always served Hawai'ian Kona and it was to die for—and hopped into Rocinante in plenty of time to drive down Route 1 to Seaclipse. As I inched along behind all the other cars on the only road that traversed the entirety of the Florida Keys, I wondered why that old man at Mayor Fred's stuck around so long to listen to Jötunheim when he obviously was as indifferent to them as I was. Was he related to someone in the band, maybe?

According to an e-mail this morning, I had four people for my one o'clock dive. I recognized three of the names: a couple who'd been diving every afternoon for the past week as part of their week-long vacation (I'd already warned them not to get sucked in the way I did), and Rany, a local who dove with me every Friday. The fourth was new, probably a tourist, named V.E. Bolverk.

Just before the bridge to Cow Key, I turned right and drove down to the coast, pulling into the large driveway that Seaclipse shared with the Waterfront. The latter was a restaurant that survived mainly because people were usually starving after a dive and would eat anything, no matter how wretched, a maxim they proved after every Seaclipse dive. I always swore I'd never eat at the Waterfront again after each time I did the Salmonella Shuffle there, but I kept going back anyhow. Bastards.

Anyhow, my couple was already there. So was the old man from the bar last night.

I nearly dropped my air tank.

This was my first good look at him—I only saw the right side of his head at Mayor Fred's—and I realized that he was missing his left eye. No eyepatch, no prosthetic, just an empty socket. Weirdly, it looked right on him. His white hair, which had been hanging loose at the bar, was now tied into a small ponytail, and he was already wearing the neoprene suit.

He and the couple were all looking at air tanks to rent. I had my own—why else do you think I drive around in a 25-year-old pickup? it's the best way to haul the tank around—but most people just rented when they dove. Especially travelers; you don't want to try and get a giant metal tube through airport security...

The female of the couple noticed me first. "Hey, Cassie!"

"Hey, Hannah—David. And you must be Mr. Bolverk. I'm Cassie Zukav, I'll be your dive-master."

Bolverk stepped forward and offered his hand. "A pleasure, Ms. Zukav. I'm sorry we didn't get to speak last evening at the saloon, but you departed before I had the opportunity to introduce myself."

I smiled. "That was going to be my line. Only, y'know, with fewer words. Why'd you stick around so long?"

"I am acquainted with the lead singer."

"Not even a relative, huh?" I chuckled. "Well, you're a better man than I am. We're just waiting on one more—"

From behind the desk, one of Seaclipse's owners, Cara Zimmerman, said, "Rany just called—he can't make it."

"Okay, then." Rany usually only made it to two-thirds of his appointed dives, anyhow. "Which one we got, Cara?"

"We've left *Harpo* for you."

"Great. Let's go, guys." Seaclipse had three dive boats, which Cara and her husband, Andy Wasserstein, had named *Groucho*, *Chico*, and *Harpo*. I usually preferred *Groucho*, but as a part-timer, I never got first pick. As we boarded the boat, I asked Bolverk, "Have you ever dived in the Gulf of Mexico before?" He had to be an experienced and certified diver, otherwise Cara and Andy wouldn't have signed him up for a dive.

"No, only in the northern Atlantic."

My eyes widened. "Really? Yowza." I cut my teeth in the Pacific, which was horribly frigid compared to what you got off the Florida coast, but the northern Atlantic was like diving in ice water. "Well, this should be nice and warm for you."

Because Hannah and David had already done the close-by dives, I went out a little further to where I knew there were some nice fish and beautiful coral reefs—David had purchased an underwater digital camera, so I went to where he'd get some good shots.

Since there were only three customers, I had to go underwater also, since you didn't dive without a buddy. Obviously, the happy couple stayed together, so I got to dive with Bolverk.

I anchored *Harpo* and put up the red flag with the diagonal white stripe that signified that we were a diving boat. We all checked each other's equipment one last time, and then we all went under.

It's so beautiful underwater. There's really nothing on land that can compare to it. There are so many different shapes, sizes, and colors, and the water embraces you and takes you in.

Bolverk and I went down by a beautiful coral reef. This one had so far remained undamaged by pollution or carelessness. Picture a cauliflower made of porcelain, and you'll have an idea what an unspoiled reef looks like.

There were critters all over the place, too, and I made sure to snap a few pictures. I got an especially nice shot of a blue angelfish. A moment later, something caught my eye. I swam over to the other side of the reef.

Something was poking out from under the sand at the bottom. It looked like something that had been deeply buried, and then unearthed by the current. The two ends of it looks to still be pretty well buried.

You found all sorts of garbage down here, but this one looked different than the usual detritus that collected. It actually looked like the tail of a lizard—but the scales were a deep, emerald green that was sharper than any amphibian I'd ever seen. And between the scales, it almost looked like a gold tinge...

Apocalypse 13

Someone less scrupulous than I would have tried to unearth it, but there were several issues there. For one thing, it was just a small tube- or tail-like piece that was buried on either side, and there was no way to tell how deep it went. For another, I preferred to leave the ocean be. I saw myself as an observer, not a participant, in what was going on down there.

After a while, Bolverk and I swam back to the boat, making a safety stop partway up. When we clambered back into *Harpo*, I saw that Hannah and David were already in the boat, the sun reflecting off the drops of water on their face and hair and on their neoprene suits.

"*There* you are," Hannah said with a grin. "We were starting to get worried."

I chuckled. "Sorry, found something weird." I turned the digital camera's display on and scrolled over to the picture of the weird lizard-tail thingie. "That look familiar to any of you?" I showed it to Hannah, David, and Bolverk in turn.

"Nope."

"Don't look like nothin' I ever saw, no."

Bolverk frowned. "It looks like nothing seen on Earth."

"So what," David said with a laugh, "you're sayin' it's alien? That's rich."

"I said no such thing," Bolverk said gravely.

There was a brief awkward pause. I started *Harpo* up and steered her back to Seaclipse.

Neither Cara nor Andy recognized the tail either. I sighed and wondered if I should've bothered getting prints of the pictures I took. Prints of my digital photography graced the walls of the Bottroff House. But I preferred ones I could identify.

Bolverk signed up for more dives for the next several days, which I took as a compliment. It was a relief, too, since I had no idea how he'd liked the dive, and I'm usually pretty good at reading people.

As I was loading up Rocinante, my phone beeped with a text message from Bobbi: "Going to Fred's to see new band. Coming?"

Oddly, I hadn't decided what I was doing tonight. I couldn't recall a Friday night where I didn't know what I was doing since I came down here. I didn't really want to go see Jötunheim again. But if Bobbi was going to be there, maybe I could get a straight answer about what was going on with 1812.

Bolverk passed me by in the parking lot. "Will I see you this evening at the saloon?"

That clinched it. I needed to know more about this guy, especially since he was the only other person who seemed unaffected by whatever mind-altering substance Jötunheim put in their amplifiers.

"You bet," I said, even as I texted a similar sentiment back to Bobbi.

Bolverk nodded, and walked off through the parking lot and continued in the general direction of Route 1. I wondered if he was going to walk all the way to Key West.

I climbed into Rocinante and pulled out onto the road, but I didn't see Bolverk anywhere. Maybe he just parked somewhere else.

That night, Mayor Fred's was *packed*. All the seats were taken, and people were jammed onto the dance floor. I procrastinated getting there, so the band was already on stage, and meandering through a lackluster version of Led Zeppelin's "Whole Lotta Love."

I found Bobbi and Jana both leaning against the merch table. Gratefully, I walked over to them.

Of Bolverk, I saw no sign. But the place was densely packed—way more than was normal, even on a Friday night—so he could've been almost anywhere in the bar, and I wouldn't see him.

They finished butchering Zeppelin and the room exploded in applause. Bobbi and Jana were among them, to my disgust.

"Hey, Cass," Bobbi said. "Aren't these guys *great*?"

"Fuckin' A," Jana added. "They fuckin' *rock*. Yeah!"

"Really?" I just stared at them. "They're *not* that hot. Certainly nothing on you guys. What the hell happened, anyhow?"

Bobbi and Jana exchanged glances. Then Jana said, "I need a cigarette."

The three of us went out onto Greene Street so Jana could suck on nicotine and we could talk in peace. Given that Jötunheim's next song was "Money for Nothing," which was a) one of my favorite songs, and b) eerily appropriate from my POV, I was just as happy to be farther away from it.

While Jana lit up, Bobbi said, "We just can't find a damn drummer, and hiring one's proving impossible. They either cost too much or they won't take the rehearsal time."

I couldn't help myself. "You guys rehearse?"

"Ha-fuckin'-ha, Zukav," Jana said. She had a thing for referring to people only by their last names. "We *gotta* get a drummer up to speed and in sync, and we can't do that with a new guy every damn weekend. Some of us have lives, y'know?"

"Since when?" I thought those words, but it was actually Bobbi who said it. "Anyhow," she continued to me, "we figured we should just take a break. Didn't realize they'd go and hire someone so awesome."

"Okay, seriously?" I shook my head. "What is the big deal about Jötunheim? I mean, they're okay, but you guys are six times the band they are."

"That's sweet, Zukav," Jana said through a cloud of exhaled cigarette smoke, "but you gotta say that 'cause you're our friend."

"No, really, I don't. If you guys sucked, I'd say so."

Bobbi regarded Jana with a smile. "She's got a point."

Jana shrugged and took another drag. "Still, these guys fuckin' rock. Pity they don't have keys."

"Yeah, I just hope we get the gig back when we finally do find a drummer. We're holding an audition in the garage Sunday afternoon." Bobbi looked at me. "Wanna come watch?"

My feeling on music has always been similar to what they say about sausages: love 'em, don't wanna see the behind-the-scenes stuff. Luckily, I had a good excuse. "Can't, I'm doing two dives on Sunday."

"Shit, Zukav, they got you doing the morning dive?" Jana was laughing at me.

"I can set the alarm."

"Yeah, and get Debbie to give you the coffee through an IV and you *might* manage to be awake before 11." Bobbi chuckled. "C'mon, let's go back inside."

"Nah," I said with a sigh. "It's just not the same in there without you guys. I'm gonna head back."

We exchanged good-nights, Jana finished her cigarette, and they went in while I headed home. Briefly, I contemplated trying another bar for the evening, but I found my enthusiasm oddly waning. I just wanted to go home and curl up in a ball.

I arrived just as Debbie was locking the front door for the night. "Hiya, Cass," she said. "We got a new one in six—big old guy with only one eye named—"

"Bolverk?" I asked in surprise. Room number six was the downstairs of the cottage next to mine.

With similar surprise, Debbie said, "Yeah. You know him?"

"Uh, he was on my dive today."

"Well, thanks for telling him about us. G'night."

I hadn't told him about the Bottroff House—which was a failing on my part, since I made a habit of talking the B&B up to Seaclipse customers. For that matter, I always talked up Seaclipse to the B&B guests.

But now I was starting to feel seriously stalked by this guy.

This time I didn't even try to go to sleep, just spent the night downloading my pictures from the dives, catching up on e-mail, web surfing, and trading insults with Captain Bottroff.

The rest of the weekend got progressively weirder. Bolverk kept signing up for my afternoon dives. I didn't make it back to where that weird tail was again, as the other divers made specific requests for other spots, and the customer was always right.

And Jötunheim kept playing to bigger and bigger crowds at Mayor Fred's. In fact, their biggest crowd was Sunday night, which was usually the second-deadest night of the week after Tuesday.

To make matters worse, the three surviving members of 1812 were there both nights, and they were all bopping to the music. Even Chet, who doesn't bop to *anything*.

I stuck around both nights, partly because I wanted to keep an eye on Bolverk—who was sitting there nursing what Adina told me was bourbon every night—and partly to see if maybe I was just missing something. Whatever it was, though, I couldn't find it.

Sunday night, between sets, I was standing in line for the women's room—something I'd never had to do on a Sunday night before—and Gunnar noticed me. Wasn't sure why—beyond the fact that, at 5'11" with a mess of blond curls, I tend to stand out—but he peeled off from these two brunettes who were hitting all over him to say, "I have been noticing you."

I stared down at him—he was half a head shorter than me. "Oh yeah?" I tried to put on my best Southern California "what-*ever*" voice.

"Yes. You are the only woman in this entire place who is not having a good time. Yet you keep coming back."

I smirked. "Maybe I'm a glutton for punishment."

"I am simply surprised." He showed perfect teeth when he smiled, and I swear to God, his eyes glinted. "Do you not find it odd that no one else in this establishment feels as you do?"

"Yeah, well, I can't stand *American Idol* or Steven Spielberg movies, either, so I guess I'm used to it." Thankfully, the line moved forward, and I was able to enter the inside of the women's room, the one place where Gunnar dared not follow. As the door closed behind me, I saw two more women glom onto him like moths dive-bombing a candle.

Okay, so the guy was the lead singer of a band that had been packing the house like no one had packed it before, but even taking that into account, ego much? He's got half of Key West falling at his feet, but he's gotta know why it's not half plus one?

I sat fuming during the second set, made worse by how much Bobbi, Jana, and Chet were enjoying themselves. First off, Chet enjoying himself was just *weird*. Though in some ways, it was worth hanging out listening to Jötunheim's drivel just to see this sight, if for no other reason than it was bound to provide blackmail material down the line.

But more importantly, these guys were totally eclipsing 1812. Every other band in the universe would be ripshit over what these guys were pulling off, but there they were, just bopping along.

After the final song—an appallingly uninspired version of "Join Together," about which the nicest thing I could say was that Gunnar played a decent harmonica—I left without even saying goodbye to anyone.

It was around three, but since it was Sunday night (Monday morning, whatever), the streets were pretty sparsely populated. Some of the bars closed early on Sundays, and the ones that were open weren't all that crowded.

So I was all alone at the corner of Duval and Caroline when the giant jumped me.

We're talking an *actual* giant here. He was at least eight feet tall, and that's *not* an exaggeration. He had a thick beard, a huge nose, and breath that came straight from Satan's ass. His arms were also the size of my entire torso, and one of them was grabbing right for me.

"Hey! Leave her alone!"

The voice came from my left, and was oddly familiar. Sure enough, it was the guy who'd asked me for directions to a strip club and commented on my height Thursday night. He was running up to the giant, screaming at him.

At least, he was running until the giant backhanded him across the face, sending blood flying out his nose and his entire body skidding across the street. A woman screamed.

I just kept staring at the giant. I'd seen some weird shit in my time, from the nixie that killed Zeke (and a bunch of others) to the dragon in the garden to Captain

Bottroff—and that was just here on Key West. You don't even want to *know* about that thing I stumbled across in San Diego...

Now that I was over the initial shock, and since my drunken admirer had been kind enough to distract the giant at the cost of some serious pain, the least I could do was take advantage.

I kneed him in the groin.

Like any male, the giant screamed in agony at that, right in my face (since he bent over after I damaged the family jewels), at which point I realized that his breath didn't come from anywhere as nice as Satan's ass.

"Step away from the lady nice and slow, chuckles."

I turned to see Lio pointing a gun at the giant. The giant snarled at Lio.

Lio pulled the trigger.

I'd never heard a gun fired in my life up until that point. My parents were crunchy-granola Southern California types, and I honestly thought everyone in Key West—beyond, y'know, law-enforcement—was too laid back to pack heat. For the record, it doesn't sound *anything* like a firecracker or a car backfiring or anything else I've ever heard. It's also incredibly fucking loud, especially when it was fired less than fifteen feet from you. If I didn't spend four nights a week listening to loud music, it might have messed up my hearing, but mine came pre-damaged.

Another scream from the giant, and then he turned and ran around the corner.

Shaking my head, I chased him, but as soon as I turned onto Caroline, there was no sign of him.

Lio ran up right behind me, holding the gun with both hands. "How the hell'd a ten-foot dude disappear like that?" he asked.

"Dunno—but thanks, Lio."

"No problem."

I shook my head. "My name's Cas—"

"Cassie Zukav, I know. Debbie told me." He grinned. "Figured you'd let me know in your own time. C'mon, let's see if any'a these fools called 911 on their cell phones."

Two of them had, as it turned out. I went over to my admirer, who was sitting up on the pavement of Duval Street, his head leaning back while a brunette woman cared for him. "I can't believe you did that," she was saying.

"You okay?"

"Yeah." The woman was holding a tissue to his nose as he leaned his head back. As I got closer, I saw that his nose was still bleeding. He was talking in a nasal voice from the nasal blockage. "I guess now we're even."

I frowned. "Huh?"

"I was *really* drunk Thursday night, and if you'd given me the right directions, I'd have wound up at an actual strip club instead of a closed museum, and Tanya here'd have killed me."

The brunette shot him a disgusted look. "You were going to a *strip club?*"

"I didn't, though! And it's 'cause'a this lady."

"So you got your nose broken for her? Jesus, Billy."

Leaving Billy and Tanya to their domestic bliss, I hung out until the cops and the ambulance arrived. Wasn't sure what to tell them, but—well, one of my closest friends was a federal agent, and I'd never hear the end of it from him if I didn't make a proper report.

That particular ordeal took a couple of hours, and I finally stumbled back to the Bottroff House at five. The captain actually sounded relieved when I showed up. "Thank God. I was beginning to grow concerned. First your uncharacteristic early returns, and now tardiness."

"I've been late before," I muttered as I took my T-shirt off.

The captain didn't even make a fuss, which told me a lot right there. "Tonight is far from a standard night."

I wasn't really in the mood for riddles. "What's that supposed to mean?"

"I mean that the occupant of the ground floor of the next cottage over attempted to gain ingress into this dwelling. However, I was able to drive him away."

It took me a moment to parse Bottroff's words. "Hang on, Bolverk was here?"

"Indeed."

"And he *saw* you?"

"Yes. Had he been a less belligerent sort, I might have welcomed another to share words with, but he seemed intent upon seeing you. He used a phrase I've heard you utter from time to time: 'low key'?"

I snorted as I climbed out of my bathing suit and crawled into bed. "Yeah, low key isn't exactly this guy's style. And he's the least of my problems tonight." As my head sunk into my pillow, I gave the captain the brief version of the night's events.

"That settles it, then. I will brook no argument, Miss Zukav—I will remain vigilant tonight, to guard against any further assaults upon you."

It was a testament to how incredibly tired I was, that it never occurred to me that the captain's notion was at all creepy until long after I fell asleep.

The next few days were shockingly normal. I did my afternoon and occasional evening dives at Seaclipse, I helped Debbie out around the B&B, I saw very little of Bolverk, and no giants leapt out at me on Duval Strreet. Apparently Bolverk did a couple of dives with Andy during the week. I tried not to be insulted.

I was almost starting to believe things were getting back to normal until I was greeted by a text from Bobbi when I woke up Thursday morning: "Jana quit 1812. Drinks after diving?"

I stared at my phone in disbelief. Bobbi and Jana had been best friends since kindergarten. 1812 was their baby. How could Jana quit?

I texted back a simple, "sure," then got ready to head to Seaclipse.

Bobbi wouldn't even talk about it during the dive. Afterward, we went straight to the Waterfront and sat at the long wooden bar. "Two beers, Jack," Bobbi said to the bartender as soon as her ass hit the stool.

Grinning, I added, "And I'll have two beers, too."

"Very funny," Jack said with a sour face, and he went and got us each just the one beer.

"I cannot *believe* her," Bobbi said after Jack handed her a full pint. "The whole week, all she's talked about is Jötunheim and how good they are, and how if they just had keyboards they'd be perfect. We're trying to audition drummers, and she's talking about this other band! So when we finally get someone, she quits on us."

That surprised me. "You got a drummer?"

"Yeah." She smiled. "Another girl, believe it or not. Poor Chet's gonna be the only guy now."

I rolled my eyes. "Yeah, he must *hate* that."

"Well, you never know with Chet." Bobbi sighed and gulped down more beer. "Anyway, it's not *just* that Jana quit. I mean, bands don't last forever, and teaching takes up a lot of her time, and it was always kinda in the back of my head that the band could fall apart, y'know?" She sipped some more beer. "But to go another band? I mean, 1812 was *us*. It's like she's not even my best friend anymore!"

Frowning, I asked, "What other band?"

"Didn't I tell you?"

"Uh, no."

"Oh, sorry. Yeah, she quit to join up with Jötunheim."

I thoughtfully sipped some more beer before making my next statement. "How do you plan to kill her and how much help do you need from me to dispose of the body?"

"Don't tempt me." Bobbi shook her head. "What especially sucks is, I got us a gig at the Hog's Breath tomorrow night." That was a completely open-air bar on Duval, about half a block from Mayor Fred's. "Looks like now we're gonna have to do it as a trio."

"Well, the Hog's Breath has a tiny stage, anyhow. Jana would've had to use the Casio, and you know how much she hates that."

"Yeah." Bobbi finished off her beer. "You wanna meet the new drummer? She's meeting me and Chet at Fred's tonight."

I stared at Bobbi as if she'd grown another head. "Excuse me? Why're you going to Fred's?"

Bobbi shrugged. "Jana's first night on the keys. When we were eight, we were both already singing and playing music a lot, and we pinky-swore to each other that we'd never miss the other one performing. There've been a few we've missed because of other commitments—and I won't be able to see her tomorrow—but I've got no excuse tonight."

"How about, 'Sorry, but you just pissed all over our friendship, so I think I'll skip it'?"

"Tempting, but it *was* a pinky-swear."

"When you were eight," I said slowly. "Seriously, you're gonna torture yourself for this?"

Bobbi grinned. "Do not mock the sanctity of the pinky-swear." Then the grin fell. "Besides, there's two other things. One is: she'll make Jötunheim sound even more awesome. And also? I want to remind her that *I* still think our friendship means something."

That drew me up short. Holding up my pint, I said, "I'll drink to that."

We risked actually eating the food at the Waterfront, and then headed back to Key West. After I changed clothes, I wandered up to Greene Street. Lio nodded hello as I passed by the Bull, and I nodded back.

"You hear if they caught the guy?" I asked.

He shook his head. "Nah, I ain't heard shit about it."

"Figures."

When I got to Greene Street, there were already people spilling out on the sidewalk, as Mayor Fred's was packed to the gills. The show hadn't even *started* yet. I didn't even want to think about what Ihor, Mira, Lainie, and Adina were going through inside.

I saw Bobbi and Chet standing with a short redhead. Bobbi waved when she saw me coming toward them. "Hey, Cass! Can you believe this?"

"No. In fact, I'm pretty well convinced this is a mirage."

"Good thing the PA pipes the music out here, too." Bobbi looked over at the redhead. "Ginny Blake, this is Cassie Zukav, our biggest fan."

I winced. "Seriously? *That's* how you introduce me? Not 'my friend Cassie,' or 'my dive-master at Seaclipse Cassie,' but 'our biggest fan'?"

Chet stared at the crowds all around us. "This rate, you gonna be the only fan we got *left*."

Ginny held out her hand. "It's a pleasure to meet you, Cassie. I've heard a lot about you."

Returning the handshake, I said, "Well don't believe any of it, I'm actually pretty damned awesome."

"Good to know."

Ihor's voice came over the PA. "Ladies and gentlemen, put your hands together tonight and now *every single night* for Mayor Fred's new house band, Jötunheim!"

Everybody around us cheered wildly and clapped. My jaw fell. I leaned over to Bobbi. "*Every* night? What about Fiona and those two guys with the beards?"

Bobbi shrugged. "Guess they'll have to play somewhere else."

So the Monday and Wednesday acoustic acts got screwed along with 1812, not to mention losing the Tuesday open mic. I mean, all right, you can't argue with crowds like this, but it still wasn't fair.

The piano opening of "I'm Still Standing" came over the PA, and 1812 had covered this often enough for me to know that it was Jana's fingers tickling the ivories. Obviously they were taking advantage of their new band member right off.

Sure enough, the next three songs were all keyboard-heavy. Jana was a virtuoso, and Bobbi was right—she improved Jötunheim's sound tremendously. But she also showed up how mediocre the rest of the band was.

At least, to me. Everyone else was eating it up, with one exception: Ginny seemed unmoved by all of this, too.

I leaned over to her after she golf-clapped while everyone was having orgasms over a blah version of "Kashmir." "It's about time someone *else* was unmoved by these guys."

Ginny just smiled.

I added, "It's like someone cast a spell over the whole damn island."

She raised her eyebrows. "Maybe someone has."

Just after she said that, I felt something brush across my nose. Looking up, I saw white flakes start to fall from the sky.

Okay, I'm from Southern California, and I live on Key West. It took me few minutes to recognize snow. Ditto most of the folks around me, since snow is just about the last thing anyone expected to find in South Florida in springtime.

Within a few minutes, the snow was really starting to pour down. And it was getting *cold*.

"I gotta go," I said. Besides the fact that listening to Jötunheim suck while standing on a street being snowed on was pretty low on my list of ways I wanted to spend my Thursday night, I had a feeling that things were gonna be bad at the B&B.

After navigating the throngs of very confused people on Duval, I got to the Bottroff House. I arrived just in time for Debbie to beg me to drive to the storage unit down on Virginia Street, since I was the only person she knew who owned a vehicle that could handle snowy roads.

Two and a half hours later, and after using the heat in Rocinante for the first time since I left San Diego, I stumbled into the snow-covered garden, my feet like ice cubes from walking through snow on flip-flops. Just getting to the storage unit and back, all of a mile from the B&B, took ninety of those minutes. The rest of the time was spent distributing heaters, extra blankets, and other stuff I liberated from the unit and tossed into the back of Rocinante.

By the time I got to my cottage, the final space heater in hand for my own room, my bones were cold. I'd never been this chilled in my life.

Bolverk was sitting on the steps.

"Shouldn't you be in your room hiding from the weather?" I asked tiredly.

He rose to his feet. "I was waiting for you, Castor Lisbeth Zukav. We must speak."

I winced at his use of my full name. My twin brother was named Pollux. Yes, really. Talk to my parents. We went by "Cassie" and "Paul" for a reason.

"Can't it wait till morning?" I asked plaintively. "I have a bed that desperately needs to have me sleeping in it." After all this running around, I doubted I'd have trouble sleeping this much before my bedtime.

"No, it cannot. Fimbulvetr is upon us, which means that Loki's plan to bring about Ragnarok has started to come to fruition."

I blinked. "Okay, basically *none* of that made any kind of sense."

"The man you know as Gunnar Rikardsen is, in fact, the trickster Loki. He is my blood-brother. I am Odin, the Allfather of the Aesir. And we do not have much time."

I remembered some of what I saw online when I was doing my search on Jötunheim's name. "Hang on—Loki, Odin—you're a Norse god?"

"Of course."

"Right, because that's the most natural thing in the world." I sighed. "Says the woman being snowed on in April while on her way to the room she shares with a ghost. All right, fine, let's get in out of the cold and you can tell me *all* about Loki and his evil plan."

Pulling my keys out, I walked past Odin up the stairs while he started to explain himself. "Fimbulvetr is the eternal winter, and is the first stage of Ragnarok. Soon Loki will be powerful enough to sunder Yggdrasil, the World Tree that binds the Nine Worlds together."

I unlocked and slid open the door only to be greeted by Captain Bottroff. "You should heed what this—this person says, Miss Zukav."

At that, I *almost* dropped the space heater onto my foot. I *did* drop my keys onto the white-carpeted floor. "You're kidding, right? The guy whose favorite epithet is 'Mary, Mother of God' is telling me to listen to the pagan deity?"

"I still believe in the Lord God and His Savior, Jesus Christ, as I did in life. But the *after*life has taught me that there is more to this world than I could have imagined. I have learned that there are other gods, and they cannot be labelled 'false' as the vicars of my youth insisted. Therefore, yes, I do believe that you should listen to what this person has to say."

"Your friend's shade speaks truth," Odin said as he took a seat in my white wicker chair.

"Jesus fuck, it's cold." I plugged in the space heater and turned it on, standing as close to it as I could while rubbing my goosebump-covered arms. "Fine, so Gunnar is really Loki. How'd he get to this point?"

Odin had a sonorous voice that was well suited to storytelling, and I found myself almost mesmerized by his story. "Loki tricked Hoder into killing Balder in an attempt to bring about Ragnarok—the end of all that is. But he failed, and he was punished. Loki was trapped in a cave with a serpent dripping poison onto his face forevermore. However, Loki's wife Sigyn remained loyal to him, and held a bowl to catch the poison before it struck him. Unfortunately, she had to periodically empty the bowl, and when she did so, the poison struck Loki's face, and his convulsions shook the very earth."

"Uhm—okay," I said, "why didn't she just have two bowls?"

That brought Odin up short. "I do not know. You would have to ask her that." He shook his head. "Regardless, Loki managed to free himself from his prison—how, I know not. But gods are only as powerful as their worshippers. When the peoples of the Scandanavian region believed in us, our power was at its zenith—but in time the Aesir were forgotten, given over for other gods. Today, we are little more than an academic curiosity, or fodder for popular fiction. Our end was prophesied to come about via Ragnarok, but instead we simply faded."

"Not with a bang but a whimper, huh?" I shook my head, the space heater having managed to get my blood actually circulating again. "Okay, fine, so you all faded away."

"Save for a few of us. I still live, obviously, as does one of the frost giants,

Geirrod, who is loyal to Loki. I believe you had an encounter with him."

"What, the lunatic outside the Bull? He's a frost giant?"

"Indeed."

"So why the hell did he want to kill *me*?"

Odin stared at me with his one eye. "Loki sent Geirrod to kill you because he sees you as a potential threat. As one of the Dísir, you are immune to his glamour—and one of the few who can stop him."

My eyes widened. "Excuse me? I'm one of the *what*, now?"

"The Dísir. The fate goddesses. The Norns are Dísir, and periodically a set of triplets is born on Midgard who are also Dísir. You are one of three, are you not?"

Now my heart was pounding against my ribcage. Yes, Mom had triplets, but Paul's and my never-named brother was stillborn.

I found myself with the need to sit down. The heater had only just started to warm up the room, but I no longer felt the cold—or, really, much of anything. I planted myself on the edge of the bed, since Odin was in my only chair. In a very quiet voice, I said, "Yes, I'm a triplet."

"Just so. Why do you think you are able to speak with the shade or survive an encounter with a frost giant?"

Before I could elaborate on the role that two other people played in my driving Geirrod off, Bottroff finally spoke up again. "If such is the reason behind our ability to communicate, Miss Zukav, then I, for one, am filled with gratitude."

I stared at the captain. In nine months, that was the nicest thing he'd said to me.

Unable to entirely parse this, I forced myself to focus on the point at hand. "Okay, hold it—the band's using magic?"

Odin nodded. "Loki is using a glamour, yes, to make his music more appealing. It is a minor glamour, not strong enough to affect me as the Allfather, nor you as a Dís. He was unable to revive worshipful interest in the Aesir—our time has passed. The Christians were little more than conquering fodder for Vikings in our heyday, but now you are everywhere."

I held up my hands. "Don't look at me, I'm Jewish." I sighed. "All right, so he formed a rock band. Figures—fan dedication's probably stronger than a church would be anyhow. So why here? Why Key West?"

"Because, as I said, the next step is to sunder Yggdrasil. And one of the roots of the World-Tree is the ficus around which the saloon on Greene Street is built."

I put my head in my hands. "Of course it is. So, fine, how do we stop him?"

"There is a counterspell that may be cast while Loki casts the spell to sunder the World-Tree. He will cast it tomorrow night—Fimbulvetr must last for at least a day before he may attempt it. You must cast this counterspell."

"Whoa, whoa, whoa!" I stood up. "You're the Allfather, the big badass of Norse myth. I'm just a tall chick with bad hair. Why aren't *you* casting the spell?"

"Loki is my blood-brother, and we swore never to harm each other. You, however, have made no such vow, and as a Dís, you can easily cast the spell."

"Oh, I can, can I?" This was getting insane. Insaner.

"Yes." He rose to his feet. "I must depart. I will return in the morning with the components you will need to cast the spell and instructions on how to cast it."

"Uh, okay, but I've never cast a spell before."

Odin slid the door open. "You are a Dís. You will be able to." With that, he left.

"Okay, then," I told the closed door. I turned to the captain. "You really believe this?"

"I believe that it is snowing heavily, a phenomenon I have never encountered in a century and a half. I believe that these musicians you have described are enchanting the good people of this island. I believe you were attacked by a vicious monster. I believe that the gentleman who just departed has a notion as to the reason for these occurrences and also the method by which they may be rectified."

"So you're saying I should see this through?"

"Yes. Yes, I do."

I collapsed on the bed. "Yeah, me, too."

My dreams that night were filled with random images of Bobbi and Jana in a catfight, Gunnar giving Bolverk the finger while standing on Mayor Fred's stage, the Gulf of Mexico totally frozen over but Cara and Andy still trying to dive in it, Geirrod shooting Lio in the chest with a big shotgun, Ginny, Chet, and the rest of the crowd at Mayor Fred's giving Jötunheim a standing ovation, and a bunch more.

When I woke up, I frowned. Ginny *wasn't* into Jötunheim. How was she unaffected?

I put on the sneakers I hadn't worn since December and the long pants I hadn't worn since I arrived on the island and put them on. The snow was still coming down and piling up in the garden. Seriously, this was the first time my legs weren't exposed to the open air in nine months.

"What a fucking nightmare," I muttered. "This is gonna cripple the island. We don't have salt, we don't have plows—hell, most of the people who live here don't own *socks*."

I trudged through the snow to the main house in order to get some of Debbie's killer coffee. Several guests were in the dining room, scared and subdued. Nobody knew what to do, and probably the whole island was shutting down. I had a text on my phone from Cara saying that Seaclipse was closed, to my lack of surprise. I doubted that any business was going to be open. Plus, how were deliveries supposed to get here on unpassable roads?

Then again, the world was going to end tonight, anyhow....

I trudged through the frozen tundra back to my cottage with an entire pot of coffee and then fired up my laptop to do a litle online research before Odin came back. Sure enough, Norse mythology tracked frighteningly well with everything Odin said and the whole eternal-winter thing.

When Odin arrived, he had the spell components: a bunch of really stinky herbs, a mortar and pestle, a electric mini-stove, and a familiar-looking lizard scale.

"You took that from the tail-thingie we found last week!"

"Indeed. It is from the Midgard Serpent, the creature that surrounds your world. That it has allowed itself to be seen is another omen of Ragnarok's imminence."

"Joy."

I spent the entire day in my room with Odin and Captain Bottroff going over how to cast the spell. Apparently, I had to get the mix of herbs *just* right, say the incantation *precisely* (in a language I totally didn't know or recognize), and time it exactly to when Loki cast his spell, which would be him singing a song with a set of lyrics in the same weird language as my spell.

But no pressure...

Debbie managed to provide enough food for me and Odin, as well as the other guests, though she wasn't sure what she was going to do Saturday, since there weren't going to be any deliveries.

That night, I drove to Mayor Fred's. Duval Street was eerily not crowded. A bunch of hearty souls were trudging through the snow drifts to the few bars that decided to open up—which was maybe a quarter of them.

Rocinante was able to slowly plow its way through the snow, and when we turned the corner onto Greene, I just parked right across the street. I couldn't park right in front, because it was packed with people. Even though snow was still coming down, *hundreds* of people were trying to cram into Mayor Fred's.

But this time, unlike last night, there was a clear path from one part of the entryway, past the ficus, to the stage. That meant I had a clear line of sight, although I'm pretty sure it was so *Loki* had that same line of sight...

Ginny Blake was in with the crowd outside, and when she saw me and Odin climb out of the truck, she walked right over.

I was about to ask her what she was doing here, but she wasn't paying any attention to me. She stared at my companion. "Hello, Odin."

"Greetings, Sigyn."

Son of a bitch. "*You're* Loki's wife? The one not bright enough to have two bowls?"

Ginny frowned. "Excuse me?"

"Never mind—no wonder you're immune to his glamour."

She smiled. "What wife can't see through her husband? In any event, after spending eternity protecting him from that serpent, he repaid my loyalty by abandoning me when the cave collapsed and he was freed. So I have followed him in the hopes of watching him fail." She turned to Odin. "I assume you are here to expedite that failure, Allfather?"

"Not I. I swore an oath not to harm my blood-brother, and I will not go back on it."

Ginny's eyes widened. "You mean there's a chance he'll *succeed*?"

I sighed. "Hope not. I'm casting the spell."

Staring at Odin, Ginny asked, "Are you out of your mind? She is a novice."

"She is a Dís. She can cast the spell." Odin's voice was absolutely flat.

"I don't care if she's one of the Norns, she's never done this before. The fate of all the Nine Worlds is at stake, and you're risking it on a promise you made to *him?"*

Odin stared down at her with his one eye. "Yes."

Ihor's voice sounded over the PA. "Welcome to snowpocalypse, ladies and gentlemen!"

"You don't know the half of it," I muttered.

"Tonight and every night, it's Jötunheim!"

The crowd cheered like crazy. This time I could see them—same short blond muscular guy up front, same other three, plus Jana on stage right behind her usual keyboard setup of a standup piano and two sets of electronic keyboards. They opened with an old Jethro Tull song called "Hunting Girl" that used to be an 1812 standard.

While they played the song, and I wondered why Jana was going around throwing her old band's music for these guys to play, I started putting together what I needed for the spell. As the song spiralled to a finish, Loki held up a hand. "All right, I need some quiet for this next one."

As he spoke, Jana started playing a quiet, dirge-like melody very low on the keys, set to "organ" mode.

Slowly, the crowd started to quiet down, until there was total silence—something, I gotta say, I'd never heard in this part of Key West before, not even at four after the bars closed—save for Jana's organ playing.

Then Loki began to sing a song in a language I didn't recognize.

Except I *did* recognize it. Odin had been giving me the words all day. I lit the mixture in the pestle, dropped the scale from the Midgard Serpent into the flames that licked up from it, and then started a chant of my own.

I had no idea what the words *meant*, but I'd been practicing them all day until Odin was ready to kill me (and I him, believe me), and dammit I was gonna say them *right*.

Even as I said the words, I could feel—well, *something* pulling at my chest.

Loki saw me standing at the entryway. Everyone else in the bar was mesmerized by the music and didn't even notice me standing there with a flaming pestle in my hand. He finished what sounded like a verse of his chant, then looked at me with obvious annoyance. "I was wondering where Geirrod got off to. Couldn't even kill a Dís. Can't find good help these days, it seems."

I just kept chanting. Maybe he could afford to do his spell piecemeal, but I wasn't risking it. The pull on my chest got weaker as I went, which I hoped was a good sign.

"But there's nothing you can do, little Dís. Oh, if Allfather was doing what you're doing, I'd be doomed, but he won't harm me. His insistence on keeping his word is so charmingly old-fashioned, isn't it?"

Then he sang another verse, and the pulling on my chest grew worse.

Sweat beaded on my brow even though it was so fucking cold. I had come here wishing I had something thicker than a denim jacket, and now I was wishing I'd thought to throw it off before I started casting the spell.

The pull grew stronger, like someone had reached into my ribcage and was trying to yank my heart out through it.

I kept chanting. I wasn't about to miss anything.

"Haven't you learned *anything*, Loki?"

That was Ginny, who my peripheral version told me was standing just behind me and to my left.

"Sigyn!" This time Loki cut off in mid-verse. The pull on my chest disappeared, and I kept the chant up, louder this time.

"Yes, Loki, I'm still alive. And you are about to fail to bring about Ragnarok *again*, just as you did last time. Oh, and you can rest assured that I will *not* be there to stay the poison from your brow again."

"I won't need it, *dear* wife of mine," Loki snapped angrily. He sang the next verse, and the pull grew even worse.

Thanks a lot, Ginny. If you were trying to distract him, that *totally* didn't work.

Suddenly, just as a hand touched my shoulder the pull stopped. The words, which were a bitch and a half to pronounce right even after a day's practice, were now coming easily, as if it was a language I'd spoken all my life.

And Loki stumbled on the stage.

"You're going against your word, old man?" Loki asked with a sneer.

Only then did I realize who was touching my shoulder.

"Yes," was all Odin said in response.

"We are blood-brothers! You swore an oath, Allfather!"

"And now I am breaking it. As you broke yours, many times. What good is my word, if existence ends because I held it?"

"What good is existence if your word while living in it means nothing?"

When I finally got to the end of the chant, I decided to answer Loki's question before taking the final step. "Words ain't no good if the music sucks."

I threw the pestle at the ficus. It sparked and shattered, yellow flame shooting out in all directions. The pull on my chest increased, and I fell to the floor.

Loki collapsed on the stage.

Wind whipped through Mayor Fred's, a cold, bitter wind that the body heat of hundreds of people couldn't warm. It blew out the flames caused by my shattered pestle. Then the entire world went white, as if we were all suddenly buried in a snowdrift.

I heard voices: Loki's, Odin's, Sigyn's. I had no idea what they were saying, but I heard them as I lay there on Mayor Fred's floor, unable to move. I struggled to get up, but whatever force had been pulling on my chest all this time was keeping me from moving.

After several seconds of struggle, I closed my eyes, shivering from the bitter cold.

When I opened them, I was in my bed.

Captain Bottroff's ghost was standing over me. "At last, you awaken. Even one with your prodigious ability to slumber should not be in such a state for so many days."

I swallowed. "Days?" I sat up, realized I was still in the outfit I wore to Mayor

Fred's on Friday night, minus the denim jacket, which was hanging on the back of the wicker chair.

"Yes. It is now Sunday. I will fetch the gentleman—he wanted to know when you awakened."

A breeze, and then the captain was gone. I sat up slowly, my stomach growling. Looking out the window, I saw that the sun was shining and there was no sign of snow. I could see the garden clearly, though some flowers seemed to be missing. I guess they got frosted to death or something.

First thing I did was get out of bed. That took longer than it should have, as pins and needles shot through my legs, and I had to stand at the side of the bed, hand braced on the mattress, for several seconds before I felt confident enough to actually walk.

My arms and legs felt like they were made of jello, as I shakily pulled my shirt over my head. Removing my bra proved an act of dexterity almost beyond my means, and I sat back down on the bed, not trusting myself to remove my pants while upright.

By the time Odin showed at the sliding door, I'd managed to get into a bathrobe. I cursed the fact that my bathroom only had a shower stall, since what I really needed was a long bath. For one thing, I wasn't sure I'd be able to stand in the shower for more than a minute or two without collapsing.

He slid the door open. "It is good to see you well."

"'Well' is a relative term, but I'm alive. I guess it worked?"

"Yes." Odin nodded. "I have accepted responsibility for Loki and Geirrod."

I frowned. "What does that mean, exactly?"

"No Midgard jail may hold either of them, and your enforcement officials cannot arrest someone who does not actually exist."

Nodding, I said, "Yeah, okay, good point."

"I must take my leave of you, Castor Lisbeth Zukav."

I winced again. "Will you stop that, please? It's 'Cassie.'"

For the first time since I met him, Odin smiled. "Very well, Cassie. I hope you continue to use your gifts as a Dís wisely."

"I didn't even know I had gifts."

Bottroff spoke up, then. "Yes, you did. And rest assured, sir, that I will endeavor to keep Miss Zukav on the proper path."

"You have *got* to be kidding me." I put my hands on my hips and stared at the captain. But I was smiling.

"Be well, Cassie." And with that, Odin departed.

My cell phone had been in my pants pocket, and had long since lost its charge. I plugged it in to find it had a dozen messages.

Half were from Bobbi. I called her back, and we filled each other in on what had been going on. Well, as much of it as I was willing to talk about in a phone call. Bobbi had become a dear friend in the past nine months, and if there was anyone I could talk to about being a Dís, it was her. But not now.

Eventually, we got around to talking about 1812. "Mayor Fred's actually asked us back. Without Gunnar, Jötunheim has just sucked. We're starting tonight."

"As a trio or a quartet?"

Bobbi hesitated for several seconds. "Dunno yet. Jana and I–" She sighed. "We got some stuff to work out."

I didn't know what to say. Jana's quitting wasn't entirely her fault, thanks to Loki's glamour. On the other hand, nobody *else* in 1812 quit and joined Jötunheim. That was something those two were gonna have to figure out.

We promised to have lunch the next day to catch up in more detail, and I promised to tell her everything. Then I called Seaclipse, and worked out my schedule going forward. I told Andy that I wasn't up to working today, but I'd be okay tomorrow.

That night, after a not-nearly-long-enough shower in which I did *not* fall down and a huge meal provided by Debbie, I went to Mayor Fred's. Jana wasn't on the stage, but Chet, Bobbi, and Ginny were. I took a seat near the ficus tree. I suddenly felt protective of it. Adina got me a pint of beer, and Ihor came over the PA.

"Ladies and gentlemen, back after a brief absence, Mayor Fred's favorites, 1812!"

Bobbi walked up to her mic. "Good evening, Key West! This one's for our biggest fan."

And then Chet walked up to his mic. He wore sunglasses, like usual, so I couldn't tell where, exactly, he was looking. But I chose to believe he was staring right at me when he started singing their first song: "I Put a Spell on You."

The Soul Collector is a familiar face to fans of Patrick Thomas' Mystic Investigative series. In this case he faces his most dangerous battle yet. A group of Nearly departed come back as one terrifying monster with the potential to destroy the world.

MANY HANDS AND OTHER PARTS

A case of the Soul Collector
By Patrick Thomas

They say many hands make light work, but the hands that worked to send these folks to meet their maker were definitely involved in the dark variety.

Of course these days when people went to meet their maker, an awful lot of them must be ticking him off because he keeps sending them back. Well, him or somebody else. Either way it's changed the world by making death the not so final frontier.

There were some many different kinds of the dead returning that academics had begun cataloging them. I did too, but my reasons had more to do with not perishing rather than publishing. By my last count there were 113 different kinds of dead from abominations to zombies.

"What could have done this?" Detective Fowler said. He was a tough guy. I could see him start to gag from the sight and the smell, but he didn't let either stop him from doing his job. Fowler didn't even look away as a sign of respect to the victims. Not a lot of cops would go to those extremes. "Even forensics is having trouble figuring out where one corpse starts and the other ends."

This was as bad a series of murders as I had seen in my years as a federal soul collector. I didn't envy the crime scene folks. I'd seen a few things before I was made official that were worse, but it is always best not to bring those things up in polite company. Too much vomiting usually follows.

"I don't think it is a what, but rather whats," I said.

"You think more than one kind of dead are teaming up to kill?" Fowler said.

"No." It had happened before, the nearly dead working together to get their jollies. The ironic part is when one of their victims comes back to take them out. Not that all the dead come back. No one has been able to figure out yet why so many have been returning to the mortal world or why some do and others don't. A lot of us have our suspicions, but the feds don't like us to spread rumors. "I think it is an incorporate."

"You think a corporation is employing dead to kill for them?" Fowler said.

I shook my head. "It is a fairly rare type of Nearly." Slang term for the nearly departed. "It happens sometimes when bodies are buried together. They come back, not as individuals but as parts of a whole new creature made up of body parts of each of them put together in the order they were buried. It's happened a few times with mass graves." One of them almost wiped out Rwanda and is still a poorly kept secret. The other is the real reason we nuked Sarajevo.

"Did you ever deal with one of these incorporates before?"

I nodded. "Twice. Once it was just the carcass after the souls were taken out. The other time it took out three soul collectors before we were able to take it down"

Fowler let out a long whistle. "Damn. I thought you soul collectors could take out any of the dead."

I shrugged. We have that reputation, but it wasn't that simple. Soul collectors had an affinity for the dead and the power to remove and store souls. The big problem with the Nearly is they were already dead, so they couldn't be killed again, only trapped. Remove a soul from a corpse and it stops moving. Just blow it up and it can take on new forms. In Sarajevo they learned that the hard way. Now they have an angry radioactive cloud that is held in only by some wards. Those spells go down, that cloud is coming after the rest of humanity. The incorporate in Rwanda they trapped in a bomb crater pit and poured tons of cement over it. They've had to reinforce the cement several times as it regularly breaks through the encasement. There simply aren't enough soul collectors on the planet to put it to rest.

"Think you will be able to take this thing out?" Fowler said.

"Depends how many souls are bound together." Removing a soul is a difficult task. It's dangerous to do more than one at a time. It is possible to do it against an entire group, but one mistake and it turns deadly. The most I am able to do safely is three and that is with total concentration. When you are fighting a Nearly, you can't concentrate solely on one task or you will wind up dead.

"Let's see if we can get some video of what did this, so we can see if I'm right and if I'll need back up." It took us a couple hours, but we got some footage from a bank ATM that caught it in a few frames. I was right about the monstrosity. By my best way of figuring, there were at least eight souls trapped in the hulking mass of flesh. Unfortunately it wasn't as if the eight souls were joined together like Siamese Twins in a neat and orderly fashion. There were arms and legs and heads and other parts randomly scattered about a central mass like the body had been melted, then swirled before hardening again. The thing looked more insect than human.

Removing eight souls was more than I could handle. When you remove from an incorporate they all have to be pulled out at the same time or the remaining ones pull the soul back in. Worse, when a collector is doing an extraction, their soul is linked with the one they are taking. We are able to tap into the power of our souls while we are still alive. There is always the danger of the Nearly pulling us out, but that's a remote chance one on one. With an incorporate it becomes likely. Soul cages can only hold one soul at a time. All eight souls would have to be removed together, broken apart from each other and put in eight cages simultaneously.

As much as I hated to admit it, I needed back up. Preferably at least seven other collectors. Problem is there are barely a hundred of us on the North American continent. It would take a day or two to get that many together. All I could hope for is that this thing stayed dormant until the cavalry arrived.

"Fowler, I need eyes in the sky, which means I need to get your air support up," I said.

Fowler laughed. "We are a small town police department. We don't have any helicopters."

"Then call the Staties and have them put some up," I said.

"What part of small town police department don't you understand? The Staties not gonna jump on anything I say unless there is nationwide new coverage," Fowler said.

"Call them and give them my authorization number. They will have helicopters on the way within the hour," I said, handing my business card with the authorization code written on it and ID number.

"Why are the State Police going to be listening to one federal agent?"

"Simple. The federally sanctioned soul collectors have an unofficial policy. Anyone who refuses any soul collector in the line of their duty does not get assistance from when they ask for it." Unlike most federal agents, we can say no. "Do you think the governor wants to explain to the voters why the soul collectors aren't helping when one of the Nearly starts running amuck?" I said. "Besides if this thing gets loose in a populated area, we could be talking hundreds or thousands of deaths. The governor doesn't want to explain that either."

Fowler nodded and looked down at the card. "There's no name on here."

"Your point?" Names have power. Years ago I changed who I was entirely. These days I have a designation, but no name. It's safer that way. And because soul collectors are such a valuable commodity, the government has no problem paying me in cash.

Fowler was impressed that they put three birds in the air. I was able to coordinate with the pilots about what I was looking for. There were two things. The first was any sign of the incorporate. The second was any large freshly dug holes in the ground. I hadn't heard of any incorporate that hadn't risen from a mass grave. That meant someone had buried eight people together and the incorporate had likely dug its way out. We find the hole, we might get a clue as to what caused them to rise.

Since there were eyes were in the sky, I took to the streets. I started by walking around the neighborhood of the murder with Fowler trailing behind me. I was hoping to sense the incorporate, but had to be fairly close to manage that. My ability to sense the dead was a little further than line of sight, but not by much. And it doesn't matter if the Nearly are hiding inside a building or underground for me to feel their presence.

The one thing normal folks don't realize is how much death is around them every day and everywhere they are. We passed by a stoop where a man and a woman were passionately kissing. Standing next to them and staring like he had a broken heart was the ghost of a man clutching a ghostly portrait picture to his chest. It was a wedding photo of him and the woman. Sometimes the dead care about something so much in life that they just can't move on.

I knew better than to stop or intervene and kept on searching. Two hours later, I had found nothing but sore feet.

"Fowler, I need to widen the grid. Drive me around the area," I said. We got in his patrol car. The way sensing works is kind of like scanning a face in a stadium without software. It's not a good idea to go by the bleachers at 60 MPH, so we were doing 20 around the city much to the chagrin of the citizens who would normally be honking and flipping off a driver going so slow. Those same people were much more hesitant to do it to a police car.

One of the cars that past us had a driver that was brave enough to flip off the detective. As he past us, I felt death pouring off him like a bad aftershave.

"Follow him," I said.

"What, for flipping you off?" Fowler said.

"No. He's killed. A lot." The taking of a life leaves the killer with a certain residue. It is why even if we get the Nearly problem under control, soul collectors will still be useful in murder investigations. We can tell just by looking at a person if they have killed, not to mention if it was recently or frequently. This guy registered on both the recently and frequently scale. "Run the plates. Find out if he has a record of military service." He could have recently returned from overseas which would give him a legitimate reason for all the death that clung to him.

Turns out he had never served his country. The recent model car was registered to a Thomas Branagen and had an Off Star system. We were able to make a call to the company and tie into the GPS tracking system on his car. Since we had his address, we broke off and headed for his house. Someone who had killed that much needed a place to get rid of the bodies. He might not have done it at the house, but it was someplace to start.

We went to the front door of the neat little duplex. It even had a nice little white picket fence. I knocked lightly and rang the bell, nobody answered. I smashed in the door with my left hand. That's the dead one. Not part of the original equipment, but it has its uses.

"We don't have a warrant," Fowler pointed out, trying not to stare at my dead limb. I get that a lot, but almost nobody has the balls to mention it to me. Fowler only looked for a moment and to his credit already had his piece draw to back me up.

"The courts have ruled that soul collectors in the course of an investigation can determine the need for entering a private dwelling. Falls in the same loophole as imminent danger. No warrant needed," I said. "We are looking for anything that says he had killed anyone here." We checked the house, then the backyard. It was a bust, just a little 40 x 100 lot with a neatly manicured lawn with no empty graves dug up and the house was clean as a whistle.

"We need to run a check and see if he owns any other properties nearby," I said.

Fowler called it in. Turns out Branagen didn't, but his mother had a little cabin in the woods outside of town.

"I recognize the name. She has been missing for about three months," Fowler said.

I got on the horn and got one of the eyes in the sky to head to the address. Too many trees to get a good look at the ground, but the pilot was able to see that something had knocked down a row of trees leading out of the woods.

"Let's get over there. I think we'll find the grave we're looking for," I said.

Fowler turned on the bubble gum lights and siren then sped towards Branagen's mother's cabin.

"Fowler, we need your soul collector over at Thomas Payne Elementary. We have word of twist mass of multiple Nearly chasing a man on school property," the police radio blasted. Fowler slammed on the brakes and we did a 180.

"My niece and nephew go to that school."

I called the Off Star company, gave them my ID number and asked for the last location of Branagen's car. They told me that it had been in an accident with the air bags deployed, but no one had answered when they called to see if anyone needed help and gave me the nearest address.

"That address is two blocks from the school," Fowler said and the speedometer hit ninety.

We were the first law enforcement on the scene. Teachers and students were fleeing from the school, crying and screaming.

There was one woman who seemed the lone calm head in the crowd. She was barking directions, making sure everyone got away safely.

I went up to her and flashed my badge. "I'm a soul collector. I need to know what's going on in there."

"It is horrible. Massive flesh and limbs. It trapped a bunch of students in the auditorium during a play. There is maniac in there with a machete and a gun blocking the emergency exits. He promises to kill anyone that tries to get out. The thing is throwing children around like they are rag dolls and calling the thing mother."

"Which way to the auditorium?"

The woman pointed and I started running, Fowler on my heals.

Looked like my backup wasn't going to make it in time.

I came in the backdoor and it was pretty much just like the woman said. Kids were huddled on one side of the auditorium. There were a few battered little bodies lying around, but they were breathing. I'd be able to tell if they weren't. On top of the stage was a man with his arm around a woman's neck, his machete to her throat. He had emptied some shots into the incorporate, but really hadn't done it any harm.

"Why is the thing stopped?" whispered Fowler.

"My best guess they are back because he killed them and the threat of him killing someone else is enough to hold him at bay, but for how long I don't know," I said.

"You mean that thing can think?" Fowler said.

"On the most basic level, yes. Right now it is more about emotions. It's a combination of fury and sorrow over him killing them, so the thought of him killing another is enough to give us a window to stop it."

"I got a head shot. I can make it," Fowler said.

"No. The blood of its intended target will only get it moving again. And because it is the focus of the incorporate's reason for existing, it might be able to absorb it into its body, which would make it even harder to stop. The living and the dead don't mix well," I said.

"Then what do we do?" Fowler said.

"I have a plan. I am going to take his soul," I said.

Fowler actually turned his head away from the subject to stare at me open-mouthed. "I thought taking the soul of the living is almost impossible and illegal."

"Not impossible. Just difficult. And very illegal." No DA was going to charge a soul collect over stealing the soul of a lunatic holding a bunch of kids hostage. Plus, the few DA's who've put away soul collectors for reasonable actions insure that city gets no aide from the rest of us. We've had a couple of nut cases that went way over the line. Those don't fall in the protected category. "However the if the incorporate thinks he is dead, it might stop it. Or even better, be put to rest."

"Can you do it from here?" Fowler said.

I shook my head. "Not with the incorporate between us. I am going to have to get closer. To take the soul from him while he is alive is going to take a lot of concentration. If he turns either of the weapons on me, shoot him and I will try to take his soul before the incorporate attacks," I said.

Fowler nodded. "I got your back. Be careful. I can see my niece in the crowd over there, so we have to take this bastard down."

I walked to the middle aisle with my hands out to my side. I had my thumbs holding a soul cage against each of my palms. A soul cage is basically a glass sphere or marble about the size of a golf ball. Tinted glass has properties that with the right magic can hold a soul. Led to the legends of genies. They don't do wishes, only killing.

"Mom, stop it. I'm sorry. All of you just leave me alone!" Branagen whispered. The incorporate made a sound partway between a growl and an earthquake.

"How about we talk about this," I said loudly. It got the attention of Branagen and he trained his gun at my head.

"That's close enough. Take another step and I'll put a bullet in you," he said.

"I wouldn't do that if I were you. I'm the only thing in this room standing between everyone and that incorporate. I'm a soul collector," I said.

Branagen snorted. "Bullshit."

I turned over the palm of my right hand and activated the soul cage. It puts on a pretty light show which is hard for anyone but a soul collector to duplicate.

Branagen's entire expression changed. "Thank goodness you're here. I didn't want to do anything to this woman, but that thing was chasing me. I didn't know what else I could do."

"I understand." I understood he was lying through his teeth, but I still had to get his hostage away. "First thing I cannot stress enough is that any killing or blood will attract it to whoever committed said violent act. If you hurt that woman, it will be on you faster than a zombie on fresh brains. What I need you to do is put the gun and the blade on the ground and let her walk away."

"If you do that you will save me?" he said.

"If you do that I will do my best to stop the incorporate from hurting any innocents," I said.

"Okay." The man took his hand off the woman's neck and she ran away. He bent down and put his weapons on the floor.

"Step back from the weapons," I said. Even as he did so the incorporate started moving forward again on the far side of the auditorium I was in. I had already started the magic with my light show so it didn't take much to extend a tendril into his chest. Branagen screamed bloody murder. It's damn painful to have your soul ripped out. Unfortunately his screams only made the incorporate start running toward him, although what it did was nowhere near a normal gate. Almost a combination of rolling and waddling. I managed to collect Branagen's soul an instant before the incorporate got to him. In fact, the monstrosity caught him before he hit the ground. The incorporate just stood there with seven hands holding the body. It shook him and realized he was lifeless. There was a sound like the grinding of metal and bone before it threw the body into a wall. The neck twisted at a bad angle and there was a loud snap. I had planned to return his soul so he could be tried, but the bastard killed at least eight people, including his mother. I wasn't going to lose any sleep over the way it turned out.

I was hoping at this point that the souls would give up the ghost so to speak and leave the monstrosity they had become. It didn't look like that was happening, although it did seem to be shutting down all higher motor functions. That might be okay for a while, but sooner or later something would rouse it from its slumber and it would start killing again. Murder victims tend to have a lot of anger issues.

I turned to the students and teachers. "Alright," I whispered. "I want everyone very slowly and quietly to walk out of the building. Try not to make any noise." The teachers followed my instructions and very quickly got everyone, including the wounded students, out of the auditorium.

Fowler walked up beside me. "What do we do with it now?"

"I've got an idea that some would say is incredibly brilliant and others would say is incredibly stupid."

"Which do you think it is?" Fowler asked.

I grinned. "I will let you know after I find out if it worked or not."

I took out eight soul cages and laid them out on the stage while standing in what would be considered the orchestra pit in a larger auditorium. The incorporate would likely poorly react to any of its eight souls being forced out, but there were other possibilities. What I had been hoping for was with its act of vengeance done, that the souls would decide to try to move on to the hereafter. I was thinking maybe that was still possible with a little nudging from me.

Apocalypse 13

Collectors are able to see the souls of anything living and I was able to make out the miss mash that was the incorporate. Most of them were twisted and intertwined like a bunch of stereo speaker wires that had been put away by a three year old and an army of angry kittens. However one of them was only wrapped around the outside once. It looked like it had been the soul of a child.

I reached out with my power and gently nudged it in an attempt to untangle it from the others. It took a while, like untying a shoelace that had become knotted too tightly. Persistence paid off and I got it freed from the others. I picked up one of my soul cages, but I didn't activate it. The idea of spending eternity inside a glass sphere wasn't a pleasant one. Although the incorporate had killed, it was lacking conscious thought. If I could get the souls to move on, it would be better than caging them. The human race has at many times in its existence been subject to the herd mentality. That doesn't necessarily change with death. I pulled the little soul out from the rest and then let go of it. It shimmered and floated, then simply moved on from our plain of existence to the next.

I smiled as I don't often get that outcome when I am called in.

I stood and did nothing. I saw one of the souls pull itself apart from the others and follow the little soul into the hereafter. The remaining six souls started moving and unwinding themselves from each other. It took a while, but one by one they moved on or almost all of them did. There was one soul remaining in this misshapen monstrosity and it wasn't going anywhere. As the last remaining soul, it now had control of the union of misshapen flesh. I saw one set of eyes snap open and there was intelligence there. The nightmare of skin and bone turned towards us and all the mouths I could see were grinning evilly.

"Federal soul collector," I said. "Stand down or be destroyed."

"I want my Tommy," it hissed out of one face, but I could make out eight separate laughs moving in sync and a horrible harmony as the creature came straight for me.

I hadn't put down my soul cage and my magic was already prepared. I grabbed hold of the remaining soul and yanked her out, pushing her deep inside the soul cage. Without the others to anchor her, she was no harder to pull out than a typical Nearly. Matter of fact, she was easier because she still believed herself to have the power of eight souls when all she had was the power of eight bodies. There wasn't even much of a struggle. Once I locked the soul remaining inside the cage, the nightmare lost cohesion and the bodies fell apart to a gooey rotten mess of mismatched rotting flesh.

The stench was overwhelmed only by the sight. Fowler moved over to a garbage can and ended up vomiting in it, this being beyond his tough guy endurance. He gained his composure quickly and came over to me with a handkerchief covering his mouth.

"So you won, I take it?"

He didn't see any of the soul show. "Yep. It's all over except for the cleanup," I said and turned to leave.

"You don't help with that part?" he said.

"Nope."

I could see Fowler's spirits drop. He had been a good guy and had a help. I don't often get allow that well with the locals. He didn't deserve to get stuck with taking care of these remains. Then again, no one did.

I stopped and turned back. "Why don't you call it in and have someone else take care of it. I think I'm going to need your help with other matters so you're not going to be available to clean this mess up."

Fowler beamed and did what I said. "What do you need my help with?"

"I'm hungry and I don't know this burg. I figured you would know a good place to go for lunch or an early dinner," I said. That and I could use his help to figure out who the victims were and notify their families.

"Good idea, but I can't believe you are actually hungry after seeing and smelling that thing fall apart."

"Aren't you? Because if you're not, then you're welcome to stay here and help."

Fowler grinned. "Actually a might bit famished myself and I know the perfect little diner. Let me check on my niece and nephew. After that, chow's on me."

In Bullets and Brimstone *Patrick Thomas and John L. French teamed up to introduce us to a world where crime in Hell is literally hell and sometimes the devil and his right hand men need help from a monster hunting Baltimore cop to make things right. In* From The Shadows *they bring together pulp characters The Nightmare and Nemesis for adventure and romance. Now in "A Plague on the Land" John takes the same Baltimore cop to The Realm of Eire to save the love of the Goddess of Retribution Nemesis.*

A Plague On the Land

A story of The Nightmare and Bianca Jones
John L. French

Everyone needs a place to unwind, to relax after a long night at work, to meet with those who share similar interests and to discuss common problems. After hours, when the lights went out and daylight was not that far away, Moran's became such a place. One by one, without seeming to disturb any doors or windows Moran may have locked, the hunters of the night gathered. Men and women who hid in shadows and clothed themselves with darkness in their crusade against crime. This is where they met before assuming their civilian disguises, to spend some time with others like themselves. This was their brief chance to relax. By common assent, little business was discussed, maybe a warning here or a word there about which criminal was plotting what crime and who was seeking whom.

"When did it start?" Seamus Moran wondered as he watched a pint of his best seemingly disappear from the counter. "When did the Dark Ones choose my place and why?"

Those were two questions Moran could never answer. He could not remember a time when they did not gather, when spectral laughter was not heard every night after hours.

"Maybe it's something like a family curse," was his thought as the flash of a fire opal drew his attention. He poured its owner another large Bushmill's then returned to his musing. "My cousin Paddy has the same kind of crowd, less violent though. This sort would not be permitted in his place."

Thoughts of Paddy and his place uptown caused Moran to think of home. Not his apartment above the bar, but of that ancestral place from whence he and his came.

Moran was of the Gentry, the fair folk of Eire, that mythical land that was the Spirit of Ireland, a land that was currently in sore distress.

Moran had first thought to consult with Paddy, but the more he heard and the worse the news got, he knew that this was not his cousin's fight. If there was any truth to the tale, it was a killing matter, and the taking of life was something the elder Moran would not do.

"Now these in here …" Moran scanned the shadows of his bar, barely able to make out his costumed patrons, "most of them have no qualms about pulling the trigger when it would do the most good." There were exceptions - the green one was a man of peace, the pink one killed when she had to but mostly avoided it. Otherwise these champions of Justice were killers all.

Justice was what was needed - Justice for his people, Justice for his land. Maybe he could find it here.

Which one? Few of his afterhour's patrons would believe that Moran was anything more than a short barkeep who served them drinks. They were men of cold steel and science, accepting only what they saw or could prove. To them ghosts were luminous paint and witches just deluded women. But there were those who knew differently.

"You look lost in thought, Seamus."

Such as the Nightmare, the man who just spoke.

"That I was, until yourself came along." Moran sighed, fully aware of what he was about to do. "Could I ask a favor?"

"If you want to peak under my mask, it'll cost you a drink."

"Maybe the next time, this is … can you stay after the rest have gone? It's … serious business, your kind of business."

"Look around, Seamus, they've already left. There's no one in place except you and me."

"How do they …"

"Trade secret."

Dawn was near. Michael Shaw, aka The Nightmare, sat unmasked in a booth waiting for Moran to bring breakfast. Over eggs, bacon and a cold glass of orange juice with which to welcome the morning, Moran made his plea.

"I hate like the devil to ask this of you, Michael."

"There's no harm in asking, Seamus. I can always say no."

"That you can, and after hearing what I have to say you probably will. If so, no hard feelings. You and your money will be welcome as long as there's a Moran's, however short a time that may be."

"Well, if there's a threat to my favorite watering hole I'm half convinced already. Now what's the problem?"

"Michael, there's trouble back home."

"So I've been reading."

"Not the Rebellion. That's a fight that's been going on for centuries and may go on for more. It's not Ireland I'm speaking of, it's Eire."

"They're not the same, I take it?"

Moran shook his head. "Every country has a physical plane - England, the United States, Ireland - and a spiritual plane - Albion, America and for Ireland, Eire.

It is the soul of the Land, and Ireland's soul is blighted."

Shaw's eyes widened as his mind leaped. He sensed a revelation coming, one that would lead to new adventures and fresh challenges. "And you know this how?" he asked as he tried to repress a smile in what was a serious matter.

"It, Eire, is the land of my birth, the land I left when I came to America and the United States, the land to which I dream of one day returning."

Shaw lost his struggle as his smile broke free. "If you're from Eire, then given your size, that would make you a ... leprechaun?"

"Close enough, Michael Shaw. And if it's my pot of gold you'll be asking about next, well, if you do this for me and make it back then you will have earned your chance at it. All I'll ask is a fair head start and if you catch me, it's yours."

"Seamus, I'll never spend the money I have. I don't do this," Shaw held up the mask of the Nightmare, "for the money. None of us do."

"Why do you do it?"

"Because, my friend, it must be done and we few are able and willing to do it. Now tell me, what ails your land and what must be done to save it?"

***

In another bar, some miles and many years away, two women met in a secluded booth. One was tall and dark and beautiful. The other was small, fair-skinned and while the man she loved thought of her as beautiful, she herself did not.

"I'm surprised he lets us in here," the smaller woman said, indicating the diminutive man behind the bar.

"It's not us Paddy objects to, Detective Jones, it's our methods. He thinks that there's always another way. If everyone believed that ..."

"We wouldn't be needed. But tell me, why does the angel of vengeance need the help of a Baltimore cop?"

"You're much more than a Baltimore cop, Detective."

It was true. Despite her small size and slender build, Bianca Jones hunted monsters. Not just the two-legged kind that preyed on the weak and helpless - killers, rapists, drug dealers - but the terrors from dark places that saw humanity as cattle and play things. She was very good at what she did, but this skill was dearly earned and she was always aware of the dreadful cost of failure.

"Granted, but that doesn't answer my question. Why do you need me?"

"You accept who I am, then. Few do."

Bianca smiled. "In Baltimore we do more than wait for monsters to come to us. We research and prepare. We want to be ready to meet a threat when it arises, not try to develop a plan while half the city is being destroyed. So yes, I've heard of you. Nemesis, goddess of retribution."

The woman in black returned the smile. "One of my many names, but it will do for now. As to why I need you ..."

Nemesis drew several tattered pulp magazines from her bag and threw them on the table. They had the title FROM THE SHADOWS emblazoned across the top front and each garish cover featured a man dressed in black wielding oversized pistols while fighting some menace or the other. The captions at the bottom read "In this issue, another exciting adventure of The Nightmare."

Bianca picked up one of the books. "The Nightmare, I heard of him. A character like The Spider or The Pink Reaper."

"Would it surprise you to learn that he was real?"

"After what I seen, little surprises me. I assume there's a point to this?"

Nemesis gave little sign of hearing Bianca's question. "He was much like you, Michael was. No special powers, just an ordinary human doing extraordinary things. He too fought monsters and once helped bring down a god."

Bianca knew the look on Nemesis's face. She saw that look whenever her husband glanced her way. She felt it on her own face when she looked at him.

"You were in love with him."

"I still am and always will be. Yet he is in trouble and I cannot go to him."

Bianca looked at the date on one of the pulps. "If he was alive back then, by now he must be ..."

The woman in black shook her head. "Where Michael is is beyond time. When he entered it was somehow closed to all those like me. That he could pass through shows that the way was not barred to mortals. Michael went to save a world but without help he will fail."

"All this time, is he still ...."

"The realm of Eire is outside time. I have known of Michael's peril since he left this world. Unable to help him myself, I have waited long to find someone who could, a mortal like him who would dare challenge a god. If you are willing, I could send you to him. That, at least, is within my power."

"And so is bringing me back, I trust."

Nemesis nodded. "If you are successful. If not, there's little point."

Bianca sympathized with the woman across from her. To rescue a child she had stormed the gates of Hell. To save her love she had given up Heaven. But she was a practical woman.

"You're asking me to risk my life and leave the city I've sworn to defend unprotected just to save your old boyfriend. Why should I?"

"A fair question, Detective Jones. You just told me that you like to be ready to meet a threat when it develops. If, in the future, there comes a dire, desperate situation, would it not be a good thing to have the goddess of vengeance standing at your side?"

"Favor for favor, then?"

"It is the way of the worlds, Detective."

"Given the circumstances, call me 'Bianca.' And after you order us another round of drinks, you can explain just what I'm about to agree to."

***

The Nightmare stood alone in a dark, blasted landscape. Where there had once been green fields was nothing but brown earth. Burned stumps stood where trees had grown and houses were nothing but ruin and rubble.

Apocalypse 13

There was no sign of life – human, animal or otherwise.

With a pistol in his right hand, the Nightmare carefully approached what had been a village. As he grew close he was met by the odors of decay, pestilence, of burned bodies and spilled blood. Not wanting to look, he searched what was left of the villagers' homes. He found what he had expected, signs of sickness and slaughter.

Some had died of a wasting illness, their lives slowly drawn from them, their emaciated bodies still lying in their beds. Other had died more quickly, slain by knife and sword. Still others had been set afire, their contorted, blackened bodies telling the Nightmare that they had been alive when fire was set to their flesh.

"Seamus," thought the man in black, "what have you gotten me into? At least I can't say you didn't warn me." His mind took him back to Moran's just after the bartender had asked his help.

"Those of us who have left Eire have always maintained a connection with it. We are of the Land and the Land is of us and there's no escaping that. It was a grand place and it was said the Lord made it so that a bit of heaven might be on Earth."

"If it was so grand, Seamus, why did you and your cousin leave it?"

"Aye, and a damned good question that is. I cannot speak for Paddy, that one has his own reasons for everything, but as for me, why does any boy leave a home where people love him and he has all he needs? For adventure, for the challenge, so that the boy might become a man. But if it's a good home you never really leave, do you. There's always a little piece inside you, to encourage you in the good times and comfort you in the bad."

Seamus tapped his chest. "Eire was always right here. And feeling it, knowing that it was but a door away, was enough for me. But now, Michael, that feeling is gone and there is a deep hole where once it was. Something bad has happened, but I do not know what."

"How can I help?"

"I can't go back, Michael, I've tried, but the door won't open for me nor for any of my kind. But for you, a noble man with a just cause, it might. You are not of the Land, so maybe it will not reject you as it did me. Find what's wrong. Stop it if you can. And if you cannot, if all is lost and the Soul of Ireland is gone then you must act as the avenger you are and kill the thing or things responsible. For if you do not, then once it has finished with my Land it will move on to others and one day find yours."

Shaw thought for a moment, then asked, "Seamus, in Eire, is there a god of sleep?"

"There are several, Angus for one, Epos Olloatir for another. Why?"

Shaw checked his guns, then put on the mask that covered one face and revealed another. "Pray to them if you can. Tell them the Nightmare is coming and he could use their help."

Seamus Moran then led the Nightmare to a back room of the bar where stood a door without a room.

"For two days it's been like this. Two days since I summoned it to try and go home. As I said, it will not open for me."

With a nod to the smaller man, the Nightmare strode to the portal and easily passed through it.

"To find myself here," the Nightmare said, again surveying the absolute destruction of the landscape and all who lived in it. A glow in the distance caught his attention. Dawn maybe? He waited and, when the sun did not rise to banish the seemingly eternal twilight, he walked toward the light, expecting to find the darkness that caused it.

***

"I'm back in Hell," was Bianca's first thought when she saw where she was. Then she corrected herself. Hell, at least that part of Perdition where she had met and cheated the Devil, was not this bleak. Hell was where nothing grew except pain and where Hope did not exist. This land, this "Erie" as Nemesis had called it, had once been alive and what was left of the village in the distance told her that the people who lived there had had hope for the future.

Now, though, all growth had been stunted and all hope crushed.

"And I'm supposed to find one man, one dressed in black yet, in this wasteland."

Looking around, Bianca saw a glow in the distance. With nothing else to go on, she shouldered her pack and headed toward it.

***

As he approached his goal, the Nightmare was met first by some of the odors he had left in the ruined village. The smell of sickness and burning wafted his way. Then came the sounds of battle. No, battle was not the right word, for there was no clash of steel upon steel. It was the noise of slaughter - men crying out, women screaming, babies crying. Above it all was the sick laughter of those causing it as they gleefully went about their demon's work.

"If it's laughter they like," the Nightmare said to himself, "it's laughter they shall have."

Drawing his weapons, the man in black came close enough to pick out targets and unleashed his own brand of Hell.

At first the invaders of the village did not know what was among them. There was only the flash of lightning and the sound of thunder. Each time this occurred another or their comrades fell, a hole in his head or punched through his armor. He'd fall dead to the ground though there was no enemy close enough to strike him and no sign of spear or arrow.

Then they saw it, a figure all in black, the lightning spurting from his hands with thunder following. Whatever it was, it laughed as it killed, and like the banshee's mournful cry, the laughter promised death.

But these men were not the common criminals that the Nightmare was accustomed to fighting. Killers to a man and evil to their souls, they were warriors still. Once the initial shock wore off, they turned their attention away from the murder of innocents and focused on the threat at hand. They gathered then charged, each man trusting to his fate that he would not be the one to die next and praying to the god that sent him to be the one to strike down this specter.

"This didn't work out as planned," thought the Nightmare. Though he fired as fast as he could, though with each shot another of foes dropped, those remaining came closer and closer. "They'll be close soon," he thought, "and my guns will be useless except as clubs." He thought of withdrawing, of fading back into the darkness of the night, but he was too close to the burning village, the light of the flames making that darkness too far away for him to reach before they caught him and hacked him to bits.

Better to die on his feet. Raising his guns he shot the two men closest to him. Then greeted the coming charge with a laugh of defiance.

***

Approaching the burning village, Bianca heard gunfire and laughter. From what Nemesis had told her, this meant the Nightmare was close by. A few minutes later she found him, in a fight for his life, firing his two .45s into a mass of warriors that kept getting closer no matter how many he shot down.

"Guess the lady in black was right," Bianca thought as she came up from behind the crowd of men. "He does need my help."

It was then the enormity of what she had to do struck her. "So many," she thought. Bianca was no stranger to death. She had killed both men and monsters before but only once on this scale, the zombie war in New Orleans after Katrina. There, however, she had fought the undead. Here, in Eire, her foes were living men. That they had done terrible things made it easier, but not by much.

Placing her pack on the ground, Bianca removed from two small, round objects. Knowing this day would be relived in dreams for years to come, she pulled the pins on the grenades and threw them into the crowd just as it started its charge.

Twin explosions shook the ground and blew the men closest to them into pieces. They also startled the rest to the point where the black ghost that had killed so many of them was for the moment forgotten.

Some turned to see a small, slender woman standing behind them. She was not laughing and the look on her face was unmistakable. Some sorrow and regret but mostly determination. She meant to kill them. Seeing that she held only what looked like a hollow tube, the men rushed her.

None got close enough to pose a threat. Bianca's Mossberg shotgun roared, its flechette loads tearing her attackers into pieces. Again and again she let loose tiny slivers of death and with each shot her foes fell. And when the Nightmare added his withering fire, the spirit of the warriors broke and they ran like cowards into the night, leaving the two crime fighters alone on the field of battle.

Wading through the blood and gore of the dead, the Nightmare greeted Bianca with, "Thanks. Seamus didn't tell me that he was sending reinforcements." He held out his hand. "I'm called ..."

"The Nightmare, I know, aka Michael Shaw, one of the masked vigilantes of the thirties. Later ... well, I better not say. I'm Bianca Jones, Detective Sergeant with the Baltimore Police Department. And whoever this Seamus is, he didn't send me."

"Miss Jones, or rather, Sergeant Jones. Let's see. You're a woman police sergeant, carrying a kind of shotgun I've never seen. Your clothing is not the kind that women of my era would wear and you seem to know all about me. So if Seamus didn't send you, who did and from how far into the future have you come?"

"The when doesn't matter and as for who, Leda sends her love."

That name. The name by which Michael Shaw knew and loved Nemesis. There had been evenings of bloodshed and vengeance and one marvelous night of passion. Later, after he had given his life for her and she had brought him back from the very brink of death they had separately faced down and beaten a god. She was his first true love and before this night he had had no hope of ever seeing her again.

"Leda sent you. Does that mean that in your time we ..."

Bianca shook her head. "What will be, what Fate allows, I can't reveal. But let me ask you this - what the hell were you thinking, taking on a village of crazed men with sharp weapons?"

The Nightmare shrugged. "It seemed like a good idea at the time. Back ... where I come from I laugh and start shooting. Some fight back and die, the rest run away." He looked at the bodies on the ground. "These didn't run."

"That because they're not pulp fiction gangsters who are afraid to die. These are warriors to whom death in battle is a glorious thing. Remember that the next time we face them. And please take off that mask when I'm talking to you. It's like talking to a shadow."

Thinking, "He doesn't wear a mask," the Nightmare tried to remove his, and failed.

"It won't come off."

"Odd." Like the Nightmare had only a short while ago, Bianca looked at the lifeless bodies around them. "You killed a lot of men today. How many times did you reload those cannons?"

It was then that the Nightmare realized that he had not stopped to reload. "I didn't."

"And how many round do those guns carry?"

Again looking at the dead, the Nightmare replied, "Not that many."

"Strange forces are at work here, Michael. Look at the dead."

He did. Not all appeared to have come from the Land. Many races were represented, some of them not native to the Earth they knew.

"God!" the Nightmare exclaimed.

"More than one, Michael. Let's hope some of them are on our side. Now to find out what's going on in this place."

***

Thanks to the intervention of the two mortal fighters, this time there were survivors. All had hidden in what had been vain hopes that maybe they would be spared, maybe the killers would not find them, that maybe death would pass them by. Bianca wanted to seek them out.

"No," cautioned the Nightmare, "They're frightened and who knows what they might do if two blood-stained killers sought them out. We'll stand here, weapons away, and let them come to us."

They stood and waited, the tall man in black whose very appearance marked him as a creature of the night and the small woman whose duty it was to mete out justice and vengeance. Slowly, as the residents realized that the screaming and crying had ceased and silence once more ruled their village they began to emerge from their hiding holes.

A strange lot they were, the stuff of myth and legends. Leprechauns like Seamus and his cousin, creatures smaller still who flew on paper-thin wings, beasts who could have torn unarmed men apart but who were no match for trained soldiers. Most appeared human, but there was something about them that hinted that they possibly were something more, or maybe something less.

There were twenty in all, twenty survivors in a village where maybe ten times that number once lived. As they emerged from hiding Bianca and the Nightmare saw that despite their size, appearance or nature they were united in one thing, they were all scared.

As they gathered on the main street it was not long before they noticed the pair. Some fled back into hiding. Others, noting that the newcomers had not attacked, waited. A few, seeing blood on the clothing of the two but no wounds on their bodies, counted the dead behind them, breathed a sigh a relief and said a silent prayer of thanks. One of these few approached.

He was a child-sized creature, smaller than Bianca. As he came nearer his age became evident – graying hair, a lined faced and eyes that had seen too much of life.

"You did this?"

The Nightmare nodded as Bianca answered, "Yes."

What would have been a smile under happier circumstances creased the elder's face. "Then the Mother Goddess heard our pleas. We did not think any of the Fair Ones left." He looked around, as if searching for something. "Where is your army?"

"We do not need an army," The Nightmare replied in what he called his "spooky voice."

"All this? The two of you alone did ... this?" Fear and awe was in the old man's voice. He dared to ask. "What are you?"

Bianca would have replied that they were just two people from another land sent to help. The Nightmare had a better sense of the dramatic.

"We are Retribution and Justice. We are Vengeance and Nightmare. We were sent to restore this land."

"Angus, Epos, Arian," whispered the elder as he wondered.

Knowing what it might mean to be named in a magical land, Bianca said firmly, "We are none of these. Our names are our own. And not for you to know. If you must, call us Bán and Tromluí."

The man nodded. "And I am Liam. Your names will be remembered as long as this village stands. You saved us. How may we serve you?"

The cop in Bianca took over. "Tell us what happened. When did the trouble start?"

"When has there not been trouble in Eire? Always there has been war and disease. But nothing like this. Plague and destruction have ravaged all the Land. First the pestilence comes. It kills some and weakens the rest. Then a blight steals the crops away. Sick and hungry, we are no match for the killers that come to finish the job."

"You said all the Land. How do you know this?"

Liam held his hand palm out. A small blue shape fluttered into it. "The piskies spread the news that all of Eire is besieged with warriors destroying all as they march to the sea."

"Thank you, Liam. Excuse us a moment. Tromluí and I must confer."

The elder withdrew.

"What's this 'Tromluí and Bán?'"

"Irish for nightmare and white. Seemed a better idea than taking on the names and attributes of local gods, although that may be too late after your 'Retribution and Justice' pronouncement."

"I was just ..."

"I know what you were doing, Michael. In our world it's dramatic and effective. But in a realm like this, words are magic."

"With just the two of against an army, I'll take all the help we can get. How soon do you think those marauders will be back?"

"Once they'll regroup, soon enough. They may wait for some sorcerous help."

"Then we'd best get ready for them."

It hurt her to say it. "Michael, we'd best get going before they do."

"What, but when those killers come back ..."

"If we fight to save the village, we'll lose the Land. To save the Land ..."

"We let the village die."

It was the logical thing to do, the man who was The Nightmare admitted to himself but that was no comfort at all. He would have argued with Bianca but his companion had waved Liam back.

"The heart of Eire," she asked the elder, "where is it?"

He pointed northeast. "Temair, where stands the Stone of Destiny, where lies the entrance to the otherworld. A day's journey, maybe more. You are going there?"

"Yes," Bianca admitted. "We do not know if this evil began or will end there, but that is where it might be stopped."

There was sadness in the old man's eyes and understanding in his voice as he asked, "And what of us?"

Pointing to the field of fallen men Bianca replied, "There are weapons out there. You can use them to fight and die." Then she pointed to the hills and forest behind the village. "Or you can hide and maybe live."

"A poor choice, Lady Bán."

"Your only one, Liam." To the Nightmare, Bianca said, "Let's go."

"Shouldn't we stop to eat and sleep?"

"Are you tired or hungry? I'm not."

"Neither am I, but I should be."

"Spirits at work again," Bianca said in disgust. "Come on, let's kill some gods."

***

They had been walking north for most of an hour when the Nightmare asked, "Why are we going to this Temair?"

"It's a place to start. If it is the heart of Eire, whoever's behind this either started there, in which case we may find a trail or is heading there, in which case we'll wait for him."

"What if he's still there?"

"Then we sit down with him and calmly discuss why he turned a paradise into a wasteland and ask him politely to make things right again. Either that or just kill him."

"I think we'd best kill him."

Later, after they had trekked more than half a day, "This land is barren," Bianca observed, "withered crops, burned villages, no life at all. Given what we left, I think the raiders came this way."

"I agree." After studying his surroundings the Nightmare added, "Reminds me of the Great War."

"You fought in World War I?" As soon as she spoke, Bianca realized her mistake.

The Nightmare nodded solemnly. "So there's going to be another one? Don't worry; your news isn't a surprise to anyone paying attention. It's always been a question of when, not if. I don't suppose you'd like to tell me?"

Bianca shook her head. "I've said too much already."

"At least tell me if we win."

"The good guys always do, don't they."

"We usually do, at least so far."

Bianca suddenly realized that she had the power to change history. Should I tell him, she wondered. Tell him about Germany and the Final Solution, Stalin and the Iron Curtain, Pearl Harbor and the Atomic Bomb? He's a hero. He could gather the others and together they could kill Hitler and prevent the Third Reich. There might still be war but it might not be as bad. Or it might be worse.

That was the trouble with power. Using it may not always be the best course of action. Bianca decided to leave well enough alone.

That led her to consider her presence in Eire. Was what they were doing there the best course of action? Maybe the Land was supposed to die so that a better one might be reborn. Maybe their intervention ...

"Enough," she yelled at herself, "You're thinking too much. Just do the job you came to do and get out of this hell."

Hell. If the desolation around them reminded Shaw of the war, it reminded

Bianca of the Plains outside Hell. She and her partner had gone there to rescue an innocent. The journey had forced her to face the worst parts of herself. With help she overcame them and left them on the sands of Perdition.

Now Bianca found herself on a similar journey. Walking with a partner through a mythical land. They did not tire, they were not hungry and their guns did not empty. Magic was working. Maybe they should use it.

"Michael."

"Yes?"

"When the time comes to fight, before you act, before you even draw your guns, tell yourself to become Nightmare."

"I am the Nightmare."

"Not *the* Nightmare, just Nightmare, the terror of dreams brought to life."

"This has something to do with what you said before, about words and names having power."

"It has everything to do with it."

"Worth a try. But if I'm to be Tromluí in fact as well as name, what of Bán?"

"She becomes Vengeance."

***

It could have been the same day, maybe the next. In a sunless world there were no days or hours and time was merely an illusion.

"Are we there yet?"

"Tired, Michael?"

"Bored."

"Well, if that slight glow on what I think might be the horizon mean anything, you won't be bored for long."

"Then we should start making plans for when we ... wait. What was that?"

"I didn't hear anyth..."

"You wouldn't. Back on Earth I worked and fought in the shadows. I was part of the night. Here it's as if the darkness is a part of me. There is something out there."

Bianca began to bring up her gun.

"No, don't. Gunfire will only attract attention. Let me handle this. You just keep talking."

Bianca turned to ask, "About what?" but the Nightmare was gone.

There was not much cover in the wasted land of Eire - broken stone fences, husks of trees, partly collapsed walls, but what there was was sufficient to hide a small band of men. Somehow the Nightmare knew where each of them was.

"Miss Jones was right," he thought. "We are close. This must be the first outpost." He sensed movement in the night then felt one of the lookouts leaving his post, no doubt to spread word about the intruders.

"Can't have that." Suddenly he was flowing through the darkness, travelling faster than he ever could in the mortal plane. There was no conscious thought in this, just a desire to catch the running man. When he did, he used a knife he'd taken from one of his foes from the village to silence the man forever.

There are six others. How he knew this he could not say but reaching through the night he found them, flowed to them and used his knife to end their threat. Then he was back with Bianca.

When he again appeared at her side the detective tried not to appear startled. She almost asked how things had gone then saw his cleaning blood off a wicked looking knife.

"There'll be no warning from this direction," said the Nightmare casually, as of the deaths of seven men had not affected him. "Here."

He handed Bianca a pair of matched blades – long knives, short swords – Bianca wasn't sure. "I don't need these."

"Maybe Bianca Jones doesn't, but Bán soon will. In a crowd guns are of little use except as clubs. These are best for close quarter fighting."

"And how do you know they're be close quarter fighting?"

"To quote one of my colleagues, I know."

The pair had not gone much further when distant noises reached them. The Nightmare knew those sounds from the war, they were the sounds of encamped men.

Stealthily they approached, Bianca following the Nightmare, matching him step for step, moving when he did and stopping when he stopped. Finally they reached the camp.

As the Nightmare called on the night to hide them, the pair surveyed the scene.

"Fifty, maybe seventy-five men," the experienced soldier explained to the detective. "Nothing permanent. Those tents are made to be taken down quickly. Look there." The Nightmare indicated one side of the camp. "Men preparing to leave."

"And there," Bianca drew his attention to the other side, "more men coming in. But from where?"

"Up there, maybe?"

The Nightmare pointed past the far side of the camp to where stood a castle. Temair, the Heart of the Land. It was not the fairy tale palace one reads about in stories. Instead it was a stone fortress, one that appeared easy to defend and difficult to breach.

"Liam said that Temair was a gateway to other worlds."

"From which, Miss Jones, whoever or whatever's behind this may be bringing in troops. We have to get in there."

"Any suggestions, other than knocking on the front door and asking to come in."

"I've gotten into more formidable places. But first we have to get past these men."

"Why not just go around them?"

"That would be my first choice, Miss Jones, except ..." The Nightmare pointed at the camp. Men were gathering their weapons and coming towards them. "I think someone knows we're here. We'll have to go through them."

As the Nightmare drew his .45s Bianca readied her shotgun, made sure her

.40 caliber pistol was close to hand. "We'll use out guns until they get close," she said.

"And then?"

"Then we let Tromluí and Bán take over. Start us off, Michael."

"Why not?"

The Nightmare laughed and the pair opened fire.

***

The order came from the castle. There were intruders approaching from the south. They were to be stopped at all costs.

As the men and those who walked like men gathered, they saw two figures at the edge of the woods, a tall one in black and a youth. Neither was armored. Nor did they appear to be carrying any weapons. "This won't be much of fight," most of them thought.

Then there was laughter and thunder and death came for no reason and the men knew them for what they were – wizards or gods. No matter, they were warriors and had their orders. And whatever their nature, the pair would die.

The men rushed forward only to be felled by the Nightmare's bullets or ripped to shreds by Bianca's flechette loads. Still they came, grinning in the face of almost certain death. They knew, or thought they knew, that the pair could not stop them all and sooner rather than later they would be within spear's point or sword's edge and that would be the end of them.

Bianca and the Nightmare knew this as well. As their targets came closer they killed more of them but before they got too close, Bianca said, "Now would be the time, Michael."

"Agreed, and let's pray you're right."

And as they surrendered themselves to their other selves the screaming began.

The two at the woods, the ones that were expected to die easy and messy deaths were suddenly not there. Instead each man faced that which frightened him the most, the things that haunted his dreams and caused him to wake screaming from sleep. Some broke and ran, others stood paralyzed with fright. Still others collapsed in fear.

The man who had been the Nightmare and who was now Tromluí felt their fears and fed on them. Growing stronger, he sent his night terrors further outward, engulfing those still in camp, bringing them to their knees to weep like children.

But there are men who do not fear, or if they do have the strength to overcome it. Horrible monsters, terrible beasts, skinless hags with diseased flesh have no power over them for they have caused more suffering than could ever be dreamt and enjoyed doing so. And there were such men among those advancing, men unaffected by what seemed to be a wizard's curse.

It was these men that caused she who was now Bán to draw her blades and go among them. Against her speed and skill these men had no chance and one by one were cut down. And when none stood against her Bán went down into the camp and continued her bloody work.

When it was over, when there was nothing left but the dead and empty tents,

Bianca and Nightmare slowly came back to themselves.

Bianca looked over the slaughter. "What have we done?"

"What we had to do."

"I'm not so sure. There must have been a better way." She looked down at her hands and he blades they held. Both were bloody. She would have thrown the weapons down had she been sure she would not need them again.

"What have we become?" she asked.

"Something more."

"You enjoyed doing this?" With a wave of her red stained hand Bianca indicated the dead and moaning.

"Not exactly, but ... look at how I dress, what I do, how I do it. It would be easier to strike fear into the hearts of evildoers if I could, well, actually strike fear."

"At what cost? Your life, your mind, your soul. How much of Michael Shaw would Tromluí allow to remain, and what if he chose not to stop with the hearts of bad guys? Magic has a price, Michael, just look around you to know what it costs."

Again Bianca looked at her hands. This time she did drop her blades.

"Point taken, but if we don't want to pay another installment we better get up to the castle before whoever sends down more men."

"You start for Temair, I'm going to search out this gateway to the otherworld."

"Leaving so soon? The party's not over."

"Not yet, maybe not ever, but as you said, we do what we have to do."

As Bianca walked away, the Nightmare could not help but think of how much she reminded him of someone else, although Leda would not have left her weapons, nor would she have thought about the cost of using them.

***

The entrance to the otherworlds. That's what Liam had called it back at the village. If it truly was, it might be her way back, possibly her only way back. That's not why Bianca sought it but it was how she was going to find it. Resisting the impulse to click her heels together she began repeating, "There's no place like home, there's no place like home."

She felt a tug, one which led her to the east of Castle Temair. There she found a mound of earth about the size of a hill, a round hole at its base. Through the hole Bianca sensed Baltimore, her husband Joe and the 21st century. No troops were coming from it, but how long would that last? She did what she had to do. Then, saying goodbye to all she knew and loved, she went to join the Nightmare.

***

The approach to Temair was guarded, but not well. To one whose practice it was to blend with the shadows it was an easy task in this endless twilight for the Nightmare to avoid the guards.

"But why blend with the shadows when you can become them?" asked a voice inside his head, a voice he knew to be Tromluí's. But Tromluí was a part of him, was he not? "Think, Michael, how easy it would be to slide from one shadow to the next, no fear of detection. Where there was darkness and light, there you would be, striking down your enemies, teaching them the true meaning of fear."

"At what cost?" the Nightmare wondered, thinking back on Bianca's warning. "My life, my soul, myself?"

Somehow the Nightmare knew that it was not a part of himself that answered. "You need not worry, Michael, I want nothing from you, only the fear of others."

"What have we done?" he echoed Bianca. "What have we created?" Whatever it was, it was not something he could take home with him, nor did he want it inside him.

"While I appreciate the offer, I think I'll pass," he drew his guns, checked their loads. "I'll make do with these."

That part of him that was Tromluí would have protested but as its creator, the Nightmare was able to push it away and out of his conscious mind.

He was now at the castle gates. Ahead of him was the courtyard and next the Great Hall. The Nightmare suspected that that was where he'd find the source of the Land's troubles.

"Well, Michael," he said aloud to himself, "it's just you, your guns and a laugh against who knows what. The way it should be, without the hocus-pocus. Time to play."

And with that he marched toward the Great Hall to face who knows what.

The first thing that hit him was a wave of nausea. He fought back the urge to vomit then struggled not to soil his trousers. His skin grew clammy then hot as a fever threatened to take him. An itchy rash began in places he did not want to think about.

Disease, he knew, was the first to plague the villages. But his symptoms were not plague-like, merely annoying and potentially embarrassing. His maladies did however tell him that he was in the right place.

Then he saw her, a diseased-ridden hag with more sores than skin. Lesions on her body oozed pus when they did not leak blood. She smelled of putrescence and decay. On seeing her, the Nightmare was glad that he could kill from a distance, for he had no wish to get any nearer to the creature than he must.

"Madame," he said politely, "I think its past time that you saw a physician."

What was probably a cackle came out as a death rattle followed by a prolonged cough. "I doubt if any would heal me, young man. I am the reason for their profession and the source of their wealth. I am Cailleach, and I am Sickness Herself."

Leveling a .45 in her direction, the Nightmare said, "And I have a cure for that sickness."

The diseased goddess laughed again, phlegm gurgling in her throat as she did. "You would think to kill a god? Destroy this form and I will find another."

"And in the meantime the Land will have a chance to heal."

Cailleach smiled, if a show of bleeding gums and blackened teeth could be called a smile."So be it," she said and when the Nightmare fired she made no move to avoid her fate.

He shot her twice, in her head and heart. As she collapsed and began to decay, the Nightmare thought he heard her say, "Beware the stranger and your other self."

Before the Nightmare could consider these words he heard,

"He told us you would come. Where is your other?"

Turning, the Nightmare saw a man at the far end of the hall. He was armored. A sheathed sword hung at his side and in his hands were a shield and spear. The man was tall and well muscled, the image of the perfect warrior.

"You must be War."

The man shrugged. "War, Death, Destruction - it's all the same is it not?"

"Who are you and why do you plague this land?"

"I am called Elphane by some and as for plagues, they were Cailleach's doing. I brought war and destruction. As for why ..."   It seemed to the Nightmare as if the warrior god had tried to speak but could not. He did, however, turn and look at the doorway behind him.

Pistols in hand, the Nightmare advanced, expecting Elphane's attack at any time.

"Were we to fight, dark one," cautioned the god, "you would lose."

"Were I to fire these, you would die."

At this Elphane smiled. "I can throw this spear faster than a man can blink and it always flies true. My shield is such that nothing can pierce it, indeed, whatever force strikes it is returned threefold against my attacker. And when I draw my sword it cuts so clean that you will not feel your head leave your neck. As I said, dark one, were we to fight you would lose."

Bizarre plans ran through the Nightmare's mind. Could he catch the spear? Could he fire and not hit the shield? If his bullets did strike the shield could he then run in front of the god so that they struck him? Rejecting these ideas he simply asked,

"And if we do not fight?"

"Then how could you lose?"

Nodding in understanding, the man in black holstered his .45s. As he approached the far doorway of the Great Hall Elphane stepped aside. To the Nightmare's questioning glance he replied, "I am the god of death and destruction, not a porter. Enter of your own free will. Beware the stranger and your other self."

That phrase again. Who was the stranger? Was it the "he" who had warned Elphane of his coming? And was his other self Tromluí or could it be Miss Jones? What had become of her and would she somehow betray him?

The room which the Nightmare entered was smaller than the Great Hall and was empty of all but a chair and the man sitting in it. If man he was. He was dressed in white and shone with an inner brightness that made the torches on the walls unnecessary. There had been boredom on his face when the Nightmare came in but that disappeared when he saw the man in black.

Immediately sensing that this being was the one responsible for the troubles plaguing the Land, the Nightmare decided not to waste time. Drawing his .45s he fired but as he did so a shadow rose up before the shining man and seemingly swallowed the bullets.

"You didn't think it would be that easy, did you?" the man asked. "Meet your other self."

At the man's words the Nightmare knew the shadow creature for what it was. It was Tromluí, that part of him that he had rejected.

"You came to this Land to stop me and to stop me you took part of the Land into yourself. And when you rejected it you not only gave me the means to stop you but to use that part of you to enter your world when I am done ravaging this one."

From outside the castle there came the sound of thunder and from the doorway the voice of Bianca Jones.

"Your gateway to other worlds just collapsed." To the Nightmare she explained, "Several grenades going off at one will do that to a hole in a hill. We're probably trapped in this world, but then again, so is he."

As Bianca spoke, the Nightmare noticed that she carried a spear in one hand and a sword in the other. "How did you get those?"

"I'll explain later. In the meantime, who's our new best friend?"

"Fools. You are in the presence of Apollonius of Tyana, the true Messiah over that Nazarene pretender. Long have I wandered the many planes of existence, looking for a world such as this, one whose mortal plane is so beset with strife that I can usurp its very gods and cause them to do my bidding. Know this, I needed that gateway only to bring in warriors with which to overwhelm this land. There are other paths which I may trod. Your souls for one."

And the shade of Bán rose up next to that of Tromluí.

"Your own selves will devour you and through them will I gain access to your world."

As the two spirits began to advance Bianca turned to the Nightmare. "Trade you," she suggested and at his hesitation added, "Trust me."

Seeing no other choice, he agreed.

Tromluí which was Nightmare itself enveloped Bianca, filling her being with horrors which would have overwhelmed anyone else. But these terrors paled in comparison to those which the detective has faced in real life. She was a Baltimore City cop and had seen it all – men gunned down for no reason, women brutalized beyond belief, children raped and murdered. Bianca had fought monsters and had walked the plains of Hell. Nothing scared her anymore save the possibility that she would one day fail the people and the city she loved. And since she had lived that fear every day for the past few years, experiencing it again had little effect on her. Powerless over her, Tromluí faded away

As the Nightmare faced Bán he remembered what she as part of Bianca had done to the soldiers outside the castle. And in remembering, smiled. Now and then he saw in this spirit of vengeance an aspect of Nemesis, the goddess and woman whom he loved. Whispering softly the name "Leda" he let that love shine through.

And as Bán had been born of Bianca, and Bianca had been sent by Nemesis, the spirit felt the love. With no vengeance to take, Bán faded.

"Is that all you got?" Bianca asked. Saying "catch" she tossed the sword to the Nightmare.

"Fools," Apollonius said again and unleashed his powers against them. Heat seared one, cold froze the other. They would have fallen, should have fallen but their belief in themselves was stronger than any self-named god. Her skin blistering, Bianca drew back her arm. Barely able to feel his limbs, the Nightmare advanced with his sword.

Bianca let loose the spear that always flew true. It pinned the would-be messiah to his chair. The Nightmare moved closer. One swing and Apollonius did not even feel his head leave his neck.

"Did we win?" asked a very frostbitten Nightmare. Feeling in his fingers and toes was gone and it felt as if his arms and legs were next

"If the bad guy's dead I think so," answered Bianca, her every nerve ending screaming in pain, "but right now it doesn't feel like it."

"F-fire and ice," said the Nightmare through shivering lips. "We're in a magical realm. Do you think ..."

"Worth a shot. It's that or die."

Crawling over to each other, they just managed to embrace before losing consciousness.

***

It was hours, or maybe just minutes later, when they awoke. Both were seemingly healed, the Nightmare with some small tingling in his fingers and Bianca with a decent tan for the first and only time in her life.

The headless body of Apollonius was still in its chair but, like their pain, was beginning to fade.

"That's never a good sign," Bianca said.

"Like us, he was a stranger to the Land. Now we have to find our way back. Any ideas?"

Before she could answer, Elphane came into the room. "May I have my weapons back now?"

"That reminds me, Miss Jones, you never did explain how you got them."

"It seems that there are two answers to my riddle. One was not to fight and the other ..."

"While he was bragging about his weapons I kicked him in the balls and took what I needed," Bianca explained.

"Of the two, I liked your answer better, dark one." Elphane looked at what remained of the corpse. "Still, you managed to free the Land from the stranger and for that you have my thanks."

"And mine as well, Michael."

At the sound of a familiar voice the Nightmare looked around to see a smaller than average man.

"Seamus, but I thought ..."

"With that one gone," Seamus indicated the now almost vanished body of Apollonius, "the way once again opened, my way, at least. I understand it will take some digging to repair this lady's handiwork." He turned to Bianca. "Seamus Moran, my lady, at your service. And may I say it's nice to meet a lady of the proper height for once."

Taking the proffered hand, Bianca said, "I've met your cousin."

"Then you know that good looks run in the family. That is, they run from Paddy and run to me. Ready to go back, Michael?"

"Wait, what of the Land, what of Eire? How will it heal itself?"

"Rest assured, my lady, the one thing we have is plenty of fertility gods and goddesses. The Land will heal amid much pleasure. Michael, it's time I saw you home."

"Past time, I'd say, Seamus, but what of Miss Jones?"

"She'd be more than welcome. She'd fit in well with your group. But hers is a different path. And now if you're ready?"

"A moment, Seamus. Miss Jones, thank you for your help. It was a pleasure fighting at your side."

"Likewise, Michael."

"Give Leda my love. Maybe one day ..."

"Maybe. One never knows. Goodbye, Michael."

"Goodbye, Miss Jones."

***

In a New York tavern, many years away, two women again met in a secluded booth.

"He's safe then," asked a woman in black.

"As safe as anyone who does what he does. And from what I've read ..."

"One never knows, Bianca. The past at times is as fluid as the future. But for now he's safe back then. And I owe you."

"Damn straight you do. I just pray I never have to call in the debt."

A smallish man who looked very much like his cousin came over to their table. "Excuse me, ladies."

"Yes, Paddy?"

"Many, many years ago a man dressed in black with a wicked laugh came to me at closing time and begged a favor. He asked that if two deadly and beautiful women should ever come twice to my bar I was to give them these," he handed them sealed envelopes, "and serve them this." Paddy filled their glasses from a bottle that was old when he was young and the Irish had first learned what to do with the juice of the barley. "Drinks tonight are on Michael Shaw."

Bianca's message was simply "With all my thanks."

Nemesis's message was simply "With all my love."

And for that moment and many more, the laugh of the Nightmare echoed in their minds.

Inter dimensional experiments can be deadly as Edward J McFadden III shows us in this Science Fiction tale of death and destruction. Can astronauts from the International Space Station save a damaged planet and help humankind survive?

Counting Sheep Among the Stars

Edward J. McFadden III

1
Frying Pan

City by city, the Earth had gone dark, and the memory of those final days haunted Commander Valentina Kordova's every waking moment, doubly so during her brief periods of sleep. Known as Val to her two shipmates on the International Space Station, the Russian Commander was strapped in a hammock that was strung across Tranquility Node Three, which she had made her private quarters. She stared out a tiny viewport, the blackness of space and the gleaming stars all that was visible from her limited vantage point. She couldn't sleep, and she imagined dancing sheep jumping from star to star as she mentally counted back from 100 the way her father had taught her.

But there would be no sleep this night, and she doubted Flight Engineers Skip Jennings and Guy Brasic were having better luck. At 0800 Greenwich Mean Time they would begin their preparations to abandon the space station, the place they had called home for almost six years. Using the Soyuz capsule docked at the station as a lifeboat, the two astronauts and one cosmonaut would fall to an Earth they no longer recognized as their home.

That was plan A.

Kordova turned a white pill over and over between her fingers as she considered the other option. They had eaten the last bits of food—*their last supper*—and then the commander had handed out the pills that would put them to sleep and ensure that they never woke. Kordova still hadn't decided for sure which path she planned to take, but she was fairly certain all three of them would be on the capsule when it left the station. Both Skip and Guy were military trained space veterans, and giving up just wasn't in their DNA.

Counting Sheep Among The Stars — Edward J. McFadden III

They all could have given up many times over the last six years, as they struggled to survive on the space station alone, no Earth-side support, rationing food, drinking recycled water, breathing manufactured air, and tolerating each other's failing mental states and increasing body odors. A last minute supply launch as the Earth had fallen into chaos had bought them a few more years, but now they were forced to deal with the inevitable. They had to return to Earth and face head on what the rest of Earth's inhabitants had endured.

Val lifted the pill to her lips, and for the first time actually considered swallowing it. She thought of her three children, her husband, and somehow it seemed easier to just take the pill and join them in whatever beyond they awaited her. But there was still too much discipline, too much pride, for her to leave her two shipmates to their own devices. She knew how to pilot the capsule best, and without her, Skip and Guy's chances for survival went down exponentially.

She cupped the pill in her hand, released herself from the harness that held her in place, and floated across the compartment toward a communication station on the far bulkhead. She flicked on the display screen and cycled through a series of files before she found the one she was looking for. It was a private, encoded message from Roscosmos, the last communication the station had received. NASA had gone dark within 24 hours of the singularity event site materializing, and aside from a few garbled messages, the Americans hadn't been heard from. If the President and other leaders were hiding beneath the mountains hoping the dust would clear, they had chosen to stay silent about it.

An image of a bearded man filled the screen and a tear slipped down Kordova's cheek, then drifted away. Her husband, Gleb, was also a cosmonaut and had worked at the Roscosmos Mission Control Center. She paused the image, letting his face fill the screen. It had been the last time she had seen him. A few more tears came, the droplets floating in the air before her. She hit a button, and the image unfroze.

"Val, are you OK?" he asked, his eyes frantic. Val had known the instant she had seen him that things had gone very wrong Earth-side. There was a pause in the tape as she had responded, but her response wasn't recorded. "Things here have," he paused, and looked off camera. "Things here have deteriorated. We are still unsure as to what has happened, but we think the EU had an experiment go wrong and…" he paused again, and his face disappeared from view, and never returned.

Communications and video they had received prior to this final message had shown a collapsing civilization and a dying world, but all Kordova and her crew could do was watch as the atmosphere filled with green smoke and the oceans turned black. There had been no earthquakes, no crashing mountains, surging seas, or hurricanes. In fact, there had been no natural disasters at all, but the images of the panicking and dying masses had told them all they needed to know. The damage and killing had been caused by creatures that no one understood and the green smoke they needed to breathe. The devils had systematically killed and destroyed every living thing they could find, and though Kordova and her shipmates knew there were most likely pockets of survivors around the globe, they also understood that in such small numbers they were powerless against the demons that by all accounts had crawled from whatever disaster the EU had created. The images of the creatures she and her crew had seen ranged from bug like organisms that ate their victims from the inside out, to huge, mangled, dinosaur-like beasts that stalked the Earth, crushing anything that crossed their paths.

Then there was the green smoke, which the creatures needed to breath, but that killed humans and most animals after a few simple breaths. The space station was equipped with spacesuits that had been designed for the Mars mission, and were much more advanced than the Extravehicular Mobility Unit (EMU) spacefarers had used for many years. The new suits were much lighter, had a sleeker life support backpack, and could provide air into perpetuity via advanced oxygen scrubbers. Everything was powered by a new top-secret high-tech battery locked into the life support backpack so the astronauts couldn't examine it.

As the screen before her filled with static, Val floated across the compartment and looked out the tiny observation porthole again, the stars looking back at her like millions of dead eyes. She peered downward through the thick glass, and she could clearly see the volcano of green light spewing from the Earth where CERN had been. The light wasn't flames, but the incandescent glow of the green smoke as it bellowed from the rent in space-time. That would be their destination. They would try to figure out what had gone wrong and fix it, or die in the attempt.

The end times had laid waste to the Earth, cleansing it of man. But Jesus had not come.

2
Fire

"Brace for impact!" said Commander Kordova, as she prepared her crew for landing.

Their morning had started with an early scare when the electronic docking claw wouldn't work. But after two hours of rerouting systems they finally managed to free themselves and begin their voyage home. They had breathed pure oxygen while Guy played with the landing claw, so Val had ordered them to put on their spacesuit helmets and life support backpacks as a precaution.

Their fears that the landing parachutes that would allow them to soft land their ship had been damaged, or were covered in ice, had proven unwarranted. When they had opened, and as the spacefarers felt the pull of tension on their harnesses, the three companions forgot, for a couple of minutes, what they would find upon their return home.

All space station modules had been closed off, and all systems turned over to the computer, so the station theoretically could remain in orbit for years due to the large solar arrays that captured the suns energy above the green horizon. With the station modules sealed from one another, it could sustain damage in one part but still not be destroyed. Guy had asked Val why it mattered, and she had shrugged.

Val shifted in her harness. Her spacesuit was uncomfortable and she hated wearing it, but something told her they were going to have the suits on for a long time. The capsule *thumped* upon impact with the Earth, and teetered, and for an

Counting Sheep Among The Stars   Edward J. McFadden III

instant the crew thought the capsule was going to tip over. After a few tense seconds the ship settled itself, but on a fifteen degree incline. They had landed on something.

As Skip reached up to open a comm. channel, the capsule was rocked to one side as if it had been hit with a battering ram. The space ship fell on its side leaving Guy and Skip looking down at Val as they hung in their seat harnesses. "What the hell..." said Skip, as the interior of their vessel echoed as something pounded on the hull. Val and her crew strained to see through the tiny porthole, but they could see nothing but green sky and black clouds.

An eye filled the porthole, and Guy screamed. A red pupil rolled against a black cornea and settled on Val, and then narrowed. The capsule rocked, and the red and black eye splattered against the window, pieces of skin and eyeball sticking to the glass. They were jerked in their harnesses as the ship was lifted from the ground, and then they were free falling, and Skip and Val realized what was happening before Guy because they held tight to their restraints.

The capsule landed on its side and Val shrieked when she heard the crunching of metal. The space travelers looked about their vessel, but everything appeared intact. Silence fell, and they waited for several long minutes, expecting at any moment to be tossed like a pebble. Red light from the warning klaxon spilled across the cabin, painting everything in a ghostly red glow. "Check yourself out before you climb out of your harness. Make sure all the seals on your suits are tip-top and I want a ship status report ASAP."

Static filled Val's headset, then "Yup," from Guy, and "10-4 Commander," from Skip. While Skip cranked up their communications and tried to verify their location, and Guy checked ship's systems, Val pulled a key from the pocket of her spacesuit using a short tether, and unlocked the storage container bolted under her seat. Within were three Ash 12 machine guns and five MP-446C Viking handguns, spare magazines, related holsters and shoulder straps for all eight guns, a knife, and a bottle of Russian vodka. Val smiled at the thought of the dead soldier at Roscosmos that had put together their last shipment of food and supplies, and smiled.

Val strapped on a leg holster they had modified to fit over their spacesuits and slipped a Viking into its cradle. Then she slammed a magazine containing lightweight supersonic bullets with aluminum cores into one of the Ash 12s and pulled back the bolt, loading a round into the chamber. They would load all the weapons, but they would be fired only when absolutely necessary, because reloading would be very difficult while wearing their spacesuit gloves. They had wrapped their trigger fingers tightly with duct-tape, which made it possible to fire the weapons with their gloves on, but it was still a challenge.

"Val, I didn't pick-up anything. I mean, not even any distress beacons. If anyone is alive they don't want anyone to know," said Skip.

"Are we where we want to be?" asked Val. They had plotted a course to touch down in a small valley in the Alps, just south of Geneva. The coordinates for the valley had been sent via an encrypted message from Roscosmos before they lost contact, with no explanation. Val deduced that the landing site had been chosen because of its proximity to the singularity event site, but Guy and Skip felt there must have been other reasons. Their plan was to utilize the capsule as a base, and search the area.

"Think so. I only had power for a few minutes, and we were tossed pretty good. But we should be pretty close to our mark," he said.

"We're dead here, Commander, nothing but a trickle," said Guy, static filling their spacesuit comm. channel. "We got nothing left. All systems are down. The batteries must have been damaged. We've used up what little juice we had, so we're gonna have to pop the hatch manually."

Val nodded, Guy and Skip collected their weapons and the three spacefarers fumbled around the cabin and each other. The spacesuits were difficult to maneuver in, especially in tight spaces, but thankfully their years of training had made functioning in them like riding a bike. Guy loaded the extra guns, the knife, and the bottle of vodka into canvas bag, and tethered it to his belt.

"OK. Everyone ready? Heads on a swivel," said Val, as Skip popped the hatch, and thin green smoke rushed into the capsule. They waited a few minutes, letting the emerald gas surround them. Their suits were working, and Val looked at each of her shipmates in turn and smiled.

First hurdle cleared.

Skip inched through the hatch, then disappeared from view as something with yellow fur darted across the hull and pulled Skip out as if he was a ragdoll. "SHITTTTT," yelled Val, as she thrust herself upward along the steel footholds until she was halfway through the hatch. A creature that looked like a tiger with a head full of eyes and teeth was getting ready to take a bite out of Skip when Val opened-up with the Ash 12, peppering the creature with bullets. She cringed behind her visor, the empty shells bouncing off the capsule's hull. The creature fell to the ground and Skip got up, moving like a child who had been bundled up by his mother so he could play in the snow.

Val was through the hatch in an instant, followed by Guy, and in the space of thirty seconds the two astronauts and one cosmonaut had their backs facing the capsule as they peered into the green gloom.

"That was close," said Skip. "Thanks, Val."

Val wondered if she had done the man a favor, or a disservice. Through the gloom they could see creatures of all shapes and sizes massing for an attack. It was as if their presence had sent out an alarm. They had plummeted from the sky, and every beast for a 100 klicks saw and heard their landing.

"What now?" asked Skip.

"Let's get back in the capsule, and use it as cover. We can—" Val was cut short by the sound of shrieking mortar fire. Fifty yards from the capsule there was an explosion, then another, then a third. The monsters were scattering, wailing as they went, but then came another menace. The ground rumbled every few seconds as something very big came their way.

But then like angels floating through green clouds people in blue biohazard suits burst from the haze, beckoning them to follow. Val motioned for Guy and Skip to fall in behind her as she ambled toward the newcomers. She didn't know who these people were, but they were people!

"Guess we know now why the Russians wanted us to land here," said Guy, as they disappeared into the green mist.

Their new friends moved fast, threading in and out of dead trees and scorched earth. When they reached a small cleft in a mountain face, the leader stopped, went to Skip, and pulled his faceplate close to his. "Follow us," yelled a man with deep-set green eyes and curly black hair. "The passageway is very tight, and if you rip your suit, you're dead." Skip gave the man a thumbs up and relayed the information to his companions over their suit-to-suit comm. channel. Val was mildly annoyed that they thought Skip was the leader, but knew they had bigger problems than sexism.

They inched along the tall rock face, and after a few minutes, some people split from the group and began fanning away into the smoke, firing cover rounds. Then their leader slipped behind a large stone, and they entered a cave. The tunnel followed around many curves, and narrowed to no more than five feet in width when they came to a ramshackle steel wall that looked like it had been welded together using old cars and other pieces of scrap metal.

The man with the curly black hair tapped four times on the door. It slid open, and they passed through. The steel wall was more than four feet thick by Val's count, and she considered how much work it must have taken to create. Once inside, the leader took off his biohazard hood, took a deep breath, and smiled. "We have some power in here, and life support." Val looked at Guy and Skip who both looked skeptical. "There are guys from CERN here. We have geothermal systems. Trust me," the man said with a French accent that made Val blush a little.

"Me first," she said, as she popped the seals on her helmet and took it off. After taking several deep breaths, she nodded at Skip and Guy, and they did the same.

"My apologies, Commander. I am Louis Callilett," said Louis, as he extended his hand to Val.

"No apology necessary," said Val. "I am Commander Valentina Kordova."

"Ah, a Russkie," said Louis. "Fedor will be so pleased. This way."

The tunnel widened considerably before narrowing again, and Val could see that their camp wasn't very big. "How many people do you have here?" she asked.

"Not many. Nineteen men, seven women, and two young boys. We fled up here from Geneva as soon as the rip appeared. Jacob knew what it was right away and got supplies from CERN, where he worked. Several of the people here are scientists, and a few are soldiers. The soldiers raided their base as they fled, and we met up with them because Rafael loves Gina, and Gina was with us," he said, smiling.

"How did you make this place," asked Skip, motioning around him.

"It looks like more than it is, really," said Louis. "All the tunnels and antechambers are natural. Once Dr. Jenkins setup our geothermal power source, things got easier. Keeping the creatures at bay while we got the supplies and completed the place was the hardest part. We lost more than half our people in the effort. And it was important that we didn't attract attention to ourselves. That's how some of the major installations got wiped out. Some of these things can chew through rock."

"Dr. Richard Jenkins?" asked Skip. "He is an American scientist?"

"Yes, we are very diverse here, because of CERN, mister...?"

"I'm Skip Jennings and this is Guy Brasic."

"Nice to meet you," said Louis. "Are you hungry?"

"Very much so," said Val. "Do you have food?"

"Never enough, but we do have a garden where we grow things under lights, and some of the demons are edible after intense long-term cooking to get the toxins out. And thanks to our geothermal power, we also have plenty of distilled water."

After they had eaten and washed up, they were given clothing and didn't ask who the prior owners had been. They sat in a large stone chamber with most of the adults who lived in New Geneva, as the inhabitants called it. They had been introduced to everyone, but it was impossible to remember all the names, and Val and her crew were feeling quite overwhelmed.

"Louis told you the basics, but you must have a million questions, so shoot!" said Elva, the widow of Jacob Dovtor, the man who had founded New Geneva, but who had died building the barrier wall at the cave's entrance. Elva led the group now.

"Everyone keeps referring to the singularity as a tear. What do they mean?" asked Val.

"Jessica," said Elva, and motioned for a young lady with long blonde hair to come forward. "Jessica saw the entire thing with her own eyes. She was so afraid my husband helped her, and she followed him."

The demure women seated herself in front Val, and said, "I was sitting at a café, having a coffee, when there was this sound like all the air was being sucked from the world. To the north a green slit opened in the sky. For a moment, it looked like a door opening with green light spilling through. As it got bigger, I fainted. When I woke, Jacob was tending me."

"The cause..." Elva paused for effect, and looked around. "Some feel a comet coupled with a planetary alignment caused the rip in space-time, creating a singularity. A place where physics as we know it don't make sense." She paused, looking at the spacefarers. "Most believe CERN caused the rip with one of their accelerators, as do we. Many thought God had brought on the apocalypse, and breathed the green smoke willingly, so they could join their deity."

Silence. Val looked at Guy and Skip. This was what they had been told. "How did my people know about this place?" asked Val.

"Fedor notified his government of what we planned to do. Some of the creatures are smart. Real smart. And many of the world's top secret facilities were already being overrun. So they took a chance. Plus, we are practically on the edge of the event site. If it keeps expanding at the current rate, it will overtake us in approximately two more years. What better place to mount an offensive?"

No one spoke, and Val looked around at the dirty faces. Many looked tired, but most also looked defiant. "Any idea how we can close the rift? Remove the singularity and stop the creatures and smoke from passing through?"

"We had hoped you would ask that," said Elva.

A tall German stepped forward. He wore glasses with a cracked lens, but his keen brown eyes sparkled. "My name is Gustoff Greyhelm. I am a particle physicist, and I worked in the CERN complex. We were running an extremely difficult experiment in the Large Hadron Collider the day the anomaly appeared, so I think we caused it. Like most rips when under stress, it has expanded. The singularity is huge now, so one can walk directly into it. Three have. None have returned. In fact, I don't think any of them made it all the way inside. The closer you get to the vortex of the singularity, the higher the temperature gets, and the more intense the winds get. Their biohazard suits melted and ripped before they could pass all the way through. Your spacesuits, however, might make it. Much of this is speculation based on transmissions we received from the three who entered the singularity, but to say our data is incomplete would be a huge understatement."

Val looked at Skip and Guy, and then asked, "Enter it? Why?"

"To close it," said Gustoff.

3
Salvation

There would be no counting sheep on this night, and the absence of stars in the cold blackness above made Val shiver. She lay on the floor next to Skip and Guy, their valuable spacesuits stacked behind them. The natural cave room was angular, and barely fit the three of them and their equipment. The sound of Skip's gentle snoring eased Val's mind as she ran what she had learned over and over in her head.

The plan was simple. Three people, presumably her, Skip, and Guy, would try to enter the singularity, and as soon as they reached the vortex, they would detonate a device to create an explosion, spreading charged particles that would apply force from within the anomaly outward, reestablishing enough symmetry between dimensions to close the hole. The obvious problem with the plan was that someone, or three someones, would have to die to make it happen. Due to the instability of the singularity event site, there was no way to detonate the device remotely, so at least one person would have to stay behind.

She would have to be the one to go, and Skip and Guy would have to accompany her. They knew how to operate the spacesuits and were used to maneuvering in them. Her head hurt, but as she drifted off to sleep, her gut told her she was in for a surprise.

***

Several days passed while Val and her crew rested and strengthened their bodies, and steeled themselves for what was to come. After ten days, they were summoned to Val's administrative office, which was nothing more than the front corner of her small living space. She had a wooden table and two chairs, but everyone sat on the floor because there weren't enough chairs. Louis, Fedor, Dr. Jenkins, Dr. Tairy, Val, Skip, Guy, and Elva sat in a tight circle, the bottle of Russian vodka at their center. Everyone looked a bit uncomfortable as they sipped their vodka and tried to look casual while doing it. Val, seeing the nervous eyes and worried glances, asked, "What's happened?"

"Skip," said Elva.

Skip took a long pull on his vodka, and looked at Val. She saw something in his eyes that she'd never seen there before: shame. "We all think you should stay behind."

Val reared back like she had been tapped in the face with a light jab. Her eyes opened even wider when she figured out why they wanted her to stay. "I am not a goddamn queen bee!" she shouted. Guy and Skip looked at one another, and couldn't help but share a smile.

"More like saving the human race, but call it what you want," said Elva.

Val got to her feet and paced around the group. Her mind raced as she ran through the men she had met the prior night. *I bet Fedor is to be my mate,* she thought. Her mouth fell open, and then tightened as she started to scream, but closed again when the harsh logic of the situation struck her. "And who is to be my mate? Fedor?"

"To start, if you choose," said Elva. Val looked at Fedor, who blushed and looked away. Elva continued, "There are nineteen males, seventeen of whom are fertile. There are seven women, only three of whom are fertile." She paused, and let the silence stretch out. "Then there's the fact that we need you to lead this place. I lead because Jacob asked everyone to follow me. You should lead the human race back to the surface, Val. You."

Val had never been religious, but her mother had raised her as a Christian, and in that moment she prayed that her dead husband and children would show her the way.

"Elva, I..." A large man with a dark black beard had entered the chamber. He froze when he saw Val. They looked at one another as if they knew each other, the burly Russian transfixed, his eyebrows knitted, and his mouth fell open a little. "Valentina?" he said, still not believing what he was seeing.

"Nikolai?" said Val, as she threw her arms around the man and hugged him tight. Turning to the group she said, "We were at flight training together."

Nikolai broke the embrace and looked at Elva. "Sorry to intrude, but you wanted a report as soon as the advance crew was back." Elva nodded for him to continue. "Nothing's changed other than the space capsule is gone. If we're careful, we should be able to get them to the edge of the event site."

"Thank you," said Elva, and Nikolai retreated with a sideways glance at Val.

"We have a long march to get to the event site's edge, no? Seems like those things get drawn to us like kids to candy. How can we make it?" asked Skip.

"We know a few secret ways. Plus, in our suits the beasts have a much harder time sensing us. Very little scent, is what we figure. When you arrived, your entrance sort of gave you away," said Louis.

"And who will go in my place?" asked Val.

"Terhan Estani. He's about your size, and is one of our soldiers. You—if you accept the offer to lead—will decide who leads the mission. We can provide an escort to the edge of the singularity, and then they will be on their own."

Everything that made her who she was fought the idea that she would become a baby machine. She was a warrior, had bested men twice her size, and now they wanted her to stay pregnant for the rest of her life, by a series of men she didn't know. That would change, of course, and she did know Nikolai. And to be the leader. That showed a level of respect that made it hard for her to look at things from only the baby angle. Her three kids had been born without complication, and the more she thought, the more it made sense. Also, somewhere deep inside she knew her husband Gleb would understand.

But that didn't mean she had to like it.

"Skip and Guy will flip a coin to see who leads," said Val, and she turned to Elva. "This special bomb is ready to go?" Elva nodded. "And your people are ready to guide them to the site?" Elva nodded again. "They leave at 0800 tomorrow," said Val. She could barely contain her emotion as she looked at Skip and Guy. Then she strode from the room before she started to cry.

***

As they got closer to the singularity event site things got even more hairy. They had used a secret passageway that let them out in the northern foothills of the Alps, just south of the event site. Geneva was gone, and in its place a huge green smudge covered the ground and extended into the sky. Green smoke seeped from the site, and the closer they got the thicker it became.

Skip, Guy, and Terhan had said goodbye to their escorts that morning, and Skip had never felt as alone as he did when the six people wearing blue biohazard suits disappeared into the haze. It was the end game, and he, Guy, and Terhan were about to make their last move.

Skip had won the toss, and he brought up the rear. Terhan was on point, and though he was having a difficult time getting used to the spacesuit, he was doing OK. Guy hadn't spoken since the others had left, and he was no doubt thinking the same thing Skip was: these are the last moments of my life, and I need to make them count.

Shrieks, growls, and constant chirping sounds filled the smoke all around them, but so far they had dealt with only a few minor attacks. *We've been lucky*, thought Skip, but no sooner had that thought floated through Skip's mind when they were engulfed by a strong gust of wind and Terhan fell to the ground, which probably saved his life.

A slender creature that looked faintly humanoid flew through the air right above where Terhan had been standing. Skip squeezed the trigger on his Ash 12. A burst of gunfire struck the creature in midair, and it fell to the ground in a heap.

They tightened their formation; Skip watching their backs, Guy their center, and Terhan still running point. The number of creatures around the event site was immense, as they roamed free between this world and the other. Several times, they had been forced to wait behind a large rock, or in a ditch, as hordes of demons—of all shapes and sizes—passed them by.

The howling alerted them to the attack, but they only had seconds to prepare.

Apocalypse 13

Large creatures that resembled deformed giraffes with purple-orange skin, two heads, and six legs, stampeded toward them through the haze, and Skip fired, followed by Guy and Terhan. All three men emptied the clips of their Ash 12s, covering each other as they reloaded. When the creatures began to back off, Skip and his companions retreated into the mist, piles of dead demons all around them.

A tall, slender creature with two arms and five eyes stared at Skip from a few feet away. Then there was a popping sound, and the air was pulled from the area like someone had activated a huge vacuum. The creature blinked out of existence like it had never been there.

There was more gun fire, and Skip saw Guy facing two demons that were glowing against the pale green smoke. Their pink skin looked raw, and they each had multiple legs and arms, and a big head with a single red eye. Guy's Ash 12 rattled, and the creatures split apart, dividing every time a bullet hit one, and within seconds Guy was under a mound pink flesh.

Terhan screamed, and Skip turned just in time to see him dragged by the leg into the green smoke. Skip knew Guy had the bomb, and so he headed for the pile of creatures that were trying to pull the astronaut apart.

Beneath the mass of bodies, Guy was firing his Viking, and blue blood and pink flesh splattered Skip's white spacesuit as he started pulling creatures off his friend. The things had sharp teeth, and Skip was careful not to let them rip his suit.

Guy wasn't so lucky. Several seconds passed as Skip tossed creatures, and Guy shot them, but in those few seconds, the green smoke seeped into a rip in Guy's suit and his eyes bulged from his head. He reached out toward Skip, the small box containing the bomb in his hands. Through the rounded faceplate, Skip could see Guy's face turning red, sores and gashes appearing all over his head.

"You do it, damn you. You do it!" he screamed, as blood spewed from his mouth, splattering the inside of his faceplate. Then he was gone.

Skip looked down at his friend, and thoughts of what would happen to his corpse sent a shiver up his spine, but he didn't have time for pleasantries or sentimentality. Skip grabbed the device and ran as fast as he could, the spacesuit weighing down every step, as he looked for Terhan, but all he found was a thin trail of blood, and then a spacesuit boot with Terhan's foot still in it. Skip barely gave the appendage a second glance as he rumbled forward.

A group of monsters was forming around Skip, and he knew that if he didn't reach the event site soon, he never would. A bolt of lightning ignited the air around him, and Skip dove to one side, barely avoiding the explosion. Two huge legs appeared in the vapor, and Skip pointed his machine gun upward and opened up, screaming as he emptied the Ash 12's magazine again. When the Ash 12 was empty, he threw it away, got up, and ran, his ears ringing. There was a gust of wind, and the Earth shook as the beast Skip had killed fell.

Two bat-like creatures with long knurled talons streaked from the green smoke, and Skip drew his Viking and blew both from the air with two clean shots. More creatures were gathering, and Skip ran forward blindly into the event site.

There was no beginning and no end, and Skip felt like he was under water, all his movements slow and exaggerated. There were trees, and the buildings of Geneva, but they were up-side-down, and most had huge chunks missing. Creatures of all shapes and sizes moved around him, but they didn't seem to see him. The wind had picked up and his internal cooling system was running at maximum.

Skip didn't know how far he had walked, but every step was an effort, and it felt to Skip as though the wind itself was trying to keep him from his goal. It whistled by him now, and on he walked, fearing every step would be his last, when finally the wind began to lessen, and the pressure on his chest began to ease. "The eye of the storm," he muttered to himself, as he crossed a large patch of grass, which squeaked and yelped as he walked on it. Above him buildings hung in the air, and his vision began to flicker, like every other frame of visual space had been removed.

Then he was there, standing before a clear hole that looked like a tornado. He thought of his wife, the way his house used to smell when she cooked, and the scent of her perfume. Then he remembered Val, and stepped forward into the vortex, and detonated the device.

4
Of Things to Come

Seven years later...

Val smiled and looked to the sky, a patch of stars visible through a break in the green haze. Perhaps her great-great-grandchildren would be able to count sheep and fall asleep beneath the stars without a breathing apparatus, but for her, and her children, the difficult life would continue underground while the Earth healed itself. Weeds sprouted all around her as life began to reassert itself on the mountain-side, providing oxygen.

By all accounts, the rip had closed and the singularity had disappeared. Val didn't know for sure what had happened, but once the rift closed, the demons and green smoke stopped coming, and the demons started dying. There were some creatures, however, like the dog-sized scorpion-like beast, which adapted to the oxygen atmosphere, and would be a constant reminder to humans of what had happened.

With most of the creatures removed as a threat, scavenging efforts began in earnest, and Val and her people had made contact with several other outposts around the world. Children were being born, and Val herself was pregnant with her fifth child since returning Earth-side, her third with Nikolai. That made eight in total, her first three having perished in what everyone now called The Awakening. It had been science that caused the apocalypse after all, and science that had saved them—religion had been irrelevant. Val hoped that put religion behind them as a species, but it had been a rebirth, and even the most hardened heathen couldn't deny that.

Val imagined a day when she would be able to stand by her children on the surface, counting sheep as they jumped from star to star, and telling of the days when it was just her, Skip, Guy, and the vastness of space. And how others had died so that they could live. Maybe that day would come, maybe it wouldn't, but at least now she looked down a road that was heading toward the highlands instead of the deepest of valleys. It would take hundreds of years, maybe thousands, before the oceans returned to their clear majesty, and once again teemed with benevolent life. But teem again they would.

That fact, that hope, made Val laugh, and she threw up her arms and pointed toward the heavens, and the sheep dancing among the stars.

Samantha Mills and Briana Vandenbroek envision an environmental disaster like no other. Clean, uncontaminated water is scarce, rationing is in force and the fae's control of the weather is not making the situation any better. Into this world comes an agent hired to steal an envelope and make a simple hand off that turns out to be anything but simple.

MIRROR, MIRROR

Samantha Mills & Briana Vandenbroek

As Miranda drove up the Coronado Bridge she felt a surge of paranoia. The gray waters churned beneath her, several shades darker than the storm clouds churning overhead. Even this strip of bay, quarantined from the danger of the open ocean, seemed to exude a malevolent energy. Any day now, another earthquake off the California coastline might destroy what was left of the beach community.

If a storm didn't do it first.

She practically held her breath for the two mile stretch and imagined she could hear the highway groaning beneath her car. The city council was still in budgetary deadlock. There was no telling when the next round of repairs might be approved.

But the only alternative to the bridge was to detour south and drive up the Silver Strand, the narrow isthmus providing the only land route to Coronado. Miranda shivered at the thought. The creatures inhabiting the Strand could tear through her little car without breaking a sweat.

For the hundredth time she ran the pro/con list through her head.

Pro: Bateman was paying her a lot of money.

Con: Their mark had set up camp at a luxury hotel in the middle of the freaking bay.

Pro: Bateman was paying her a *lot* of money.

All she had to do was steal an envelope from her mark, and hand it off to her contact outside the hotel. Easy enough, right? Along with her instructions and a dummy packet, she was given a photo and a name: Hammond Peterson. Bateman was vague about the contents, but explicit about the need for discretion. And when you need discretion who else do you turn to but a professional thief?

If Bateman made good on the second payment she'd be able to pay back Smitty ... and Mr. Mylo, and maybe a few of the others to whom she owed her money or her life. Just because you were damn good didn't mean the clients were lining up.

Times were rough all over.

"Water water everywhere..." She whispered; it was one of granny's mantras. She'd been resorting to them a lot lately.

She passed a figure standing off to the side, arms raised above his head and his face upturned to the sky. Though she couldn't see his face, she knew his eyes would be shut and his lips moving in silent chant. Weather control was not a simple magic. It took total concentration to hold back or bring forth a storm of this magnitude; the newscasters were warning residents of fist-sized hail stones, torrential rains, and listing the potential flood zones from which to steer clear. Not that anyone would be stupid enough to go out in this weather once it was on top of them.

Well ... except for Miranda.

At last the bridge angled down. She breathed a sigh of relief as she rumbled back onto solid earth and passed through the remains of the old toll booth plaza.

Coronado was quiet and largely abandoned. Private security forces patrolled the town, hired by the remaining locals to ensure vagrants remained safely on the other side of the bridge.

And there, at the center of the island, loomed the Villa Del Agua— the wealthy man's way of pretending he could still control the world, even as it fell down around his ears. It was built into a contrived mountainside which, along with some fae-bought sky shielding, protected the structure from the storms that wrecked ocean level buildings. The hotel boasted spacious rooms, loose staff, rare foods, and most importantly, clean water.

Miranda drove herself into the protected parking structure at the bottom of the hill, making sure there was a strong light shining on her windshield where she parked. She walked out of the structure into the chill, salty air and her hair began to curl.

She got about one flight up the hillside stairway before a scene outside the parking structure caught her attention. She leaned over the rail for a peek, and immediately regretted it.

The security car caught her eye first. It was the guard's personal car made to look authoritative: aka a tan sedan with a magnetic light on the roof. The guard stood next to the passenger door wearing the typical Coronado uniform: black slacks, jacket, and combat boots. He loomed over a vagrant.

Even in the wavering light the man's condition was apparent. A thin, weak body beneath his ragged clothes. Patchy hair and beard. Swollen face and hands, probably his ankles as well.

Saltwater poisoning.

Miranda's stomach turned. The security guard glanced up and saw her watching. He didn't look malicious, only tired. His job was to clear the riffraff before they ruined a wealthy client's appetite. Nothing personal.

The sick man had a small jug at his side, unlabeled. Had he been kicked off the water ration for some crime? Had he been robbed? Something had driven him wild with thirst. Wild enough to drink ocean water perhaps?

Miranda had only been that thirsty once, bone-dry two days before her next water allocation. She remembered struggling to restrain her tears for fear of further dehydration. It was a lesson of conservation she never wanted to repeat.

The guard spoke calmly. "I think you have a party to get to, ma'am."

Miranda needed no encouragement. She fled up the staircase.

At the top she was greeted by a four-story facade of white wood paneling and sloping red clay roof tiles, a stark contrast from the concrete parking structure. The palm trees and vine-encrusted trellises over the walkway were likely fake, but convincingly lush.

She nodded as she passed the waiting valet, who frowned at her flushed cheeks and decided lack of vehicle. If she had to make a speedy exit she didn't want to wait around the entrance for her keys, and if the valet thought she was just cheap then so be it.

Miranda entered the hotel lobby, and a world that was normally out of her reach.

The room was dominated by a sweeping central staircase in pure Spanish colonial style. The wrought iron banisters had a delicate, curling design that belied their strength. Colorful mosaic tiles were set into the risers supporting cream-colored steps, and the dusty red floor tiles were arranged in a traditional basket weave design.

That would have been impressive enough, but the place was also wired. Completely wired. False windows showed a gorgeous sunny beach outside, at odds with the impending stormy weather. There were media screens embedded in every wall, tastefully contained within antique picture frames. And they all had the same public service message playing. There was currently no audio, but she didn't need it. This particular pitch had been running for two months.

The man on screen looked young, but he could have been a hundred years old. Narrow face, slender build, impossibly colorful eyes. Fae. He was a director of distribution. His suit cost more than Miranda would make in a year. And she wanted to punch that smarmy smirk right off of him.

"This summer we enter our third year of El Niño, and the warm current shows no sign of abating. Six hurricanes have traveled up from the equator this year— and six hurricanes have been deflected by your hard-working weather guards. Unfortunately due to increasing attacks by insurgents, we have been forced to heighten security around our grocery trucks. We are asking for a tiny three percent raise in the shipping tax to keep the dole going without interruption…"

What a surprise. Election season was coming and there were complications with the food dole again.

Seventy years since the eruption at Lake Toba sparked a chain reaction around the world. Seventy years since volcanic winter wiped out nine tenths of the population. When the Fae first came forward, offering their magic to cleanse the world and bring it back to right, everyone saw them as the saviors of humanity. They selflessly dedicated themselves to seeking out havens from the chaos, and nurturing these little pockets of safety into towns and cities where life could resume with some echo of normalcy.

Over time, the humans realized just how indebted they had become to their fae saviors. The fae held back the elemental disturbances wreaking the rest of the country. The fae were the only ones who could open road access to water reserves up north.

The fae supplied the seeds to farmers, the water to irrigate them, the trucks to deliver produce back to the city... Fae generosity quickly grew tiresome.

There was never any clear evidence of profiteering, but that didn't stop the disgruntled from spreading rumors or acting out. As for Miranda, after a lifetime under continually rising taxes and pretension, she didn't trust them as far as she could throw them.

She shifted her attention to the lobby desk before anybody could spot her disgust. Granny's words came down like drumbeats against her temples: *Look natural. Look bored. Fit in.*

Some things were easier said than done when you were raised on a barley farm.

"Miranda! You made it!"

Miranda turned toward the familiar voice with relief. "Tasia!"

The cocoa-skinned woman flowed down the staircase with practiced grace. She strode over to Miranda and grabbed her hands, leaning in for a cheek to cheek kiss. Tasia's dark coloring offset Miranda's strawberry hair and farm girl freckles. Neither woman was especially lovely on her own, but when the two appeared together they turned heads.

As they were doing now.

Look natural. Fit in.

Good thing Miranda was here in the role of visitor and not native.

"I had quite a drive," she said, with a theatrical shiver.

Tasia pouted. "I wasn't sure you'd make it. They're saying the storm might be coming too fast for the weather guards to hold it back. Some of the guests had to cancel!"

Not my guest, I hope?

The possibility that Miranda had braved that dreadful bridge only to miss her mark was disheartening, to say the least.

"You know me," she said. "Fashionably late. But shouldn't you be getting ready?"

Tasia laughed. "I'm always ready!" She patted Miranda's arm. "You're right, though. Gary's got me rubbing elbows when the party starts but I'm going to sneak out after an hour so I can suit up and stretch out. I'll have to leave you alone a bit, babe."

"I kind of figured," Miranda said dryly.

Tasia embraced her in another unstoppable display of affection, turning curious heads once again. "I know you hate these shindigs. It means a lot to me that you came."

"Oh, don't worry about it..." Miranda patted her friend on the back, feeling her friend might be hamming it up a bit. Then again, that's what made her such a great distraction; she knew how to keep everyone's eyes squarely where she wanted them, on herself. And without Tasia's contrived invitation, it would have been a lot harder to crash this party. The Villa Del Agua was stringent in its reservation policies and she wasn't exactly prepared to leave a credit card at the desk.

Before releasing Miranda from the ridiculous hug, Tasia whispered *"He's in Room 322."* She stepped back and in a normal voice announced, "I have to go back, but go talk to the concierge for your room, it's under my name. See you in the solarium!"

Tasia inflicted one more kiss on the cheek and then hurried back up the grand staircase. Miranda headed for the lobby desk, where a large sign was hung prominently overhead bragging, *Grade A Level Water Ration. All of our tanks are clean!*

"Well," she said. "That's nice."

***

Miranda had changed into her best clothes before she left, so she threw her overnight bag into her room and ran back downstairs. The solarium, it turned out, was even more impressive than the lobby. It was located at the very back of the hotel, on a cliff-side extension of the second floor. In better weather the glass-paned ceiling was translucent. At the moment a false vision of white clouds and clear sunlight were projected overhead.

The room was warm and delectably humid. The swimmers would find it oppressive but the guests reveled in it, and the guests were the ones paying. Lush greenery, indistinguishable from the real thing, adorned the walls and dripped with soft glowing bubble lights strung up on wires made to look like vines. The support columns were likewise bursting with electrical fruit. Cocktail tables were spread throughout the novelty jungle, piled high with expensive hors d'oeuvres and picked at sparingly.

And then, of course, there was the centerpiece to it all: the six lane, twenty-five meter competition pool, surrounded by more gorgeous paving stones. With the world's freshwater still so polluted by ashes and volcanic poisons, people had to make due with saltwater and chemically sanitized waters for cleaning (and recreation if you were rich, or foolhardy).

Miranda stood near the edge for a moment, mesmerized and horrified by several hundred thousand gallons of seawater. The briny scent tickled her nose and visions of public service announcements came to mind. They had terrified her as a child. Those calm, smiling fae came on screen every evening, advising parents to closely monitor their children at bath time lest they swallow the water or suck on a sponge.

Her mother dragging her out of the irrigation canal, shouting, "You stay away from it! You only drink what I give you to drink!"

Miranda gave the pool a wide berth and distracted herself by noting where each exit was placed. She travelled half the room before she spotted Tasia chatting up some slick-haired businessmen. As her eyes adjusted to the dim light Miranda scanned more and more faces around the pool. She couldn't quite peg it, but there was something odd about this group… and then it hit her. This appeared to be a humans-only affair. The attendees all looked wealthy enough but there was not a single member of the political class in sight.

Poor Tasia. The meet and greet wasn't quite as prestigious as she'd thought.

"There you are!" Tasia called. "Gentlemen, this is my *dear* childhood friend, Miranda Mackenzie…"

Schmoozing. What a chore. Miranda pasted on her best vaguely-interested smile, snatched a glass of wine from a passing waitress, and suffered through a series of upper-middle-class complaints.

Could you *believe* that they might rebuild that rundown district destroyed in the last quake? I thought they were going to raze it and put up a new park! Why waste money on cheap houses that will just fall again next time? Why not just relocate the residents?

Investments in farmland had stabilized for the first time in a decade. Do you think some of that extra tax money will finally go to broader crops? When was the last time we got a batch of oranges?

They had a crew sent out to retrieve an uncontaminated iceberg for the state's Yuletide celebration (can you imagine the number of personal favors *that* must have generated?), and then wouldn't you know it, a tidal wave hit the boat and by the time a second crew could brave the weather the damn thing was down to the size of a fridge.

Oh, it was all so very difficult wasn't it? Miranda remembered bad summers when the kids did all their chores at night while it was cool, and cherished little sips from the canteen after noontime naps. Tasia glanced at her occasionally, aware of her friend's social opinions, but Miranda kept that smile screwed on tight.

And then, the moment she'd been waiting for.

"All right, darlings," Tasia said. "It's time for me to slip into something a little more comfortable."

They laughed and groaned polite protests. Miranda leaned in and feigned regret. "You're lucky I love you, leaving me alone with these stiffs!"

Tasia hammed up her exit, waving and blowing kisses. As soon as her friend disappeared through the door, Miranda made hasty excuses to the businessmen and hurried to the back of the solarium.

Her mark might be in the solarium already, or he might be in private quarters. It was time to find out.

She ducked into a supply closet, the only spot nearby that she was likely to get any privacy. She set her satchel on a shelf full of cleaning fluids; a little frisson of excitement ran through her as she reached in and pulled out a small box a little larger than her fist. All six sides were made of flawless glass, revealing an interior of swirling green smoke. She held it between her palms. It immediately warmed at her touch. She leaned close and whispered, "Devirosh." Her breath fogged the glass for a moment and cleared.

A face began to form in the smoke, and a smile tugged at Miranda's lips. The years passed but he always appeared with the same face. It was the face her mother had introduced her to. It was the face her grandmother had loved. Bright eyes over sharp cheekbones and the shadowed hint of a goatee.

He eyed the room, flitting from pane to pane around the box. His voice emerged faint and wispy. "What a glamorous job you have, Miranda."

"You know me," she said. "I've got them begging on my doorstep."

"Mm. What do you need, blood of Eleanor?"

"To find the man from that picture and the large manila envelope. Both may be in Room 322. He probably won't leave something like this lying around for the maids to find, but maybe we'll get lucky. At the very least I'd like to see where he is, and the layout of the suite." She had already discussed her purpose and cover story to the djinn, but his type of talents required that they be within a particular radius. It was too bad, otherwise she could have done this from her own home! As it was, if Devirosh could verify that Peterson was watching the swim meet, then she could search his room without interruption.

"Let us take a look," Devirosh said. His eyes drifted shut. His face softened against the glass and sank back into smoke. The smoke in turn cleared, and in its place was the vision of a hotel suite. The perspective was high, looking down on a rumpled set of sheets and a grand media screen on the opposite wall. They were looking through the mirror over the bed.

And there it was, exactly as Bateman had described it. Peterson had the envelope sitting on the coffee bar by the door, for goodness' sake, and he was standing in front of the mirror trying to fix a haphazard tie. The guy was clearly not familiar with necktie technology, because he kept frowning halfway through and pulling it apart. He looked ... ordinary. Messy black hair with an out-of-date cut. Slacks and a dress shirt, but no matching suit jacket in sight. He wasn't exactly the rich bozo she'd been expecting, but he matched the photo and Devirosh would know if any glamourie was at work.

Her curiosity about the envelope was growing by the minute.

"Bingo," she said. "You've got a lock on the room?"

"Of course," the djinn murmured.

All she had to do then was wait until their mark arrived downstairs, and she and Devirosh could get down to business! *I ought to find a bigger mirror.*

As she reached for the knob, the door swung open and a maid stared at her with the hesitation of somebody about to offend a patron. "Ma'am?"

Miranda picked up her satchel and dropped the cube into it in one smooth motion. She slung the bag over her shoulder and brushed past the waitress with a breezy smile. The woman's protests died with a resigned sigh.

The party was in full swing. During her brief departure the solarium had grown *packed*. The twinkling lights were brighter, showing off the guests' expensive suits and cocktail gowns.

And then Miranda in her all-purpose black dress and a giant handbag. She took a breath and strode further into the fray. An announcer's jingle sounded over the room's hidden speaker system. The crowd began to quiet and a man's voice wafted through the fake trees. "Hello! Welcome to the fourth annual Coronado Swim Display..."

Miranda tuned out the ensuing grovel as the music switched to an uplifting American tune and lights shone toward the solarium doors. The women swept in one by one, casting off their robes and taking positions at the head of the pool. Tasia, always the charmer, walked in with a glittering public relations smile on her face, taking a few extra seconds in the limelight to throw winks and kisses at the audience. She had a beautifully toned body and the ability to rock it.

Miranda abruptly lost interest in Tasia's bathing suit as the room shook around them. She heard the tinkle of broken glass and the splash of a swimmer tipping into the pool too early. She couldn't even hold her own footing and knocked shoulders with another guest. A couple of women nearby tittered nervously.

"Sorry," she said to the man beside her, "I'm just passing... through..." Miranda faltered at the sight of Peterson.

Of course she had to bump into him!

"That's all right," he said. "Force of nature!" He patted her on the arm. Bateman said this guy was a bureaucrat of some sort, but Miranda was struck once again by his appearance. He seemed so naive, so *unrefined* for this type of party.

"You look about as out of place as I feel," he joked. He stuck out a hand. "I'm Hammond."

And awfully bad at flirting with women, if that's what he was trying to do.

"I'm here with a friend," she said coolly. *Try to look like you're not analyzing every facet of his appearance, Miranda!*

He withdrew his hand and said, "Oh right, right, of course. I'll leave you be."

He shuffled off through the crowd, uncomfortable and smiling nervously each time he brushed past somebody. Who the heck was this guy? Another thief, perhaps? Maybe he ripped off Bateman and this was a repo job. Maybe the guileless bumbling was a sham personality.

She stopped herself. That didn't matter. He was out of his room, that's what mattered. She wandered toward the exit, smiling apologetically as though she were looking for someone in particular. She cast periodic glances back at Peterson to make sure he was settling in for the show.

He wasn't. The man barely even glanced at the near-naked swimmers lining up at the pool. He was working his way through the audience with a purpose. He tapped a man on the shoulder, leaned in close to him, and murmured some sort of instruction. He straightened, wound further into the crowd, and did it again with somebody else. The men he spoke to apologized to their companions and started walking toward the exit.

Damn! Peterson wasn't here for the show at all. It was a front for him too, and whichever businessmen and politicians he was meeting up with.

Mental note: that was the sort of information it was nice to have up front. Either Bateman didn't know what the bumbling bureaucrat was doing here tonight or he was playing things close to the vest.

And then she spotted Gary Madsen peeling off from the other coaches. A glance at Tasia on the starting line showed that she saw it too, but she lacked Miranda's surprise. Was Gary involved too? He was directly involved with administration, what did he have to do with this?

Miranda made up her mind. It was time to stop asking questions and start getting answers. She slipped out via one of the side exits. The corridor was narrow but refreshingly cool after the mugginess of the solarium, and the music and commotion from the party were abruptly silenced by the closing door. Once outside the soundproofed common room, Miranda could hear the storm's fury building beyond the shielded walls. It made her heart skip a beat. It was so easy to pretend that the world wasn't out to get you when you were surrounded by sunny skies and glowing fruit.

She shook her head as she ducked into the ladies' room. It was empty and sported not one, but two full-length mirrors on either side of a love-seat. Perfect. She brought out the communication box again and sat down on the edge of the love-seat.

Devirosh floated up against the glass with a lazy smile. He blinked slowly. "You wish to travel now, child?"

"No," Miranda said. "First I wish to observe."

The djinn receded into smoke, and the outlines of Peterson's room reappeared. The mystery package was still sitting on the coffee bar. Damn! She should have gone for it right away instead of mingling with those pompous idiots! The lack of work lately must be making her soft in the head. A moment passed, and Miranda thought she could make a grab for it after all— but then Peterson entered the room. Two women and three men, including Gary, followed him inside. They looked out of place squeezing into the little suite. No doubt they all had much larger rooms booked for themselves.

Peterson stood with his back to the mirror, protectively close to the coffee bar. His guests formed a semi-circle around him. Miranda prepared herself for an hour of talking heads, but it quickly grew apparent that Peterson's guests were as impatient to get things over with as she was. After a minute of obligatory chatter an older gentleman holding a martini glass interrupted Peterson and gestured at the envelope.

Peterson nodded and turned to pick it up. His hands trembled a little as he broke the seal, and he took a deep breath. Just as he began to lift the contents out, his guests crowded around him and blocked the line of sight from the mirror.

"Dammit," Miranda muttered.

The reaction to Peterson's reveal was swift and dramatic. Shocked expressions, even physical recoil. One woman went weak at the knees and sank onto the foot of the bed. Somebody else darted to the door and checked that the locks were all thrown.

Immediate argument erupted, and Miranda was startled by the red-faced fury of the man with the martini glass. He tossed his drink back in one swallow and gestured wildly at the young man.

Miranda frowned, and came to a decision. "Can you bring me their sound, Devirosh?"

"Of course," the djinn whispered. He added, "It will be an effort."

"I understand," she said.

Devirosh's sigh came like autumn leaves in a breeze, and sound issued from the little communication box.

"— right in front of me, and I still can't believe it!" Mr. Martini finished. "How the hell are we supposed to pull this off?"

Peterson focused on the rotund man. "Paul, you wanted hard evidence; this is it. You've all indicated certain sympathies to the cause, so prove it. Combined we have the resources. We can't do this without you, without *any* of you."

The woman on the bed shook her head slowly, eyes still trained to whatever had riled them all up. "I think I speak for all of us Hammond when I say... we're playing a dangerous game here. We can't just rush into this you know, planning something this big will take time."

"We could get in trouble just for *listening* to you," another man exclaimed.

"They can't arrest us just for *listening*, Santiago."

"I'm not talking jails, I'm not talking juries, I'm talking black bags."

"It's not black bags you have to worry about, it's black dogs. Great big hellhounds made out of the ground!"

"Out of the ground?"

"Made out of– I don't know, mushrooms or something! Out of thin air! I don't care where they come from! Fae can make whatever they want!"

Peterson calmly waited out the bout of hysteria that had clutched his audience. He tucked the papers back into their manila cover for the moment.

Paul abruptly bulldozed the conversation. He raised one hand and declared, "We aren't having this conversation here."

"Paul–" Peterson started.

"No. There's a boardroom off the second floor club. It has silence capabilities. Nobody says another word till we're warded."

This met with murmurs of agreement. Peterson moved as if to put the envelope inside his coat, but Gary grabbed his arm, chiming in for the first time. "No," he said. "It's not coming with us. I'm not being found with that."

"*Thank* you," Miranda said.

Devirosh's lidded gaze drifted up through the reflection. "Your opportunity is nigh, child."

"Yes," she said wryly. "I gathered."

She stood and positioned herself in front of a mirror. She held the communication box out, about a foot from the reflective surface. Devirosh pressed against all six sides of glass, green smoke deepening and writhing, and then he let out another one of his autumn sighs. The smoke abruptly dissipated, and tendrils spread out like cracks into the bathroom mirror. The scene wavered for a moment, then anchored, and Miranda had a full-length view into the hotel room.

Everyone had filed out. Peterson took a final glance around the room and tucked the envelope inside the nightstand drawer. He pulled the door shut on his way out, and Miranda could hear the hard click of the deadbolt, as well as the little beeps as he set an electronic lock for good measure. Miranda stepped forward into the mirror, and the encircling arms of the djinn.

Traveling with Devirosh was traveling in deafening silence, numbing cold, blinding dark. While mere seconds ticked outside in the real world, inside time stretched the length of a dream. Miranda curled inward, held womb-like by a vise grip wreathed in fog. Devirosh cradled her and sheltered her on a plane she could never see, and his breath stirred her hair.

She floated through wisps of memory, old affections and yearning. It might have been sensual, if she didn't know it was her grandmother he recalled.

And then she finished her step. She automatically ducked her head to fit through the shorter frame, and hopped down from the dresser to the ground. She shook her head to clear the last wisps of protective fogging. Perhaps one day Devirosh would show her the world Eleanor adored...

No time to waste on wondering this time. Miranda grabbed the package and turned right back across the room.

Devirosh waited patiently in the still smoky mirror, hints of eye, shoulder, torso. He was even less material than before, his connection to her world strained by the effort of transporting a physical body.

This was not their first grab-and-dash. Miranda knew better than to dawdle.

She climbed back up onto the dresser. "My room," she said, and stepped into the mirror.

The journey felt significantly more strained the second time around. Miranda tumbled through thinning soup, pulled by slippery fingers. Sounds leaked through the djinn's shielding, high-pitched keens like birds were trying to speak.

She stumbled out of the mirror and onto the bed in her hotel room, shivering at the memory of that sound. The packet was cold against her chest, and a tiny film of ice crystals evaporated on contact with the air. She crawled down to the floor with her back against the bed, trying to catch her breath.

When the urge to let her teeth rattle had passed, Miranda set her prize down on the ground and dug her cell phone out of her bag. She pulled up the newest number and sent the prearranged message to her contact: *The show went great! On my way home.* A few moments later she received the confirmation: *Great dear, see you soon.*

Miranda had it. The job was all but done. She only had to slip out of the building, get in her car, and go to the drop-off point. Easy snag, easy money. No one was expecting a guest to willingly go out in this hellish weather, so no guards would be posted where she needed to be. And with the portable shielding Bateman had given her, she could safely get out and back to the hotel in thirty minutes tops. She'd eat an expensive dinner with Tasia, retire to her room like any other non-suspicious tenant, and take a nice, hot bubble bath.

But ... she had it.

This curiosity thing is going to get me killed someday.

"Devirosh," she said, "please keep an eye out for suspicious movement."

The djinn was increasingly translucent, but scouting took only minimal effort for him. He nodded and dissipated. Her headboard mirror turned into a security camera hub, slowly cycling through various prominently placed mirrors in the hotel as she sat back up on the bed.

Miranda lifted the flap and pulled out the papers that had garnered so much attention.

Not just papers, but photos too.

There were aerial shots of lush fields, clear blue skies, fresh running water, unfenced expanses. Picture after picture of untouched perfection. Names scribbled across corners, random numbers ... Latitudes. Longitudes. Time stamps.

It took her a moment to make sense of what she was seeing, and then she was glad she was already sitting down. She breathed, "You've got to be kidding me." *These are real places! Clean places! Why haven't we been told about this? Why aren't we living out there?*

She was shaking as she put the pictures aside, trying to swallow the feelings of betrayal that rose as she read through the documents. Soil testing, weather reports, it was all here. If these reports were to be believed, then her entire world was a lie.

How the hell had Peterson gotten his hands on all of this? Was he an auspiciously placed paper-pusher? Did he have connections?

Between the fae's real estate monopolies, their selling of magics for ease of living or guarantees of protection from further natural disasters, and their total control of the market in the form of company stores, they owned just about every aspect of human life. Most didn't question it; this lifestyle had existed for generations, and after all it was the fae who gave them the chance to survive in the first place.

Or had they?

Those crazy bastards with their secret pamphlets and stupid slogans were right after all! The fae were lying to everyone. They swore there were no more clean places left in the world, but they knew, they had to know. It was their greatest illusion, and Peterson wanted to blow the lid off of it.

To break the back of fae control was a terrifying prospect, but it was impossible not to consider, once the phase of knee-jerk denial passed. Could it really be done?

Miranda thought she was going to be sick. No wonder Bateman had been vague on the details. Did the man even know what he'd sent her to steal?

Granny swam up in her mind, severe and practical.

This is why you don't ask questions. You need money, you take a job. You take a job, you do the job. That's life, little girl. You always do this, you always blow things out of proportion!

Okay, calm down Miranda. Maybe these weren't real. Maybe they were more trumped up reports by the conspiracy theorists.

But then why hire a thief? If it was trash just handle it the usual way: call them terrorists in the news and leave it at that.

Now she wondered how many of those news feeds were cover-ups too.

Obviously Peterson had something he wasn't supposed to have, and somebody leaked word of it to Bateman. Who was Bateman anyway? To whom exactly was she delivering this information?

Miranda was about ready to rip her hair out when Devirosh made a sound for her to look up. She twisted around. A familiar form caught her eye in the mirror. Tasia was striding down a hallway, her hair damp, her terrycloth robe billowing around her, her expression absolutely furious.

There was no way the swim meet was over. Tasia's race, maybe, but she should be down there watching the other girls and rubbing elbows. Something was wrong.

Miranda's chill returned and she asked, "Devirosh, where's Gary?"

The djinn found him quickly, and Miranda's fears were bolstered.

Gary was walking briskly down another hallway, caught in epileptic bursts as Devirosh flitted from mirror to mirror in pursuit. At his side, quite clearly, was Hammond Peterson. They were alone, and speaking intently.

Miranda froze at a glimpse of hotel room number 434. Then 436 and 438 in rapid-fire succession. They were on this floor, and they were coming toward her room.

At least, there was no time to assume otherwise... if she was wrong she'd feel sheepish later. Miranda shoved the papers and photos haphazardly into her oversize shoulder bag, along with Devirosh's box, and ducked into the bathroom. Just as she crossed the threshold from carpet to tile she heard the little *swoosh* of a key card deactivating her door lock.

She shut the bathroom door, and held her breath. Devirosh floated, calm as ever, in the mirror over the sink, awaiting the first sign that she required escape.

Miranda slowly pushed against the button lock on the door. She winced at the whisper faint click.

On the other side of the door, voices rose.

"Since when does Paul Johnston answer to the Water Board?" Deliberate, furious. Peterson in a mode she had not encountered.

"Since the Water Board bought majority shares in Johnston Pharmaceuticals. Don't be dense, man. I'm trying to help you out here."

Gary was quiet and persuasive. He probably bore the same expression he used to calm Tasia down when she got in a snit. Miranda leaned in with her ear to the door jamb to hear better.

"No," Peterson insisted. "Paul's a firecracker, I know, but I trust him."

"I hate to break it to you, Hammond, but your trust is easily won."

Out in the hallway, a familiar stomping reached their room. With dramatic flourish, Tasia threw the door open, and slammed it shut behind her, gasping: "Gary, what are you *thinking?*"

"Natasia, I am serious. You wait downstairs or I swear—"

"Why are you even talking to him? And here? Gary! This room is rented in *my* name! Where's Miranda?"

Peterson now: "What the hell is going on here?"

Miranda heard the distinct thwack of a club to the head, then Peterson collapsed to the ground and began to groan. Her heart rate spiked— oh shit oh shit.

"Jesus, Gary, you didn't have to do that!"

"We discussed this. You did your part, now let me do mine."

Miranda grabbed the doorknob and twisted, hard. No time to question her decision, just go, just step, just rush inside.

Tasia exclaimed at the sight of her, automatically grabbing at the gaping edges of her robe. Gary's eyes narrowed and he dropped a slender desk lamp to the floor. Peterson was on his hands and knees, clutching at an oozing welt across the side of his neck.

"Come on." Miranda yanked at his arm and he struggled to his feet, not yet questioning the fresh company.

"Bateman?" Miranda guessed.

"A friend," Gary acknowledged.

She nodded. "Thanks again for the invite, Tasia." Damn, the line was supposed to come out chilly but she couldn't keep the heat from creeping in.

To her credit, Tasia looked genuinely wounded. But to her credit, Tasia could be a good actress. Miranda got Peterson upright and wedged one supportive arm under his. He stared at her, comprehension dawning. Not the whole thing, she was sure, but he knew he'd been sold out.

"We've got to get out of here," he slurred.

"It's not like that." Tasia ignored him entirely. "You needed a job, I knew somebody who needed a hire. How is that not mutually helpful?"

Miranda took a step back, dragging the wounded man along. "Do you know what he had, Tasia? Do you understand what you're taking down?"

But the question was pointless, because Miranda already knew the answer. Tasia would never understand, because Tasia had never gone thirsty when her dole was used up too soon. She had never gone hungry because they needed a home more than food. No matter what stories Miranda shared with her they were just stories, exaggerations, unfathomable. If you were thirsty, buy water. If you needed money, get a better job. If you couldn't get a job then go on the fae work roll and move to a subscription farm (where you'd never be able to pay off the plane ticket that brought you there but at least you had food and water, right, that's what you were complaining about in the first place, *right?*).

Tasia opened her mouth to blab a justification but Miranda didn't hear her. Gary saw it on her face: imminent departure.

Miranda thrust her arm further under Peterson's, dragging him back by the chest.

Gary reached under his dinner jacket and produced a gun from his waistband.

Tasia let out a startled shriek at the sight of it.

Miranda stumbled back, through the bathroom door, banging one elbow sharply on the porcelain sink, but she didn't feel it, not yet.

One shot rang out, and a chunk of wood and plaster blew out of the door jamb. Tasia was shouting again. Gary knocked her down and she fell silent.

"Devirosh!"

Miranda continued to fall back. She squeezed her eyes shut and she hit the shower doors...

...the frosty glass, barely reflective, another shot ringing out behind them and a distorted male voice, crying out in frustration...

...and Miranda could not feel Peterson anymore, she was trapped in a vise, momentum opening her way through a mirror world thickened into sludge. The djinn's hold on her was weak and slipping. A triumphant keen began in the darkness around her, rising to a pitch that threatened to burst her eardrums. Feathers buffeted her from all sides and something that could only be a talon nicked her collarbone.

And then, without the usual sense of warning, Miranda was dumped back out to the real world. She fell through a wall mirror, smashed a vase on a decorative table, and landed on her shoulder. Peterson followed immediately after her, crushing her legs.

"What the hell was that?" Peterson demanded. At least the cold had snapped him back into focus. He rubbed at his arms, staring at Miranda as though she'd bite.

"D-Devirosh," Miranda chattered, "where are we?"

She couldn't even see the djinn's face in the hall mirror, only hints of green smoke. His voice came whisper-low and apologetic. "I am sorry, beloved child... I cannot carry two, not with three requests in a day..."

He fell silent. She secured the clasp and clambered up, adrenaline driving away the last of the chill. "Up," she said. "Up! Now!" She pulled at Peterson's arm.

"I *am* getting up—"

A door opened, at the farthest end of the hall. Gary stepped out. He aimed down the sights of his gun.

Peterson cursed and in a moment they were running, injuries forgotten, nothing more important than that bright, neon emergency exit sign a hundred feet away.

Another shot went wide as they reached the door. Gary had lost all pretense at subtlety. Framing Miranda was out of the picture, and there didn't appear to be much of a Plan B.

They skidded into the emergency exit stairwell. Peterson jumped at the crash of thunder overhead, the sound echoing through the stairwell as Miranda cast about for something, *anything*. She grabbed up a broom resting in the corner, and wedged it against the door before they sprinted down the stairs.

"Who *are* you?" he demanded. They thudded onto the landing and twisted around to the next set of steps.

Miranda felt obliged, at least as long as they continued to flee. "They hired me! I didn't know who, it was the fae— or Gary's people trying to impress the fae. They thought I was out, they thought I was delivering the papers! They thought I'd get back in time to find your body!" They passed the third floor entrance. "Gary, anyway, I don't think Tasia knew he was pinning it on me."

"My documents!" Peterson gasped, rocking to a halt on the second floor landing. "We can't leave them up there!"

"No, I have it all." Miranda felt like an absolute maniac, but she had to know, and right now. She used Peterson's momentum to twist him around and slam his back to the wall.

"Hammond," she said. "You have to tell me, and tell me honest: what do you want to do with this information?"

"You've seen it?" He nodded, dismissing his own question. "I want to go there. I want to bring everybody I can. We shouldn't have to live like this."

Miranda let out a shaky breath. "Right answer. God help me, I believe you."

She crooked her finger for silence, then eased open the second floor door. She peeked around, half expecting a blow to the face. But the corridor was bright, and cool, and precisely how she remembered it.

"Shouldn't we take the exit all the way down?" Hammond whispered.

For a criminal mastermind, she thought, he wasn't very bright. "To a back alley? He might have people watching, whoever was at the rendezvous point I bet. We need a more public route."

Miranda was rattled by the silence of Devirosh. He usually chimed in by now, offering advice even if he could not travel. Had she pushed him too far?

They entered the solarium through the side exit, and it was like stepping back in time. The dinner party was going strong, as though nothing had happened, as though a lunatic wasn't wandering the upstairs halls firing a handgun. As though Miranda wasn't carrying the most important paperwork since the Declaration of Independence in her handbag.

She grabbed Hammond's hand and led him through the crowd, as the next set of swimmers lined up at the head of the pool.

They were halfway across the room when the front doors to the solarium swung open. A bright rectangle of light cut a swath through the atmospheric glow of the bubble light jungle. Gary walked in, trying to look nonchalant and failing. He spotted them and began weaving his way through the crowd, ignoring all attempts at polite conversation aimed his way.

They tried to turn around, to go back the way they'd come, but the oblivious guests kept pushing forward toward the pool, eager to see the next race.

Faster than she could have imagined, Gary was there. He pressed his gun to Miranda's back, and she froze. "Let's go, you two. I'm done playing games!"

He directed them toward the nearest exit, one hand gripping her arm. But as they turned, Hammond yanked his gun arm up, surprising Gary into pulling the trigger.

The shot went through the roof, shattering glass. People began to back-peddle from the edge of the pool. One shout, then two, then a tide of screams as the two men wrestled for the weapon.

The gun went off again, and something hot splashed Miranda's arm. Hammond collapsed.

Green smoked curled around the edge of her vision and she turned to the pool. A face flashed across the water and was gone. Someone screamed as Gary raised the gun at her, and she jumped into the shimmering, distorted reflection of her attacker.

Travel was turbulent, and hot, and it wasn't seconds but an agonizing summer in the desert, sand scouring her skin, the full burn of the Arabian sun. Miranda tried to scream, but her throat was parched, she was dying, she was mummifying inside and out, and her dry throat was going to swell up and choke her.

Miranda fell onto a dense cloud of green smoke, and it buoyed her somewhat, but it was icy cold, so cold that at first she thought it a brand new burn. The cloud carried her across a foreign sky and its icy fog wove inside her bones.

She tried to open her eyes and barely managed to crack them. For a moment she saw... something vast, something overwhelming. She did not understand, and panic kicked in hard.

And then his face appeared over hers, strained but benevolent. And Devirosh whispered, "I'm sorry, Eleanor..."

Miranda hit the world hard. She finished falling back, and she smacked her head into a pane of glass. A stick dug into her right thigh. Her fingers were clutched into claws from the cold, and— she was alone.

Miranda opened her eyes. She was in her car, awkwardly splayed across the front seat. Devirosh had dropped her right through her car window, hot damn.

The parking structure lights bore down harshly through her windshield. Even in the yellow cast she knew the substance splattered across her arm. Blood. Hammond's blood.

With shaking hands she worked the clasp on her bag, one try, then a second before it opened. She felt past the papers; those would have to wait. She found the little box by touch, but it remained cold in her hand as she drew it out. The dread in her heart was confirmed. A thick crack ran a full circuit around three sides of the cube. The glass was about to fall apart in her hands.

Goodbye, Devirosh.

Miranda bit back tears. She pushed the box and bag onto the passenger seat and yanked on her seat belt. She turned her key. The engine roared to life.

She had information that could get her killed. The fae were onto her. Their human sycophants knew her face. Her friends couldn't be trusted. And she was about to face Venetian streets and hail the size of her pounding heart.

One thing was certain: it was time to get the hell out of Coronado.

Matt Schiariti tells us a tale of caution. An angry bitter man is given the gift of three wishes. Can he handle them wisely?

HOLLOW
(BE CAREFUL WHAT YOU WISH FOR)
Matt Schiariti

"I'm sorry sir. This card has been declined."

Tom McNulty stared at the pharmacy technician behind the glass window for several heartbeats. She was everything he hated and loathed about the newest generation. The girl couldn't have been more than 16, chewing a wad of bubblegum the size of a golf ball. She had a look in her eyes that told him she was assessing him, mocking him silently.

Judging him.

"That can't be possible," he replied through slowly clenching teeth. "I just paid the bill."

The blue haired teen made a face then swiped the credit card again. The magnetic stripe reader beeped once again. She looked at him one more time as she swiped the card.

The same result.

Declined.

"It's still not working, *sir*," she said through a mouthful of pink gum. The word 'sir' came out like a curse. She looked over his shoulder at the ever growing line of people behind him. They were getting impatient.

"Come on, guy," one of the older customers grunted. "I ain't got all day. Go hit the ATM if you can't put it on the plastic."

As if I haven't thought of that already, asshole.

Tom didn't have the funds in his account to cover the co pays. With pay day a week away trying to put it on his credit card was the only solution. But that obviously wasn't working which only added to his sour mood. His ailing mother needed the medications but he just didn't have the money. His credit cards should be fine but the machine said otherwise. He did just pay his credit card bill after a long conversation with the annoying associate over the phone but had to pay a hefty late fee.

Another person who doesn't know their ass from a hole in the ground, Tom had thought angrily as he listened to the foreigner's indistinguishable English over the phone.

"What's it to you?" Tom spat over his shoulder. He rifled through his walled looking for another credit card. This was the third one he tried. All declined.

"What's it to me?" the burly man with the graying beard and pock marked face countered. He looked to Tom like he'd spent one too many days inside the bottle. *Just another of the great unwashed. Another worthless person who's got nothing to offer society.* "We've all been waiting in line for ten minutes while you try to pay your bill, that's what it 'is to me'. Either pay or get outta here, buddy."

"Look, mister," the tech said through a half inflated bubble. "We've got customers out the wazoo lining up. You either have to pay or you have to go."

Tom stared at her. He knew somewhere in that dimwitted brain of hers she was belittling him. He would never behave like that to an elder. Ever. In that moment he wanted to reach through the service window and bash her skull into the desk repeatedly until she apologized. But he couldn't do it. He knew he had to conform to society's liberal rules. The very thought made his jaw clench.

Bitch, he thought. *You're the one that's worthless. Not me. If more people were like me this world would be a better place!*

Tom took the useless credit card she slid to him over the worn down fake granite counter top angrily and shoved it in his pocket. The burly man with the craggy face was no more than two inches away from him when he turned on his heel in a barely contained rage to leave the useless pharmacy.

"It's about time, loser," the man hissed as Tom walked by.

Tom grabbed the door handle with a trembling hand, his knuckles white and turned around.

"Screw you people! You're all worthless! Every last one of you!" Rivulets of spit shot out of his horribly maintained teeth as he spat the words to all the patrons and employees of the pharmacy and exited into the cold November storm.

***

The frigid, wet weather was perfectly in tune with Tom's mood. He pulled his coat collar tighter around his neck as he leaned into the driving hail and rain that threatened to blow him over with its fury.

It wasn't unlike the fury in his head.

"Assholes," he said to himself. "Every last one of them. They don't know anything about respect. If I had it my way I'd give them all a good lesson." Tom's monologue was getting attention by the passers-by as he walked the two blocks from the pharmacy to his apartment where his mother was waiting. He didn't even notice their gawking until he walked right into one of them.

"Hey, watch where you're going jerk!" an older woman in a fur coat yelled at him.

Tom stopped short and was about to give her receding form a piece of his mind when a sudden blast of cold water doused him with ice and slush from the waist down. It took his breath away.

He looked down at his water darkened shoes and his sodden pants, gray turned to near black with the cold water. They were saturated. Probably ruined.

A car door thudded shut brining his eyes to the curb. A man got out of a massive SUV, his titanic truck tire sitting in the puddle that caused Tom's last cold and wet predicament.

"Hey! Look what you did to my pants!" Tom screamed at the larger man. He was running his hands up and down his legs, displaying the damage the large bald man's ignorance caused.

"Not my fault you were walking too close to the curb, moron," the man smirked and hit Tom with his shoulder as he walked past. No apology. No concern. Not even a helping hand up.

The man was gone by the time Tom got up.

"Son of a *bitch*," he cursed to himself. Tom walked up to the front door of his building when he realized the large ignoramus had already turned the corner. He knew it wasn't worth it. Just another one of the great unwashed that could use a lesson.

Tom placed the key into the front door of the old building angrily and stomped up the dark, dingy stairs to apartment 3C where his mother would be awaiting medications that weren't going to come.

***

"Tom? Tom is that you?" His mother called from the spare bedroom. Her voice was slurred and slightly frantic.

"Yeah, it's me mom," he said throwing his keys down on the kitchen table.

He looked around his apartment. It was an extension of his mood, of his personality. It was spartanly furnished. He just bought the bare minimum of what he needed to function somewhat normally. A ratty leather couch sat in front of a beat up old console television in the living area. The kitchen had an old 50's style metal and Formica table surrounded by two chairs in the same style. All the walls and carpeting were dark browns or reds, the color of old blood. The tan window shades were always drawn, keeping the room in an eternal twilight no matter what time of day.

It was just how he liked it. It was like a womb.

"Did you get my meds?" she asked impatiently causing a coughing jag.

Tom sighed and walked to the spare bedroom.

His mother had been with him for the past several years. She had severe stroke and was unable to take care of herself totally without help. They couldn't afford an assisted living facility. Mrs. McNulty was a widow and Tom had no brothers or sisters. The only other surviving member of his family was his Uncle Franklin but he was always traipsing off to parts unknown looking for buried treasure and trying to make his fortune. The man thought he was the second coming of Indiana Jones. He thought he was some type of relic hunter. Tom knew better though. He was a rank amateur who couldn't stay routed to the same spot for more than two weeks. Uncle Franklin was a complete and utter failure both as a fortune hunter and as a human being.

"No, mom. I didn't," Tom said from the doorway of the spare bedroom. His mother was propped up on a medical bed with the curtains closed tight. The only light in the room was that which dribbled in through a crack in the old plastic window shades and the eerie translucent glow from the ancient black and white TV that was always tuned into the Spanish channel. His mother was addicted to telenovelas. Tom couldn't understand why she was so enamored with TV shows filled with foreigners who didn't even speak the language.

He was half way through explaining how the morons at the pharmacy had screwed him over when she interrupted him.

"Worthless," she hacked. "You're completely worthless. I should never have had you, Tom," the diminutive old silver haired woman scorned from beneath her plethora of blankets. Her mouth was in a permanent rictus of a scowl. Tom always thought it was fitting. Her face was a perfect representation of what was on the inside.

"Thanks, mom," he sighed.

"Aborted," she continued as if not having heard him. "You should have been aborted. I've regretted having you since the day you were born. If your father..."

She was interrupted by a knocking at the door.

"I gotta go get that mom," he seethed and left her to her venomous words as he closed the bedroom door behind him.

**

"I'm coming," Tom yelled at the incessant knocking on the door.

Another impatient jerk with no respect.

When he opened the door he was greeted with a man wearing a brown uniform complete with matching jacket and hat.

A delivery man.

"You Tom McNulty?" the portly man said from the apartment's hallway, still looking down at his clipboard. He had a package the size of a shoebox sitting on the floor between his dirty brown boots.

"Yeah, that's me." Tom replied, eyeing the man's deep set eyes and ill kept goatee.

"Got a package for you. Here, sign this," he said, thrusting an electronic clipboard at Tom. "Whoa, what a dump," he added under his breath.

"Excuse me?" Tom said after taking the clipboard.

"Nothing," the man replied with a disingenuous smile.

Tom finished signing and handed the clipboard back to the judgmental man standing before him.

Who the hell are you *to be judging me?* Tom thought to himself as the man handed him the manila wrapped parcel.

"Have a nice day, *sir,*" the delivery guy scoffed, having taken one more look at the interior of tom's dark, dank apartment and shaking his head before he disappeared down the murky hallway.

"Dickhead," tom mumbled as he shut the door.

He looked at the box after he placed it on the kitchen table. It looked like it was through a war. The manila wrapping paper was thick but worn. It was covered with all manner of dirt and muck the likes of which Tom couldn't even begin to guess at.

On closer inspection he noticed an international rubber stamp that said 'Tunisia' on it in shit brown lettering.

"What the hell?" Tom whispered to himself. Who would be sending him a package from that Far East?

"Tom? Tom!" his bedridden mother called from the bedroom. Since the door was shut it sounded like it was emanating from under the depths of the ocean's surface. "Who was that?"

"Just a delivery guy, mom! Just watch your show," he called. *You old bat.*

Tom sat at the scratched kitchen table and stared at the package. It wasn't some mistake. He double and tripled checked the hand written address on the faded yellow packed. It was his name and address. No mistake. He couldn't be sure but he thought he recognized the handwriting.

Curiosity getting the better of him, he took a knife and slit the burlap string that held the package securely together. Inside was an ornate carved box. It looked like it had once been shiny but the ravages of time and weather made it look old and weather beaten. Also inside was a letter, also aged and weathered looking. Tom thought the paper was probably white and of decent stock at some point but the elements gave it a beat up, antique appearance.

He unfolded the piece of paper and began to read to himself.

Dear Tom,

I've done it! I've finally done it! I've found my fortune! Enclosed herein is an item of such antiquity, of such value that I can honestly say, once it's sold at auction, we'll be set for life, boy-o! This is the thing I've been looking for my whole life. It's the culmination of countless years of searching. It's the result of nearly a lifetime's worth of hard work and sacrifice. When those slugs at Oxford get a load of this they'll rue the day they ever made fun of Franklin McNulty I can tell you that!

I'm sending this to <u>you</u> my dear boy because I know you can keep it secret and away from prying eyes. Let's just say I didn't come by it by the most legal of means. But that's just between you and me, yes?

Please, keep this in a safe place. I can tell you all about it when I arrive back in the states in several weeks. I have other business to attend to in country but I promise that as soon as I can I'll be on the first plane to New York and I'll tell you all about it then.

Oh and one other thing. Please do not take it out of the box! I know your curiosity will try to get the better of you but please, don't give in! This is a very old artifact and it has to be handled with the utmost care. Try to put it somewhere where it won't be in danger of falling or getting trampled upon.

I'm in your debt for this, Tom!

Yours always,

Uncle Frank.

***

Tom stared at the loopy hand writing for quite some time before he placed the letter back on the kitchen table.

What had his loony old uncle gone and gotten himself into now? And who did he think he was getting Tom involved in it? If Tom knew his uncle half as well as he thought he did, Uncle Frank probably bedded some rich sultan's teenaged daughter or broke into some museum or private collection in order to get his hands on whatever it was that the ornate box held. He probably had half the country looking for him.

Tom almost had a mind to toss the thing in the nearest dumpster and be done with it, damn the consequences from his delusional uncle but he couldn't bring himself to do it. He was, quite frankly, curious in the extreme.

Tom put the contents back together and placed it over the kitchen sink where he knew it would be safe.

***

Tom couldn't get his uncle's letter and package out of his mind. He flipped aimlessly through the channels trying to distract himself but distraction couldn't be attained. His curiosity was not to be denied.

He went to the pantry and retrieved the box, the manila packaging feeling like aged parchment in his hands. Tom couldn't be sure why but his pulse was hammering in his chest.

He sat at the kitchen table and took the ornamental box out of its surrounding packaging. It felt very heavy for something that wasn't quite the size of a shoebox.

"What the hell is in this thing?" he whispered to the empty, dark room. If it weren't for the faint sounds of his mother's relic television coming from down the short hallway Tom would have thought he was the only person in the universe at that point.

He reached out with a shaky hand and opened up the old wooden box. The smell and weight of ages of limitless time greeted him when the box was fully opened to reveal what was inside.

Tom looked upon what he could only describe as some sort of ancient stone tablet. It was intricately carved out of some stone he couldn't even put a name to. It was the color of rust, of old congealed blood. Dust covered the age's old stone carving. Leaning closer he blew on it to better see what was carved into the stone in a bas relief. The dust that issued forth from the tablet had a smell he couldn't quite describe. It smelled...ancient if a smell could be quantified in those terms. It tickled his nose and caused him to sneeze.

"You're not getting a cold are you?" his mom bellowed from the bedroom. "The doctor says I can't get sick! You'd best keep away if you're getting a cold!"

Bitchy old bat, tom thought to himself.

Apocalypse 13

"Tom, this soup is cold!" she continued in her phlegmatic voice. "Get your useless hide in her and warm it up!"

Tom sat up from the kitchen table with a sigh. It was difficult, but he was finally able to tear his eyes off of the carving. He decided he'd give it a better look once he was done attending to his mother.

Her glassy eyes stared at him as he walked into the cold bedroom with slumped shoulders.

"Jesus H. Crist, Tom. First you screw up my meds at the pharmacy this morning and now you're trying to feed me cold soup? Is there *anything* you can do right?"

Tom leaned against the door frame, lost in his own thoughts. Every word his mother had just said going in one ear and out the other, completely ignored.
The letter his uncle sent him kept going through his head.

"....*please do not take it out of the box!...*"

His mother's complaints were like the buzzing of bees or static from a TV that's been left on after the broadcast had been stopped for the evening. It was only background noise as the visions of the old stone carving flitted through his mind's eye.

The more he thought about it the more the picture came into focus. It was odd since he couldn't quite make it out while he was looking at it but now that he was away from it was as if a camera was finally coming into focus.

"Tom! Do you hear me? Have you been stuck dumb *and* deaf now too?" His mother's caustic words finally broke Tom out of his reverie.

"Yes, mom. I hear you," he said tonelessly. He walked over to her and took a pillow from beneath her head. It was weighed down with countless months of sweat and dead hair.

"Tom?" nervousness strained the old woman's voice, the rictus of her face transforming from a scowl into a look of fear. "Tom? What are you doing? Why do you look like that? What are you doing with my pillow?"

Tom didn't know what she was seeing but he knew what he was feeling. She was just like all the rest. Not like him. She, like every other person he'd ever met in his life was against him. She had used and abused him for years. She treated him like shit. She treated him more like a beast of burden than a son. No, his mother was no better than the rest.

Tom had had enough.

He took the pillow and slowly, almost ceremonially, placed it over her waxen, palsied face.

"Tom! Tom!..." the words were cut off and muffled as he placed the rank disgusting pillow over her face and applied pressure.

The frail woman put up a meager fight, her last reserves of adrenaline allowing her scrawny, gray skinned hands to snake out from beneath her rumbled covers and grab as his wrists but it was no use. Tom was much stronger. She was old and frail.

Weak. Useless. Not like me. If she were like me I wouldn't have to do this, his inner voice said to himself.

His mother managed to rake a pointed, yellowed fingernail across his hand. The blood beaded at first then finally broke free of its epidermal prison as it ran down his hand onto the pillow that was taking his mother's miserable, overlong life. Tom didn't feel it. He was focused on finally being released from the shackles the woman in the bed had on him.

It only took several minutes but the fight finally went out of his tormentor. With a few applications of additional pressure to be sure Tom knew deep down that his mother was dead. He looked down at his bloody hand, a small river of viscous crimson streaming but it didn't matter.

All that mattered to Tom now was to match the picture in his mind's eye with the carving on the stone tablet.

***

Tom walked the length of the hallway to the kitchen and sat down. He left a trail of his blood in his wake but it didn't matter. He was interested in one thing: looking at the stone tablet.

The box was opened before him and he leaned in for a closer look. He confirmed what he saw in his mind moments before ending an old woman's miserable life.

Carved into the dark russet stone was a humanoid figure. Tom couldn't believe how intricate the stone work was. It was obviously the result of a master craftsman. The details were intricate. Sublime. Perfect.

The humanoid had a head in the shape of an upside down triangle, complete with snake slit eyes, lupine nose and a cruel mouth.

The body was muscular. Its shoulders were broad, its chest muscular.

Those weren't the most curious features, however.

Below the waste the body, if one could call it that, tapered into a point at the bottom. The creature didn't have legs. In a surreal moment, Tom thought of the Tasmanian Devil from the Bugs Bunny cartoons. It had the same form as when the whirling dervish cartoon character would speed around the landscape and its legs disappeared in a miniature tornado.

Words were inscribed below the figure but Tom couldn't make them out. They were in a language he didn't know. The thought occurred to him that it was in a language that man had not seen in eons. It had the look of the ages about it.

He leaned in to get a closer look, reaching for it tentatively with his cut hand. It was then that a fat drop of his blood dripped onto the stone tablet. The stone issued a hiss—or what it a sigh?—when it came into contact with the dusty stone.

Electricity filled the room. Light issued forth from the tablet, like rays of sunshine coming through fat spring rain clouds only in reverse. They issued upwards, not *from* above, as they cast the room in an eerie red glow.

A low thrumming sound filled Tom's dank closed off apartment. It was such a low frequency that it was felt more than heard, like feeling the rotor blades of a low flying helicopter approaching from miles away before the noise actually registers in the ear.

The noise caused Tom's head to hurt. He grabbed his head and screamed, falling off the chair as it threatened to consume him. Crushing pressure crept up on his skull. It was like someone had his head in a vice and was increasing the pressure tortuously slow.

He began to sweat and convulse on the cold decade's old kitchen linoleum when a crack of thunder issued forth and then all was quiet.

Tom blinked his eyes several times. The pain in his head was gone. He almost cried with the sudden relief from the pain and its intensity. Once his hearing came back to him he could hear the sound of his mother's television in the distance and something that sounded like the buzzing of locusts.

He pulled himself up to sit in the kitchen chair when he saw it.

The humanoid figure that was carved with such pain staking and almost loving detail in the weathered stone was floating above the kitchen floor above the tablet.

Tom thought he'd gone crazy.

He reached out, against his better judgment, to touch what was before him when a spark of heat seared through his hand.

"Oh, my God," Tom said in a small awe-struck voice. Tom didn't believe in God, but it was purely a reflexive utterance.

"No. Not God," came a booming voice. It threatened to explode Tom's skull from the inside out. It had an immensely low and gravelly quality to it. The cruel mouth didn't move but Tom knew the creature before him was its origin.

"Am I crazy? Am I really seeing this?" Tom said more to himself than the demon in front of him.

"Perhapsssss," the Demon entity hissed. "But I am here." It added.

It sounded to Tom like there was a legion of creatures generating that voice. It swirled about him like he was in the center of a circle of people, all hissing and talking to him, saying the same things only a slight time delay between each one.

"Are you...the Devil?"

"No," the creature spoke/hissed directly into Tom's consciousness. "The Devil was but a concept undreamed of while I walked the wastes."

"What are you?"

"I am that which existed before. I am that which exists now. I am that which will continue to exisssst..."

Tom felt himself being caressed by the myriad voices speaking directly into his head. And the eyes. The red smoky eyes threatened to consume him.

"You have made the pact of blood," the creature continued. "You have but to ask it and it shall be yourssss. Three times. Three wants granted."

Tom almost laughed at the absurdity of it. Three wishes? A genie?

"Ok," Tom laughed. The cackle that came from his mouth was saturated with mania. It wasn't a health sound. "I could sure use a glass of whiskey right now."

"As you wisssh. You have asssked and I ssshall grant," the creature said with a guttural growl that was more felt than heard.

A highball glass of brown liquid formed in front of Tom's very eyes on the kitchen table. He reached a shaky hand out to it and felt the tingle of static electricity and a mild head as his skin came in contact with it.

Tom raised it to his lips, the trembling in his hands threatening to spill the smoky brown contents. He looked into the Demon's eyes but saw nothing there to indicate if it was a good or bad idea to take a sip. Tom took an inhale of breath to fortify himself and took a sip of the drink. He swallowed the warm liquid, a trail of pleasant fire trailing down his gut and opened his eyes to gaze once again at the motionless demon.

I'm still alive.

"I shall fulfill two more requesssts," the demon said matter-of-factly.

Tom finished the whiskey in one long pull, the fiery liquid stealing the moisture from his esophagus. He coughed from having downed it too quickly before he sat back and thought with his arms crossed in front of his chest.

"My mother. I need that body gone. The smell will cause the neighbors to call the cops and that's the last thing I need. To be stuck in jail with scumbags, rapists and morons."

"Granted," the creature growled.

Tom ran to his mother's room. Before his very eyes he watched as the body of the woman who gave him birth, the body of the woman who treated him more like an unwanted pet than the fruit of her womb disintegrate before his very eyes. Her body turned to ash then drifted away into the ether, the blankets falling flat on the mattress once the body that held them aloft disappeared.

Tom was back in the kitchen, his eyes as wide as saucers.

"One more requesssst. Choose wisely," the creature telecommunicated to Tom's mind.

He thought long and hard. What would his third wish be? Money? Women? No. Too cliché. Too contrived. Tom knew those things wouldn't solve the issues of his miserable existence.

What request could possibly make his life worth living with so many morons and jerks out......?

That's when it hit him.

Tom thought of all the altercations he had with people that very day alone. The girl at the pharmacy with her judging look. The man in the line behind him who critiqued him with his eyes. The lady on the street. The man in the huge SUV who doused him in slushy frozen water on the sidewalk.

His mother.

He thought back on all the people who belittled him growing up and into adult hood. He thought about the bullies. The stupid people. The great unwashed.

None of them are like me. That's the problem. None of them are like me but they should be.

The demon hovered patiently above the tablet while Tom ran through the litany of disappointment and stupid examples of humanity he'd encountered over his near four decades of life.

He settled on his third and final wish.

"I want everyone in the world to be like me. Every last one of them. I'm tired of being put down. I'm tired of people judging me, belittling me. I'm tired of them thinking they're better than me. If everyone in the world was like me then I wouldn't have to try to fit in. I wouldn't have to try to conform to society's strict rules of what's normal and what's not. Let the bastards conform to *me!*" Tom announced triumphantly.

"Isss thisss what you truly want?" the demon asked. "Isss this your heart's desire? To have every single living breathing human walking the earth to be like you? Do you want them to be remade in your image? Using the very depths of your sssssoul as the template?"

"Yes," Tom said emphatically without a moment's hesitation.

"Your wish is granted," the demon said emotionlessly.

Tom didn't' know what to expect but nothing happened. Did he think he'd feel different? Did he expect the clouds to part and impart some type of divine event upon him? He didn't know.

"Nothing's happened."

"It'ssss happening right now. You have but to look out your window or turn on your television to see the world that is being recreated in your image."

Tom rushed over to the living room window and threw the shade open with a snap. The November sky was turning a dark gray color as night descended but the street lights cast the street in a bright blue glow.

"I don't see anything happening!" Tom said hysterically.

Did I waste my one last wish? What the fuck is going on here?

Then he saw it.

Two groups of twenty-somethings were walking down the street in opposite directions. At first it seemed as if nothing was happening, just two separate groups of friends about to pass each other like ships in the night.

But when they reached each other they stopped. It started out as some pushing and shoving. Tom could barely hear anything because his windows had been painted over from the outside years ago and he never addressed the problem but he heard the unmistakable sounds of yelling. It was like trying to hear a conversation through a thick wall.

It wasn't long before the pushing and shoving turned into out and out brawling. Fists were flying, kicks were thrust. The two sets of twenty year olds were beating each other to death. They used anything in the street they could get their hands on to enact their brutal and bloody screenplay.

"What the fuck?" Tom said in horrible fascination as he watched the sheer brutality of perfect strangers, seemingly with no prior problems with one another beat each other to death.

It wasn't long before people driving by stopped dead in the middle of the street, exited their cars and joined the orgy of violence.

"This has to be some kind of mistake!" He screamed.

Not long after he uttered his words, Tom heard the sounds of yelling and fighting coming from the hallway. He rushed over to the door and opened it a crack only to see his neighbors on the floor in the hallways scratching and clawing and biting each other. He thrust the door shut and locked the doors.

"What the hell is going on out there?" He yelled at the motionless demon.

"The humans of the world are being remade in your image. It is just as you assked."

"This can't be happening," he choked out.

Tom ran to his old console television and stabbed the on button. He tuned it to the local news station.

What he saw was nothing he could have possibly imagined, even in his worst nightmares.

"....we repeat. Random acts of violence of been reported the world over," said the screaming anchor man from behind his news desk. Over his left shoulder, live footage from all over the world was playing out a macabre and bloody opera. London, Tel Aviv, Sao Paolo. Every city that flashed up in the little square at the upper right of the news broadcast showed people beating each other to death with their fists, legs, teeth and anything else they could find.

The harried anchorman continued.

"...we urge you to stay in your homes. Lock your doors. Do not answer the door for anyone! This is not limited to the United States. This is all over the *world*. The President has decreed a state of emergency...do not, under any circumstances leave your..."

The anchor man was cut off when a lovely young woman—the evening meteorologist, if Tom remembered correctly—jumped over the news desk and grabbed the older man by the throat. She had nothing but hatred and maniacal aggression in her eyes. It wasn't long before the 'Please Stand By. We Are Having Technical Difficulties' graphic replaced the brutal imagery on Tom's television.

A loud knocking was sounding on Tom's door as he tore himself away from the TV to look at the demon.

"I said I wanted everyone to be like me! This isn't what I asked for!"

"It is exactly what you asked for. I asked you if you wanted to use your soul as a template and you agreed. My part of the bargain, sealed in blood, has been fulfilled."

"But why is everyone killing each other?" Tom pleaded.

The demon cocked his head at Tom as if misunderstanding before saying, "Your soul is black, Thomas McNulty. It is blacker than The Before. It is blacker than the After. You are a walking, murderous shell of humanity. You are *hollow*. You assked for people to be remade in your soul's image. I have given you what you wanted."

"No!!! I don't want this! I take it back!"

"You cannot. The rules, sealed in blood, were explicit. Three wants. Three desires granted. Thisss is the world you wanted. Thisss is the world you wished. Thisss is the world remade in your image."

The door burst open as the Demon absorbed itself back into the ancient cursed stone as if it had never existed.

The woman from the street and the man from the SUV tore down Tom's door with bloody knuckles, tearing each other's hair out, ripping at each other's eyes before they saw him and closed in on him with murderous intent.

"No! Nooooo!!!!!" Tom screamed. The sadistic man and woman threw him down onto the ground and began to pull, rip and tear at his flesh with their hands and teeth. His last remaining minutes on Earth were nothing but a cascading wave of agony.

As Tom's screams became more harried and filled with pain, a voice issued forth from the evil tablet, the epitaph of Tom's excruciating final moments.

"Your wish has begun the end of the world, Thomasssss McNulty. It has been sealed in blood. You should have been more careful in what you wissshed for."

And so it was that people the world over tore and bit and brutalized their fellow man until humanity was no more.

What would happen if a large meteor was slated to crash into earth and everyone knew it was going to happen? David Lee Summers tells us the story of a Burgermeister struggling save his Alpine village as earth faces catastrophic destruction from above.

A Garden Resurrected
David Lee Summers

Wilhelm Baumgartner hiked along a well worn trail through dense forest until he came to a familiar clearing. Grass carpeted the ground and a soft breeze whistled through the trees, but otherwise, it was eerily silent, lacking the familiar sounds of birds and creatures scurrying through the undergrowth. Baumgartner looked up at the deepening blue sky, then went over to a smooth rock and sat down. With a sigh, he wondered how many more blue skies he would see over the idyllic clearing where he often came to be alone and think.

He retrieved a pouch of tobacco from his pocket and tamped the shredded brown leaves into a battered pipe. Baumgartner was burgermeister of the nearby village of Kleinstadt, nestled near a lake in the Bavarian Alps. Kleinstadt, along with the rest of the world, faced extinction. Frankly, Baumgartner felt the rest of the world could go to hell, but he cared a great deal about the future of Kleinstadt and his family.

The balding, potbellied man lit the pipe and watched as smoke swirled bravely skyward, as though it could ward off the evil that came from above. Tobacco was difficult to obtain in the mid-twenty-first century, and he realized his supply might soon be cut off entirely, but he needed to come up with a plan for the next day's council meeting. Smoking helped him think.

As the burgermeister smoked, the sky darkened. Even before the first stars appeared, the meteor grew visible. It wasn't as big as the full moon, but it was nearly as bright. Astronomers predicted it would hit the Earth in just a few days. It was unlikely it would hit anywhere near the little Bavarian valley, but disaster loomed nonetheless. Even if it hit the Pacific Ocean, which was the scientists' best guess, the amount of water vapor thrown into the atmosphere would cause clouds and rain for years. Food production would be difficult if not impossible. Tsunamis would devastate coastal cities. Earthquakes and volcanoes were expected. Commerce would be disrupted, if not shut down altogether.

Unless the meteor fell directly on Kleinstadt, the town would survive for a time but, isolated as it was, the burgermeister knew the village would eventually run out of supplies. The people had been stocking up, but unless the impact was much less catastrophic than predicted, they would have two or maybe three years, presuming the town's population didn't blossom. He didn't worry about new babies being born. Babies were always a blessing. He worried about outsiders arriving, seeking the relative safety of the valley.

He inhaled the smoke deeply and blew it out in rings, watching them, as they appeared to encircle the meteor. The villagers needed something that would discourage people from raiding their town. Also, if they ran out of supplies, they might need to find more. That would mean going to other towns that wanted to keep strangers out. They needed an advantage against those villages—something more than guns. Everyone had those. He hated to think about that, but as burgermeister, it was his responsibility to be prepared for all contingencies.

The breeze returned, sending a chill along Baumgartner's arms. He looked at the pipe and saw that the tobacco was nearly exhausted. He stood and returned to the trail, unhappy that he had no better answers than when he arrived. As he hiked back to the village, he caught glimpses of the nearby, ancient castle. Legends told that before World War II—before the Nazis—a Graf named Schaefer had occupied it. There were stories that Graf Schaefer had been a vampire. The burgermeister began to wonder if those old legends could be used to his town's advantage. He knew just the person who could help him find the answers.

* * *

Instead of going home, Burgermeister Baumgartner went to the house of the librarian, a thin, gray-haired man called Jung. The old man opened his door a crack and peered out over the top of wire-rim glasses, as though already afraid of invading outsiders. When he saw the burgermeister, he threw the door open.

"Pleased to see you, sir," said the librarian. "May I offer you a brandy?"

The burgermeister licked his lips, then nodded. "Yes, I think that would be very welcome about now."

"What brings you out tonight? Thinking about the coming disaster? It seems you've done as much as humanly possible." The librarian stepped into the kitchen. When he returned, he handed a snifter of brandy to the burgermeister.

"Have I?" Baumgartner took a sip and found enough courage to forge ahead with his question. "What do you know about Graf Schaefer? The legends that he was a vampire?"

The librarian lifted his bushy eyebrows, then took a generous gulp from his own glass. He stepped over to an armchair and sat, indicating that the burgermeister should take the room's other chair. "According to the records, the Schaefers oversaw this valley for centuries. They were good rulers, but reclusive. When the Nazis came to power, they swept away much of the old royalty, including Graf Schaefer."

"That's the official history. There's more to the story, though, isn't there?" The burgermeister leaned forward.

The librarian nodded. "There are no records of a Schaefer marriage. No records of a young Schaefer attending school in Kleinstadt ... or anywhere, for that matter. It lends credence to the idea that there was only one Schaefer who ruled this village for centuries."

"But weren't there specific legends saying he was a vampire?"

"A lot of whispers, but nothing in the official record. It's said he had no garden at the castle, no cattle pens. So, rumors started about how the Schaefers' ate." Herr Jung shrugged and sat back, steepling his fingers. "During the days of the black plague, deaths were, of course, blamed on him. In more recent centuries, it's harder to find records of how he fed ... if he was, indeed, a vampire."

"Perhaps he lured visitors from outside to his castle." When Jung didn't say anything, Baumgartner took another sip of his brandy. "How did the Nazis sweep Schaefer aside?"

"A Nazi administrator appeared one day and announced he was in charge. The graf was never seen after that."

The burgermeister nodded. "Hitler was familiar with the occult. He and his men would have known how to dispatch a vampire."

"If he was a vampire, they could have found him during the daytime and driven a stake through his heart." The librarian's eyebrows came together. "But how do these stories of a long-gone boogyman actually help us?"

"I don't know." Baumgartner took a deep breath and let it out slowly. "In a way, it's just idle dreaming—a hope that we could spread his legend again and keep outsiders away. Perhaps people in other villages would help us in our time of need, fearing the wrath of the vampire." The burgermeister took another sip of brandy. "Even if there was a real vampire, I'm sure he's long gone. When a stake is driven through a vampire's heart, he falls to dust, doesn't he?"

The librarian snorted. "You've been watching too many old movies, my friend. The idea was simply to pin the vampire to the ground so he wouldn't walk. The stake didn't destroy the creature. It just immobilized him."

Baumgartner's eyes widened. "Then you mean Graf Schaefer may still exist?"

Jung sighed. "If he was a vampire—if the Nazis didn't burn him—then yes, he might still exist, but those are a lot of uncertainties, my friend. I think you need to get some rest."

"Could he be resurrected?"

The librarian picked up the brandy and took another deep swallow. "There are ancient texts in the basement of the library that tell how such a thing could be done, but" —Jung narrowed his gaze— "these are all just old stories. There's no guarantee it would work. Even if it did, why resurrect a vampire?"

"A legend is a difficult thing to pin our hopes on. But a real vampire? No one would dare bother us if Schaefer were resurrected."

Jung held up his hand. "Presuming we could do this, how do we keep a vampire fed in this world after the apocalypse? Wouldn't that be suicide?"

"Why would he turn to the village when there's so much carnage outside? Do your books not also tell of ways to ward off vampires? If we make it easier for him to seek his prey elsewhere..."

A slow smile crept across the librarian's face. "I see where you're going with this."

"Check the books of arcane knowledge. Meet me at the city hall tomorrow during the council meeting and let me know what we need to resurrect the good Graf. Let me know if this plan has a chance of working." The burgermeister finished his glass of brandy.

"Promise me you'll go home and get some rest," said the librarian, standing.

The burgermeister shook his head. "Soon. I have one more stop to make before calling it a night."

* * *

Baumgartner returned home and retrieved his car, then drove as close to the old castle as he could. He put new batteries in his flashlight, then hiked up an overgrown trail to a rusted, iron gate. The old castle had been fenced off years before to keep people from going inside. The castle had not been maintained since World War II and it was falling to ruins. Tucking the flashlight under his arm, the burgermeister found the gate's key on an old ring he carried. It opened with a shriek.

Calming his beating heart, the burgermeister stepped through the gate and continued into the courtyard of the ancient castle. If Graf Schaefer had indeed been a vampire, it seemed likely he would have slept in an underground chamber. Baumgartner shone his flashlight around the overgrown courtyard. Some doors clearly led into the castle itself. Some clearly went into storage chambers. He walked over to one door and tried it. It was locked and none of the burgermeister's keys worked. Another door was hanging loose on its hinges. He touched it and it fell with a thud that echoed in the empty courtyard.

Shining his light into the gloom beyond the door, Baumgartner saw a set of stone stairs that led downward. The burgermeister tried to swallow, but his mouth was dry. He continued inside and descended the staircase. Near the bottom, a piece of stone crumbled and he nearly toppled the rest of the way down. Seasoned hiker as he was, he kept his balance and reached a dark, damp chamber at the bottom. His flashlight touched several stone crypts.

One of the crypts stood open. Within were the remains of a man who appeared mummified. The burgermeister looked around at the damp, moldy walls and noted how strange that was. The worms and bugs should have eaten anyone buried in this place long ago.

Baumgartner crept closer and the hairs on the back of his neck stood on end. Parchment skin clung tenaciously to the mummy's skull. Its mouth was open in a silent scream revealing sharp, white incisors like the fangs of a dog. An iron stake was driven through the chest of the mummy, pinning it to the crypt. The burgermeister was surprised the stake was not wooden, as he had seen in so many American and British movies. Joy at the discovery battled with fear and revulsion. He backed away from the crypt. Confronted by the certainty of the vampire, the burgermeister wasn't sure whether he was seeing the village's salvation or its damnation.

* * *

"A few of us could go to Munich and steal a tank from the army base there." The suggestion came from a councilman named Fiedler, who was a commando in Afghanistan, early in the twenty-first century.

"Why don't we just hire some mercenaries from Libya," suggested a councilwoman named Krebs. In addition to serving on the council, she was the wealthiest person in town and managed Kleinstadt's only bank.

The burgermeister held up his hands. "Neither of those ideas will work. Who can get past the entire army to steal a tank? Even if we could afford Libyan mercenaries, how are we going to feed them? How do we keep them from taking advantage of us?" He shook his head. "I propose we implore Graf Shaefer for help."

At that, the audience in the council chamber literally erupted. Some people crossed themselves to ward off evil. Others shouted that Baumgartner had lost his mind and should step down. About a dozen people stood and walked out of the council chamber.

Fiedler leaned forward. "The Nazis dispatched the graf years ago. I'm sure he's dust by now."

"He's not," shouted Baumgartner over the noise of the crowd. "I saw him myself just last night. He is merely staked to his crypt."

At the burgermeister's words, an uneasy silence descended on the crowd.

"Herr Jung tells me we could resurrect Graf Schaefer," continued Baumgartner.

Krebs pointed at the burgermeister. "You tell me hiring mercenaries is foolish, but you talk of bringing back a vampire?"

"Mercenaries will consume much food. A vampire" —Baumgartner shrugged— "only needs a little blood, and there will be much blood outside this valley."

Fiedler sat back and rubbed his chin, apparently giving the idea some thought. "But can we control this creature?"

Baumgartner looked out at the audience. Spotting the librarian, he held out his hand. "Herr Jung knows the records of our village better than anyone."

The librarian stood up and looked around nervously. "I have studied the records. Wreaths of garlic and holly are effective at turning a vampire away."

Frau Krebs sighed and folded her arms. "Brilliant, Herr Jung. It'll be like a French gourmet's Christmas in June." Nervous laughter followed by a discontented murmur arose from the assembled crowd.

Baumgartner glared at the councilwoman and banged his gavel. When the crowd was silenced, he turned to the librarian, urging him to continue.

Herr Jung nodded. "Having a supply of blood handy could be used to appease the vampire." This brought gasps from several people. He smiled slightly, then held up his finger. "I will also point out that if a vampire kills his entire food supply, he will die as surely as a human who eats all the crops of his field or kills an entire herd."

"I believe it is worth the risk," said Baumgartner solemnly.

The people in the council chamber resumed their murmuring, but this time it was quiet, as though considering the plan.

Frau Krebs shook her head. "This still sounds like fantasy to me. Even if the vampire exists, even if he can be controlled, how do we know he can even be revived?"

The librarian removed his glasses and made a show of cleaning them. "I have found a spell..."

He was interrupted by another outburst. Herr Fiedler stood up. "I will not be part of some foul Satanic Ritual."

The librarian calmly shook his head. "This is no Satanic Ritual, Herr Fiedler. These magicks are far older, going back to the old gods. We must summon elemental spirits such as the valkyries."

Fiedler folded his arms and sat back in his chair. "This still sounds as though we are dabbling in dangerous territory."

"Any more dangerous than breaking into an army base?" asked Baumgarner. He turned to Krebs. "Any more dangerous than hiring mercenaries?" The room had fallen silent, expectant. The burgermeister took a deep breath and sat back. "All in favor of attempting to resurrect Graf Shaefer and imploring his aid?"

Fiedler and Krebs looked at each other. After a moment, they slowly raised their hands.

"We will need blood," interjected the librarian, "lots of blood."

The burgermeister turned to the hospital's administrator who sat in the front row. "I'll put you in charge of that."

The doctor frowned, but nodded. "We'll hold a blood drive."

* * *

The burgermeister was cautiously optimistic as he returned home that afternoon. The hospital said the call for blood was going well. Herr Jung thought they could try the ceremony the next day. Baumgartner opened the door and found his wife seated, facing the door with her arms crossed. "I want you to speak with your daughter," she said coldly.

Baumgartner smelled sausages and saurkraut from the kitchen, but he knew he wouldn't get any until he went upstairs and found out what his daughter had done that was upsetting his wife. He pursed his lips and gave a curt nod. "Yes, dear."

He trudged upstairs and knocked on his daughter's door.

"Come in," called Heidi Baumgartner.

Cautiously, the burgermeister opened the door. He saw his eighteen-year-old daughter in a form-fitting black dress cut low, revealing ample cleavage. "Is it true?" she asked wide-eyed. "Are you going to awaken Graf Schaefer?"

Baumgartner swallowed. "Yes, we are going to try."

"I want to go, but Mama says I can't."

The burgermeister looked around at her bookshelves. They were lined with tales of vampires. Everything from Anne Rice's tales of the Vampire Lestat to Stephanie Meyer's *Bella und Edward* books. He sighed and stepped into the room. "I saw the Graf. He is but a desiccated husk of a man. He is not the romantic figure of these ... fantasies."

"Perhaps not now," said Heidi, "but what happens after his life force is restored? Herr Jung showed me pictures. Graf Schaefer was a very handsome man..."

"That was long ago," said the burgermeister. "What makes you think I would deliver my own daughter into the hands of a vampire?"

"Not just handsome, but rich," she persisted.

The burgermeister loosened his tie. "Rich will mean nothing after the asteroid hits."

"He could make me immortal," she persisted. "You would never have to worry about losing me after the catastrophe."

Baumgartner ground his teeth, then looked up at his beautiful daughter. She was, indeed, his most precious possession. She was the entire reason he fought for the town to survive. He loved Kleinstadt and the lake. He loved the mountains and forests, but the reason he fought for survival stood in the room with him. Finally he nodded. "You may come along." He held up his finger. "But don't tell your mother, and I want you to put on some more modest clothes for dinner."

She bent down and kissed her father on the cheek. "Yes, Papa! Right away."

* * *

The next night, as the sun sank below the horizon and the asteroid loomed large and bright in the sky, Burgermeister Baumgartner and his daughter along with Herr Fiedler, Frau Krebs and the librarian arrived at Castle Schaefer's gate. All wore strings of garlic around their necks. As Baumgartner unlocked the gate, Herr Fiedler and Frau Krebs retrieved an ice chest from the car. Inside was a gallon jug of blood. Heidi Baumgartner hastily removed her garlic necklace while her father wasn't looking and straightened her hair.

Forming a solemn procession, they made their way up the hill, into the courtyard, and then down the crumbling steps into Graf Schaefer's crypt. Herr Jung lit torches that lined the craggy walls, casting the room in an eerie, flickering light.

Heidi Baumgartner looked into the crypt and gasped at the sight of the mummified form. "He'll be more handsome once he's rejuvenated, I'm sure."

"I don't care whether he's handsome or not," said Frau Krebs, "as long as he keeps this village safe in the difficult times to come."

The librarian blew dust from a stone plinth and placed an ancient leather-bound volume on its surface. Opening the book to the marked page, he began reading old German that the burgermeister could not understand. After a moment, the librarian looked up. "The time has come to remove the stake."

Baumgartner swallowed and took a tentative step toward the crypt. He grabbed the iron stake and pulled. It wouldn't yield. "What the devil did they use to pound this thing in with? It's stuck fast." He looked over his shoulder. "Give me a hand."

Fiedler and Krebs stepped up and grabbed the stake. All together they began wiggling it back and forth, lifting a fine cloud of dust from the mummified form of Graf Schaefer. Heidi Baumgartner sneezed.

Apocalypse 13

"Careful," cautioned Herr Jung. "You'll rattle the poor man apart."

"It's no good," moaned Baumgartner. "They must have hammered the stake into the stone of the crypt."

The librarian stepped around the plinth and examined the body. "If the stake won't come out of the body, we must remove the body from the stake." He directed Frau Krebs to take the vampire's feet. He placed Herr Fiedler at his hips and had the burgermeister take the head and shoulders. "Lift him very gently and lay him on the ground. If I understand the book correctly, this will help. Not only will he be free of the stake, but he'll be on his native soil."

Very carefully, the city councilors of Kleinstadt lifted the lightweight, mummified body of the vampire and placed him on the ground next to the crypt. The librarian resumed his place behind the plinth and read another section of the ancient text. Baumgartner recognized some of the names such as Odin and Freya. He recognized the names of valkyries such as Brynhild, Gudrun and Sigrun. There seemed to be other names, gods or other beings of power from around the world—Iktome, Amatsu-Mikaboshi and Shiva. After a few minutes of recitation, the dry and frail corpse began to glow with a soft, greenish light.

"The time has come," said the librarian. "A little blood into the stake wound."

Frau Krebs opened the gallon container of blood and poured some into the wound.

"A little into his mouth, too," urged the librarian.

Frau Krebs did as the librarian instructed.

The librarian continued to read from the book. As he did, Baumgartner saw the flesh begin to glisten and fill out. The old wound pulsed and became like red clay, flowing closed. The hollow eye sockets blinked twice, then the whites of eyes appeared. The third time, there were blue irises. There was a deep, intake of breath and then a moment later, a piercing scream escaped the body. Herr Fiedler stepped back, covering his ears.

Graf Schaefer thrashed about as the muscles expanded like balloons. Tufts of white hair sprouted on the mummy's bald pate. The librarian kept reading, shouting now over the screams of the being thrashing about, stirring up a cloud of dust.

"More blood," called the librarian. "He needs more blood!"

Frau Krebs knelt down beside the vampire and lifted the gallon jug of blood to his lips. He drank greedily for a moment. One gulp, then another. When he took the third, he gagged and spit it out. "Goddamn it! That shit's cold!"

The members of the town council gathered around in wide-eyed silence, staring at the frail old man on the floor. The vampire looked around at those people assembled. Heidi Baumgartner screamed.

The vampire blinked. "What's the matter with her?"

Heidi took a deep breath. "I thought this ceremony would give you your youth back."

The vampire chuckled. "I wish that were true. I'm over a thousand years old, young lady. I'm no Clark Gable." He took a deep breath as though savoring air for the first time in a long while, then took another look at Heidi. "Young lady, you should put some more clothes on. You'll catch your death in this damp crypt."

Heidi Baumgartner blushed bright red, then shrank back into the shadows.

Graf Schaefer looked around at the others. "Who are you? Are you the members of the Nazi Party I was told to expect? If so, the answer is still no. You may not build one of your filthy death camps in my village."

The burgermeister knelt down beside the vampire. "No, we're not Nazis. They have been out of power for over a century. I'm Wilhelm Baumgartner, burgermeister of Kleinstadt. These other people are members of the city council. We have come seeking your aid."

"A century, you say." The vampire shook his head. "It took you long enough." He held out his arms. "Help me off this dusty floor and let's go find someplace more comfortable to talk."

Baumgartner and Fiedler helped the ancient vampire stand. He brushed dust from his jacket and trousers. He looked into the shadows and held out his hand. "Fräulein, please come out. I mean you no harm."

She stepped from the shadows. "I don't think you're quite what anyone expected."

He shrugged, then looked over at the book on the plinth and at the stake stuck fast within the crypt. "It seems clear you knew I was a vampire."

"We just didn't expect you to be so ... old," said the burgermeister's daughter with a shudder.

He smiled sadly. "All things age and change, even vampires." He climbed up two of the steps. "Now tell me, if you are not Nazis, why have you awakened me?"

As they climbed the steps and entered the courtyard, the burgermeister pointed up into the sky. "The world faces disaster."

Graf Schaefer nodded slowly. "A portent of evil from the heavens. It has been a long time since I have seen such a thing." He looked around at the town council. "I helped Kleinstadt survive the black plague. I will help my town survive this new crisis."

"I'm delighted by your cooperation," declared Frau Krebs. "Help us and we will help you find people to feed upon."

Graf Schaefer turned and took the banker's hand. "You sound as bad as those Nazis," he said gently. "They thought I would delight in having a death camp in this town." His gaze grew more intense and Frau Krebs gasped as the vampire tightened his grip. "I am not here to cooperate. You will do what I say, or you will not survive."

Frau Krebs nodded rapidly and the vampire released her.

"I am but one old vampire who requires a garden carefully tended," continued Graf Schaefer. "I will do everything I can to help my garden flourish." He reached out and touched Heidi's cheek.

The burgermeister shuddered, but one look at the sky reminded him that a gardener who covers his crops is not such a bad thing when hail falls from the sky.

Apocalypse 13

* * *

The asteroid hit the Earth two days later. The devastation was much worse than expected. It hit the Pacific Ocean near the East Coast of Asia, shutting down Chinese and Korean manufacturing. Nuclear power plants melted down. Tsunamis virtually destroyed every city on the West Coast of North America. The impact triggered earthquakes all around the globe.

Even the secluded valley that protected Kleinstadt was not unaffected. Tremors caused the remains of Castle Schaefer to tumble to the ground and set rocks sliding from the mountains. Several houses in the village were destroyed. Before the castle's destruction, the graf had secured other quarters and under his tutelage, the villagers were already rebuilding the shattered homes.

Clouds darkened the skies over Kleinstadt, but the winds kept radiation and other contaminants from raining into the lake. Herr Jung cautioned that as the oceans grew contaminated, there would be an increasing chance of problems from the rains, but for the time being, they were safe.

A week after the asteroid impact, a dozen men rode through the Bavarian Alps, looking for gasoline to feed their starving motorcycles and food for their starving bellies. They wore spiked helmets salvaged from a World War I museum and thick woolen coats to protect against the chill air. They came to the top of a rise and saw Kleinstadt below. Even from the distance they could tell the town was virtually untouched. They saw fruit trees near the lake and it looked as though people were building greenhouses. "What a lovely jewel," said the leader and motioned for them to continue down the road.

A mile further on, they came to a sign announcing that they were about to enter the Village of Kleinstadt. Just beyond the sign was a telephone pole. The lines were useless because of the catastrophe, but someone had hung an ancient, rusted cage from it. Inside was a mummified figure in tattered clothes.

"Isn't that cute? They think they can frighten us away," said the leader.

"I've heard of this place," said the man next to him. "These are the people crazy enough to awaken a vampire to protect them."

"It's the middle of the day," said the leader. "What can a vampire do now? We ride in, get food and ride out again."

One of the men shouted and pointed to the cage. "Look! Look!"

"What is it, Klaus?" The leader looked where the man pointed.

The mummified figure arose and opened the cage door. It bared its fangs. "Leave my village in peace."

The leader paled and directed the bikes to turn around and return the way they came. They pirouetted in a shower of gravel. As they hurried down the road, one of the men lost control. The bike spun out from under him and he landed in a heap, in the middle of the road. Another biker noticed and turned back to help. The rest rode on, heedless of the accident.

Graf Schaefer emerged from the cage. The perpetual twilight after the asteroid apocalypse allowed him to walk during the day, but only as a shell of his nighttime form.

The biker who returned was the one the leader called Klaus. He drew a percussion-cap pistol and aimed it at the approaching revenant. "Stay back. We'll leave, but I've got to help my friend."

The vampire stopped. "Why were you with those men?"

Klaus looked back the way the bikers had gone. "Two days ago they rode into our town. Goetz and I were the only ones left. The choice was ride with them or die."

Graf Schaefer nodded. "Retrieve your motorbike. You may enter Kleinstadt."

Klaus blinked back surprise. He looked down at his fallen comrade. "What about Goetz?"

"Is he a good man?"

"Better than me," said the biker. The man called Goetz stirred and began to sit up. Klaus spoke softly to him. A moment later, he helped Goetz stand.

"You may take him to the village," said Graf Schaefer. "You will be watched. If indeed you prove good men, you may stay."

The two bikers looked at each other, then nodded.

* * *

Graf Schaefer watched as Klaus helped Goetz limp down the road toward the village. Goetz's spiked helmet lay on the ground where it had fallen. The vampire stepped over, and picked it up, then looked toward the village. He still loved Kleinstadt, but the garden had gone untended too long. It needed an infusion of new life and new blood. He smiled to himself as he remembered the meaning of the word apocalypse. It meant a lifting of the veil, a revelation. These men would be Kleinstadt's much-needed apocalypse.

Grey is a nasty alien who would happily see every earthling destroyed if it meant he could get off this planet. Sadly he has the means to accomplish his sick goal. A djinn and a werewolf are the only ones who might be able to stand in his way in Terri Osborne's tale of earth's best defenders.

A Djinn, A Werewolf, and Grey Walk Into a Bar
Terri Osborne

"You're too late."

Oh, that little demon spawn of a freaking alien Satan. "What have you done now, Grey?"

"What do you think, djinn?"

"Blowing up Earth this time, or just screwing around with the humans?" There were a lot of things he'd attempted in the three hundred years I'd known the little terrorist. All he wanted was to leave Earth in his rearview mirror. Whether Earth survived the process was completely irrelevant. Tunguska? That had been Grey trying to signal his people. Disappearance of the honeybee? Yeah, that was him, too. The Bureau was still trying to figure out what he'd been attempting with that one.

Grey's face smiled. Mind you, it was just as fake a smile as the skin over that ugly mug.

I didn't have a chance to come up with a comeback before Fen ran into the bar and stopped beside me. "What is it, Fen?" He gave me that look. He hated that I didn't even need to see him enter the room to know it was him. "Fen, you're a werewolf. We've been partners for twenty years. Do the math."

He shook his head and gave a short laugh that wondered if he'd ever learn, which was par for the course. "There are sirens all over out there. Jumpers on the office towers. People refusing to come out of their houses. Net's saying the Americans are talking lack of faith in all of the peace negotiations. Russia's gone insular and belligerent all of a sudden. What the hell's going on?"

I pointed at Grey. "Aren't you going to say hello to our old buddy?"

Fen glared, a flame of anger in those dark eyes. "How the hell did you get out of Area 7?"

"Does that really matter right now, Fen?"

"Yes, Fenrus, does that really matter?" Grey's left eyebrow raised, and his voice took on a menace I hadn't thought him capable.

To answer his question, it didn't matter. And Fen knew it. My partner walked over and put the handcuffs on Grey.

"Really, werewolf?" A bright light began to glow around the cuffs, and they dropped open from Grey's wrists, clattering to the floor like so much useless garbage.

"Grey, you're coming with us."

"Werewolf, I'll go wherever on this useless rock I choose. Nothing you can do will stop me."

One thing I liked about working with Fen, his fuse with arrogance was even shorter than mine. "Listen, you little grey alien," he began, quickly swiping his hand over his head in a gesture I knew meant he'd had enough. "I don't give a damn what you think you can and can't do. I've seen what you've *tried* to do, and it's a joke."

"You've seen what the humans are doing to each other out there, and you call me a joke? Your compassion is astonishing."

"*You're* lecturing on compassion, Grey? Now *that's* the joke." I said, reaching toward the Glock on my hip. It wasn't much, but a bullet to the kneecap had a better chance of stopping Grey than a foot chase through the back alleys of Milwaukee at that point. "Come on, before I get the brass to give me the force fields. You're going to reverse whatever you've done and we're going to send you back to Area 7 tonight."

"Reverse this? Whatever would make you think I could do that, djinn?"

His use of 'could' instead of 'would' gave me a moment's pause, but I set it aside. "Because you're going to reverse it, Grey. It's that simple."

It took Fen wrestling one of the little terrorist's arms behind his back to get him to come along. Grey was the one who'd crammed those long arms of his into a human skin. If we used that weakness to our advantage to get him to cooperate and come with us? I wasn't going to feel all that guilty about it.

The alleys near the river weren't quite as industrialized as other areas of the city, but the cold white of the halogen security lamps on the surrounding buildings wasn't making me feel comfortable as I walked toward the door. Of course, the maze built into the bar made it a lot more complicated than it needed to be, but we finally made it back to the bookshelf that served as the bar's hidden entrance. "The local FBI is a couple of blocks over. We should be able to get him to ARBI from there." I pulled out my cell phone and dialed the secure line to Cathedral Square as soon as I had a signal.

"Cathedral of St. John the Evangelist, how may I direct your call?"

No matter how hard she tried to hide it, Shannon's English accent still bled through. It had been a while since I'd been in Milwaukee, though. To hear a Midwest accent fighting with the British was strange to my ears. "Shannon, tell the director we've got him. We'll be there in a few minutes. Anything unusual?"

"Nothing that's getting through the shielding."

Fen's questions about what he'd heard on the radio came back to me. "What do you mean? There aren't jumpers on the Cathedral, are there?"

"There were. The attempted suicides are becoming more than the hospitals can take, Raina. There's a group holding candles out on the lawn. They're talking about the end of the world. The assistant director came back from getting dinner talking about how he didn't deserve to live. He said he felt better as soon as he walked under the shields. What is going on?"

I looked up and saw Fen standing at the opened door. His expression was one of curious concern. All I could do was shrug. "I don't know. Grey's done something, but he won't talk."

"Get him over here. We can bring Cassandra in to have a little chat with him."

I couldn't help it. I cringed. Bring in the greatest truth-teller in all of the Realms to deal with a career criminal? I also liked the rather perverse nature of it. If anyone could get the answer out of him on how to reverse whatever he'd done, it would be Cassandra.

But that still meant we needed to get him to the Bureau. If there were people attempting suicide all over, that was a bad sign. What the hell had Grey done?

"We'll be on-site in fifteen. Can we get the force field generators in place in time?"

"Consider it done. Ta."

Ending the call, I put the cell back in my pocket and re-aimed the gun at Grey's back. We walked out the door and into a spiritual wall like I'd never experienced before. It was a wave of emotion that hit me like a kick in the chest by one of those professional wrestlers on television. I had to stop. I couldn't breathe. I couldn't even think. Despair rolled over me in waves, each one growing in intensity. No matter where I looked, I couldn't see a smile or hear a laugh. It was as though the shine had gone off of the world. Nothing was…alive. "Fen, can you feel that?" I looked over to find my partner doubled-over. His black hair was almost reaching the ground in that pose. All he could do was groan.

Grey, that son of a bitch, just stood there smiling at both of us like the spectre of death.

"What the hell have you done?"

He walked over and looked me in the eye. "Hell on Earth."

I fought to recover my breath. It was a hard battle. The weight on my chest from the pressure of the emotional current was unlike anything I'd ever felt, and that was saying something. If this was what was descending on the humans? No wonder they were trying to kill themselves.

Still, I was a djinn, and I was ARBI. Weakness had to be temporary. If the enemy knew where to hit you, they'd use it to their advantage at the next opportunity. And if anyone would use any advantage he could get, it would be Grey. Every vertebra in my spine screamed in agony as I pulled myself upright. He wasn't going to win, not this time, not ever.

"Why are you still here?" I asked.

Grey's smile quirked at the corner. "What?"

It hurt just to talk, but I forced the words out. "You could have escaped any time you wanted, but you're still here. Why?"

"Perhaps I want to see the look on your precious face when you figure it out."

The sound of a bullet moving from the magazine to the chamber of Fen's gun came from behind the little demon. "Maybe we'd like to see the look on your real face when I put a bullet between those bulbous eyes."

Grey didn't even try to turn around. "Always the predator, eh, werewolf? What will you do when there are no more prey left to hunt? What will you be then?"

Fen's voice had a snarl to it. "Something you won't be. Alive."

"Are you sure about that?"

"Outside of taxes, it's the only thing I *am* sure of."

Grey's lips thinned. I could have sworn there was a glint in his fraudulent eyes. With a slowness I didn't think he could manage in his human suit, the little alien turned around to face Fen. "Death, the ultimate equalizer. Why try to fight it? What do you have to look forward to, werewolf?"

I could see Fen trying to fight it. "The end of you."

"And that will make things better?"

Fen was somehow holding his ground as Grey inched toward him. "Yes."

The annoying part was that the little terrorist had a point. The world was turning to Jahannam. We'd all be fighting to survive the pit soon enough, and we wouldn't even have the courtesy of being in Hell. What was there to look forward to?

Grey pulled something out of his pocket as he slowly approached Fen. When he held it up into the harsh white light, admiring it as though it were a precious pet, I realized what he'd done.

"Where did you get the damned Box?"

The laugh was haughty and annoying. I wanted to kill him on the spot. "Now the djinn realizes the danger."

Fen's eyes were still lost.

"Pandora's Box, Fen. He's opened it. Where did you get it?"

"You don't think they just keep us prisoners in Area 7, do you?"

I swallowed hard. He was right. Area 7 was maximum security *everything*, including storage. If Pandora's Box was going to be in ARBI custody, that was where it had to have been kept. We had managed to put the ingredients of our own demise together without even realizing it. Such hubris to think we could keep the criminals away from the dangerous artifacts.

Fen pulled up short with the gun, tucking it back into the small of his back. His breathing was still labored. "I'll take that."

Grey's fingers closed around it. For a brief second, I thought his actual fingers might have been peeking out, as they seemed so much longer than human fingers. "I don't think so."

"How is it not affecting you?" I had to ask. Fen and I might have been fighting it, but Grey had been at the center of the hopelessness hurricane when he'd unleashed it. How had he not been blown away?

"He's not human," Fen said. "That's it, isn't it? You could open the Box without fear because it would only affect humans."

"Or creatures created by human deities," he said, turning that devilish smile on me. "I have nothing to do with this planet except to be stranded on this horrible rock."

I stared at the ground, trying desperately to bring my thoughts under control. The lowest scum sucker on this planet, who was only here by accident, was talking down to me like I was a child. I was stuck with my partner in a back alley in Milwaukee while that same scum sucker caused humanity to destroy itself from within. And there didn't seem to be a damn thing I could do to stop it. My vision was slowly starting to blur. I couldn't help it. The tears were welling up. I was a failure as a djinn. I was a failure. My brain fought with itself over ways to get the Box back into custody, and nothing surfaced.

Fen whimpered. It was barely audible, but I could hear it. I lifted my head, and caught his eyes. That same puppy dog look that got him so many girlfriends was writ large over his face. Those eyes were the size of baseballs. The question of what we were going to do hung heavy between us.

What were we going to do?

An image appeared in my mind, one that was from millennia ago, of Solomon's temple. My brothers and sisters had been imprisoned and forced to help Solomon build the thing. Long days, even longer nights for the djinn, we'd been enslaved to make it happen. And we'd persevered. We'd made it through that period with our souls intact. It had been a nightmare, but it had been survivable.

As this would be. I just needed to get the Box away from Grey.

A siren somewhere in the distance brought me back to reality. I caught Fen's eyes again, and glanced toward Grey's knees. If we both hit him, we had a chance. But we both had to do it. There was fear in those wolfen eyes. He wasn't due to transmog for another two weeks, but the wolf was so very close to the surface in those eyes. If the Box was affecting the wolf, we might be able to use that. "Fen?"

There was a pleading in his eyes not to do it, but I gave Fen a hard stare in return. We were going to do this. We had to. No arguments, no concessions, no excuses. Finally, I could tell by his look that he had come around. I slowly began to bob my head, counting off the beats until we could hit. Three would be obvious. Everyone expected that. Fen and I had come to a long-standing arrangement that we always went on five. And, when five came around, Fen went low and I went high.

Grey never saw us coming.

The Box clattered to the ground, and Fen kept wrestling Grey on the hard concrete. I scrambled across the ground to where the Box had come to rest and grabbed it. The lid had slid off, but there was nothing left to come out. I couldn't resist looking inside. There was a bottomless feel to the Box, as though I could have fallen inside and never found a boundary. So that was how it had held so much. Only a craftsman the likes of Hephaestus could have created such a box. Contrary to popular belief, it wasn't some clay pot. It really was a box. And it was beautiful.

One side effect of the hit was we knocked the fake human skin Grey had been wearing off-kilter. There must have been a micro force field of sorts used on his skin, as there was suddenly an odd blue-green light that filled the alley.

"Raina, a little help?"

Fen was busy wrestling with Grey, who was slowly coming out of the skin. I could see Grey's pale iridescent flesh poking through. His long arms were going to be a problem. I shoved the box deep into my coat pocket and got into the wrestling match. When I would get an arm pinned, Grey would kick and knock Fen for a loop. Those stick-thin limbs had some serious force behind them thanks to the years building up strength in Earth's gravity.

"Get his legs."

"Yeah, tell me something I can actually do."

One long leg came back up and knocked Fen in the back of the head. Fen reached back and grabbed the ankle, and judging by Grey's telepathic scream, Fen got some of his thicker fingernails into the flesh.

You see, that was why Grey liked to venture out in human skins when he escaped. He didn't have a mouth of his own. Also, his actual flesh supposedly (if I believed the geeks at Area 7) had three times the number of nerve endings as human flesh.

"No more borrowing others' voices, Grey. You're going back to Area 7, and this time you're going to stay there."

Fen, being the brilliant boy I had trained him to be, pulled the micro-cuffs that had been specially designed for Grey out of his back pocket. We'd have tried them earlier, except they didn't work when Grey was wearing a skin. Now that we had him out of it, though...

Fen pulled him up by his wrists. Grey bitched and moaned telepathically the entire time.

When the adrenaline from the fight wore off, the emotional wave hit me flat in the head. This time, I was a little more prepared for it. I managed to steel my brain against the onslaught. My heart, however, raced a mile a minute.

Fen and I walked side-by-side until we reached the ARBI. When Fen's defenses against the emotional waves needed reinforcement, he handed Grey over to me, and vice versa. The entire trip was filled with sirens, gunfire, and other sounds that I didn't want to even try to identify. It took what felt like an eternity, but we got Grey into the doors of the Cathedral and into the hidden entrance to the Bureau. Blessedly, the second we got into the Bureau, I felt the shields goto work. The waves of horrible emotion were left behind us at the door. The pounding began in my skull within seconds.

Shannon was sitting right behind the doorway at the front desk, her red hair a beacon against the black marble wall. "How is it out there?"

"Not fun," I said. "If it's not jumping off a building, it's shooting something or trying to get shot by something. Please tell me we have the force fields in a cell."

Shannon nodded. "Cell 22-A is ready for you."

Fen and I walked Grey back to the steel cell door together. The officer on duty, a tall blonde who gave off that shapeshifter vibe that I'd long since learned to ignore from Fen. "Keep this son of a bitch in there until he dies."

"And then some," I added. "Maybe another century after. Can we use cryo on him?"

Grey turned that bulbous head of his toward me, his black eyes glassy. The shock hit me telepathically.

"Yes, you little demon," I said. "You're lucky I'm not in charge of the Bureau."

As soon as the door was shut behind him and the fields were activated, I turned around and walked back toward the front door.

"Raina, where are you going?"

"We have to fix this, Fen." I pulled the Box out of my pocket. "There has to be a way to fix it." Screwing up my courage, I walked back out into the park, staring up at the Cathedral's bell tower. There had to be a way to put the evil that Grey had unleashed back into the bottle.

My heart stopped at the sight of a rocket trail moving behind the tower. I hadn't even known there were still missiles on that trajectory. Who was America launching against?

Then it hit me. If those were newer missiles, I had maybe fifteen minutes to figure out a way to stop humanity from surrendering to the hopelessness. If there was a way to detonate those warheads before they found their targets, we might be able to stop it. The trick was going to be getting humanity to *want* to stop it.

Who was I kidding? I was just a djinn. This was one for the brainiacs in the Bureau.

Fen stumbled out of the Cathedral door. "Raina, come inside. The shielding will...oh, dear God." He got to the curb, knelt down, and retched. I wanted to help him, but it just seemed so pointless at that moment. What good was a djinn or a werewolf against the massive power that Grey had unleashed? Still, my brain tried to focus on the problem. After three thousand years, I wasn't ready to go up in a nuclear mushroom cloud just yet.

How had hopelessness been put into the box in the first place? Zeus. The ARBI had a considerable amount of resources, but we didn't have a Greek god on the payroll. As far as I knew, they'd all moved on centuries ago. The Box was created by the old magicks, and that only meant one thing. A creature just as old could be the only one to even attempt a repair job.

We had Lilith, but she had taken PTO to some other plane of reality and wasn't expected back in touch for another week at best. With her, it was hard to be sure of anything.

Baba Yaga? No, she wouldn't have had the first clue of what to do with the Box. It was too old for her somewhat limited skills.

King Daghda the Second? Even if he allowed a djinn to set foot on Irish soil, I had no way of knowing what his Hunter might do. She was still part human, after all, and judging by the way the Box was affecting regular humans, it was too much of a risk. Besides, we didn't have time to get the box to Dublin.

Shannon had walked through the Cathedral door shortly after Fen, and curled up into a ball in tears on the sidewalk. "Who's here, Shannon? Do we have *any* of the Old Ones here?"

It turned out to be Fen's voice who answered. "Besides you?"

I turned around and looked into those sincere black eyes of his. The pain was still strong from exposure to the emotion wave. A swath of red caught my attention from his forearm. "Fen, no. Not you, too."

He pulled the bloodstained sleeve back, showing me the cuts. He'd told me one night over a drunken bout of post-traumatic stress about attempting suicide when he realized what he'd become, only to have the wounds heal before he could bleed out. It had been the most depressing night of his life up to that point. "I can't do this, Raina."

I walked the three steps and put my hands on his cheeks. "Please, Fen. We need you. *I* need you. You can't walk out on this. Not now."

The voice that left his mouth was nothing I'd heard in the twenty years I'd known him. "Help me. Help us." In all of my centuries, I had never heard a werewolf beg.

I tried to look at Shannon, but I couldn't pull myself away from Fen's pain. "Is there anyone on site as Old as I am?"

"No," Shannon said between sobs.

So, it had to be me. It came down to the last known djinn in the Realms to save the world, and I was it. Don't get me wrong, there wasn't a bit of what was going on that I liked. It went against everything I had been born for to help mankind. That was the job of the malak. After a thousand years of playing with the same toys, however, the novelty had worn off. How many times could you screw around with humans and still have it be fun?

Then Solomon had entered the picture. He'd trapped us, made us do his bidding. I was stuck. Whether I liked it or not, I had to help humanity. Eternity was a long time when you were me. My brothers and sisters were long gone. They'd tired of Earth and decided to leave the humans to their own devices.

Fen always joked that I had an overdeveloped sense of responsibility. Did I have any choice but to prove him right?

"Give me the Box."

"Raina, do you have any idea what it'll do to you?"

I couldn't help but laugh. "Do you? Fen, I know what'll happen if I sit here and do nothing. Don't ask me to stand by and watch you die."

"How can you be sure you'll live?"

I looked at the Box on the sidewalk. For millennia, it had held back the one thing that could destroy mankind. That tiny little box. I reached out and picked it up. The inlay work was so intricate it would have rivaled even the best artisans of the modern era. Mother of pearl graced the edges, and carved into it were figures that I could only assume represented the Fates the Box contained. How Pandora had ever been tempted to open the thing in the first place was a mystery.

Just touching the thing gave me chills. The Box carried the weight of history as well as its contents. It belonged in Area 7 where it would be secure forever. It had no right being in my hands in the middle of America. It had no right to be opened a second time.

"Raina?"

There were symbols carved very subtly into the lid, so subtly that I was willing to bet the brain trust at Area 7 had never even realized they were there. It was an ancient language, older than Greek. How could Hephaestus have known such symbols?

Box in hand, I walked back through the door into cold marble corridors of the Bureau, making my way to the interrogation chamber. In one wall was an enchanted panel that looked like a painting of Mona Lisa, but was actually a translucent marble. Yes, the Bureau did like its marble facades. I touched the wall beside it, and it sensed me, who I was, what I was.

On the other side, Cassandra leaned casually against the interrogation table, her dark hair pulled into a professional bun at the nape of her neck. "Grey, you're going to tell me what will reverse the curse of the Box, aren't you?"

Grey's large skull turned toward her, his black eyes still glassy and vacant. I could feel the "screw you" waves coming off of that iridescent head.

"Come on, Grey," Cassandra continued. She had a blessing of a voice, one that coaxed the truth out of mortal men. Grey, unfortunately, was neither mortal, nor a man.

So I wasn't going to be able to back out of this. There was no time to wait for Cassandra to coax the answer out of the little demon.

"All right, here we go."

I walked back outside with the Box and moved so I was in the middle of the park. I wasn't sure why, but something told me not to be near any buildings. Maybe I'd watched *Highlander* one too many times, I don't know.

Placing the Box on the ground, I sat in a lotus position before it. I took the lid off, studying the symbols for some hint of what I might need to do. It looked like it might have been Old Aramaic, but it had been centuries since I'd last had call to read anything from those sources.

It was time to wing it.

"In the name of Allah, my creator. In the name of all of the deities who are or have been worshipped by the people of this world, I ask what sacrifice will be necessary to return that which was loosed into this container."

I wasn't sure why I thought I'd get an answer, but waves of despair only increased in intensity.

"In the name of Allah, and all that is sacred, I offer myself in service to restore the order of this domain. My life is forfeit if that is what is required. Please, take what is necessary to ensure the continued existence of the humans."

I sat and waited. Nothing happened. I could still hear the screams and wails of despair in the distance. Gunshots and sirens had become the theme song for the evening.

"We don't have time for this." I grabbed the Box's lid and jammed the corner into my wrist. My eyes crossed from the pain, but I gave the Box a blood offering. "Restore this planet. Save them from themselves. Please, take from me whatever you need."

My stomach started to turn. "Please restore this planet."

I turned to look back across the park at Fen. "Please. Help them."

Time had to be growing short. The nukes had to be close to the targets. "Please."

My vision blurred as I tried to see if I was even hitting the Box. I was getting weaker by the second. Finally, I collapsed into a heap on the grass.

**

The next I knew, I was waking up in a black marble room. "The Bureau?"

"Yeah," Fen's voice sounded relieved to hear me.

"It worked?"

"Kind of."

I tried to turn my head to look at him, but it just hurt too much to move. "Define 'kind of.'"

"Well, we're all here, aren't we?"

Feeling was beginning to come back to my limbs. I could sense stitches in my wrist. "The Box?"

"Back in Area 7 where it belongs. And yes, it's full of your blood now. It was sealed before they took it out of the park."

"What happened?"

Fen finally walked around the bed I was in and pulled up a chair. "They were able to stop all but two of the nukes before they hit Russia. The planet's got a mild nuclear winter going, but we're still here. The djinn put the genie back in the bottle."

He wanted a groan at that bad pun, but I wasn't about to give him the satisfaction. "What about Grey?"

"Back in Area 7 where the little demon belongs. There are three layers of force field security on him. Cassandra got him to admit to everything. He won't be leaving Area 7 ever again."

"Do we have any idea how long he lives?"

Fen shrugged, a move even more exaggerated by the sight of his white shirt against the black marble wall behind him. "Not a clue."

Shannon picked that moment to knock on the door and poke her head into the room. "Raina? I heard you were awake."

"Bad news travels fast," I said.

My vision cleared just enough to see her making moon eyes at Fen. One of these days I might figure out what it was about my partner that turned human women into puddles.

"Have you told her yet?" Shannon asked.

Fen's lips thinned. "I was trying to figure out how to say it."

Oh, that sounded good. "Fenrus Gévaudan, how long have we known each other?"

He crossed his arms over his chest, and I could see the cuts in his arms had healed. "Fine. You do know the price you paid for that stunt, don't you?"

The feeling came back a bit more. "Well, I feel like I've been hit by an entire convoy of trucks, so it couldn't have been that easy."

"Your immortality."

My entire being stopped in its tracks. "My what?"

"Your immortality. You're human now. No more djinn tricks."

I leaned back against the pillow and stared at the ceiling. My immortality for the planet. My eternity for Fen's life.

It was an acceptable trade.

High school can be hell as the daughter of The Magister discovers when black magic is running amok and Dad is otherwise occupied. An eleventh grader really shouldn't be responsible for saving the world, right?

Black Market Magic
Hildy Silverman

Rob Emmerson was a colossal dick.

Now, as a first-semester senior in high school, that meant he was destined to be popular and get laid on a regular basis. It also made him the focal point, for better or worse, of nearly every student's emotions. Since high schoolers are pretty much constructed of equal parts furious emotion and raging hormones that put Rob in a very dangerous position, at least to those of us who really understand the power of such things.

So I guess I was a little less flabbergasted than my classmates were when, on a crisp, autumn morning, he wound up Rob-kebobed on the flagpole in front of my high school.

Those who arrived first at school, which included me, were greeted to the gruesome display of a vertically spitted Rob. Amidst the mayhem of screaming, tears, hoots, and flipping open of phones to snap MyTube videos, I walked up for a closer view. Not that I really wanted to - though shoving a pole up Rob's obnoxious ass had occurred to me on a few occasions, the actual sight was not nearly as amusing as it had been in my imagination.

The flagpole was only about seven feet tall but there was no way in the world an ordinary person, or even a gang of them, could have physically hauled Rob up there and slammed him down hard enough to accomplish the job. That meant magic was involved, which eliminated about half of my schoolmates and nearly all of my teachers as suspects. I glanced around, wishing I could risk a quick bit of levitation to study the scene closer, but there was no subtle way to manage it.

This was definitely not the time to clue the rest of the Central High School for Magi-Mortal Integration in on the presence of the Magister's daughter.

Okay, relax, I know his rep. But my father does what everyone should recognize as good work - he enforces the laws of appropriate magic usage. In fact, *he's* the guy who took care of that filmmaker who screwed up the story of that pretend dark lord older folks still call the best trilogy in the history of ever (point of fact, the Demon Who Wears Your Face was really responsible for those accursed prequels. My father sentenced him to a century of *It's a Small World* repeat rides. The Demon begs for death every hour on the hour).

My dad is just another magus in this world as far as most of our kind and mortals know, so long as you don't screw up and start throwing the kind of nasty magic around that makes mortals start reaching for their pitchforks and nukes. If anyone makes the mistake of crossing that line, well, that's when dad becomes a lot less regular magus and a lot more *holyshitpleasedon'tARRRGGGH* scary.

As for me, his Heir, my powers are still developing. They Manifested earlier than most of my peers' but they're not all in yet. However, what I have I wield pretty well. Usually I'm trying *not* to use them in the face of constant temptations, such as the skewered dingus I was staring at now.

There were a few times when ol' Rob did something, like try to cop a feel of my eleventh-grader behind, when I'd wanted to scorch his heart to a cinder in his chest. But I'd always held back, because my mom taught me early that zapping people we don't like is not the best way to handle our problems. Oh, and because I don't want my father to ever be put in the position of having to sentence me. Like, *ever*.

Someone else obviously lacked my restraint.

"Everyone, move back to the side of the school. All together...Cinda Wickerson, get away from there!" Mr. Dennison, the principal, grabbed me by the back of the neck, turned me around, and marched me off to join the other students he'd already corralled. I winced at his grip and up came that urge to do something involving scorching. I resisted the temptation and obeyed.

As I stood with the rest of the milling, giggling, weeping, and stunned silent, I decided just staring at Rob's sorry, flapping remains wasn't doing anyone much good. I closed my eyes and turned my focus to Listening into the thoughts of those around me.

At first, there was just babble, which wasn't unusual in the face of something shocking. I sifted through the jumble of voices until I was able to make out bits of sense:

Jesus! How'd that even happen?
Just perfect. We don't have a shot in hell of winning Saturday's playoffs without Rob.
Thank God, now I can take a piss between classes without Rob flicking lit matches at my head!
Robbie, oh, Robbie, I'm so glad I gave it up to you last Friday, before it was too late!
Robert, baby, I'm so glad I gave it up to you last Saturday, before it was too late! (Yep, those were two separate girls' thoughts).
Da–amn. That wasn't supposed to happen!

Bingo! It was hard with all the etheric chatter but I used the techniques my dad had taught me and managed to isolate the thinker.

I picked up a stunned sensation, seasoned with a little triumph, horror, relief and just a sprinkle of regret. Since thoughts don't come with instant identifiers like a familiar tone of voice, I didn't recognize the thinker right off the bat. However, if

I probed a little deeper, I would...

The thoughts stopped, abruptly, as if someone had dropped a brick wall between their owner and me. I opened my eyes wide, startled by the interruption, and snapped my head around. *Oh, hells no! No one here has the juice to block me.*

My scalp tingled and my mouth went dry. *Unless someone does?*

Whoever it was shouldn't, that's for damned sure. Even though I'm not a full-blown Magister, and won't be until my dad passes the proverbial torch upon death or retirement, I'm naturally a helluva lot more gifted than other magi are.

I glared at each of my schoolmates in turn, but not one gave away a thing with their expressions. The magi just looked lost in their own contemplations, torn between wondering which of them might have pulled this off and what might happen once word spread among the mortal majority.

As for the mortals, most of the ones that even bothered to glance my way just gave me the stink eye of *what are you staring at, weirdo?* Even after nearly twenty-five years of school integration, it was still an Us and Them situation on the group level.

But there were exceptions, progressive thinkers like my mom and my buddy, Doug. He flashed me a lopsided grin. Maybe not the most appropriate response given the circumstances, but with all the mortal/magi tension rippling around us, I appreciated it nonetheless.

My bestie, BethAnne, was too busy listening in on cheer captain Sandy Flygel's loud gossiping with her crew of Barbie girls to notice me. Judging by the expression on BethAnne's round face, their conversation was probably about her, and not exactly complimentary. *Another problem for another day*, I thought, accepting that a long session of building up Bethie's busted morale waited in my not-too-distant future.

I darted a few looks at the teachers and Principal Dennison – nothing there, either. *Crap!*

Soon the cops, firefighters, and EMTs arrived. We were all ushered from the scene into the auditorium to give statements. Not surprisingly, the mortals were questioned and sent on their merry ways first, while the magi students were grilled for at least an hour longer before being released home for the rest of the day.

I took advantage of the extra time to pick through thoughts again but though I went as deep as I dared without arousing notice, I didn't pick up the signature of that last thinker I'd heard. Either he or she was still blocked or had slipped away from the police round up and left the building altogether. *Double-crap.*

***

The administration offered us counseling for a week to deal with our feelings about Rob's graphic demise. Within two weeks, though, everyone had fallen back into their familiar patterns of classes and cliques, bonding and bullying.

I considered telling my dad about the incident so he could order his team of enforcers to be on the lookout for some possible rogue magic use. He's been so busy, caught up in some major investigation into all the extreme and deadly weirdness going on everywhere these days. He didn't share the specifics, but the new lines around his eyes and mouth told me I was probably better off not knowing the details.

I decided to hold off and see if Rob's death was a onetime violation that the mortal police would handle or Dad could deal with after the holiday.

Yeah, life stayed pretty normal for a while. Right up until cheer captain, Sandy Flygel, fell out of the sky.

She landed smack in the middle of an outdoor Halloween party thrown at Doug's place, just to the left of the barbecue pit.

Sadly, standing just to the left of the barbecue pit when it happened? Doug.

I had only come through the gate into Doug's backyard two minutes before Sandy screeched her way down into Doug, driving them both about ten feet into the dirt. It was so fast (not to mention unexpected) that I didn't even have time to look up, let alone cast anything to intercept her.

Again, it was a lot funnier to picture a plummeting cheer captain in your head than to actually witness it. In my imagination, a whistle sound would have accompanied Sandy's plunge, one that surged into a loud *zoo-o-o-m*, followed by a *boy-yoy-yoing* upon impact.

Of course, my cartoon scenario would have ended with Doug and Sandy crawling out of a Sandy-shaped pit covered in dirt but no worse for wear, ending on Doug glaring at Sandy furiously while she shrugged an apology.

In reality, no one crawled out of the crater her impact left. A peek inside revealed two broken, bloodied bodies hopelessly tangled together. Not a lot of *ha-ha* value in that image, trust me.

Now, I didn't much pine for Rob and was indifferent at best to Sandy's nonexistence, but Doug was one of the good guys, mortal or magus. He always kidded around with me, invited me to his annual Halloween shindigs, waved to me when we passed in the hallways. He had no shame in our friendship at all. Frankly, he'd shown me a whole lot more affection than most kids officially considered my own kind offered me.

I'm a lot of weird, even to other magi, who innately sensed I had something else going on. Combine that with the so-called *natural* revulsion many mortals feel toward my kind and it's little surprise I could count my friends on one hand — with a couple fingers folded down.

Whatever. They'll all answer to me someday, whether they like me or not.

Doug hadn't let bigotry get in the way of hanging with me. Now someone had thrown a mortal Barbie girl on him from upwards of a hundred feet. I was *pissed*.

"Hey, I think one of them's still alive!"

I ran to the edge of the hole and listened. Sure enough, there was a low moan coming from Doug.

"Doug!" I called. "Dude, are you...all right?" I knew it was a stupid question but wasn't sure what else to say.

He just whimpered and my stomach muscles clenched like fingers curling into a fist. Death was close, so I didn't waste time waiting for words Doug couldn't form. I closed my eyes and reached into his mind. *Doug, I'm sorry*, I told him. *You're not alone, dude. I'm here.*

His mind had nearly shut down, but I made out: *Cinda. I don't know...what's going on? So dark...hurts...!*

Tears welled up behind my eyelids. I squeezed my eyes tighter shut to keep them from escaping. *It'll stop soon.*

Guess...had it coming. For...that asshole. Who groped. You.

I shivered, not from the cold approach of Death this time, but rather the reverberation from contact with a tainted soul. Startled, I probed deeper and found the tarlike stain on Doug's psyche.

He'd killed. And he'd done it with magic.

But he was mortal.

Doug, I sent urgently. Time was short and nothing made sense. *How did you kill Rob?*

His thoughts were hazy, dreamlike, which was good in a way because he didn't waste any neurons wondering how he could avoid incriminating himself. *Got sick of his bullshit. Waiting for him. To call me a magus-lover or...toss my ass into...locker. Putting gross hand. You. Last straw. Wasn't supposed...fatal though. Oh well.*

I didn't ask why, I asked how. Doug's why's only made me cry harder. I'd had no idea he cared about me that much. Now it was too late to matter.

Oh. Bought...spell for. Five hundie. Hocked my...bike and...Grandma? Hey, you're back!

I broke contact just in time, rocked back on my heels, and landed on my butt in the grass. Damn it, I could've used another couple of minutes but Doug was going, and if I stayed with him – well, I might have wound up wherever Grandma was myself. I whispered a quick farewell and added a blessing for smooth passage into What Comes Next.

I wiped my eyes quickly with the back of my hand, stood up, and walked out of Doug's yard, ignoring the screams and frantic yowling into cell phones by the other partygoers. I didn't feel like hanging around to make more statements to the cops.

I struggled to focus on what Doug had said about killing Rob. He'd bought a spell. A straight-up mortal had purchased and used magic, black magic to boot. That was most Not Cool. Someone (or several someones) was peddling magic to mortals and *teenage* ones yet. I'd never heard of such a thing being possible but was willing to bet it was a hanging offense. Probably a hanging, stoning, burning, flaying and *whatever-else-dad-conjures-up* offense. What magus would be stupid enough to risk *that*?

***

I walked home in a haze of grief and pondering. My mother looked up as I came into the family room and said, "Hi, Cinda. Didn't expect you back so early."

I debated whether to launch into an excuse for why I'd voluntarily returned before curfew, since she couldn't read my mind and find out for herself.

My mother is mortal. My dad took a progressive stance and married out of our race, a move that nearly prompted his mother, the previous Magister, to disinherit him. If his sister hadn't removed the only other Heir option by dying in a hit-and-run before her powers Manifested, he'd never have succeeded Grandmother. Still, she'd never acknowledged Mom or me before she died. To her, I was just the mutt her son had disgraced his lineage by siring.

Anyway, knowing Mom would wind up reading about Doug's death-by-cheerleader in the news tomorrow, I decided to come clean. Sort of.

"There was an accident at Doug's party. This girl, Sandy, uh, I don't know, got high maybe?" I winced at the nasty of my pun. "Anyway, she must've climbed up on the roof and jumped."

"Oh, my God!" Mom clapped a hand over her mouth. "Is she okay?"

"Oh, no," I said, trying to maintain a matter-of-fact tone of voice. "She's dead. So's Doug. She landed on him, probably broke his neck when she..." I couldn't keep it up. Those damned tears started flowing and my throat closed up until only a little croak came out.

"Baby." Mom was off the sofa and had her arms around me so fast that, if I didn't know better, I'd think she had the power to teleport. I leaned into her soft warmth and hugged her, sniffling to keep from getting nose leakage on her lemon detergent-scented sweater. She rubbed my back and murmured loving things until I felt like I could stand and talk again.

I went into the kitchen and grabbed a napkin to tidy my face. "Where's Dad?" I snuffled.

"He's at a meeting."

"Another one? Geeze, didn't he just have one on the weekend?"

Mom combed her fingers through her hair, revealing a few lines of gray in the lower layers. Those were new. "He has...so much to juggle these days," she said, avoiding my eyes. "He's summoned the coven leaders tonight to iron out some, er, final plan."

"D'you know where he's holding the Circle?" I asked. "I really have to talk to him." Even with all the whatever he had going on, Dad would surely agree that a body count of three and mortals using magic was bound to attract all the wrong kinds of attention.

Mom frowned. She so wanted to tell me it was too late to start wandering around at night and too dangerous to boot. "You think something other than drugs or general teenage stupidity is behind your friends' deaths, don't you."

I sighed. Couldn't keep much from a Magister's wife, mortal or not. She'd seen and heard too much during their twenty-plus years of marriage. "I think it's kind of a bizarre coincidence that three kids died in horrible, barely-explainable ways inside of three weeks, yeah."

"You need to track your father down right this minute? He'll be home in a couple hours." She glanced at her watch and tugged at her hair some more. "Well, five. Or so."

I didn't have to read her thoughts to watch her go through the following cascade analysis: *teenage girl out alone at night in woods, equals future victim of crazed raping axe murderer.* "I'll be careful, Mom. You know that."

She factored in: *daughter is magus and Heir to one of the most powerful magi currently walking the Earth.* Add in said father in the same woods as daughter, along with representatives from each of the thirteen covens. Equals very little chance of daughter ending up raped and axe murdered.

Mom swallowed and forced a smile. "Okay, honey. He's at the Pine Brook campground. Where Andy's camp used to have their summer picnics?"

I remember going to my kid brother's Family Day picnics at his camp every August. Back before my powers Manifested, back when I could still pretend I was just another pre-teen magus or, on some occasions of which I'm kind of ashamed, just a mortal girl. Now I longed to be *that* girl again.

I took the car keys off the hook by the door and said, "Okay, thanks. I'll be home in a little while."

Mom fiddled with her hair some more, obviously still worried but trying not to show it. Despite all she knows about Dad and me, and what we can do, she can't help but be concerned about us. I felt sorry for her because of it. Knowing how capable someone you love is in your head, and actually having totally confidence in their ability to protect themselves in your heart, are not at all the same things.

"Love you." I smiled.

"Me, too, sweet baby," she said. She managed a little smile but couldn't resist adding, "Please be careful."

I waved my reassurance and headed back out the door.

The car ride over gave me a little more time to think about the current sitch. Mortals can't wield magic, period. Dad explained that to me back when I first asked why he didn't teach Mom to be a magus so she wouldn't feel left out of that half of our lives.

"They can say the words and mimic the gestures and wish really hard," he'd told me, "but it's just not going to work. Magic is a part of us, of what we are as magi. Either it's in you or it's not. It can't be learned."

If that was true, and I had no doubt he knew, then it stood to reason spells couldn't be sold to mortals and have any real effects. This meant the person selling had actually cast the hex that Doug used on Rob...and had sold his or her services to someone else, who'd then had Sandy hurled into Doug.

That had to be it. A magus assassin-for-hire, swindling mortals into thinking they could buy magical power of their very own.

An icy chill passed through me.

I pulled over into the shoulder and closed my eyes to process. I spoke aloud to help organize my thoughts. "If a magus is scamming mortals and killing to make it appear legit, he or she is likely still hanging around school soliciting more customers. One of those customers is someone who bought black magic to get back at Sandy and Doug, like Doug got back at Rob, and is likely another kid. This means, if I tell Dad, he's going to sweep into my school and start ripping through everyone's minds until he finds the pusher and the user. And kill them both a lot."

Now, I wasn't overly sympathetic to the magical black marketer, but the mortals who were buying? They could be innocent enough, like poor Doug, just pushed too far by constant bullying and easily tempted into take drastic revenge.

What if Sandy's assailant was another friend of mine? Dad wouldn't show him or her any mercy. He couldn't, because if the mortal majority found out that there was a way to make themselves into *de facto* magi, or believed it was a possibility, the threat to world order would be beyond toleration.

We all only barely walk the tolerance line as it is. If the Were or vampires felt genuinely threatened by seemingly empowered mortals, or mortals found out a magus was slaughtering mortals as part of a fraud...my throat closed up at the thought of the slaughter that would follow.

Prejudice doesn't just come from thinking you're better than others, my parents told me. Just like a lot of bullying at the microcosmic high school level, much of it comes out of jealousy.

Think about it. You'd be hard-pressed to get your average mortal to admit anything but disgust for the vampires living in the ghettos on the outskirts of their cities. Yet for some reason, they keep creeping into vamp territory, hoping for a quick bite and conversion. Ordinary humans may not like the bloodthirsty killing spree aspects of vampirism, but they sure as hell were jealous of the super strength and endless life.

Jealousy and bigotry dance cheek-to-cheek. Something told me they were also the keys to figuring out the motives of whoever killed Sandy and Doug.

Maybe Dad would just wipe the user's memory, but even that caused brain damage. Memories of one thing inevitably tangle up with others, so you couldn't neatly erase some thoughts without taking out, say, all of the math someone had ever learned, or their ability to walk and chew gum at the same time.

I pounded the steering wheel with the heels of my hands. *I already lost one friend to this black magic peddler, damn it!* I wasn't going to serve up any others to my father. Besides, I would be Magister someday. Stopping the magus behind these violations, my own self, would be good practice.

I turned the car around and drove home. Told Mom that I'd gotten an update on Sandy that made me realize I'd overreacted, that it was just a stupid stunt for MyTube that went horribly wrong, and went up to my room.

Once in my favorite skulls-and-flowers pattern jammies, I lay down on my bed and stared at a thin crack in my ceiling, deciding what I was going to do to fix things. It took almost all night but by the time I closed my eyes and dozed off, I had something resembling a plan.

***

Over the next week, I observed my schoolmates very carefully. A few casual convos with other magi students left me confident in my assumption that none of them had taken Sandy and Doug out.

I poked into the mortals' thoughts next - rude, I know, but necessary - sorting those who knew and liked Sandy from those who knew and hated her. Out of that subset of ten, I determined which ones hated her enough to be glad she was dead. I tried to whittle down further to those who were glad Doug died or, at least, didn't care that he had.

That's where I hit a roadblock. All but three considered his loss the only downside of Sandy's plunge to Earth. Not helpful, unless Doug's death had truly been unintentional. That was unlikely, given his prior involvement with the black marketer.

Unless...

Maybe the seller set it all up, so that before a buyer figured out he or she didn't retain the magic purchased, the buyer was eliminated? In which case, Doug's death might not have been part of the second *customer's* plans at all.

I started from the top, refocused on those who were well and truly glad Sandy was dead and left Doug out of the equation entirely. Out of the set of possibilities that netted me, I poked around for magical residue. Out of this subset, I isolated for traces of black magic.

Five hits. Five mortal students had come in recent contact with black magic.

Then came the awkward part: I had to come in physical contact with each one in order to probe deep enough to figure out if they'd merely been in the presence of black magic, perhaps during a negotiation with the seller, or if they'd actively absorbed the dark stuff.

I found all sorts of ridiculous reasons to brush up against each of the five. I pressed against one guy in the lunch line, who called me a whore-witch. I bumped into a girl while pretending to text and walk, and got called a stupid bitch-witch for it.

Some mortals are just *so* witty.

In gym class, I had no problem 'accidentally' colliding with my last, least-favorite suspect during dodge ball, my bestie BethAnne. I bounced off her and then the ball slammed me in the gut and I dropped onto my behind.

"Out!" shouted Ms. Weiss, our gym teacher. I barely heard her, in fact, hardly remembered getting to my feet and limping off the court to the sidelines wondering where all my breath had gone.

Not because of the gut-punch from the ball, though. It was because of the black magic I'd sensed oozing from BethAnne's pores. It was enough to make me want to hurl the cardboard-like pizza slice and watery lemonade that had been my lunch.

My heart sank as I watched the rest of the game, my knees hugged up against my chest. I knew BethAnne had *hay-yay-yated* Sandy, even more than I did, probably more than all the other non-Barbie girls who despised her nasty, uppity, flawlessly assembled self.

Sandy had utterly humiliated BethAnne back when she tried out for the Cheer squad last month. BethAnne later told me she'd given a great audition but Sandy and her Barbies just laughed her off for 'dancing around like a baby elephant.'

BethAnne is a little on the curvy side, true, but she felt it was really because the guy Sandy had a thing for sat next to BethAnne at lunch a few times. *Jealous bitch*, BethAnne had said. *Someone ought to knock that princess right out of her tower.*

Then someone had.

I suppose that's why I'd held off probing BethAnne's psyche until last. I knew she had motive but didn't much want to know my best friend was a stone-cold killer. Besides, she'd had nothing against Doug, since much like herself he didn't let a little thing like my magi heritage get in the way of our friendship. There's no way BethAnne would've used a Sandy missile to take Doug out, at least not on purpose. Then again, if my revised theory was correct, Doug's death had been an unintended consequence.

Further speculation was pointless. It was time for confrontation.

I cornered BethAnne in the locker room after the other girls were already changed and headed off to class. "Wait a sec," I said. "We need to talk."

"You didn't even hurt me," said BethAnne with a grin. "Forget it."

It took me a moment to realize she meant when I bumped into her during the game. "Not about that. About Sandy."

To the horrible horror of my already horrified heart, BethAnne's smile got bigger. "Yeah, you saw that, right? I wish I'd been at the party but, you know, I had my Language Arts test the next morning. Did she scream all the way down?"

Now that was not a BethAnne thing to say. Sure, she may have hated Sandy with the wattage of a thousand fiery nuns, but she was overall a friendly, somewhat shy girl. Not one to wallow in the pleasure of another's bloody demise. "Not as loud as Doug did," I lied, and waited for her reaction.

BethAnne's smile wobbled. "Oh, yeah. That sucked." Under her breath, but not so low I couldn't hear her, she added, "Can't believe I didn't stick the landing."

"What do you mean?" I took a step closer to BethAnne.

Her eyes darted to the right. "Nothing. I've got to get to Chem." She tried to squeeze around to my right. I slammed my hand against the locker bank behind her and blocked her exit with my arm. She blinked at me. "Excuse me, Cinda."

"I'm afraid I can't." I took a deep breath, tried to get my nerves under control. *This is your my future career*, I told myself. Someday I'd be the Magister and shaking down rogue magic users would be a part of my job. Best learn to woman-up now. "What did you do to Sandy?"

"Me?" BethAnne's eyes opened wide enough to show the whites around her blue irises. "What could I possibly do? I wasn't even there!"

"You didn't have to be. You just had to know when and where Sandy would be before you sent the curse."

My eyes bored into BethAnne's. I heard her panicked thoughts: *what does she know? How can she know? This isn't what I paid for!* Emboldened, I hissed, "Do you have any idea what you've done? You're a friggin' murderer!"

"I...it wasn't supposed to be, you know. Fatal." BethAnne shrank back against the lockers and I saw fear in her eyes. I wasn't sure if it was the fear of discovery or that she could sense my aura of power, which I freely emitted in order to shore up my attempt at being intimidating.

"And what did you think would be the outcome of dropping someone umpteen hundred feet from the sky?" I demanded.

BethAnne's cheeks flushed red. "She was only supposed to fly up far enough to scare her into messing herself, then land in the middle of Doug's party with a load in her panties." She stared down at her shoes. "She'd never have lived that down."

"She didn't *live*, period." I planted my other hand against the lockers, cutting off BethAnne's second attempt to dart away from me. "Neither did Doug." My nose practically squashed into hers.

BethAnne's lower lip quivered and she blinked against a sudden rush of tears. "That should never have happened. Doug was really cool. I just...I don't know how it went so wrong! I said everything she told me to say, used all the right ingredients, and performed the ritual." She shook her head and closed her eyes.

That gave me pause. *She* said and *she* did? So did that meant it wasn't the black market magus who'd cast the spell? It seemed BethAnne really did it herself. But how? Unless everything BethAnne had done was just for show and the magus had cast the real hex?

BethAnne abruptly shoved me backward and sprinted for the gym. I staggered against a bench but managed to stay on my feet. Then I beat said feet after her.

I ran into the gym where the class after ours was already running laps. One of the runners slammed into BethAnne and both of them staggered toward the center of the gym floor -

- which imploded, temporarily deafening me and probably everyone else in the room, and resulting in a huge, gaping hole toward which the off-balance pair stumbled.

I didn't even think. I let instinct guide me, my father's lessons rising to the forefront of my brain. He would lose his crap over making a public display of power like this. What choice did I have?

I made the quick gesticulations for focusing hastily summoned magic and chanted, "*Instigare pedus!*"

BethAnne and the runner's tangled feet slammed flat on the ground as if they'd turned to magnets and the floor was a giant metal slab. They teetered, upper bodies dipping dangerously low over the precipice, but with their feet firmly stuck, they were able to deny physics and snap themselves back upright.

The hole wasn't too happy with that. It yawned wider, like the mouth of a starving crocodile, the splintered flooring along the rim forming jagged teeth that loosened and slid into the darkness below.

I waved my left hand through the relatively simple motions of a levitation spell and held the pair of screaming teens in mid-air as more hardwood crumbled beneath them. Even the couple other magi in the room gasped - either startled by the bold public use of magic that was a no-no on school grounds, or maybe appreciative of the amount of *mojo* being expended.

Who in the hell's doing this? I wondered. Someone with a hell's worth of power, for sure. I took a quick survey of the rest of the room; saw nothing but open-mouthed high schoolers and one stunned gym teacher. Except there was a shadow over by the bleachers that didn't look quite right...

The shadow flexed and a whirlwind rose from the hole, reaching up toward the floating pair.

Oh, no you did not! I thought. The more magic I exercised, the more easily it flowed. I barely had to mumble a Word to draw BethAnne and her unwilling partner toward me as if a big rubber band attached them to my outflung hand.

I felt a powerful jerk, as though someone had pulled the rubber band harder from the opposite side. My feet left the ground and I found myself hurtling after BethAnne and the runner toward the center of the mini-tornado.

Not good, not good, very bad! I forced down panic, shifted my focus from the spinning death ahead of me, and the bottomless grave beneath. Concentrating on the shadowy figure obscured by the bleachers, I summoned up a Reverb spell and threw it with all my will.

Now, I'm still learning and a Reverb spell is an upper-level bit of magic. But I also had a huge reserve of natural power and stark raving terror to tap into.

The Reverb surged up from inside me with such force that I produced actual sparks from the fingertips of my outstretched hand, and felt as if I'd turned myself inside out. My body twitched like a prisoner's post-electric chair frying, but I was still able to track my spell as it slammed into its intended recipient. A scream tore through the maelstrom.

I managed to expand my levitation spell to include myself before we all plunged into the pit below. It took every scrap of power I had left to land BethAnne, the runner, and myself a safe distance from the hole that used to be the middle of Central's gym. Fortunately, as BethAnne put it, I stuck the landing.

Out of the corner of my eye, I watched the shadow I'd spotted earlier tear free of its hiding spot by the bleachers. It condensed into the form of a woman as it flew. Her howls grew more enthusiastic as she sketched an arc through the air, arms and legs flailing, grasping for something, anything to slow her trajectory.

There was nothing.

She plunged into the hole, leaving only the echo of her screams in her wake.

The gym was utterly silent for all of a minute. Then a boy who'd been standing somewhat apart on the sidelines stomped forward. The runner who'd collided with BethAnne had shoved her away (not into the hole, fortunately) and was shaking in his sneakers. He didn't have a moment to gather his wits before the furious boy from the sidelines – I recognized him now as a senior nicknamed Spark – marched up to him and started pounding on his chest with his fists.

"Damn it, Donny! It was supposed to be *you*! Why aren't you down there?" He punctuated each word with another fist slam.

Donny barely had the wherewithal to grab Spark's wrists. When he finally succeeded in intercepting Spark's blows, Spark kicked Donny in the kneecap.

"Ow!" cried Donny. "Are you nuts? What is happening? What the hell is going on?" He was *thisclose* to a total mental meltdown.

"You dick!" Spark's spittle peppered his face. "I know you blew that twink Eric behind my back. Jeannie *saw* you, parked behind the mall last Saturday!"

"Aw, you know better than to trust that hag. Anyway, what does that have to do...giant hole in the floor! *Tornado!*" Donny babbled.

Spark kicked him again and Donny landed on the floor, hugging his knees to his chest and rocking.

I tore my eyes away from the soap opera and went over to BethAnne. She stumbled toward me and I had to catch her to keep her from falling over. "I didn't do that." She pointed a shaking finger at the pit, and I knew without a doubt that she was telling the truth.

"That magus who went flying into the pit," I said, "is she the one that sold you the spell against Sandy?"

BethAnne nodded, too freaked out for subterfuge. "Doug recommended her to me. Said she gave him the magic to teach Rob a lesson."

"Teach him a lesson? Doug *speared* Rob up the wazoo! That's a little more than a lesson." I still couldn't fathom my sweet buddy actually reveling in the impalement of anyone. It just didn't make sense, although he'd probably been shot up with black magic the way BethAnne apparently was. Yeah, that had to be it. No one could contain that much foreign evil and not be warped by it, no matter how fundamentally decent they started out.

"What in the hell is going on in here?" The gym teacher, Ms. Weiss, spun me around to face her. Her face was taut and white, her eyes blazing. "Cinda, you know better than to spew magic on school grounds!"

A few kids started screaming again. Others burst into tears. A couple took the route of hysterical laughter. Way too many pointed at me and whispered loud enough for me to make out words like, "devil" and "witch" and "burn."

Uh, oh.

Before I could try to worm my way out of the whole mess, which I couldn't even begin to figure out how to do, the entire room fell silent again. And still. Not a person moved. Even the bits of shattered flooring stopped caving into the pit.

Double uh, oh.

I turned away from Ms. Weiss's frozen, furious face and met the much-more animated but equally furious face of my father, the Magister.

His eyes blazed with power, colors shifting in his irises like a kaleidoscope. One glance at the frozen tableau of crazy around us told him magic had broken out where no magic should be, and he was Most Displeased.

"H-hi, Daddy," I said. I tried to smile at him, but only managed to make the corners of my mouth twitch.

He folded his arms across his chest. "Explanation. Now!"

I cleared my throat a few times and gave him the full download. There was no reason to compound my little tragedy of errors by lying now. He was being nice by not ripping all the information right out of my brain and giving me the chance to use words instead. I didn't dare offend him by uttering a single false syllable.

When I finished, he rolled his eyes heavenward. "Goddess help me," he said. "It's a good thing your mother mentioned your concerns about the goings-on in this school when I got home at dawn."

Refocusing his eyes on me, he said, "Let's just postpone the whole lecture on how you totally screwed the pooch by not coming to me in the first place until later, shall we?"

"I knew you were busy," I mumbled. The excuse sounded so lame now that I cringed when it came out of my face.

"I'll consider not grounding you until you Inherit because you're still learning," he added, lips set in a narrow line. "I suppose I should've been keeping up with the news on these suspicious deaths." He shook his head. "Shouldn't have let myself get so distracted by what's coming if I don't..." He broke off and stared into the distance at what appeared to be some relentless horror only he could see. Underlying the expression of fury on his face was something I was a lot less accustomed to seeing there – fear.

Before I could stop gulping and ask him what was up, he blinked and returned his attention to me. "Anyway, there are recriminations enough to go around. For now, our focus needs must be on covering this mess back up. Starting with." He pointed to the pit and crooked his forefinger.

I heard a faint whine that grew into a louder and more enthusiastic scream until (after several minutes) the magus my Reverb had hurled toward the center of the Earth flew back up. She froze, hovering above the hole.

"Shut up already, will you?" My father rubbed his shadow-ringed eyes. He's not what you'd call a morning person, even when in the best of moods. In which he was not.

The magus's mouth snapped shut. Her eyes lit on my father and she started dogpaddling in the air, frantically trying to return to the comparative safety of her endless fall. As if she'd get that lucky now.

Finally, she realized the futility of her struggles, and just hung her head and hovered limply in midair. "Magister," she muttered.

"*Hashik Hashkor*," said Dad.

I puzzled through my shaky knowledge of Old High Magish and came up with *shopping night*. That didn't sound right. "She's been selling magic on the black market," I said. "Somehow she actually instilled magic into mortals. I didn't think you could do that."

"*She* can." My father scowled. "She isn't selling magic *on* the black market. She *is* the Black Market."

"Huh?" I said, cleverly.

Dad nodded at the floating magus. "She is the embodiment of the mystical black market, *Hashik Hashkor*. She carries magic from place to place, sells aspects of her very self into others in exchange for money, sexual favors, political gain – whatever she desires at the time. She's not even always a she," he glared at her again, "but has probably chosen that form in the mistaken belief I'll go easier on a female manifestation."

"Oh." Wow, I knew we had some weird beings among our kind, but a person who was a market...or was that a market who was a person? My head swam.

Dad tapped his steel-toed boot on the floor. He was still in his regalia from leading the Circle, right down to the full-circle, crimson-trimmed black cloak of his office. "You want to attempt to explain your actions here, or should I just blow you up a few times first?"

Hashik Hashkor winced. "That won't be necessary, Magister. I was just - it is what I am. How can you expect me not to do what I am?"

"That's your problem. It's bad enough when you sell yourself into our own people to augment or alter their abilities; it's something else entirely when you infuse mortals with magic. That's a criminal trespass I've only warned you against on *seven separate occasions*!" The air around him rippled, shot through with scarlet sparks.

"Y-yes, Magister, but these were just some token revenge spells. Why, they were hardly noticed." She laughed awkwardly.

"Really?" My father spread his arms to indicate the remnants of the gym and repeated in a voice of gravel, "Really."

"I was going to tidy up this mess afterward." Hashik Hashkor fidgeted (not an easy thing to do while levitating).

"And the boy speared on the flagpole? And raining down cheerleaders?"

"Just one cheer - look, things got a little out of control." She spread her hands wide. "It wasn't me, Magister. I only infused those little shits with temporary magic. *They* did the castings, caused the fatalities, and left the messes behind!"

"And this surprises you *how*?" Dad waved his hands in aggravation, leaving sparks of static in their wake. "They're *teenagers*, you half wit! They're nothing but surging emotions and raging impulses. Of *course* any magic they perform is going to fly out of control, especially if they're revenge-minded! Any being in existence as long as *you* should have anticipated *that*." The lights in the gym blinked on and off in time with the words my father emphasized.

Hashik Hashkor blanched and hugged herself. "Forgive me, Magister. You're right, of course." She added, mostly to herself, "Shouldn't have tried to maximize my profits with resales."

Resales. Things were starting to make more sense. "Is that why the kids who used up their infusions were the next victims?" I asked. "The magic you gave them was only temporary, enough to fuel one curse."

"Black magic tends to strike back at the vessel that dared contain it as soon as it gets the chance." Dad confirmed. "Since mortals have no natural magic to protect them, they were left defenseless once she drew back her aspect and sold it into the next customer." He shot a disgusted look at Hashik Hashkor. "Conveniently, any dissatisfied customers-*cum*-potential witnesses are thus automatically eliminated."

"Poor Doug," I shook my head slowly. "He wasn't evil. The power he borrowed, it just took his crazy hormone-fueled anger and twisted it into the darkest form possible. I knew the real Doug would never have killed anyone."

"The same can be said for your other friend." Dad brushed his fingers over BethAnne's frozen, tear-streaked cheek. He may be many things, but heartless isn't one of them, at least not toward innocent girls he's taken ice-skating with his daughter.

Except BethAnne wasn't innocent anymore. She was responsible, at least on some level, for a death by black magic. She couldn't escape the cosmic backlash of that, not completely.

I put my hand on my father's arm. "Daddy, please." I didn't even try to stop my tears. I needed every weapon in my daughterly arsenal. "Isn't there something you can do to save her?"

My father looked at me and, for a moment, his expression softened. "I'll see what I can come up with, sweet pea," he murmured.

He raised his head, features hardening as he refocused on the rogue magus – market – whatever-she-was. "First things first, though." His voice remained low, took on a dangerous edge. I used my good sense to take a giant step away from him.

"Very well, then," snarled Hashik Hashkor. "You think the Inevitable coming for this run-down rest stop of a world is the only threat you face, Magister? Arrogant mortal-lover!" She expanded, her mortal form fading into something huge and nebulous. Her final words were garbled by the transformation, but I made out, "...do you a favor...end your worries...end it all!"

The expanding black formation sparked and laser-like spears of red and silver shot through and down from the ragged mass that must have been the true form of Hashik Hashkor. The floor began to buck again, knocking several of my frozen classmates over. Beneath her, reddish light projected from the gaping hole in the gym, as if someone were shining an incredibly powerful, but thin beam of light up from somewhere far, far below.

The light grew brighter and wider, and a heat accompanied it that made me throw my arms across my face. Something exploded and gurgled up from the center of the gash in the earth. Eighth grade Earth Science knowledge about the planet's molten core and magma and spewing volcanoes bubbled to the forefront of my panicked brain.

The earth quaked and the bleachers rocked crazily. The only reason I didn't wind up in a heap with everyone else is my father took my hand and levitated us a few inches above the rocking ground.

Still, I couldn't help but scream, "She's drilling into the core! She's gonna kill us all! Daddy...!"

My father was on it. He stretched his left hand over the edge of the hole, closed his eyes, and issued a single command, "*Sigelum*."

I felt, rather than saw, the power he released with that one word. Before the echo of it faded, the light from the hole shrank and faded back. The gurgling lava flow retreated just before it crested the gym floor. The earthquake subsided.

Dad lowered us back to the once-again stable section of the floor. He arched one eyebrow at Hashik Hashkor and dispelled her remaining aura of magic. She snapped back into woman-shape with loud, multiple *cracks* of hastily rearranged bones.

Hashik Hashkor opened her mouth, either to beg for mercy or start shouting more spells, but my father forced it shut again with a casual wave.

"Your suffering will be threefold, in accordance with each of your violations." His lips peeled back in a wolfish grin. "At least now I don't have to worry about hiring entertainment for the next Samhain gathering."

Hashik Hashkor couldn't scream, but her eyes bugged out so far I thought they were going to roll free of their sockets. My father pointed at a space just to her left and tore a bit of Reality apart.

The space next to Hashik Hashkor parted to reveal a rift of such blackness that to look into the utter absence within was to invite madness. I quickly looked away and so only heard the awful sucking sound, followed by a slam of finality.

"That'll hold her for now," said Dad.

I dared to look back and, sure enough, Hashik Hashkor was gone. My father strode to the edge of the pit, peered over, and asked, "Any innocents fall down there?"

I shook my head. "Nope. I stopped BethAnne and that Donny guy from taking the deep dive."

Dad nodded. He shot me a stern look. "You know Hashik Hashkor could've killed you. She - it - is an entire black market of magic, not to mention one of the cockiest outlaws among our kind."

"And I'm the Magister's daughter," I said. Sometimes the best kid-versus-parent offense is a good defense (especially if it includes a large helping of buttering up).

"So you are." I saw a little twinkle of pride in his still-stormy eyes. "You handled things as well as could be expected, given the circumstances *and* your poor decision not to alert me right away."

This was about as much of a pat on the head as I could reasonably expect, so I said, "Thanks."

"You're still not leaving the house for a month. Straight home from school, get your homework done, no watching TV. or web surfing. Mystical studies and then bedtime. Clear?"

I nodded. Arguing with a pissed-off Magister is an exercise in stupid, even if he is your father.

Dad sighed. "Okay, then. Go to your next class. In a few minutes, this will be cleaned up."

I cocked my head to one side. "How?"

"I can't bring back her victims, but when there aren't more, they'll be written off as bizarre, isolated incidents." He looked sad. It's killer to have so much power and yet find yourself powerless when it really counted. I understood that better now that I'd lost Doug and nearly lost BethAnne - even the most powerful of us have limitations. "But this physical evidence? That I can take care of. Any leftover can be blamed on that unusual, but not impossible, earthquake that struck a few minutes ago. Messy, but not disastrous - or obviously magical."

"What about everyone's memory?" I waved at my gym class. "Are you going to wipe them all?"

"That's more complicated." He rubbed his chin. "I think I'll go with a fogging spell. They'll know something odd happened, especially the magi kids, but when they think about the specifics, all they'll remember will be jumbled, written off as hysteria from the earthquake. The mortals will come to dismiss the whole thing." He shrugged. "They usually do."

"That works," I said. "Thanks, Daddy. And again, I'm really sorry. I shouldn't have tried to field this myself."

He rested his hands on my shoulders. "You'll be me someday, Cinda," he said, gravely. "This kind of thing will become your responsibility, all the time, every time."

He hesitated. "Trust me when I tell you, it comes sooner than you want. And once it's yours, there's no turning back, no shrugging it off, no avoiding the nastiness of it all. You don't want to rush into it before you have to. If I could...if I had a choice, you wouldn't ever." He broke off and turned away.

My throat muscles tightened again, in empathy this time. Sometimes even the Magister can't hide his real feelings.

And I knew, or at least sensed, something was coming. Something *else* that he didn't think he could stop, even with all his power and the power of the thirteen covens behind him. Something...final.

Feeling what he felt, even for a moment, made me want to run out of that gym and keep on going, as far away from my future responsibilities as possible.

"I'll see you at home," Dad said, erasing all trace of emotion from his voice. He raised his hands.

I felt the floor start to rumble and left him to clean up the mess I couldn't. That I didn't have to.

Yet.

It's not enough that a ghoul and a shaman have to save the world from dragon fire in Robert Water's tale of terror and despair. Their biggest problem is that dragons have been extinct for years so they want to know how on earth are people in a suburb outside of Baltimore getting Charred in the first place.

Indeh
Robert E. Waters

There was a time when the thought of eating human flesh disgusted me, when I was a boy living a simple and *human* life in Arkansas. That was thirty years and ten lifetimes ago. Now, even the burnt, black remains of dilapidated storefronts and the stagnant smell of sulfur cannot dull my appetite. And as my boss Joe Littlecloud waved his wrought-oak staff over smoking wooden beams and whispered some ancient Apachean script, my hollow stomach churned at the hope of spotting a severed limb or a cooked thigh among the ruins. I was embarrassed and tried changing the subject.

"I see no bodies," I said, failing miserably in getting food off my mind.

Littlecloud continued to wave his staff and mumble, but he nodded agreement. In time, he said, "No, no bodies at all. Very strange."

He knelt down, his long, boney frame creaking beneath his bear-fur cloak, his alligator-skin cowboy boots twisting in the ash as if he were stamping out a cigarette. He reached out and ripped off a piece of dry wood from a broken kitchen table. He put the wood to his nose and sniffed. "Sulfur," he said. "Can you smell it?"

I nodded. I have to remind myself that humans do not possess the sensory powers of us ghouls; their senses are limited, for the most part, to their immediate surroundings. I, on the other hand, smelled the sulfur before we even got out of the car, and I smelled the burning flesh a mile before we arrived. A lot of people had been burned alive here last night.

But *where* were the bodies?

Littlecloud threw the wood away and stood up. He pointed to a massive pile of twisted metal, shattered plank board, and resin siding. "Come," he said, his hand shaking slightly, "let's take a look over there."

I followed, keeping a jaundiced eye upon the desolation we passed, hoping to see a bit of flesh or a mangle of loose intestine. My mind, however, wandered to my boss as he picked his way through the rubble. He was disturbed, shaken by what was around him. In the ten years I had served as his assistant, it was rare to see him so visibly upset.

Joseph Littlecloud is an Apache shaman, or *diyin* as they are most commonly called. He is an investigator for the FBI-VPA, the Federal Bureau of Investigation of Violent Paranormal Activity. Possessed with bear spirit, he believes that he is the reincarnation of a murderer and wife beater, returned to earth to atone for his sins. I cannot attest to such things myself, you understand, for I have only been afflicted with my condition for little over thirteen years, having been captured and *turned* by an Egyptian necromancer for his own nefarious gains. My name is Horus Ruth, and my life is confined to taking notes, making calls, interrogation, canvassing, coffee-making and grave-robbing. I have my own demons to exorcise. But a good assistant knows when his boss is troubled, and I tried to steer our investigation in a different direction, hoping that that would help Littlecloud wrestle with the matter at hand.

"Perhaps this was arson, Joe," I said, a spring in my step and light in my gruff voice. "It isn't uncommon in these trying times, you know."

He nodded. "No, it's not, but I don't think so. It's not *common* for arson to affect an entire community, is it?"

He knew I knew the answer to that, but Littlecloud liked to argue points even when their falsity stared us in the face. It was a game we played.

"Divine Intervention?"

I got a smile out of him on that one. Littlecloud was definitely not an atheist or even an agnostic, but he possessed the practical sense to know that in the two millennia that humans, undead, and *fae* had co-existed in the world, there was little need for the Gods to show themselves and cause trouble. We were all doing a fine job of mucking things up ourselves.

"I wish it were as simple as that, Horus," he said, stopping before the pile of metal and wood and resin that was the focus of his attention. He held up his staff once more. "But no. Divine intervention did not play a role in this, and I think the answer may lay here."

He closed his eyes and began his whispered chant again. I turned away and surveyed the entire expanse of the destruction, fighting the pain in my stomach and trying to ignore the myriad blue-and-red lights from the police and EMT vans that sat on the perimeter, waiting to swoop in and take their own best shot at trying to figure out what had happened. Littlecloud and I knew that they would fail... as first-responders in such desperate times almost always fail.

The town in question was Reisters Mill, a relatively small community on the edge of the Wild Zone that encircled Baltimore City. In the last few years, it had signed a mutual-protection agreement with the city in order to trade and share resources in an attempt to bring some sanity and order to an otherwise tenuous situation. The world was, in effect, on the verge of collapse. Its economic and social structures had deteriorated to such an extent that the only way human communities could survive was through these "buddy" systems. From all accounts, the agreement was succeeding, and in fact had just recently thwarted an attempt by a vampire prince to take over the mayor's office and infect the political system. But now this: the entire town within a three mile radius had been leveled, as if some nasty comet had run its tail along the ground and then swooped back up into the clouds. But this was no celestial or natural phenomenon. No volcano or earthquake had come to call, no nuclear or hydrogen attack had done this. This was something else.

Littlecloud moved in his usual way, raising his staff up and down, walking around the pile and flicking his arm out as if he were punching the air. I watched him closely, looking for signs of The Change, that delicate moment between human and animal flesh, when a shaman of his prowess could (quite by accident) shift into his animal form and be stuck in that fashion for some time, thus posing a threat to himself and to others. Littlecloud had mighty powers and was usually capable of controlling himself, but he was upset and anxious in a way I'd not seen in a long time. The last time was in Cleveland, as we investigated the goings-on of a local witch who was sacrificing babies to maintain her youth. Littlecloud was so angered by the events that he began to shift without control. I pushed him into the Cuyahoga to cool him off. When he came out, he beat me vigorously with his cudgel for several minutes, and then spent the next few days apologizing profusely. He even broke the law by allowing me carte blanche access to a local cemetery. I was a kid in a candy store.

Years later, he confessed that his behavior was a sign of his sin. "An abuser beats and apologizes, beats and apologizes," he said, a tear in his eye. "Please help me stop this madness."

I've tried ever since.

I was just about to intervene again when the pile shifted. It was Littlecloud that saved me. He grabbed my tattered denim jacket and pulled me aside as the heavy metal beams tumbled away to reveal a smashed car. In the front seat, on the passenger side, sat a woman, bereft of clothing and hair, but singed fully black as if her body had been cooking for years in the hot Peruvian sun. Her skin was so taut and tightly stretched across her old bones that she seemed more fake and leather than human. At first I thought she was a mannequin that had somehow found its way into the vehicle. But then she moved, violently, rising up in the seat as if her lungs were filling with air. She fought against her seatbelt, raged against it, as if it were some hideous snake constricting her body. She moved back and forth and she bellowed and barked and twisted her head left and right. When she saw us, she stopped, poked her ravaged head out of the shattered window, and spoke through battered teeth.

"Hydrastigor!" she said, belching the word. "Hydrastigor lives!" And then she pulled back, filled her lungs, and pursed her lips like blowing a kiss.

But it was not love that flowed from her mouth. It was fire, a long red cone of the hottest flame I had ever felt. Littlecloud pushed me down and shielded us from the breath with his bear cloak, whose hairs singed but did not burn. Even underneath my boss's body I could feel its heat, hot, roiling and persistent. When it stopped, Littlecloud jumped up quickly and ran to the car. The woman was about to blow again when he struck her thrice in the head with his staff and silenced her forever, letting her thick blood and brain matter run down the side of the car.

He opened the door and let her body fall to the ground. I moved over to it quickly and studied her blackened skin. It was wrinkled like beef jerky, but smooth as if it were glazed with a gentle honey sauce. I ran my hand down the line of her back. There was still a lot of good meat beneath that tough skin. My mouth watered, but my tiny undead heart skipped a beat.

"Is she... Charred?" I asked.

Littlecloud knelt beside the body, a tear in his eye. "Yes," he said, "and you know what makes Charred, don't you?"

I nodded. There was only one thing in the world that turned people into what lay before us.

"Dragon fire!"

***

It is times like this that remind me of my Lord Byron... "*Thy gnashing tooth and haggard lip, then stalking to thy sullen grave, go and with ghouls and afrits rave, till these in horror shrink away, from spectre more accursed than they.*"

No one in the world is more accursed than The Charred, those unfortunate souls who have fallen to dragon fire. They do not burn to cinder and fill clay urns like anyone else who finds their end in flame. No, they live beyond life, like me, but are confined to serve their creator as puppets in whatever nefarious goals their master has in store. Some would claim that I had served in such a capacity, but ghouls and vampires and any assortment of other undead have a certain level of freewill that they may exercise at any given time: If things get too rough, we can end our lives in many painful ways. Not so The Charred, whose service to their maker is like an unthinking computer program or a clockwork toy that continually runs itself into a wall because it has no control over its movement. And that is the most heinous curse of all: Knowing that what you do is wrong, but not being able to do anything to stop it.

The Charred lady that we had confronted in the ruins of Reisters Mill had apparently been created by a dragon named Hydrastigor.

"But it makes no sense," Littlecloud said when we returned to his office on Pratt Street in downtown Baltimore. "Dragons are extinct. There hasn't been a sighting of one in over a century, and if it were a dragon, it would have easily been spotted in the sky, even in the darkest of night. No sightings have been reported."

"Perhaps it was a wurm," I said, finishing off the last juicy morsel of skin of the woman's left leg. Littlecloud had allowed me to tuck a piece of her away before the cops rolled in. I licked my lips, feeling refreshed and confident. "They have been known to attack towns."

Littlecloud shrugged. "Then where were the holes? The sunken roads or hollowed out buildings? Wurms don't breathe fire either, at least none I've ever seen. No. That Charred lady was from dragon fire. There's no other explanation."

But of course, there had to be another explanation. Littlecloud was right: Dragons were extinct, rubbed out years ago by a world fed up with their drama and relentless pursuit of world domination. Such great, terrifying beasts as Ryxasus, Gunga-Mop, the Italian white winged Domitian, the great Incan goldtusk Pachapraxys, the Saharan snub-nosed Baragog. Each had seemed unbeatable in its time, bringing the world close to the apocalypse, but each, in turn, hunted down and destroyed. Not even a single egg remained from any of their mighty clutches. Dragons were gone, finished, confined to bedtime stories and product logos.

"Have you ever heard of this Hydrastigor?" I asked, chucking the cleaned femur bone into the wastebasket beside the desk.

Littlecloud shook his head. He fiddled with a small dream-catcher that he had acquired recently at a flea market. He turned his attention to an Apache Ganh Dancer headdress, an elaborate piece with richly colored feathers and vampire teeth fitted into the top to represent fingers reaching into the cosmos to join human flesh with the great Mountain Spirits. It was an important symbol for his people, his culture, and he always turned to it when he was deep in thought, whenever he was close to making a decision on what his next move would be. I waited patiently for him to speak, knowing that it would be fruitless to continue the speculation.

He rubbed his fingers over the delicate feathers, then turned and took a seat at his desk. His sharp face was calm, but his eyes were fierce. He was about to tell me something I did not want to hear.

"Well, we have to assume that this was a dragon attack, but we have to be cautious about making that declaration public until we know for sure."

"It may be too late by then," I said.

He nodded. "And the Bureau is going to be on our ass and quick demanding answers. We have to play stupid until we know for sure. Whatever this Hydrastigor is, its designs are sinister, that's certain. We have to move quickly, and we have to be smart about it. I have to make some calls first, talk to my people, sort things out. I have a theory, and I pray to Yusn Life-Giver that I'm wrong, but in the meantime, I need you to work your contacts. I need you to contact *one* person specifically."

I nodded. One of the reasons Littlecloud had picked me as his assistant was because I knew every undead around. My contact list in the non-human realm is expansive, and I always make a point to keep my contacts strong. "Okay, who do you need?"

He told me.

I jumped up, grabbed the femur from the wastebasket and shook it at his head like a bat. "Fuck you!" I screamed. "I'm not doing it!"

***

But of course, after an hour of Littlecloud's cajoling and pleading, I relented. It's rather disgusting to see a human beg, on his knees and cupping his hands together like he's praying to God. Littlecloud is certainly no Christian, but he takes it upon himself often to remind me that I used to be one before I was turned into this grey, sallow-skinned monster standing before you now. He also has no problem reminding me that he saved me from certain death from an evil necromancer with his own designs on world domination.

The person that he wanted me to talk to was that very same madman. It was the intelligent thing to do, I had to admit, but that didn't mean I had to like it.

Ish Kann Makatsup was an Egyptian-born merchant who had fallen into some bad magic back in the disco era (who hadn't?). Rumor had it that he was at the university in Iran during the American hostage crisis. He had been radicalized by the experience but decided that strapping on a bomb was a bit too tame for his tastes. He much preferred calling on Anubis to bring forth the new Caliphate. A few years later, I was travelling in Egypt with a team of students from the University of Memphis, when I foolishly did a bit of sight-seeing on my own. I was nabbed, killed, then resurrected and made an undead slave. I will not go into details about what the son of a bitch made me do, and I was thankful that he was eventually brought down. If it had been me, I would have killed him on the spot and picked his bones clean, but The Hague wanted to make an example of him, to put him "on display" as a warning to future generations. So now he sits in a padded cell in the Paranormal Oddities wing of the Smithsonian in Washington, DC.

I caught the train down to pay a visit.

His room is tiny and bereft of anything save for a few chairs, a table, a toilet, and a cot. He's given allowances to move around freely in his room and can go outside for a few hours of exercise daily with hefty hermetic mage security and SWAT team surveillance. He's a kind of Charles Manson persona, saying very little that ever makes sense, his eyes always filled with some faraway madness. But I had interviewed him before and I had a presidential license to do so whenever I wished. Ish Kann Makatsup was an ass in the world, as Shakespeare might say, but there were few who knew more about ancient lore and dragons than he.

"I hate the very sight of you, you know," I said to him as we sat at his table. He had been put into a straightjacket. "In fact, I hate you so much that I would not lick one hair on your boney arm."

It was a serious insult from a ghoul, but he didn't seem to care. He smiled. "You were one of my finest." His Arabic accent was as thick as ever. "One of the greatest ever. That's why I named you Horus."

"How kind of you," I said, fidgeting a little. I crossed my legs. "I was surprised that you named me after your daughter as well. Ruth is an uncommon name for a Muslim. More of a Jewish name, no?"

I knew that would piss him off. He shook his head, a jerky, frantic motion. "I considered it the finest name I'd ever heard. You should be thankful. She was a lovely girl."

I gritted my sharp teeth. "Let's get to it, Ish. I'm not here to stroll down memory lane. What do you know of a dragon named Hydrastigor?"

He tilted his head back and looked at the ceiling as if the answer were written there. He blinked several times, his breath steady and thoughtful. He said the name over and over, blinked again and then closed his eyes. He stayed that way a long time, then opened them and got that quizzical look he often wore after achieving some great breakthrough in the lab.

"Hydrastigor... there was once a dragon in Eastern Europe. Hungary, maybe, or Romania. Mid to late seventeen hundreds I think. Her name was Minaminata. A rather small dragon as I recall, a mix of green and black scale. She loved human blood, believed it kept her strong and youthful. She ruled a small kingdom, but she had been cursed with a very large clutch, thirty eggs by my recollection. An ungodly amount, and that ultimately proved her doom. Twenty-five of the eggs were destroyed, and *she* met her fate in the Borgo Pass, fifty silver-tipped arrows in the chest while protecting the other five. Although no claim to her death was proffered, many believed it to be a certain vampire whose biography was written by that mad Irishman, Stoker. A tragic, tragic ending..."

He drifted off, lowered his head as if to sleep.

"Ish!"

He jumped awake. "Oh, yes. Well, the reaming eggs were retrieved, but as they were being crushed, the last of the five burst open and out sprang a newborn, wild and untamed, incapable of imprinting on its mother, and thus a restless, uncontrollable chick. A nasty little fire-breather, it was, killing about a dozen on that day alone."

"Then it survived?"

Ish shook his head. "No, that's the thing of it. It was cornered in a barn a few weeks later and torn to pieces by pack-hounds, its remains dried and ground into dust, scattered to the wind."

"Then it has nothing to do with Hydrastigor."

Ish shook his head and stood up, looking silly and comical all wrapped in tight white burlap. It was rather embarrassing to see him in that condition. In his day, he was so powerful, so larger-than-life. Now...

"Maybe not," he said, "but there is a limerick that Romanians sing to their restless children even today to make them go to sleep..." He hobbled back and forth on his old, skinny legs, bouncing as he moved, humming it out in his mind before he opened his mouth. "... *neither flame nor teeth could end its reign, and into oblivion it crawled, but know you this, little child of mine, when Hydras returns and finds you awake, he'll snatch you from your mother's arms, and carry you to your endless rest...*"

His words trickled off into indecipherable mumbles, but the essence of what the limerick meant staggered me. It could not be true, I thought. How could it be? There had never been a case of disembodied dragon spirit. Never!

The old Egyptian stopped mumbling, turned to me, and said with a wry smile, "Your boss is in big trouble, Horus."

I did not reply. I got up and walked to the door.

"Get me out of here, Horus," Ish said as I buzzed to be let out. "You can't handle this thing alone. No one can. I'm the only one who knows what this thing is. Let me go, plead to the president, use your influence, get me out and I will help you."

"No!"

He charged me, bared his teeth and grunted a sickly moan with a half-hollow mouth. Three darts burst from tiny holes in the wall and struck his atrophied legs. He stumbled and fell to his knees, lingering there like an old Q-tip teetering on the edge of a bathroom sink.

I slipped quickly through the opening door and let it shut tightly behind me. I turned and looked at my old master. He stared at me through dark, groggy, wet eyes. I could, if I wanted to, use my influence to plead for his release. It would not work, of course, but I could try. But no. His days were done. He would never breathe free air again.

And yet, I couldn't help but feel the weight of irony at his words. If what he was suggesting were true, if this Hydrastigor was the Hydras in the limerick, then only a used up, sniveling little Egyptian priest with designs to rule the world, might well be the only person who could save it.

Suddenly, my usually insatiable appetite was gone.

***

I found Littlecloud at the annual Gathering. It's an old tradition that many Native American tribes try to maintain despite being scattered to the four winds. It's a festival of thanksgiving, of communion, of coming together to worship the old gods and the old life-ways, to sing, to dance, and to drink lots and lots of booze. The biggest and best are held in the Northwest, near Seattle and Portland, and draw thousands. Those on the east coast are often no more than small affairs, maybe two to three hundred attendees in total. Littlecloud sat near a bonfire, wearing his Ganh mask. He was not dancing; he was too proud and fearful of ridicule for that. He sat there, cross-legged, staring through the eyes of the mask, looking like a dragon himself, speechless and unmoving.

I told him about Hydrastigor.

Around us the incessant hum of music, voices, dancing, and drums accentuated Littlecloud's silence. I could not see his eyes, but I imagined them darting back and forth through the hazy sensations of peyote, which he often took to divine entities and motives on the ethereal plane. I tried it once, but it doesn't possess the same potency to one who is already dead.

Littlecloud sniffed and moved his hands to pick up a pipe sitting next to the fire. It was an elaborate but beautiful piece, a foot long, fastened with beads and feathers and intricate patterns of Pueblo and Zuni myth. I'd seen him smoke it before. He used a blend of peyote, hemp and fine Kentucky tobacco. He puffed once, twice, three times then laid it down again.

"Do you know what the Apache call themselves?" he asked. He had told me this before, but my mind was on other, more important concerns. "No," I said.

"We are the *Indeh*," he said. "We are the dead. Not like you, no, but our way of life, our homeland, our connection to Yusn Life-Giver had been, at one time, destroyed, as we were ripped from our homes and forced onto reservations. We were the dead, walking in a dream."

I sighed. "Things are better now, though, right?"

He nodded. "Perhaps, but what has become of the world?" He lifted his arms and waved them about as if he were offering up the shadows cast by the firelight. "We have merely transferred our status to it. The world is *Indeh*, Horus, and we are merely its custodians, glorified crypt-keepers, barely stemming the tide."

Gloomy fuck! I watched him pick up the pipe and take another puff, thankful for the first time in a long while that I was a ghoul. Humans are often very depressing, like Littlecloud, brooding about the end-times, about the collapse of their world. But in times like this I like to remember my Bible: *Man may come and go, but earth abides.* And so it would be for us all. Even I would find my end at some juncture down the long and winding road, and I hoped to God that when that time came, I'd have a fleshy arm bone in my hand, a warm glass of human blood, and a *Beatles* song in my heart.

I grabbed the pipe and dropped it to the ground. "No more of this hollow talk, Joe," I said, using my best stern-father voice. "It's time to go to work. A dragon has returned, and we do not know where it is, we do not know what it wants, but -"

"I know who it is, Horus, and I know what it wants. I've seen him in my dreams."

Almost on cue, the drums and dancing stopped. Littlecloud couldn't have planned it better, and in fact, it wasn't because of what he had said, but because of the flashing lights and sirens heard in the distance. Police cars were approaching, and even though a Gathering was sanctioned and legal through local law, many felt uncomfortable with White Eyes around. The dancers dispersed and the music stopped. The festival was over... at least for now.

"Who is he?" I asked, ignoring the uniformed men approaching through the darkness.

Littlecloud removed his mask and turned to look at me. "His name is Pedro Nightwing. He is *Ilkashn*. And..." a tear fell from his eye, "...he is my brother."

***

Well, you think you know somebody and then they drop an anvil on your head. Who knew Littlecloud had a brother? I certainly didn't.

The police had arrived to take us to another town that lay in scorched ruin. This one was on the east side of Baltimore. Same pattern, same distinct smell of burned flesh and sulfur. No bodies.

Hydrastigor had struck again.

"So this brother of yours," I said in the back of the squad car as we were being driven back to our office. Littlecloud had been pensive during the drive. "Who is he exactly?"

He looked at me, the tear that he had shed earlier now dry and almost indiscernible on the streaks of red-and-white clay that lined his face. He had not bothered to clean them off before getting into the car. "Pedro Nightwing. Jicarilla Apache. A former *diyin* shaman imbued with bat power. One of the finest human beings I've ever known and my blood brother."

"So, he's not your real brother." I was actually relieved to hear it. I'd spent too much time with Littlecloud *not* to have known of a long lost sibling.

He shook his head. "But I don't make the distinction. In my mind, he is my brother. We grew up together, lived on the same reservation and in the same village until the Dissolution Act of 1972 which eliminated all reservations and tried to absorb Native Americans into the population at large. We went to high school and Columbia together; we even earned our respective powers under the same shaman.

We broke our skin and mixed our blood. He is my brother and will be so until we die."

"You said he was *ilkashn*," I said. "He's a witch?"

Littlecloud nodded. "We went our separate ways for a long while, but then something happened to him. I do not know what. When next we met, he had been accused of killing his parents. It was in all the papers; perhaps you might have heard the stories? This was before you and I met, before you became a ghoul. The Springstone Murder case? They were brutal, gruesome. Pedro was accused because of his erratic gift. As I said, he has bat power, and a bat *diyin* can be restless, unsettled, swift of spirit and cunning of mind. A bat shaman is susceptible to ethereal suggestion and possession, and Pedro became the primary suspect in the murders because of the pentagram found in his parents' basement. It was believed that he had been trying to summon a demon and consume its spirit, to devour its strength, you see, as *ilkashn* often do. He was accused of demonic possession, subdued and thrown in jail."

"Was he found guilty?"

"No. When I heard of the arrest, I went to see him. By then, I was already in the Bureau, so his case had been handed over to me. I went to see him as a friend, but also as someone charged with finding evidence of his guilt. He knew why I was there; he saw right through me. And he resented it. He resented my success, my position in society. You see, he'd never fully integrated into white society, despite doing well at Columbia. He never quite fit in. I think that's why he turned to darker pursuits. Through magic, through witchcraft, he found that connection he lacked in the real world.

"I was young, arrogant, and honestly more than angry at him for bringing shame to his family and to our people. We argued. He let his bat power overtake him; I let mine overtake me. We fought violently, quite literally destroying the interview room. It took twenty guards and more than a few tranquilizer darts to end the brawl. I left and never saw him again.

"He was tried but acquitted. There was never any hard evidence tying him to the murders. He was released and then disappeared. Until now."

"And now he's hooked up with this Hydrastigor."

"He *is* Hydrastigor! Your Egyptian madman was right on that, Horus. This restless dragon spirit has lived in the ethereal plane for centuries, looking for an empty vessel through which to return. He has found his chance in Pedro Nightwing. It is a sad and lonely existence to be cut off, disconnected with the world, Horus. These two lonely spirits have found each other, and they will not stop until the world suffers for its sins. They will not stop until I am dead."

"You? Why would they care about you?"

"Pedro wants my bear spirit," Littlecloud said, as we rolled up in front of our office.

"What for? He's got dragon spirit now. What power can bear spirit give him that he doesn't already possess?"

"Courage," he said, getting out of the car and tipping his hat to the driver.

"A sense of place. A patience that he currently lacks. It is true that a bear spirit can be violent and unpredictable, as I have shown over the years. A bear is a bear after all. But it also has a connection to the earth that Pedro does not possess. Remember, Horus, that for a human being to acquire an animal power, the animal must offer itself to that person; a man cannot simply go into the woods and say, 'I'm here... come to me'. But he can steal the power from someone who possesses it, as a witch often does. He has damned his soul forever, Horus. Yusn Life-Giver will not accept Pedro's soul in the end, but I doubt seriously the witch cares right now. No, he will pursue me until he has stolen my bear."

"Then we have to go into hiding," I said, stopping him before we entered the building. "The Bureau will have to protect you."

Littlecloud laughed and shook his head. "They can't. The matter has progressed too far. The only ones that can stop him are you and me."

"Okay, then how?"

He got that pensive look again and turned his face up to the clouds that were gathering over Baltimore. It was near one in the morning.

"I have much meditation to do, Horus," he said, putting his hand on my slumped shoulder. "And you have to eat. Go, now, and feast. Fill your belly and then return here at six sharp. It will all be clear by then."

He patted me on the shoulder, tried to smile, turned and walked into the office. A spring was back in his step, but I could tell by the way he held his arms tight against his sides that he was afraid.

So was I.

***

I ate in much the same way I imagined Jesus had done at the Last Supper. It could very well have been my last supper too. So I dined in a nearby graveyard and then found a nice, sturdy mausoleum in which to take a power nap. Baltimore is not like New Orleans, where the ground is so saturated that most of the coffins rest above ground, so it can be difficult to find proper accommodations for an evening's hunt. God, I love New Orleans!

But I ate handsomely and then slept, falling into a fitful sleep to the ring of distant sirens. Those sirens seemed very close, and yet I was so used to hearing them that I didn't pay them any mind.

Big mistake.

I awoke, surprisingly, on time and made my way back to the office. That's when I realized the sirens had been for us.

The entire block had been quartered off and at least a dozen cop cars surrounded our building. They had moved in SWAT as well, with hermetic security toughs and an ex-werewolf pit-fighter who had turned state's evidence against the mob. I had met the beast once at a seminar in Pittsburgh, but we didn't get along. This was some serious firepower, and I immediately understood why.

The entire front of the building had been blasted out and debris from the offices within was strewn across the city roughly two hundred yards from impact. I suspected that many in uniform circling the debris field suspected that the blast had come from outside, some "thing" crashing its way in. Such was not the case. The blast had occurred inside-out, like one might experience with a clever bank heist. The distribution of rubble and the blast patterns on the bricks were clear evidence. The thing that had done this had walked into the building as a man... and had left a dragon.

Hydrastigor had struck again, and this time, he had taken my boss.

I could have cried as I searched the office for Littlecloud's body. I almost wished it, as I knew the alternative was far, far worse. But there was no body. Just the stagnant smell of sulfur and... Nothing else. My spirits lifted a little at that. No charred body smell, which made sense with the attack occurring so early in the morning. No one had been in the building, save for a few custodial members and Littlecloud. No burnt flesh meant that he was still alive. Yes, alive! But where was he?

I was about to leave when I stubbed my gnarled toes on a small package near the rumpled desk. I bent to pick it up. It was a piece of ruled notebook paper tied around a small hammer. I opened it up, and a piece of gravel fell to the ground. I picked it up as well and read the note. Just one letter. One letter had been written on the paper, clearly by Littlecloud's hand. The letter Q.

I rolled the gravel between my fingers. There was only one quarry in all of Baltimore that mined this kind of gravel. I smiled.

I crumpled up the note and tossed it to the floor. I took a step to leave, and my foot came down on a loose nail in one of the floorboards. I cursed, and then instinctively took the hammer and drove the nail head home. I tossed the hammer down and walked out, vowing to make some serious renovations to the office when this was all over.

***

Hydrastigor had unleashed hell upon the world. By the time I reached the Hunt Valley Quarry, his Charred army was on the move.

Thousands of them, more than I had even expected from the two attacks near the city, they leached out of the abandoned quarry tunnels like some gross, multi-bodied black mamba seeking food. Their deadly breath lurched out in gulps of sulfuric air and set alight everything in their path. It reminded me of zombie attacks I had been involved in near Paris when I worked for Makatsup. But this was far deadlier, their fire destroying everything and Charring fleeing mothers, fathers and children, and swelling their ranks. It was an army that grew as it spread, and the towns of Hunt Valley, Padonia, and Timonium were in danger of being wiped out.

Air and surface assets had been moved in to meet the threat. Helicopters and fire tanks (as if that would help!) circled around the growing death salient, trying to pick off stray Charred with explosive rounds from scores of SWAT and military ranks. I was rather impressed by the human showing. Usually it takes awhile for them to mobilize, but apparently they were not blind to the threat. Perhaps Littlecloud had actually called in his suspicions before being nabbed. It would be just like him to feign independence, and then move in like gangbusters. Joe Littlecloud was a private investigator, true, but he was an Apache first, and they tended to work in strength.

I found it rather easy to slip past the massed combatants. Even the Charred whose mission was to burn everything in sight. I was little more than a tiny blip on their radar. I was dead after all, so to them, I was near kin. I took advantage of this, killing violently each one I encountered, sending my claws across their throats and bellies, spilling what little remained of their innards. I was leaving many good meals behind, but I had to buck up and focus. My boss was in danger.

I found the mouth of one of the tunnels and proceeded down. It was dark, pitch black in fact, but I have thermo-graphic vision, and thus I see rather well in the dark. I pushed aside a few stray Charred who had been left behind from the initial rush; these were mainly old men and women who could not keep up. It was not worth wasting time killing them; they would soon meet their fate somewhere out there.

It seemed like I walked for miles below the earth, letting my nose guide me. The stink of sulfur and charred meat was overwhelming. It was difficult to detect anything else, but there were occasional breaks in the stench, just enough to let me get a bead on exactly where the worst of it was coming from. I took those passages specifically.

A little further along, the tunnel began to lighten, then lighten more, until it was clear that I was moving toward an open space. Then I heard talking, arguing in fact, just as clear as watching TV. Back and forth, back and forth, like a heated political analysis show. I recognized one of the voices.

I entered a large chamber, roughed out by years of earth scrapers. Two rail tracks ran the length of the room, emerging from a side tunnel and escaping through another. Abandoned coal cars lay everywhere, beset with thick quarry dust and rust. The air was dense, difficult to breathe, but I did my best, and hid behind one of the cars. Smoke from a dozen candelabras positioned strategically around the room gave off a fine smoke that obscured my vision, but I squinted and could make out two shapes, one dancing around like a deranged monkey, and the other chained to a large wooden wheel; he was beat up and blood ran down his face.

It was Littlecloud. He laid spread eagle on the wheel like the Vitruvian Man, tiny gashes across his exposed arms, legs and chest. If it were Easter, one might imagine Jesus all nailed up on the cross with a crown of thorns, but this was no messiah. It was my boss, and he was in a world of hurt.

Pedro Nightwing struck an imposing figure. His hair was blood red and flowing down his back, turned that way I assumed from the dragon power controlling his body. A silver streak of white ran the length of it, accentuated in the faint cave light. He was taller than Littlecloud, but skinnier, gaunt like a shade or specter. One could almost see his ribs peeking out from beneath his cloak. In his hand he carried a staff, much like Littlecloud's, but smaller and more club-like. He danced around my boss, moving it up and down, chanting something I couldn't understand. *I seriously have to learn their language.*

Littlecloud reared up as if he'd had a heart attack. He screamed, then the sensation subsided and he lowered back into place. He breathed heavily, panting, pulling on the chains. He shook his head. "You don't have the strength, Pedro," he said. "I'm stronger than you are."

"Maybe at one time, Joe," said Pedro, keeping his rhythm, "but not today. Today, and now forever, I will be stronger than you." The witch punched out with his staff and hit his prisoner's chest. Littlecloud reared again, and the image of his face changed, blurred into a mix of human flesh and bear snout, as if a spirit were being pulled out of his body. And of course it was. Pedro was trying to steal my boss's bear power, and he was getting close.

I needed to act.

Littlecloud settled down again, and surprisingly, laughed. "It's over, my brother. There is no more Pedro Nightwing in that frail body. Hydrastigor rules now. Whatever strength you think you can take from me, Pedro, is his, not yours. The little boy who chased me up and down the white mountains of our home, who sat with me in freezing cold streams, who bested me in wrestling, in archery, in chess, he is a dream. The little boy who told my own mother that he loved her like a son should, hugged her, and gave her his blessing when we left for Columbia. Where is that boy now, Pedro? Where has he gone?"

The question seemed to stop the witch. He paused in place and stopped waving his staff. I moved quickly.

Pedro smiled. "Nice try, Joe, but it won't work. Your great failing has always been misplaced empathy. You feel too much, and it is your undoing."

"I wonder if your mother, your father, felt the knife as you carved them up."

I was just as shocked as Pedro with those words. I moved closer, and I could tell that Littlecloud had gotten through.

The witch seemed to slump, his shoulders dropped down, and he held his staff to the ground. I could not see his face clearly, but I imagined pain.

"It was an accident, Joe. I never meant to do that. I, I was not myself."

"Just as you are not yourself now," Littlecloud said, carefully working his wrists against the chains. And for the first time, he acknowledged my presence. He turned his head and looked straight at me, and winked. "Drive Hydrastigor out of your body, Pedro, and we'll talk about this. It's not too late. Send the spirit away, like our master showed us at Columbia. Drive it away."

It seemed as if Pedro was listening, dropping to his knees and laying his staff beside him on the rough floor. He was curled almost into a ball, and I was a mere ten feet from him.

Then he raised his head violently, jerked it up with such force that I feared it would pop from his neck. In its place, however, grew the large, red and boney snout of a dragon, and his back began to move to pump like pistons in a truck, as the spiked plates of Hydrastigor tried pushing through the flesh. The witch lifted his grotesque body up and flayed his hands out and I watched them as his fingers began to fuse together in a flat mesh of claw and webbing.

I leaped on his back, not caring if I impaled myself on his horns. Now was the time to act, when the body was in mid-change, when the host was disoriented and consumed with that ecstasy that comes with *becoming* one's power. I've never experienced it myself, you understand, but I imagine it feels very similar to how I feel after taking a big, juicy bite of dead flesh after a long fast.

We rolled, and I dug my claws into his neck which grew hard and scaly beneath my fingers. He roared, and this time it wasn't Pedro's petulant, human voice. This was the voice of power, of authority, of a dragon. This was Hydrastigor.

"Release me!" he roared. The vibrations from the voice almost threw me back, but I held tightly as we rolled and rolled and rolled across the floor. His arms were flailing, trying to find purchase on anything we passed. He clawed at my eyes, bit at my throat. I did the same, drawing whatever power and strength I could. Littlecloud had been smart to send me off to feed the night before: I was strong.

We rolled into a pile of rocks, and as he tried gouging my eyes out, I found a rather plump piece of granite, squeezed it tightly in my grey hand, and sent it hard against his jaw.

It popped. The bone below the tough ridgeline of his mouth snapped, and blood flew between his razor sharp teeth. He fell silent and his eyes closed, and a faint whisk of smoke rolled out of his nose and dissipated in the thick air. He was out cold... at least I hoped so.

I crawled to Littlecloud and began pulling on the chains. He helped as best as he could. "We've got to get out of here," he said. "Work faster."

You're welcome! "I'm working as fast as my dead fingers can move."

"Where's my staff?" he asked.

"What are you talking about?"

"I left you a message to bring it."

I shook my head. "You left me a note with the letter Q on it."

"And a hammer, which any intelligent person would know that it meant for you to pry up the floorboards and discover my staff. Didn't you see the nails?"

Saw them and felt them. My foot was still sore. "Ah, no, no I didn't." I pulled the last chain away, and Littlecloud fell from the wheel. I caught him and set him down gently. He was weak from loss of blood and from Pedro trying to rip his bear power away. I knew he wouldn't be able to get out of this mine on his own.

I tried lifting him up. He pushed me away. "No, don't worry about me." He pointed across the dim room. "Get his staff."

I looked and, in the commotion, it had rolled into the shadows, but it still popped and twinkled with power. I wasn't excited about grabbing an *ilkashn* staff, but I nodded and moved to retrieve it.

As my hand clutched the handle, a massive foot came down and crushed the staff flat. A puff of dust and broken wood shards clouded around me, and I could smell intense sulfur and feel the heat of fire on my neck.

I jumped away just before Hydrastigor landed another foot.

He rose above me, in full bloom, like Atlas holding firmly the earth. He was beautiful in a way, a mix of red and black scales, shiny and bristling with tiny horns and bonelettes along the length of his impressive spine. He was almost too big for the room, his long neck and head pressing against the top of the mine. When he moved, rock dust showered down from the ceiling. I could hardly see. I shielded my eyes and tried crawling away, but his house-sized paw reached for me and plucked me off the floor. His grip was powerful, and I felt myself being squeezed like a lemon. I tried breaking free, I scratched at him. I bit at his thick skin. Nothing.

He screamed out lines of Romanian gibberish. The only word I could understand was his name, Hydrastigor, which he said often and with great inflection. My guess was that in his over-zealous, egotistical rage, he was espousing all the nasty things he was going to do to the world, as if I gave a damn. And such is the weakness of despots and madmen: wasting time with frivolous monologues.

But Littlecloud had not wasted time. During the dragon's little speech, he had turned as well, and now he rose up, eight feet at least, into a wide, muscle-heavy bear, fur as black as night, claws long and sharp. Hydrastigor pulled back his head to unleash another useless scream, and Littlecloud srtuck, hurling himself into the soft underbelly of the dragon and bringing him down hard against a pile of granite waste.

Naturally, I expected to be immediately released from my bondage. But of course, nothing ever goes right with me. Hydrastigor squeezed even harder. I went down as well, and the two titans rolled around and around the room, throwing each other this way and that, making a big production and causing me much pain. The dragon was larger than the bear, but the bear had a lower center of gravity, like a bull dog, and could not be moved as easily. Littlecloud stood his ground, moving slowly and patiently toward the dragon as it punched and clawed and bit at its assailant, landing blows that would cripple a skyscraper.

Littlecloud took the punishment, letting his old friend, his blood brother, beat him again and again. And I realized that this was just another atonement for my boss, another way for him to wipe away the guilt of past transgressions. Littlecloud was letting Pedro use him to beat out his anger, his rage. He was letting this dragon, this Hydrastigor, which had had no chance to be something special in its prior life, exact its own revenge for the loss of its chance, the loss of its mother. I was beginning to worry that my boss would allow him to beat him to death.

But as Littlecloud drew close, he balled up his fist and drove it hard into Hydrastigor's chest. The force of the punch was so great that it crushed the dragon's ribs, breaking them all to pieces. I could see the ends of shattered bone piercing through the thick red hide. The force of the blow sent the dragon into the wall. And finally he let me go.

I fell to the floor, breaking a rib or two of my own. I lay there in a cloud of dust, hearing the dragon gasp for air, and as I tried getting up, I heard a cracking, and the ceiling began to shake and rumble.

The room was collapsing. Where the dragon had struck, a large chasm opened up and grew across the wall and ceiling like a spider's web. I tried crawling away, tried calling for Littlecloud though the chaos, but my throat was dry, and the pain in my sides was excruciating. It was all I could do to keep from getting smashed from falling rocks.

Next thing I knew, I was scooped up by a big, meaty paw. Littlecloud was still in bear form, and he grabbed me and Hydrastigor and began to run, down the tunnel where I had entered the room.

I'd never seen a bear run so fast. I didn't know my boss had it in him, in fact. But his weight, his strength in that form, propelled us through the tunnel, as inch by inch, foot by foot, the mine began to collapse behind us. I tried watching our retreat, tried to ignore the mighty cloud of dust and rubble that crashed behind us, but I was too weak, in too much pain.

Somewhere along the way, I passed out.

***

When I awoke, I was on the surface with a warm Baltimore sun baking my face. Ghouls can live in the sunlight, but we don't like it. I rubbed at my cheeks like they were infested with spiders. I shielded my eyes from the light and tried getting up. The pain in my chest kicked in.

I rolled over onto my side. The sound of distant gunfire, sirens and screaming were prevalent. The Charred were still on the move, were still hunting and being hunted. The matter was far from over.

But what mattered to me were two scantily-clad men resting beside the pile of iron extract. Littlecloud held Pedro in his arms tenderly, like a baby. I managed to crawl up to my feet and walk over to them.

There were tear streaks across both of their faces. Hydrastigor was gone. Perhaps his spirit had escaped back to the ethereal plane. Perhaps the punch that Pedro had suffered had destroyed him for good. Time would tell. All that remained was a frail, beaten man, gasping for air as my boss tried to hold him closely.

"I never meant to hurt anyone," Pedro said, his eyes blinking madly. "I never meant to…"

He trailed off and Littlecloud nodded. "It's okay, my brother. It's over now. You can rest."

Pedro shook his head and coughed. A line of blood escaped his mouth. He struggled to speak. "No, it will never be over. I will never be at rest. I am the spirit of the bat, and the darkness always calls. I have forsaken my family; I have forsaken the world. I am *Indeh*. You know this, and you know what you must do."

Littlecloud nodded though it seemed as if it were the hardest thing he had ever done.

With my help, we laid Pedro down, fixed his darkening hair, and crossed his hands over his ruined chest. Littlecloud stood, raised his left foot, and placed it atop his blood brother's neck. He pushed down.

It took only a few minutes for Pedro to die. He struggled at first when his deflated lungs no longer felt air. His weak body shook, but he did not try to move Littlecloud's foot. He left it alone, and held his gaze tightly on my boss's face. They smiled at each other. They held that smile as if they were sharing a secret. A tear fell down Littlecloud's face. Only one.

When it was over, Littlecloud stepped back, closed his eyes, and took a deep breath. He was still weak and I held him tightly. We stood like that for a long while. Then he let out the air, turned and looked at me. "Are you hungry?"

I was famished.

"Then let's go home," he said, turning so that I could get a better grip on his waist. "Let the authorities handle the Charred. With Hydrastigor gone, their strength is greatly diminished. I think we've done enough for one day, don't you think?"

I couldn't agree more.

A lonely boy, bullied and outcast within his own blended family attempts to find refuge at a Science Fiction convention when he meets a beautiful girl who needs his help to save her people in Roy Mauritsen's haunting tale of adolescence.

Norman's Ark
Roy A. Mauritsen

What adults never seem to realize is that when they argue, their children can always hear them; this is true anywhere in the house, and especially when the argument is about them. And so it follows that from his upstairs room, Norman overheard the heated part of an argument between his mother and stepfather, Sam.

"He needs to learn to grow up! Those models and silly games he plays... I swear to God... I will march right upstairs and throw them out!"

"You stay out of Norman's room, Sam! I mean it."

Norman's neck burned as he stood perfectly still in his room and strained to listen.

"Those models are his father's, Sam," explained his mother. "They are the only things he has left from him. Gerald and Norman would always build things together, you know that."

From behind his door, Norman suddenly recalled his father before he got sick. A particularly fond memory of the two of them restoring a boat came to mind. He remembered taking it sailing with his father that next summer, and a distant smile lit his face.

"Norman is not a bad kid," his mother continued. "He's just not your kid. He's still adjusting to a new school and to losing his father."

"We have the money to hire people to fix things," Sam replied angrily. "We both know I don't have the time for that. If you want a boat, we'll buy one."

Sam was the vice president of human resources for a corporation that handles commercial real estate law and investments. As such, he made a lot of money. That was about all that Norman understood. That and his mother seemed less happy since she remarried. They had moved to a big new house near the corporate headquarters, several states away from Norman's small town on the east coast and all of his friends.

"That's not the point!" his mother answered in an increasingly shrill voice, as the argument continued. "He spent time with Norman, like you spend time with your own son. You might stand to include Norman a little more often in your activities, like it or not we're all a family now. Get used to it. The only interaction he gets with you is when you want him to mow the lawn. Why is it we never use our money to hire people to mow the lawn?"

"That's simple, Ellen," came the sharp reply. "It's because your son needs to learn responsibility."

"And your son needs to learn another sport?" she asked incredulously. "I never see Matt doing the lawn. He's too busy going to practice with his father."
Silence rang out like a warning bell in the kitchen, and Norman held his breath as the sound of the clock ticked behind him on his nightstand table. When his mother spoke again, her tone held both weariness and finality.

"When you take Matt to his Lacrosse game today, I want you to drop Norman off at that convention he's been looking forward. It's at that college nearby. I was going to take him, but now you can do me a favor."

"That's 30 minutes out of the way, at least!" Sam blurted.

"Well, then you'd better get going." she replied in a low voice as she left the room.

Lord Skargard looked at the mirror in his room and felt stupid in his homemade costume.

"Norman! We're leaving for Matt's game in 10 minutes." Sam's inpatient voice rose from the front of the house. "If you want to get dropped off at that thing today then be in the car."

Norman gathered up the rest of his costume and grabbed his backpack of game books. As he emerged downstairs, he did not give any indication that he had heard the argument. Stopping to say good bye to his mother, he was surprised to find an extra forty dollars pressed into his palm. She smiled gently at him, like only his mother could, and told him to have fun.

As Norman approached Sam's SUV, he could hear Matt complaining. "Aw, come on Dad, HE's coming with us?" Norman ignored the complaint as he opened the car door to see Matt and his friend Tony, both decked out in their lacrosse gear, sitting in the backseat. Norman threw his backpack in the back cargo space of the SUV, ignoring Matt's polite request, "Watch the sticks, dickwad," and squeezed in next to Matt, who reluctantly gave him room to sit. Norman was a big kid, not really overweight, but it was going to be a tight fit with the three of them in the back. Glancing across the car, Norman gave a polite "Hey Tony," getting little more than a snorting laugh in reply. Resignedly, he turned and looked out the window. *This is going to be a long ride,* he thought. And things would only get worse next year when they started their first year of high school together.

Like every other time he rode in the car with his stepfather, Sam listened to the news or to some talk radio show. "— Global warming is for idiots," Sam grumbled at the radio broadcast. "Hey Matt, global warming is a scam. Don't let any of your democratic teachers try and trick you into thinking otherwise. There is no such thing as global warming."

"Got it dad," Matt replied eagerly. Norman was sure Matt would be parroting that back in class Monday morning. Then it started, "What are you supposed to be, Darth Vader?"

Norman pulled his gaze away from the window to see Matt and Tony staring at him with malicious grins.

"It's just a costume," Norman replied. "It's one of my characters from a game."

"Pretty stupid looking, Dork Vader," said Tony. Both he and Matt laughed, high fiving each other.

"Dude, your stepbrother is such a nerd," Tony added.

"I know, right?" Matt agreed.

"Your costumes aren't much better," said Norman. "What are you supposed to be?"

Matt pushed into Norman with extra force as the SUV turned a corner, squeezing him uncomfortably against the door. Norman's costume crumpled.

"These are sports uniforms, dickasaurus. Something you wouldn't know anything about, because it's not some stupid wizard game and it doesn't have stupid looking dice. Why don't you go back to New York and paint your little toy models."

I wish I could, Norman thought to himself. Then he heard something on his costume come loose and realized that something must have broken when Matt pushed into him. Now Norman was getting annoyed. Tony and Matt were clearly encouraging each other, and Matt's father paid little attention as he was more interested in listening to the news.

Lord Skargard was trapped; he was outnumbered by evil slime goblin minions. Lord Skargard sought to defend himself.

"Yeah, well running around on field with sticks and throwing balls at each other looks pretty stupid to me."

Matt punched Norman hard in the shoulder. "Shut up, asshole!" The punch hurt, and would leave a knotted bruise for a few days at least. Norman could feel his eyes wet with tears. The part of his costume where Matt had hit him was certainly cracked and ruined.

"You're an asshole, Matt!" Norman raised his voice loudly, hurt and angry as he rubbed his shoulder.

"Knock it off, Norman!" Sam yelled, his eyes glaring harshly at him through the rearview mirror.

Dejected, Norman shook his head, "Whatever," he whispered. Then he quietly gazed out the window of the car, ignoring Tony and Matt. Sam changed the radio station from the news to a sports and baseball commentary of a game in progress. Sam, Matt, and Tony listened to the game, the three of them cheering and occasionally yelling at the radio. During the commercials, they each talked about players and batting averages, and Sam proudly told the two of them about his own sports stories. Norman could not wait for the ride to be over.

"Hey Matt, Norman's from New York, right?" Tony asked maliciously.

"Yeah," Norman heard Matt answer.

"Hey Norman," Tony said. "Your team sucks!"

Apocalypse 13

"It's not my team. I don't care about baseball," Norman replied halfheartedly.

Matt leaned in close to Norman. "That's why you're a loser," he said in a very real, very serious tone. Then Tony tapped Matt on the shoulder to get his attention.

"Dude, check it out—geek central!" Tony pointed out the window with a bully-ish gleam in his eye.

They had finally arrived at the college where the convention was held. Around the entrance to the convention building, all manner of people had gathered. Teenagers, college students, older men and women, even families with children. Many of the people within the crowd were dressed in costumes. Some costumes were homemade like Norman's; others were far more elaborate. Norman saw throngs of people dressed as zombies or vampires, while others wore nothing fancier than a cloak and a bright-colored wig. There were robot costumes, super heroes, science fiction aliens, and medieval knights. Norman could not wait to get out of the car as soon as he saw the convention entrance.

Tony could not wait to roll down the car window. "What a bunch of geeks!" Tony yelled out the window as the SUV came to a stop. A few people in the crowd looked over at the SUV; some even flashed their middle fingers at him in response.

"I have to get my backpack out of the back, Sam." Norman reminded his stepfather.

"Hurry up. We're already late because of you." As soon as Norman had grabbed his backpack and closed the rear door, Sam yelled out the window, "Your mother is picking you up here at 6 tonight."

Then the SUV pulled quickly away from the curb, with Tony yelling out another round of insults to the costumed crowd as they drove off.

"Finally," whispered Norman as he gave a sigh of relief. The stress of the car ride melted away as he stepped towards the convention entrance. For a few hours at least, he could forget about his stepfather. Norman would be around people that understood him. Maybe he could make some friends here; he brought his character sheets, hoping he would find other kids that played role-playing games, or someone who painted models and miniatures. This was something Norman was looking forward to since he found out about it three months ago. It was not as big as the conventions in New York he used to go to, but it was the only thing he had remotely found of interest since he moved here. Here he could find out where a local gaming store was, or a comic book shop, or some costuming club or science fiction group. Here he could connect with people, people that were not Sam, Matt, or Tony.

However, it was obvious that he would have to enter the convention without his Lord Skargard costume. The homemade costume that had survived three years of conventions and Halloweens as well as the move from New York, did not survive its first car trip with his stepbrother, Matt. It was a bittersweet moment when Norman threw his cardboard and plastic armor in a nearby garbage can. He took some comfort in the thought that perhaps after today he would make a new and better Lord Skargard costume.

Wearing only jeans, an odd pair of boots, and a black T-shirt, he stepped up to the ticket window and paid for his ticket. The lady in the booth asked him his name, and he answered "Norman" without thinking. The lady handed him his convention badge with the name NORMAN written on it in big letters.

"Next!" she said before Norman could say anything. He wanted the badge to read "Lord Skargard," but considering he was not in his costume, Norman supposed it did not really matter now.

For the next couple of hours, Norman had the most fun he had experienced since he moved. He watched previews about upcoming movies. He sat and listened happily to a panel discussion on the future of role playing games. He watched some medieval weapons demonstrations. Then, he attended another discussion panel about how to create a role playing game and get it published. Norman took notes; he had some ideas, and after the panel was over, he talked to some of the game designers about his ideas. To his surprise, they seemed very interested. One of the designers told him to contact him after the convention and gave him a business card, which Norman took very excitedly.

Later in the afternoon, Norman contently spent the remaining hours wandering the large dealer's room. The area was like a huge garage sale of everything related to science fiction and fantasy genres. Norman saw it as a flea market full of vendors selling every manner of games, posters, costumes, books, and toys. He happily spent his time browsing the tables and meeting several authors who were signing autographs at tables. He even found several local game shops that had booths there, and he took their flyers for future visits. Norman even found a place that would be holding some role-playing game on the weekends.

In the crowded dealer's room, Norman felt truly at home. He stopped at one vendor table that was selling models and books. Perhaps it was the argument he had overheard with his mother and Sam that had reminded him. Among the sorted collections of various spaceship models and monster reference books laid out on the table, Norman spied a book on boats. Next to it was a small selection of boat models. Some of them Norman had recognized as the kinds he and his father used to build, and the weight of his father's death suddenly enveloped him.

With most of the money his mother had given him, Norman bought the book on boats and one of the model boat kits, and then stuffed both into his backpack. As he did, he could not shake the feeling that he was somehow subconsciously hiding this from Sam.

As Norman left the vendor and pushed his way through the crowd of costumed convention goers, he noticed a girl dressed in a costume. In fact, he had seen her several times that day as he browsed the dealer's room. This time, she gave him a quick smile as they brushed by each other. She was dressed in a very convincing fairy-like costume with wings; Norman thought it looked very professional, like she was an actress or model dressed to promote some Hollywood movie. She was rather tall, with red hair. Norman thought she was quite beautiful, and realized he had just obviously stared completely at her breasts as he passed her.

He distracted himself by stopping at another booth to look at some pewter figurines. A silvery-sculpted wizard posed before him for all eternity, holding up a glued-on crystal ball as a golden-looking metal dragon with red jeweled eyes hovered menacingly above him.

"Pewter figurines are twenty. The pewter goblets are thirty. The pewter necklaces are twelve," the vendor said robotically as Norman admired them, hitting his head on the row of necklaces hanging over him.

Then Norman sensed someone close to him as he was looking at the figures. It was the lady in the fairy costume he had passed before. "Buy me a necklace and I'll tell you a secret, Norman."

Norman was completely caught off guard. The red-haired girl in the fairy costume was there, staring at him. She nodded towards the necklace display. "Come on, Norman. I won't bite," she added with a smile.

"Uh, sure. Why not?" Norman stammered nervously as he reached into his pocket and fished out his money. He pulled out a five dollar bill. Gulping, he fished around in his back pocket and found another wad of bills, all singles and only five of them. He looked at the sign for the necklaces. Twelve dollars, like the guy had said. He only had ten dollars.

Norman looked at the guy selling the pewter necklaces, silently pleading with his gaze and trying to nod discreetly to him that this was for the incredibly hot girl in the fairy costume with the perfect breasts and to please not let him look like an utter loser. All of that, Norman tried to convey in a single gaze. He was just about to give up and admit to the beautiful, perfect skinned beauty standing that he was too lame to even buy a cheap twelve dollar pewter necklace, when the vendor suddenly seemed to understand.

"Hey kid, which necklace do you want for your fairy girlfriend? Five bucks for the necklace, call it a convention special." He gave Norman a quick wink. Norman's face brightened, and with an enthusiastic and somewhat relieved "Thank you!" he handed over five dollars and picked out a pewter dragon claw that dangled on a black piece of string and clutched a smoky blue crystal.

He turned to the girl and held up the necklace. "My name is Norman," he announced with a broad smile, which became instantly foolish when he recalled that she had already called him by his name. But the girl smiled kindly as she retrieved the necklace from his hand. "Thank you, Norman," she replied, and stuffed the trinket in a small leather pouch on her costume. "Now, let's go talk."

The girl grabbed Norman's hand. It was a strong grip; Norman noticed that her hand was soft and warm. Entranced, he obediently followed the tall, well costumed redhead with the fairy wings through the maze of convention goers. Soon, they had left the dealer's room completely and found a small grouping of tables and chairs near a college concession booth that was serving food.

"Sit," she gestured. Norman sat. As she pulled up her chair, Norman couldn't help but ask, "Are you one of those people that walk around conventions promoting movies? Because whatever movie you are promoting, I promise I'll go see it."

The girl laughed sweetly, and Norman melted on the inside.

"No," she said. "I don't do that."

"That's a really great costume," Norman added. "Are you doing a cosplay contest then?"

"Costume?" she asked, and then realized what Norman was referring to. "Oh, the wings and stuff? No. They are mine," she answered. "I need your help Norman. My name is Isone'. I saw that you bought a book on boats and a boat model. I thought you might be interested in a project I have. Then, when I saw your name on your badge, I thought that it had to be a sign."

"A sign?" Norman's eyebrows drew together as he tried to understand. "I was going to have my badge say Lord Skargard, one of my gaming characters... but they just wrote my real name," he offered as an explanation.

Isone' leaned in. "Where I come from, my people refer to your kind as *normans*. It means normal human. If you didn't have that name on your badge, I would probably not have thought twice about it. But between the boat models and such, it was too much of a sign to ignore... to not risk a chance to talk to you."

Is she role-playing a character? Norman wondered. Maybe she had him confused with someone else. Was this some sort of convention role-playing game? "I don't really do any of that LARPing stuff," said Norman finally. "I'm sorry if there's been some mistake. You can keep the necklace though."

Norman began to get up. He felt like he was about to be made fun of. Then he paused, "How did you do that?" he asked, "Your fairy wings...you just made them flap really fast."

"I told you, they are mine," Isone' insisted. She flapped them quickly again, almost like she was annoyed. "They are real. Now sit back down. I don't have a lot of time."

Norman sat down again. This time fascinated that Isone's really great fairy costume was perhaps more real than he first thought. The large wings were clear and veined like a dragonfly's. She had two thin small antennae that protruded from her silky red hair. Now that he was looking at them, Norman realized they did not look like pipe cleaners and fuzzy balls that many of the convention fairy costumes would have been. Isone' pulled her hair back behind her ear. It was a tall and thin ear that ended seamlessly in a point. If this was a costume, it was a very convincing one. If it was *not* a costume, then Norman realized that he might be talking to a very real fairy. "I have a project that I think you could help with," the girl continued, seemingly oblivious to Norman's revelation. "With that book, you can build boats, right?"

Norman thought it sounded like a simple, almost naïve question. "Yeah... my dad, before he died," he stammered. "We used to build model boats, but we worked on real boats and stuff; we went sailing a bunch of times. Why? Do have a boat you need help with?"

"Yes. We need you to help us build a boat—a big one. Let me explain. You normans know about my people, you know us from myths and stories and legends, folklore and fairy tales, but I promise you they are all true. I'm a fairy, Norman. It's all real, dragons and wizards, all of that stuff. We remain hidden for now, but I might be able to show you. "

"I guess you look real," replied Norman, unsure of what to believe, "but aren't fairies supposed to be small? You're big for a fairy. "

Isone' responded with a bemused smile. "To answer your question, yes

Norman, we're all real. But in your time, most creatures are kept hidden away on an island. Some stay in the norman world—your Bigfoot for instance... the Loch Ness monster... beings like that. Others come and go. That's how we try to stay informed on the norman world."

Norman's eyes widened. "Really?" he asked with quiet excitement. "You aren't kidding, me right? Dragons, orcs, trolls? Wizards? All that stuff is real? That is awesome!" he shouted with a large grin.

Isone' paused, suddenly hesitant to continue. "There is something I must tell you, and it is not good news." She looked squarely at Norman. "It is very important that you believe me. A long time ago, the world had a great flood, and a norman named Noah built a boat, saving all of the animals. You must be familiar with the story."

Norman nodded, curious how Noah's ark was related to fairies.

"Well," she continued, "what you probably *don't* know is that all of the magical beasts and beings *missed* the boat. Many died from the flood that followed, but some were carried by the water to a distant island where they remain today. In time, we all became part of your legends."

The girl's eyes narrowed in intensity and her hands gripped the edge of the table. "There is another flood coming, Norman," she announced, "and this time we will be ready for it!"

Norman's head was spinning. "You want an ark? Why can't your people build an ark? Is it something that you don't want to risk being seen on TV or something? Wait, what do you mean another flood?"

"It's bigger than that, Norman." Isone' explained. "The earth's magnetic poles are going to shift soon. The global warming you normans keep talking about is only the precursor. In the next six months or so, the poles will begin to slide more quickly to a tipping point, and when it happens, the planet will actually flip with it. There will be tremendous floods and tidal waves. It's like being in a bottle of water as it gets suddenly turned upside down. There will be massive earthquakes and volcanic eruptions that will rip apart every continent. Every country will be decimated and your norman civilization will be destroyed. Only the larger mountain ranges like in your Colorado would stand a chance."

"Wouldn't this be in the news?" Norman asked. "How do you know all of this?" A thin sheen of sweat was beginning to cover his body, and he felt his hands tremble as he clasped them together on top of his head. It was just too much to believe.

"Your leaders and governments know about it. They've been working on things. But they are not going to tell everyone. They are only going to save themselves. If they told everyone, then they would have to be responsible for saving everyone. Norman, I am sorry to tell you that in six months the world you've known will come to an end."

"But how do you know?"

"Remember, I said that some stay behind in the norman world. Well, we have an expert at the North Pole that has remained in constant vigil, studying the magnetic poles as they shift. I trust his word and resources above all others."

"The North Pole?" Norman stopped and thought for a moment. Then realized this must be a joke. "Santa Claus? Really?" sad Norman. "You almost had me fooled, Isone', or whatever your name is."

"No, listen, Norman." Isone' pleaded. "Who else would know as much about the magnetic pole shift? Who would have as much vested interest in what happens to the North Pole? Let me ask you this: Most normans raise their children to believe in Santa Claus. As norman children, that's what you grew up believing. Let's say if everything is equal and true, who then would you believe? If Santa Claus said the North Pole was being destroyed by global warming and the earth's magnetic poles were shifting, then would you believe him? Or would you believe a bunch or scientists that still can't agree on whether global warming is real?"

Norman thought for a moment. He looked carefully at Isone', and for the first time he saw her as she was— a real fairy. He thought hard about what she had said. "I guess I would probably believe Santa, everything being equal," he found himself admitting.

Isone' looked relieved. Norman looked ill. The world was going to end in six months. "But why do you need me? Can't you build an ark yourself?"

"We've tried. For all of our magic, my people cannot understand technology. We're fascinated by it. But we just do not comprehend it. Did you ever see a fairy try to build a computer? It's not pretty." Isone' regarded Norman for a moment, and then she looked around to check if the tables were empty; they were. By now, the convention was closing down for the weekend. "It's like how you would not understand if I did this," Isone' said as she snapped her fingers. From thin air materialized a blue, glowing flame that rolled playfully in the palm of her hand. "Magic to us is as easy to comprehend as your science is for you to understand. Yet, you would not understand how we would do something as simple as this." The blue flame danced and twitched, shaping itself into the form of a small dragon that flew from Isone's hand and disappeared as it flew towards Norman. "But we do not know how to build an ark that will house all manner of creatures."

Norman was still marveling at the magical blue flame. He understood everything that Isone' was saying. Deep down inside he knew what the fairy was telling him. It somehow all made sense to him. Magic was real, dragons were real. The idea that the world was going to drastically change frightened him, but what Isone' told him next gave him a glimmer of hope. "There is more to this than just the poles shifting, Norman, something else you probably don't know about."

"There's more? More than just telling me that there's all of this cool stuff with fairies and dragons, and that magic is actually real, but oh wait, never mind, the world's going to be destroyed. What more could there be?"

"I said *your* world will be destroyed, not mine. Just like there are magnetic poles that are shifting, Earth has something else as well... something your science does not register, but it's a subject I am familiar with: magetic poles. These poles are a positive and negative force. They control the magical energies. In the past they have been more positive, and in recent years they have swung more negative. This means that in the past magic was more real. This was in the times of the Greek gods, then again during the Arthurian legends. Now, we are on a negative trend that has allowed technology to take over. The constant buzz of technology and industry drowns out the weaker magetic fields, but there are still pockets where magetics are strong. There's a place called Disnee that has a strong magetic field. And believe it or not, these types of conventions resonate greatly. That's why I chose to look here for someone to help us. Plus, it's a place where I can sort of blend in." Isone' flapped her fairy wings again to emphasize the point.

"So what does that have to do with...?"

"Negative magetics make for magically creating a boat next to impossible for us," Isone' replied. "Simply put, with the magetic fields so far in the negative field, our magic is not strong enough to create a boat to the scope and scale we'll need to survive. It needs to be built. And we're stuck. But with all of the research I have done on magetics, everything indicates that when the magnetic poles shift, the magetic poles will also reverse in big way. Any of the normans that manage to survive the magnetic pole shift, will not be able to rely on technology any more. It simply won't work the way it used to. Our kind will spread out and pick up the pieces of your civilization."

Isone' reached across the small table and grabbed Norman's hands. "The last part of this is belief. Please, everything I've told you is the truth. But you are not the first. It's not that we haven't tried to warn you normans. It is that normans are so out of tune with the magetic fields that many simple don't believe in it—they can't wrap their head around it. Most people, even in a place like this, don't truly believe. It's like a bird trying to explain to a rock about flying. The rock simply cannot comprehend it, even when the bird flies away. We can't convince the people who build the boats. They are too much like the rock. Your whole norman society is like a bunch of rocks. But someone like you Norman, you can still believe. We can help you build the boat, magically even. Here you would need to operate large cranes to move metal walls around; there you would have dragons to command. We just need you to translate the instructions, so to speak. In return for your help, Norman, you will survive with us to start a new world, to live a life full of magic, dragons, unicorns, and fairies. You will be our advisor, as we will need to understand the remnants of your old world. We'll give you your own dragon if you want."

Norman looked at Isone'. This had been quite a day. He was numb, but he didn't want the day to end. He did not want to go back to having to deal with his stepfather and Matt. Norman did not want to go back to his school. He did not want Isone' to let go of his hands. Norman looked at her large brown desperate eyes, and then he looked past her to the clock on the wall. It was just past six o'clock! The convention was over. He was supposed to be at the entrance already.

"Shit!" Norman said suddenly. "I have to go! My mom's picking me up. I'm gonna' be late." Norman scrambled to get out of the chair as Isone' stood up with him.

"Norman, one last thing." The fairy pulled the pewter necklace he had bought for her out of her pouch. She held it out and it glowed for a moment before it quickly returned to its normal state.

"I will have to leave and return to the island. Take this necklace. In one hour it will return to me. If you are willing to help and you believe, it will bring you back to me and you will stay among my people to build the ark. Bring whatever you can carry on you. You can bring others with you but the necklace will only bring those who truly believe. If you don't want to come, only the necklace will disappear."

Norman grabbed the necklace and quickly pulled it over his head, tucking the pewter claw under his shirt. Then he picked up his backpack.

"Uh, thanks for everything, Isone'. My mom's gonna' kill me if I'm late," Norman said awkwardly. "I guess, uh, I'll see you around."

"Sure," said Isone'. Her body seemed to dim with a twinge of sadness. Maybe she was wrong. Stepping over to Norman, she placed a long, soft kiss on his lips. Norman paused for a second to let the kiss sink in. It felt like a lifetime to him. He closed his eyes as she kissed him, Norman felt like he was floating, as far as he knew in that moment, he could very well have been.
"Wow," he murmured as she pulled away.

Isone' looked at Norman. "I believe in you," The six foot tall fairy whispered. "You have one hour to decide. If you choose to stay, then in six months I wish you the best of luck, Norman, lord of the normans." With a flitter of her wings and a spray of sparkling light, Isone' had vanished—as quickly as she had appeared.

Norman headed shakily to the entrance. As he rounded the corner, he could see the SUV waiting at the curb, headlights and hazards on. The wipers dragged slowly across the windshield with a sense of impatience.

Norman pushed through the few, straggling convention people hanging out in the entrance lobby and ran through the rain to the waiting SUV. He climbed in to find his mom waiting for him. On the half-hour drive home, he proceeded to tell his mom about his day. His mom laughed with him, and they talked about many of the things that Norman had done and seen.
Then, Norman mentioned Isone'. He described how beautiful she was. His mother was impressed, saying that this was the first good news she had heard from him since they moved here. He went on to tell about Isone' and how he thought she might be a real fairy, and Norman explained the wings and the magic fire she made. He began to explain about the magetic fields and that dragons were real, and he was about to pull out the pewter necklace as they pulled into the driveway. His mom put the SUV in park, but did not turn the engine off. The wipers beat back and forth like a robotic heartbeat, and the bright headlights glared brightly off the stark white garage doors.

"Norman," his mother started, "Sam and I had a long discussion while you were at the convention. It's just, we're all a new family now and we all have to work on getting along together. That means compromises. We're starting a new life, a successful life, in a new place with new people. It's a chance to start fresh. I loved your father very much and miss him, but Sam is good for us now, and he has some valid suggestions."

Norman listened as the back of his neck began to burn again.

"Sam and I went through your room and pulled out all of the things we thought you should maybe put away for now. A few of Gerald's things of course you can keep-"

Apocalypse 13

"What!" Norman cried. "How could you do that, Mom? I can't believe you would do that without talking to me first!"

"Sam is trying to help us, Honey. He's going to talk to Matt's coach on Monday; he thinks he can get you on the lacrosse team with Matt."

"Mom! No!"

"It'll be good for you to spend some time with Matt and his friends," his mother continued. "Maybe this is the start of something good."

"Mom, believe me, it's not the start of anything good."

"All I'm asking is that you give this a chance. It'll be good for you to get out and play some sports. Also, Sam is going to see about getting you a part time job where he works, just for the summer. That way you can have a little cash and he can spend some time with you."

Norman wasn't even listening anymore. He glared out the window in the dark, tears rolling down his cheeks like the rain rolled in rivulets down the window.

Lord Skargard looked down at the poisoned dagger in his gut. The slime goblins had destroyed his protective armor, and he was left vulnerable. Not even the fairy goddess's necklace could help. His own mother had fatally stabbed him. Only now did the mortally wounded Lord Skargard realize that his mother was obviously under an enchantment by the evil overlord.

"I'm going inside," Norman said, disgusted. He went into the house, not saying a word as he passed briskly by Sam and headed upstairs to his room.

"Give him a few minutes, Sam," he heard his mother say. Norman's room was empty of his posters. His books and games were packed in boxes labeled ATTIC. All of his paints and brushes and figurines were gone. Norman saw that his models, all but one, were stuffed and broken in a nearby garbage bag. The only model left was that of a boat, kept in a plastic display case on his desk. It was the first model he did with his dad, on the day his father had been diagnosed with cancer. He gently picked it up and put it in his backpack.

Norman grabbed a couple of other books from some of the boxes and stuffed another duffle bag full of clothes and other things. Ten minutes later, he descended the stairs and dropped his bags by the door. Sam didn't notice Norman; he had the TV on in the living room and was watching the news. There was something on the news report and Sam was giving his usual commentary. "Those global warming kooks are wasting our taxpayer money... listen to this Ellen..." Sam turned the volume up on the TV. Norman paused "The President stated that he and a joint task force of hand-picked staff and cabinet members, state governors, members of congress, other world leaders, and even private corporate CEOs will meet with scientists in an unprecedented and comprehensive closed door summit meeting to take place in Colorado, six months from today. Quoting the president in a press conference 'rest assured, global warming will not be the end of the world, but we want to best understand what the next few years will bring and what we'll need to do.'"

"Six months from now," Norman recalled. "The leaders already know." He remembered Isone' telling him. Looks like the rats are already jumping the ship, he thought. They would not be saving anyone but themselves. They did not want to be responsible for trying to save anyone else.

Norman went into the kitchen where his mother was preparing dinner.

"Mom, I'm sorry." Norman said. "I'm sorry about Dad. I love you okay?"

His mother smiled. "I love you too, son. We'll work it out. It won't be that bad, I promise." She gave him a reassuring smile.

"Can I ask you one question, but you have to be honest, okay?" Norman asked.

"Sure," his mother replied, slightly unsure about the serious tone he was taking. "Is it about girls?" she asked with a teasing smile.

"Do you believe in Santa Claus?"

His mother's face instantly soured. "Norman, I thought we talked about this tonight. We were going to focus on serious things. Besides, it's April. Christmas is eight months away."

"Yes or no, Mom, please—it's important."

"No, Norman, okay? I don't. Let's grow up a little," his mom said curtly. She sounded annoyed for a moment, but composed herself quickly, afraid that Sam would overhear. "Let's talk about something else okay? What about that girl? Do you think you'll be seeing her again; the one you met at the convention today?"

Norman paused, and then he said "Yeah, I think so," quietly, he slid a folded hndwritten note unoticed on the kitchen counter then turned and walked back to his bags. Not looking back, Norman, lord of the normans, pulled the glowing pewter necklace out from under his shirt.

Reporter Alice Minear starts the day reporting about sink holes and an unexplained metal object that crash landed in the forest near her. By the end of the day she's trying to save the world from a threat from below in Jordan Pettit's tale of an ambitious reporter attempting to get a network worthy story.

There's Something In The Earth

Jordan Pettit

Alice found herself in a most distressing predicament: She, along with her sister, Catherine and her recently met friend, Fulton, were imprisoned. Each member of the trio took to their current plight in different ways. Fulton was working on an escape plan, and to this end, was stripping any machine he could find for parts. Catherine was taking imprisonment considerably less well. She paced around the cell, struggling to form a coherent sentence, her prior efforts having yielded only one or two words at a time, most of them profanities. Alice herself lacked the energy to get worked up about it, contenting herself to sit at the back of the cell and mope.

"I can't believe this!" Catherine said, her efforts finally having paid off, "You know, it seems like bad things happen whenever I come down to see you, but this?! This is just-just-", Catherine trailed off when she turned to look at her sister, her face buried in her hand, her previous anger and frustration replaced by remorse as she went to try to comfort Alice.

"Hey," Catherine said, sitting beside Alice and putting her hand on Alice's shoulder, "it's going to be okay", she said half-heartedly.

"Cat," Alice responded, "look at where we are. We're in a cell, waiting for the end of the world. How...how is this going to be okay?' Catherine found that she had no answer for that, and, with the wind thoroughly taken out of her sails, said nothing optimistic, instead asking a question that she had been eager to have answered from the start."All I want to know is how we got into this mess to begin with", she said.

Fulton heard this and, being eager to please, not to mention fancying himself a talented storyteller, abandoned his work for the time being and jumped at the chance. "Now that's a story if ever there was one," Fulton said, "good thing you're already sittin' down, because otherwise this'd knock you right off your feet! Let's see, it all started earlier today, in fact-well actually it all started long before that, but I'll try and keep it short-anyway, like I said, all this started when I first met your sister,

Alice. It was at about nine o' clock this morning, I think…"

By this point Alice tuned out. Her life was bad enough, and she didn't need to listen to another of Fulton's stories on top of it all. Catherine, however, seemed to be hanging on Fulton's every word. If nothing else, it was a distraction from the harsh reality they'd found themselves in. Alice herself went over the events of the day in her mind, as well. She needed to know what she'd done to deserve this fate.

It began at sunrise. In the forest the light of the morning sun barely eked through the trees. It being autumn, a fairly strong wind blew the multi-colored leaves, not to mention Alice's black hair, all about. The chattering of animals and the scent of nature (and all that entails) permeated the air. The lights of the camera shined in Alice's eyes as she prepared to give her report.

"If a large, metal object crashes in the woods and nobody's around to hear it, does it make a sound?" Alice said, trying very hard not to roll her eyes, "Well, apparently not. This," she said, indicating the cylindrical object standing upright just behind her, "was discovered just last night by a Mr. Tom North while he was out camping. There is no official word on what it is yet, but the best guess is that it's a part of a satellite that broke off and fell to Earth. We'll have more on this story as it develops." A pause and then, " in other news, over two-hundred and fifty sinkholes, ranging from medium to large width and depth, have sprung up so far this week; that number handily breaks the former all-time record of one-hundred thirty-two set…last week. There's still no word on what exactly is behind all these holes, but scientists are looking into it. The mayor has revealed his plan to relieve pressure on the city's budget as well as provide more prompt disaster relief: Rather than filling each sinkhole repair crews are going to steel plate the holes. Barring further incident, repairs are estimated to be complete by later this afternoon. Still, we here at Channel 9 urge our viewers not to travel by road unless it's absolutely necessary. This has been Alice Minear for Channel 9 News; back to you, Jan."

The cameraman signaled "cut" and Alice dug into her pocket and fished for her phone, turned it on and started looking through her missed messages. Only one message, oddly enough, from her sister, Catherine. Odd, since she and Catherine had drifted apart to the point where they hardly ever contacted each other. She put her phone to her ear, dreading what it might say.

"The machine again? Come on," Catherine said, her consternation clear, "Hey, Ali," she continued, abruptly switching to an overly cheerful tone, "I know it's kind of sudden, but I just wanted to let you know, I'm coming over to visit you the day after tomorrow. I'll be flying into the International Airport by you at around nine, but don't sweat being on time too much. You know how flying is these days…Anyway, looking forward to seeing you again! Bye!"

Alice checked the date of the message, and it was as she feared: it was two days old! She rushed over to the cameraman, who was already in the process of packing up his equipment along with the rest of the crew.

"Hey", Alice said, doing her best not to look like she wasn't about to ask for something.

"…hey", the cameraman responded, already knowing full well that she was.

"So...listen, I need a favor", Alice said, rushing through each word as if time was of the essence.

"Dare I ask, what?" The cameraman said, the weariness and mild annoyance in his tone.

"Well, my sister's coming to town, and-"

"She is?', the cameraman quipped "Funny, we ain't even had a blue moon yet."

"Yeah, yeah, you're hilarious, but I need to get home like yesterday, so I need a good reason to knock off early. You followin' me, dude?"

"Yeah, I think I get it," the cameraman responded, "so what should I tell them you 'suddenly came down with' this time: Dysentery? Food poisoning? Pneumonia?"

"Ah, you're smart, you'll think of something!" Alice said, already taking off, the sound of crunching leaves carrying through the chill air as she nearly ran.

"Hey! What are you doing!?" The cameraman shouted; as ever, Alice's actions made little sense to him.

"I live nearby; it's faster to walk!" Alice shouted back, before breaking into a full run.

Although Alice was in good shape, and even ran recreationally, her home was not as close as she'd said. Therefore, when she made it up her hilly street, with its unkempt trees growing over and around the power lines strewn along the street and its pastel dwellings of varying hideousness, she was exhausted. After taking a few seconds to catch her breath, she searched in her pockets for her keys, only to discover that she'd forgotten them yet again! She tried to turn the knob, despite knowing it was futile, only to find the door was already unlocked. However, rather than being relieved, Alice became suspicious...nervous.

She never left her door unlocked. She went through the other possibilities in her mind, and the one she latched onto was that someone had broken into her house. The only question was, who: A burglar? Some crazed killer? That homicidal little terrier from down the street!? No, this was no time to panic, she told herself. There was another reason her door was unlocked. She'd been in a hurry this morning, running late as always. She probably just forgot to lock the door.

Alice knew she should call the police. But the last thing she needed was for her face to be on some tabloid webpage. As an up and coming reporter her reputation needed to be perfectly clean. Any scandal could derail her chances for a network call up. Therefore, she needed a plan. But what could she do? She had to think of something quick.

"When in Rome", she said to herself. She then skulked down the stairs as quietly as she could and began to sneak around to the east side of her house, taking cover in the tall, thick bushes lining her unkempt lawn. After a few minutes of this, she reached her goal: The one window that opened from the outside. She couldn't just rush in though, so she first looked through it. The lights were off, so she couldn't see much, but she knew from memory she was looking into her kitchen. That was when she saw something-movement, a vague shadow bounding its way around, doing who-knows-what. It looked to be heading into the living room. Reassuring herself that she'd probably saw nothing; Alice opened the window and prayed that there was no intruder.

The first thing she noticed, once through her window, was that her kitchen was an absolute train wreck. All sorts of cookware scattered everywhere, and she swore she smelled something burning. A chair had been moved over near the fridge, and said fridge had been opened, along with various drawers and cabinets around the room. As well, many of her appliances looked as if they had been altered, some with parts missing and exposed wires. So, the intruder was apparently a hungry vandal. She would be able to handle it. She hoped. Besides he was probably gone.

She made her way, quiet as a mouse, to her den. Curiously, the den seemed relatively intact. The intruder must not have found much of interest in here; so much the better, Alice thought. She made her way to the drawer underneath the deer head hanging on the far wall. She then opened the tin can on top of the drawer and got the key she hid inside it, and used that to unlock the drawer. Therein lay her gun; the deer head and the gun were both gifts from Catherine, given in the hopes that Alice would go hunting with her one day, but really, the only reason Alice held onto the things was that she hated giving up gifts from her family. Though now, Alice was more than thankful for Catherine's gifts.

Alice opened the drawer, and her heart sank when she saw what lay inside: Her gun was in there, all right, but it was damaged almost beyond recognition! At least she was sure now that the intruder didn't have it on them. Changing her tactics yet again, she grabbed the lamp from atop the drawer.

Cursing herself for being an idiot she crept forward, "It'll have to do." She was nervous and rethinking her decision to call the police, but she steeled herself for the moment of truth. She walked into the living room, and found it in a similar state as her kitchen. The intruder was in the room, hiding behind her television, and she saw what looked like a bat ear protruding above it. No matter who-what-the intruder was, Alice was ready for it.

"Hey! Get off of there, whatever you are!' Alice said, forcefully, though the intruder did not reply. "Don't mess with me! I have a lamp and I know how to use it!" The intruder grasped the top of the television with its long, bony fingers, and peeked over it with what appeared to be enormous green eyes. It was then that it complied with Alice's request and jumped down onto the floor, so Alice could see it.

"Oh, hi there! Didn't expect you back so soon!" it said, as if Alice should already be familiar with it. Alice was at a loss for words trying to process its appearance. Its massive head was home to large, bat like ears, massive, monochrome green eyes, two slits which she guessed were its nostrils, and a long mouth lined with sharp teeth, and fixated in a grin that was equal parts stupid and unsettling. Its neck was positively tiny, and its body was thin, though somewhat ovular. Its limbs were long and thin, and it had opposable toes as well as thumbs. Oh my God, Alice thought to herself. If this thing was an alien she had the scoop of a lifetime. She was going to be famous. The networks would fight over her! She'd have an office and a home on Manhattan's Fifth Avenue in no time. Thank God she hadn't called the police.

For a few moments, neither of them said anything, so Alice took it upon herself to break this awkward silence. "What-are you doing-in my-house?!" Alice asked. She cautioned herself play along with whatever he said. This creature was going to be her big break.

"Actually, I was waiting for you," the intruder said, "Sorry about the mess, I'd've gotten around to cleaning up sooner, but-"

"What did you do with my gun!?" Alice interrupted.

"Oh, well, I used it to fix your toaster," the intruder sheepishly admitted, "incidentally, I've got some going now, but, given the circumstances, I suppose it's only fair if you had it-that is, i-if you'd like it."

"I don't want any damn toast!" Alice said before forcing herself to calm down. "I want you to tell me who you are! What you are! And why exactly were you waiting for me, anyway?"

"In order: Vice-President Fulton, gremlin, and because the world may well be in terrible danger." At this, Alice's anger was replaced by a mixture of curiosity and confusion.

"Danger? From what, exactly?"

"My goodness, you are so full of questions," Fulton said, "well, I can't explain myself, but I can take you to someone who will! This way, please!" With that, Fulton dashed off to the back door of Alice's house, and Alice went with him visions of anchoring the eleven o'clock news dancing in her head. They went outside, to Alice's backyard, the cool autumn wind blowing the leaves about. Here, Fulton indicated the large hole in the center of Alice's backyard that seemed to extend endlessly down into the dark.

"Yeah, it's a sink hole, all right," Alice said, "just like the other 255 we've dealt with this week. What does that have to do with anything?"

"It's not the hole itself," Fulton explained, "it's what's at the bottom of it. We need to go down there."

Alice was very incredulous. "Uhm, Fulton? I don't know how familiar you are with human anatomy, but if I were to jump down that hole, I would die."

"That you would," Fulton responded, "which is why we're not going to do that." With that, Fulton produced what appeared to be a television remote control from the front pocket of his shirt.

"Uh, Fulton? What are you-" before Alice could finish, Fulton pressed a button, which caused what looked like an elevator to blast up from the hole. It was tall enough so for Alice to be able to stand comfortably in it.

"...Huh," Alice said, finding no other way to respond.

"Well, goin' down," Fulton said, already heading to the elevator. He gestured for Alice to come over, but she remained where she stood.

"Well, come on!" he said impatiently.

"That thing won't go down as fast as it came up, will it?" Alice said apprehensively. "The shock from the landing could kill me."

"Don't worry! You'll be fine," he said. "Quickly, please! It's a matter of national security!"

"In for a penny," Alice muttered to herself as she ran over to the elevator. Once there, she stood near Fulton, and tried to prepare herself for the fast drop as best as she could.

"Are you ready, miss...?"

"Minear. Alice Minear," she said, "and yes, I'm ready," she lied.

"Alright, here we go!" Fulton said, again pressing the button. Alice flinched, expecting to plummet at an insane speed but the elevator was much slower than she expected it to be. As they descended into darkness, a bulb on the underside of the elevator's roof lit up, allowing Alice to see. Not that there was much to see, besides Fulton.

"So, how long are we going to be on this thing? Alice asked.

"It should be another five minutes or so," Fulton said, "why do you ask?"

"Just a little claustrophobic, that's all," Alice responded, "so...gremlins," she said, looking at the creature in front of her. "That's what you are, right? Aren't you supposed to be extinct?" She'd seen a picture that looked a lot like Fulton in an old history book. She was slightly deflated. Gremlins would still make the national news but not the same way that aliens would have. Still her story would start off with '...long believed to be extinct a thriving society lives in secrecy beneath us...'

"Supposed to be, but not actually", Fulton responded cheerfully.

"Obviously," Alice said, "but what about that plague that 'supposedly' wiped all of you out in the Fifties?"

"Plague?" Fulton said, mildly astonished, "My, humans are so over-the top, aren't they?" He continued, trying not to laugh and failing miserably.

"Okay, okay," Alice said, silently wondering what exactly Fulton found so funny about lethal epidemics, "but then, why go into hiding like this, so deep underground?"

"Now that is a long story", Fulton said.

"Well, it's not like we have much else to do down here," Alice quipped, "fire away."

"Let's see...", Fulton said, going over the facts in his head, "It all started about one hundred thousand years ago. You see, gremlins once lived in a whole 'nother dimension, but one day, a massive portal opened up that sucked us all up and spat us out here!"

"You're not just making this up, are you?" Alice said, skeptical almost in spite of herself.

"If I were, don't you think I'd've come up with something more plausible?" Fulton responded, feigning offense, "Anyway, at first, all we could think of was to try to get back home, but we couldn't figure out how, even after all the time we spent trying. Being as we were a very technological society, while mankind...wasn't, so much, we mostly stayed separate, hid ourselves away. But as humans became more advanced, we became more interested. Still, we remained secretive, taking only what we thought might be useful."

Apocalypse 13

"So you were thieves?" Alice inquired.

"We preferred to think of it as borrowing," Fulton said, "and please don't interrupt, it is very rude."

"Sorry", Alice muttered.

"As I was saying, we were content to 'borrow' what we needed for some time, but as time went on, we figured that if we lived alongside humans, we could reap the benefits of their technology as well as help them to advance much more quickly. Our leaders decided to show ourselves to the American president Teddy Roosevelt as he seemed to be most equipped to deal with our existence. He was able to deal with our existence but other Americans...Well...the transition where we showed ourselves was tumultuous at first, to say the least. We never expanded beyond America fearing that our deaths would be far greater in countries with less of a 'live and let live' attitude. Our integration was helped greatly by the First World War. Yes, our skill with machines, particularly with taking them apart, was very beneficial to the Allies in those times. We ran a secret task force in Virginia to help decode enemy munitions. We were so useful, that we were called on us again to help fight the Axis Powers in the Second World War."

"Okay, so if you were so involved, how come you went into hiding again?" Alice asked.

"Well," Fulton continued, "After World War Two was over, tensions between America and the USSR shot up like a rocket. Our existence was not exactly a secret- many Americans knew about us after all-and the GRU soon discovered our tasks. The FBI, fearing that the USSR would kidnap some of us, potentially escalating the Cold War asked us to go underground. Of course, we could still come and go as we liked, but only if we stayed hidden. As we were so secretive to begin with, it wasn't too hard. But it seems, in order to keep us hidden; the government had to come up with a reason for all of us to suddenly disappear. Hence, I suppose, the alleged plague."

Alice's head spun, not only from Fulton's tale, but also from a foul stench of oil and engine fumes that now permeated the air.

"What is that reek?" she asked Fulton.

"Ah! We must be close to home", he said. Before Alice could say anything else, the narrow stone walls of the elevator shaft gave way to a wide expanse of massive machines with exposed parts, lined by long metal walkways, all lined with various workers-gremlins-going about their business. In the center of it all was what appeared to be some sort of generator with pipes extending from the machine all the way up to the top of the complex. Alice was so in awe of it all, she almost forgot about smell that seemed to permeate the world she now found herself in.

As soon as the elevator hit bottom, Fulton darted off again. Rolling her eyes, Alice followed, attempting to keep up as best she could. When Fulton, finally stopped, they had arrived at an ornate door only slightly shorter than Alice herself, which had no apparent way to open it.

"Can we—maybe not—sprint—everywhere from now on?" Alice said, panting.

"Sorry about that," Fulton said, entering a combination on a panel near the door, "Ah! There we are!" he said as the panel beeped and the door opened. He went inside, and Alice followed. Within the room there was a large, ornate desk practically buried under disheveled piles of papers.

"Mr. President!" Fulton said, "I have brought who you requested!" A blue-eyed gremlin wearing what looked like a highly decorated aviator's hat and an eye patch over his right eye emerged from under some papers, as if he'd just been woken up. Alice presumed this was the president.

"Ah, good! Very good!" The president said, as he approached Alice. "You're the first human we've let down here in some time." The president extended his hand out to her, and, not wanting to be rude, Alice shook it. The president then noticed something on Alice's hand, and retracted his own.

"Ay! Ma'am, you've been cut!" The president said, rushing over to his desk, and scattering the papers that lay on it randomly around the room.

"So I have," Alice said, "must've happened when I climbed through that window", she said to herself, "but it's fine, really, I-"

"Nonsense!" The president said, "I'll not have the visit of the first human we've had in decades be marred by injury!" With that, he finally found what he was looking for-a button, which he promptly slammed. "Paging Dr. Planck! You're needed urgently!"

"Whatever for?" A deep, tired sounding voice responded over the intercom.

"No time to explain!" The president said, breathlessly, "just get to my office as quick as you can!" The president then turned to see Alice and Fulton, both looking slightly stunned. "Sorry about that," he said, "Oh! I forgot to introduce myself! How rude of me! I am Whitney-President Whitney, I should say, and you are...?"

"Alice Minear," she said, "so...why did you have me brought down here anyway?"

"Oh, right," Whitney said, his features becoming stern, "You see, most gremlins are, if not content, then at least tolerant toward our current...arrangement. However..."

"However?" Alice repeated.

"There are some who are not. In this case, four gremlins who're locked up, and for good reason, I might add. Or rather, they were, until recently."

"Okay...so what do you need me for?"

"Well, we suspect that they have escaped to the surface, and are planning...something. We don't know what it is yet, but it can't be good. So what you need to do is find out what they're doing and stop them from doing it. Since you're an investigative reporter you should be able to figure that out."

"Could what they're doing be connected to all those sinkholes that've been popping up lately?" Alice thought aloud.

"That's very possible, and actually that leads me to my next point-You know this town like the back of your hand, yes?" the president said.

"I...guess so," Alice responded, "but I don't-"

"They'd most likely gather in a secluded place with access to a lot of machinery," The president interrupted, "do you know of any place like that?"

"Oh! The old scrapyard across town!" Alice said, "but...what makes you think they're still in town?"

"Well, gremlins, even vicious criminals, don't tend to wander too far from home if they can help it" Whitney explained.

"So, which prisoners have escaped, Mr. President?" Fulton asked.

"Well, there was-" Whitney started, before being interrupted by his door opening again. Alice turned around to see who she presumed to be Dr. Planck. Planck's eyes were a foreboding red, one scarred and nearly shut, and both sunk into his head, lined by dark circles. Part of his right ear appeared to have been bitten off, and his head sat upon an unusually long, though hunched over, neck. His other limbs were also unusually long. All this unnerved Alice as he approached her.

"Human?" he said, in a tone that made it apparent that he found her presence unusual, though not particularly interesting, "Are you who I have been sent for?"

"Uh...yeah" Alice said, still somewhat nervous.

"What is troubling you?" Planck asked.

"This right here." Alice said, indicating the cut on the palm of her right hand. Planck briefly shot the president a look, as if admonishing him for wasting his time, before reaching into his bag, and holding out the retrieved item to Alice.

"A bandage," he said, "I trust you can take it from here?"

"Yeah," Alice said, taking the band aid and placing it over her cut.

"Then I suppose my work here is done" Planck said sounding glad to finally be rid of these people. Alice, frankly, felt the same way towards Planck.

"Hold up one moment, doctor!" Whitney said, as Planck was about to leave.

"What is it now?" Planck said.

"You're going with Alice and Fulton to retrieve the criminal scum currently lurking somewhere on the surface."

"I am?" Planck said, dreading the assignment.

"He is?" Alice said at the same time.

"Of course! Always good to have a medic, after all!" Whitney said, "Oh, and Fulton? Before you go, I want you to have...this" he said, and held up a red helmet with a green visor. Fulton was at a loss for words for a moment.

"Wow. thanks so much, sir!" He said, delightedly, while putting the helmet on, "but, how will-"

"That," Whitney interrupted, "will make you my eyes and ears on the surface. I'm counting on all of you, and especially on you, Fulton."

"Yes sir!" Fulton said, saluting. He then darted off yet again, toward the elevator dragging Alice with Planck following immediately behind. Alice wishing she had gotten many more answers asked, "Who exactly escaped? Why am I going along on this rescue?"

Fulton ignored her questions, positioning her on the now tight elevator to the surface. "Later. Later."

"I hope one of you knows what we're doing once we're up there" Planck said.

"Of course we do!" Fulton said, and he pressed his trigger again, sending the elevator rocketing up to the surface again. After the three were finished reeling from their trip, Alice headed toward her back door.

"Where are you going?" Fulton asked.

"I just have to get my keys," Alice responded, "we're going to take my car and head over to the scrapyard". Once inside Alice sat down heavily on her bed. If she was going to back out-now was the moment to do so. Fortuitously-or not-the phone rang. It was her boss updating her on her schedule for tomorrow-if she felt better. Her brilliant assignment was to interview the oldest twins in Vale-age 98. Stories like that would never get her called up to the big leagues.

Decision made, Alice emerged from her house once again, her keys in hand. "Come on, boys!" Alice said, "We're goin' out to fight evil!" With that, the trio headed over to Alice's car. As Alice unlocked the doors she asked, "Who exactly are we up against, anyway?"

Fulton cleared his throat, preparing to say his piece when Planck interrupted, "Well, there's Mendel-"

"Likely the 'brains' of the outfit, if you can call him that" Fulton fought to regain control of the coversation.

"And Ford-

"The muscle, and not much else, frankly". Fulton shot Planck an annoyed look before continuing, "And the twins, Graham and Bell-"

"Two halves of one idiot".

"They don't sound that threatening..." Alice remarked.

"Ma'am believe me when I say this: there are few things more dangerous than a simpleton on a mission," Planck said, "Well, we should get going." With that, they all entered the car, Alice taking the wheel, Fulton hiding in the space beneath the dashboard on the passenger's side, and Planck hid in the space between the front and back seats.

"Drive carefully, please" Fulton said.

"I always do", Alice responded.

"I hope so," Planck said, "for all our sakes". The drive passed without incident, until they approached the scrapyard. When it was in sight, so close that Alice could practically taste it, the road was blocked by construction work.

"Why have we stopped?" Fulton said.

"Relax, I'll take care of it," Alice said, "just don't move out from under there!" That said, Alice opened her window and hailed one of the workers.

"Hey! Hey buddy!" Alice said, "C'mere!" One of the workers promptly obliged.

"Yeah, whatcha need, ma'am?" He said, his smoky breath permeating Alice's car.

"Well, I need to get to the scrapyard."

"Well, I'm sad to say, I can't letcha go there," he said, "yanno how ya said the roads'd be cleared up if there was no further incident? Well, we just got a whole load o' 'further incident' all up that way."

Alice flipped open her wallet and showed her Channel 9 identification. "I'm working on a story. It's about the sink holes and..."

Before she'd finished her sentence the flagman interrupted, "I'll see what I can do," he said, pulling out a walkie-talkie from his belt, "Hey Frankie! How's th' road lookin' up there!?" By the volume of his voice, Alice presumed he hadn't quite grasped the concept of how a walkie-talkie works.

"Should be good t' go right about...now" Frankie's voice crackled through the walkie-talkie.

"Well, that was quick" Alice remarked thinking to herself that the power of television was impressive. People would bend over backwards to let her through where anyone else would never be allowed.

"Ya don't get the State's Most Efficient Construction Company Award for no good reason," he said proudly, before becoming more serious, "Now listen: Anything that happens to you up there is on your own head, got it?"

"Relax, I'll be fine!" Alice said. The worker removed the roadblocks, and just after he'd accomplished that, Alice drove off, once again her mind darting in another direction. "We've got to be quick at the scrap yard. I just realized my sister's flight was due to land..." she glanced down at her watch, "... an hour ago." She was interrupted by her phone ringing and closed her eyes for a second. She couldn't be that unlucky. The plane couldn't have landed on time, could it? She retrieved the infernal devise and checked who was calling her. Her heart sank bit as she saw who it was: Catherine.

"Oh, speak of every last demon in Hell" she said frustrated, before answering her sister's call.

"Hi, Cat" she said, her saccharine tone drastically overcompensating for her actual frustration.

"Hey, Ali," Catherine responded, "how's my favorite sister?"

"Cat, unless there's a lot Mom hasn't told me, I'm pretty sure I'm still your only sister," Alice said dryly, "So, what's up?"

"Amazingly, my flight actually managed to be on time for once. I've been waiting on you for an hour!" Catherine said.

"Oh, I'm sorry."

"Ah, don't be," Catherine said, "I tell you what I'm going to do: I'll call a cab and meet you at your place after you're done doing...whatever it is you're doing. Where are you, anyway?"

"Uhm I'm chasing a story," Alice said, dodging Catherine's inquiry entirely. "I'll catch you up when I get home." With that, she hung up, glad to have ended that conversation. She briefly wondered what Catherine would do once she actually got to her house and saw the mess there, but refocused her mind on more pressing matters as she pulled into the scrap yard. She then got out of her car, and took a moment to stretch her legs, her feet kicking up dirt from the ground as she stepped down. Fulton and Planck soon followed suit.

"Would it have killed you to drive a little slower?" Planck said, trying to work out the pain in his neck, as well as relieve himself of his soreness.

"Well, it's not like we're taking a trip to the park," Alice said, "time is of the essence! Especially since I've got to get home to my sister. Those four should be around here somewhere if they're really attracted to metal and old bits and pieces."

They wandered the scrapyard, searching among the abandoned wreckage of nonworking cars and rusted, worn demolition equipment for any sign of the criminals they set out to track. The dust they kicked up with every step irritated their eyes. Just when they were ready to give up searching, Fulton spotted something in the distance: another demolition vehicle, a digger, but a good deal more well-maintained than the others.

"That's it!" Fulton said, "I'm sure of it!"

"We should get closer to see if that's the case," Planck said, "stay close, stay low, and move as quietly as you can." They did so, approaching the vehicle, using the rusted wreckage of cars strewn about the yard for cover. Finally, they reached one car, close enough that they could see inside the vehicle where they thought that the four fugitive gremlins might be. Fulton took a quick look over the roof of the car they hid behind, and confirmed their suspicions.

"There! I see them!" Fulton said. Planck pulled Fulton down, which caused Fulton to land on his back.

"For heaven's sake, man, keep your voice down!" Planck said.

"Did you get a good look at them?" Alice asked.

"Yes, there was one with gray eyes, two with one blue and orange eye, and a...a burlier one. I couldn't see his eyes. He was wearing a helmet that looked kind of like mine".

"Looks like we've found the idiot brigade," Planck said, "so...what's the plan?"

"I've got something in mind," Fulton said. Planck was already rolling his eyes. "Follow my lead, Doctor". With that, Fulton emerged from their hiding spot, and Planck followed, hoping against hope that Fulton knew what he was doing.

"Excuse me!" Fulton said, waving in an attempt to get their attention, "Uhm, Mr.Mendel, was it?" he said, adressing the gray-eyed gremlin, "We have...your pills! Yes!" Mendel looked back at his cohorts with the most skeptical expression imaginable, and they responded in kind. Still, Mendel decided to play along, if only for a laugh.

"These pills...what are they meant to treat, exactly?" Mendel said, attempting to hide his sarcasm while his cohorts stifled their laughter.

"Uh, well...you see, you have...vitamin deficiency! Yes, that's it! Planck actually found out about it earlier but he lost his pills, and I was just walking along one day and what should I find but those same pills!" Fulton nudged Planck, who quickly reached into his bag and pulled out a bottle of pills, silently thankful he had them in the first place, and held them up so Mendel could see.

"So, if you just let us come in there, we can give them to you, and be on our merry way!" Fulton said, hoping that the "idiot brigade" would buy it.

"I have a better idea," Mendel said, "How about Fulton takes those pills to me by himself? There's not really enough space in here for two more in here".

"Yeah! Not enough space!" Graham and Bell said, simultaneously. Fulton was very nervous, now. This wasn't going at all how he'd expected it to. Still, he couldn't back out now. He held out his hand, Planck gave him the pills, and Fulton went over to the digger, and clambered inside. It felt very strange, being surrounded by his enemies. He handed the pills to Mendel.

"Thank, you, Mr. Vice-President," Medel said, "So nice of you to come all this way just for the sake of my health, and to be our hostage".

"You're quite welcome, I-wait, what!?" Fulton said, thrown by Mendel's declaration.

Alice stooped down and whispered incredulously to Planck, "He's your Vice-President?"

Watching his incompetent handling of the affair to date she wouldn't have elected him to chief dog walker.

"The president knows that as long as Fulton is his replacement no one will ever get rid of him," Planck whispered back.

"Ah, the Vice-President, our hostage. I honestly didn't think things would go this well for us!" He said, bragging to his cohorts and rubbing in Fulton's severe error in judgment.

"Hey, what's that?" Graham and Bell said, both pointing to movement they saw behind a nearby car. "It looks like..."

"A human!" Mendel said. Suddenly, the burly (by gremlin standards) Ford shoved Mendel out of the way, taking the controls of the digger himself.

"Relax, I'll handle this" Ford said, and he drove the digger forward toward the car, toward Alice. Alice turned around, and saw the arm of the digger right above her head. The sight frightened her to the point where she froze, and time itself seemed to slow as the digger's arm descended, as she prepared for death. Just then, the digger swerved in place, the arm missing Alice and slamming into the ground, kicking up massive amounts of dust. Nobody in the yard could see a thing for a few moments.

Inside the digger, Mendel forced Ford's hands off of the controls, looking apoplectic at Ford.

"ARE YOU CRAZY!?" Mendel yelled.

"Yeah are you crazy?" The twins repeated.

"Don't tell me you're growing a conscience now" Ford said condescendingly.

"No," Mendel responded, "but think, man! She's a human! A famous one, at that! If we killed her, word would get out, and every lawman in the state, or even the country, would investigate, and it would lead back to us! Do you want that!?"

"...No" Ford responded.

"Good," Mendel said, "Now, it's time for Plan B. Follow my lead, and for heaven's sake, don't improvise, this time!" That said, Mendel grabbed Fulton and threw him out of the digger. He then opened the door and jumped out, his cohorts doing likewise.

"Well, girls, it's been fun!" Mendel said, pulling out a trigger similar to Fulton's own, "But I'm afraid that now, we must make our grand exit!" Mendel pressed his trigger, causing a plume of dust to spurt up behind the digger. The four conspirators rushed into that plume, and then vanished. Fulton was still reeling from his fall, and Alice and Planck rushed over to him.

"Are you hurt?" Alice said with concern, reaching a hand down to help Fulton.

"Only my pride," Fulton said, taking Alice's hand, "Ow! And my spine!"

"What were you thinking?" Planck said, "Are you a complete idiot?"

"Would a complete idiot have managed to steal...this?" Fulton said, revealing a furled sheet of paper.

"In this case, yes," Planck said, "let me see it!" He said, snatching the paper from Fulton and unfurling it.

"This looks like plans for some kind of sinkhole generator," he said, "Fulton, I'm legitimately impressed!"

"Hey, let me look," Alice said, swiping the blueprints from Planck, "this looks like that thing in the forest I covered this morning," she said, as if she'd just discovered a great truth, "way to go, Fulton!" she said. All this delighted Fulton; he was not used to receiving this much praise from his peers, especially not Planck.

"Don't expect this to be a trend, Alice," Planck said, settling into his usual, dour demeanor.

"Come on, boys," Alice said now fully invested in the adventure, "we're going to the forest!"

The journey to the forest went without incident. They then worked their way through the forest, through the rustling leaves still blowing in the wind, dreading what they might find. As Alice approached the device, tension grew within her. That was when she noticed that, while Planck was following her, Fulton had fallen behind.

"Uh, Doc? Where's Fulton?" Alice said. Planck let out a weary sigh.

"I don't know, but I'd better find him, before he hurts himself". Just after Planck had finished his sentence, Fulton emerged from a thick cluster of trees to the east, sporting many battle scars. He walked with a staggered gate, and his right eye was twitching, either from pain or fear.

"My God, man, what happened to you!?" Alice said.

"I had a run-in with a vicious little dog," Fulton said, weakly, "but I'll be alright".

"A dog did this to you?" Planck said, at once incredulous and condescending.

"You don't understand," Fulton said, "that was no normal dog. That was approximately eight-and-a-half pounds of pure evil covered in fur!" Alice was fairly certain of the identity of the dog Fulton was referring to, and the prospect that the dog was running around somewhere nearby unsettled her deeply.

"Guys," she said, "we should find that sinkhole machine and get out of here, quick! This way!" She led them to the generator, all the while dreading an encounter with the police, four fugitives, or worse, Mrs. Lutz' demonic terrier. The three were surprised to find that the generator was completely unguarded.

"What did I tell you?" Planck said, "Idiots". The gremlins promptly got to work on dismantling the generator. Alice was amazed by the sight: She had never seen any creature move as fast as the gremlins did while they went about their work. About two minutes later, the machine was completely destroyed. That was when Alice's phone rang again. Alice answered it reflexively, certain it would be Catherine yet again.

"Hello?" she said.

"So, as it happens, you have a sister," a voice said. Alice's eyes went wide as she remembered who that voice belonged to.

"How did you know that?" Alice said, "How did you get this number?"

"Never mind that," Mendel said, "I have news: it so happens that we're related, because I have your sister as well! Say hello, Kitty!"

"Alice, I am in deep shit here," Catherine said, "help."

"If you do anything to hurt her, I swear to God-" Alice said, furiously.

"Relax, just head over to your place, and kindly bring your merry band of simpletons along with you", Mendel said, mockingly. Fulton and Planck looked at Alice, silently wondering what had just happened.

"The idiot brigade is holding my sister hostage in my own house!" Alice said.

"That's...bad" Planck said.

"Uh, yes!" Alice said, "Don't just stand around, guys, we need to go, already!" Catherine and Alice might not be that close, but Catherine was still her sister. Alice practically sprinted to her car, the gremlins nearly failing to keep pace with her speed. Alice drove to her house breaking every speed limit along the way and a single-minded determination that the gremlins would not have expected from her before. When they finally arrived, the car's tires screeched to a stop, almost crashing into her house. She got out of her car and rushed for the door, and the gremlins followed suit. Then, they entered to find them: the idiot brigade, surrounding Catherine, who had been tied to a chair and...was that a chessboard between Catherine and Mendel?

"Alice! Thank God!" Catherine said, "They tied me up like an animal, and...and he cheats!" she said, indicating Mendel.

"It isn't my fault that you're no good at this game" Mendel said, defensively. Graham and Bell approached the board, and observed it for a moment.

"Yeah, checkmate on black in two moves" they said, in sync.

"Where? I don't see" Mendel said.

"Enough of this" Ford said, and he suddenly drew a sword and held it to Catherine's throat. Catherine's eyes went wide with fright.

"Hey, let's not do anything hasty," Alice said, quickly losing her nerve, "what can I do for you so no one gets hurt"?

"The plans Fulton stole from us," Mendel said, "return them, now!" It was then that Alice hatched a plan of her own. She didn't know if it would work, but she had to try.

"I have 'em, right here," Alice said, showing the plans to Mendel and the others, "one of you come over here, and I'll give them to you, then you give me my sister, and we never have to deal with each other again. Alright"? Without even thinking, Bell approached Alice. She gave him the plans, and he turned around to head back to his group. That was when Alice made her move. She grabbed Bell's arm in one hand, and with the other, grabbed the lamp that had been laying on the floor since her encounter with Fulton.

"Alright, here's the new deal," Alice said, wearing a slightly crazed expression on her face, "You let my sister go and turn yourselves in, or I cave this little guy's head in. And I really don't want to do that".

"You could just let me go, then" Bell said, sheepishly.

"Shut up," Alice said, "So, what'll it be"?

"Do what she says," Graham said, begging Mendel, tears forming in his eyes.

"Please?" Mendel was at an impasse, cursing his rotten luck. Finally, after taking a bit of time for mental wailing and gnashing of teeth, he came to his decision.

"Drop your weapon, Ford," Mendel said. Ford complied without complaint, "Well, it looks like you've outsmarted us. Good for you" he said, sarcastically.

"It's not like it was hard," Alice said, "now, untie my sister". Mendel did so, and Catherine went over to Alice's side.

"Right, that's that," Mendel said, "Now, let Bell go".

"Not until you're all tied up, so I know you won't try anything funny," Alice said, "Boys"? Fulton and Planck went around the room, using the rope that the idiot brigade had used to tie each of them up. Fulton held onto the remaining length of the rope, leading the four conspirators to Alice's back door. Alice and Planck followed.

That was almost too easy, Alice thought to herself. Then she looked at all of the gremlins. They were funny little creatures-and not one of them seemed to be overly smart. Maybe it wasn't too easy after all.

"Alright, boys, c'mon," Fulton said, "we're taking you home." Alice once again opened her back door, and Fulton retrieved his remote, calling up the elevator again. They all got on it, and once more it descended. As they approached the end of the line, Alice noticed that the previous stench the place had given off was gone.

The elevator finally hit bottom, and Alice, Catherine, Planck and Fulton stepped off, their prisoners still in tow. To their surprise, Whitney was already out of his office, seemingly waiting for their arrival.

"You've brought them back!" Whitney said, "Well done"!

"Yeah," Alice said, self-congratulating, "and not only that, but we also busted up the idiot brigade's little contraption up on the surface'.

"Oh, that's even better!" Whitney said, "Now, we can finally get somewhere! Guards! Escort the prisoners to their cells"!

"Finally," Planck said, "May I go, now"?

"You're excused", Whitney said, and Planck shuffled off, heading back to his office, while two gremlins, the guards Whitney had called for, approached the group. To Alice's surprise and dismay, the guards freed Ford and the idiot squad while cuffing herself, Catherine, and Fulton!

"Hey!" Alice said, "What's the meaning of this"!?

"Oh, you want an explanation," Whitney said, his smile a little maniacal, "well, I don't want to bore you with a long story, so I'll just tell you the ending: The human world is literally crumbling to dust due to massive earthquakes all over the world, caused by this baby," he said, indicating the massive generator, "and upon its ruins, I will begin construction on a new land for gremlins, infinitely more vast and glorious than any that has existed before!"

"Then why did you send us out in the first place? Why get me involved?" Alice demanded furious. She could have spent her last days in ignorance. Not apparently helping to end the world.

"That idiot Fulton put everything in motion before I could stop him."

"So what are you going to do now that we know?" Alice said, "Kill us"? Whitney seemed to take offense at Alice's comment.

"What do you take me for?" Whitney said, "Some kind of barbarian? But it was nice of you to come back down here where your police will never find you.'

He then turned to Ford and said, "Mr. Ford! Take your position"!

"Yes sir!" Ford said, and he clambered up to the top of the generator and entered the dome there. Whitney then approached Fulton, who, at this point, was torn between being bewildered and despair.

"I have to say, Fulton, I couldn't have done it without you," he said sardonically, "but I'll be needing this back" and he swiped Fulton's helmet from him. Then he turned to the guards and said, "Now, if you would, kindly remove these...interlopers from my sight". The guards heeded Whitney's command, escorting Alice, Catherine, and Fulton to a cell of their own. The trio was led down a very long hallway looking even more in disrepair than the rest of the complex. The guards finally stopped just as Alice was wondering how far the underground world of the gremlins extended.

"This is a prison?" Catherine said, observing what appeared to be more a moderately well-furnished, though small, hotel room than a cell, behind the glass wall, "Man, after I get evicted I hope I can get a room like this."

Alice turned abruptly towards her sister, "Is that why you flew out here on no notice?"

Catherine scuffed her feet across the floor, "Well, yeah. I got laid off and I can't find another job and..."

"See, it's not so bad," one guard said, while the other entered a combination on a nearby panel "but if you don't find it to your liking, don't worry; one way or another, you won't be in here for long" he said, while his partner finally completed his work, causing the glass to slide up. The three were then rather rudely pushed inside, and the glass slid down once more.

"So long, girls!" The first guard said, producing a trigger which caused the cuffs the trio were in to loosen, and fall to the ground, "Now, if you'll excuse us, we have work to do. After all, the human world won't end itself"! The guards then promptly scurried off, leaving the three all alone.

Alice, her reminiscing finished, glanced at the clock in the corner of the room. Only a few minutes had passed. It seemed time went slowly when one was waiting for the apocalypse. Fulton, having finished regaling Catherine, went back to his work, snatching the clock away from Alice's sight. Suddenly, the glass wall of their prison opened once more, and Alice saw several familiar faces standing before them.

"Hello again, ladies," Planck said, "Sorry we're late".

"Uhm...who's 'we'"? Alice said.

"Greetings once more from the idiot brigade!" Mendel said, revealing himself, Graham and Bell, "Long time no see, hmn"?

"Not long enough" Catherine said.

"This isn't some kind of trick, is it?" Alice said.

"We're double agents," Mendel offered brightly.

Alice turned to Planck-the only gremlin who'd made total sense through the whole insane day.

"This isn't some kind of trick," she demanded.

"Not at all," Planck said, "I should explain. You see, Whitney and I actually served in World War II. After the war, we were banished from earth. Some thought we should be lauded for our actions. Whitney was one of them. Evidentially he's still bitter."

"You knew this would happen the whole time?" Alice asked.

"Suspected."

"Well why didn't you tell us sooner?"

"Because he made Fulton his eyes and ears," Planck said, "and if I'd tampered with the device in some way, Whitney would've found me out. But that's not important now. What is important is making sure Whitney's mad plan fails".

"And how do we do that?" Mendel said, "We've tried just about everything, and nothing worked!"

"There is one way," Planck said, "I actually helped construct the earthquake generator, and I installed a failsafe which would cause the device to undergo a catastrophic breakdown if activated: Two panels on the left and right sides of the device that can only be activated by contact with human blood".

"Oh," Catherine said, "Okay, I have a plan."

"What is it?" Graham said.

"Cat and I run for those panels, activate them, and everyone goes home happy!"

"You can't just rush in there with Ford working the defense systems," Mendel said, "its suicide!"

"Well, how about this," Alice said, "Fulton and Doc go out there and deal with Ford, Mendel busts up the defense systems, and Cat and I go out there and bring the thing down".

"What do we do"?

"Your job's to be as annoying as possible," Alice said, "to distract Ford and Whitney while we do our work." From what Alice had seen that wouldn't be hard. The twins looked at each other for a moment, and then turned to Catherine.

"We can do that" The twins said, surprised and delighted to finally be back in sync.

"What is that thing?" Mendel said,, indicating Fulton's contraption.

"Oh, this?" Fulton said, revealing it to be a gun nearly as big as he was, "This is a little something for the president".

"What are we waiting for?" Alice said, "C'mon, boys! The world isn't going to save itself."

They ran down the long hall, toward the generator, bound and determined to succeed. All of them waited at the end of the hall, out of sight, except Graham and Bell, who rushed out to set the plan in motion. Whitney was shocked to see that the twins had escaped.

"What's the meaning of this!?" He said angrily, "No matter. Mr. Ford, kindly put these little snits out of my misery"!

"With pleasure!" Ford said, and he activated the generators' defense systems, attempting to rain bullets down upon the twins. However the closer they were to the generator the safer they were. The machine was built for long distance-not short range and Ford was essentially trying to bend the guns back on itself to attack them.

"What's a matter?" They said, mockingly, "Can't even shoot straight"? This had the intended effect of making Ford even more enraged, focusing on trying to kill the twins, to the point where he didn't even notice Mendel and Planck rushing for the generator.

"Ford, you idiot, forget the twins! We've got bigger problems!" Whitney yelled. Ford ignored him, continuing to try to murder the twins, while Mendel leapt onto the machine, tearing away anything he could get his hands on, while Planck made his way up to Ford. Whitney swung at Planck attempting to deal with the interlopers himself, when suddenly, the humans appeared, running for the generator as well. Whitney moaned, wondering how it could get any worse, when suddenly a shot rang out, passing just above his head!

"What was that!?" He said, looking around for the source of the blast, shocked at who he found, "Fulton!?" He said, backing away as Fulton approached him, but not quick enough. Fulton suddenly bum-rushed Whitney, knocking the President to the ground and pointing his weapon right between his eyes.

"You don't have to do this, you know" Whitney said, desperately.

"I know," Fulton said, smugly. He looked up at the machine, only to find two great blades had emerged above where Alice and Catherine now stood, and cried out, "Alice! Catherine! Look out!" But it was too late. Or so he thought, for suddenly the generator's upper half suddenly swerved, the blades barely missing the girls. Planck had saved them, and managed to incapacitate Ford as well.

"Hey, what's goin' on!? I can't get this thing off!" Ford said, referring to his seatbelt, which Planck had broken, "Whatever happened to 'do no harm', Doc"?

"That only applies to patients, and you nearly made me lose mine," Planck said, before exiting the dome. "Now, girls!" he yelled down to Alice and Catherine.

Alice and Catherine were more nervous now than ever, but they steeled themselves. This was the moment of truth. They each ran their hands along the generator's blades, drawing blood, and placed their hands on the panels on the sides of the machine. After they had done that, the pipes at the top of the machine broke off, and an alarm sounded. Alice, Catherine, and every gremlin in the complex promptly fled for safety, except Ford, who could not, and Whitney who would not.

A series of explosions had begun to erupt from within the machine.

"Hurry up, Planck!" Alice said. Debris was raining down on all of the gremlins jammed into the tunnel. "We're going to get killed out here."

"I am trying!" Planck said, frantically typing in numbers on the panel. After a few more seconds, he succeeded, and they all crammed themselves into the office, the door closing behind them. The sound of explosions continued for a few minutes more, and then, silence.

"Is that it?" Alice said. The door opened again, and they all exited the room to find the smoldering remains of the generator, blood seeping out from under the broken device the only sign of Ford and Whitney.

"We did it!" Alice said, "Yeah!" The others expressed similar sentiments. Then, Fulton had a realization.

"I guess..." Fulton said, "this means that...I'M president now...wow".

"Not just yet" Planck said.

"Oh, right," Fulton said, clearing his throat, "As my Vice-President, I pick...Dr. Planck"!

"What, me?" Planck said, a bit stunned, "I figured Mendel..."

"Yes you, and rest assured, things'll be a lot different under us".

"Well, as much fun as all this has been," Catherine said, "I think Ali and I need to go home now, 'cause I, for one, have had enough excitement for ten lifetimes."

"Alright" Fulton said, and he escorted the girls to the elevator once again. Alice and Catherine got on the elevator, and Fulton got his trigger once more.

"Well...I guess...this is...goodbye" Alice said, with a twinge of sadness.

"...For now" Fulton said, smiling and activating the trigger again, sending Alice and Catherine to the surface.

Early the next day Alice dressed with special care and grabbed her pocketbook.

"Hey, where're you going?" Catherine said.

"Work" Alice responded, shrugging. When she was out the door, she got out her phone, and called a fellow anchor.

"Hi, Steve" Alice said.

"You sound pretty good for someone with strep throat" Steve quipped.

"I lied," she said calmly. "I was off following a hunch and the boss man wanted me to do a local color piece." Alice said.

"Well?" Steve asked impatiently.

She withdrew the plans for the earthquake device from her purse and smiled to herself "and have I got a story for you."

KT Pinto knows that it's hard to throw a good party. It's even harder when you're a Goddess throwing a party for dark deities and all anyone can talk about is Time.

By Invitation Only
KT Pinto

  Hosting a memorable party is not as easy as one would believe. People tend to think you just throw together some food, put out some paper plates, and invite random people, and you have a proper social gathering.
  Well, maybe that's how *some* hostesses have a party, but that's not the way I do it. I throw spectacular events, whether they be huge galas or a simple brunch for two. Some petty people say that I plan such events to make up for my spotted past. I ignore them; envy is a deadly sin and some other entity more powerful than I am will make them eventually pay for their words.
  The most important thing of all when planning a gathering is, of course, the guest list. If you invite the wrong people, a party could go from being a fun, energetic experience to a tense, draining one.
  I've been hostess more than enough times to make up my primary guest list rather quickly. My ilk was not what artists portray in their light, airy paintings of divinities. No happy sun goddesses, no nature women who dance joyfully, no matrons of hearth and home... it's not anything against them, but there is a point where beings can just be too nice. Imagine a room full of deities who are too polite to voice an opinion about *anything*! Then you just have hours upon hours of talk about the weather (which many of them create), and the latest fashions at Valhalla. That is a party death sentence; I've seen it happen. I've also been at gatherings with both the "light" and "dark" ladies together. It is always a large party (it has to be with so many guests), and you would think that there would be enough space for them to avoid each other. But an exchange of words in the ladies' lounge usually created more disastrous results at such a party than a golden apple at a wedding.
  My guest list is a little more colorful: Goddesses who speak their mind, whose ideas of romance leans more towards bawdy tales in dark alleys rather than hearts and flowers. Women who dance with passion and lust than with sensuality and seduction. They walk through the realms of death and destruction, chaos and fear, anger and crisis...
  And, in all honesty, some of these goddesses are just downright fun bitches.
  Why no men, you ask? Well that's a rather gauche question, but a logical one.

Men tend to change the dynamic of any situation, usually not for the better. But all you need is one male in a room full of females - and this happens with deities, humans, monsters, fay, and daemons - and chaos ensues.

Besides, the basis of my party is a ladies' tea. Males wouldn't know what to do with a cucumber sandwich and you don't want to know what they think a fingerbowl is for!

So my guest list varies only slightly from gathering to gathering; why mess with perfection? The next on the list of importance came location. Again, that was a pretty simple choice for me. I had never been banished from Eden, unlike my ex-husband and his second wife. I had left of my own volition. This meant I still had the key to the back gate, and the gatekeepers tended to look the other way when I came in. This is why I always offer the leftover food and slaves to them at the end of a gathering. One thing I've learned in all my centuries as hostess: be nice to the working man. If you're nice to them, they are there for you. A lot of hostesses don't feel that this is necessary. I'm sure they'll change their tune when they have to deal alone with a party crasher, a broken appliance, or a sudden apocalypse (and I'm speaking from experience on all three!).

There is a lovely clearing in the Garden where I sometimes host my Tea. It is serene, filled with the aroma of sweet-smelling flowers, and is big enough for my exquisitely laid out table, a comfortable conversation area, a space for dancing, and a place for Baba Yaga's house to rest (yes, I've tried explaining the no pets rule, but there's no getting through to the old woman).

Arranging the seating is a painstaking task under normal circumstances, but when you have goddesses who may not fit the norms of seating rules, it becomes neigh impossible... unless you are skilled like I am. I mean, how many hostesses would think to give up their seat at the head of the table to Kali, whose flailing hands tend to disrupt others when she got excited about a topic? Or who would make sure to keep the beer away from Sekhmet, who still remembers the hangover from all those millennia ago? Contrarily, a good hostess must make sure that the brandy is always within arms-length of Pele. And only an amateur would believe it was a good idea to let the Erinyes sit all together, sisters though they are.

These things and more were always on my mind when I plan out a tea. Luckily for me, I didn't have to worry about the food. My first few parties I tried to keep the purity of the event and do it all by myself, but even a goddess like me has to admit that there is just so much I could do alone, especially with all the different food tastes that everyone has. I interviewed a lot of caterers before finally settling on Hermafro Caterers, an all drag-queen catering service. I wasn't fazed by their fashion choices - hell, if Thor can wear dresses, why couldn't others? - but I was completely blown away by their food. They even managed to make raw meat taste good... or at least as good as raw meat could possibly taste. I used them at every event I had; their variety of culinary skills made the chances slim that the selection would ever get boring.

With the food taken care of, I could focus my attention on the invitations. You would think that invitations wouldn't be that important, especially in this day and age of magic missives and the internet, but nothing says class and style like a griffon-delivered, engraved invitation. Besides, there are certain things that must be asked of my guests, beyond requesting timely replies. I insist on clothing being worn at all times; when you invite Sheila na Gig to your events, this is an important request. As beautiful as the naked form is, it is not appropriate at a tea party. No pets also has to be specified on the invitation, as goddesses are known to be accompanied by birds, dogs, spiders, snakes... this is a tea party, not a meal at the great hall of Camelot (that's a party hosted by Morang LeFey or Morrigan, not by me!). My final request was to politely ask that they don't call forth their elements while at the tea. Many of these goddesses control messy elements, like primordial ooze, lava, blood, night (a curtain of night can be rather cumbersome on such a light, casual event), and other untidy things. And the most important thing about invitations: make sure that Eris not only has an invitation placed in her hands, but that she signs a form saying that she has received it. It takes a brave griffon to deliver this particular invitation.

The last thing to consider is a theme. Having the guests and location and food is fine, but for what reason would your guests want to be at your event? I mean, there are just so many times you can invite people over for no reason, even with the great offerings of food and company.

I have had quite a few successful themes over the years: the *Through the Looking Glass Gala*, the *Black and White Brunch*, the *Bring Your Human Pet Party*... that's not to say I didn't have some duds. Even an established hostess could miscalculate her guests' reactions to a theme. I had really thought the *Day of the Dead Dinner* would have been a big hit, but had neglected to tell some of the afterlife deities that bringing their charges was not a part of the theme. Corpses and rotting zombies do not do anything good for one's appetite.

The theme of my most current gathering was easy to come up with, because it was a Yule celebration. Even though many of our guests were from different cultures around the world, we all had changing-of-the-seasons celebrations. Because I was a Judeo-Christian entity, as well as a Pagan goddess, who's earthly home is in the northern hemisphere, my Yule celebration was held in late December, a few days before the Christmas holiday.

Of course, I didn't plan something as simple as a yuletide tea... any mere mortal can do that! My tea was called the *White and Green Gathering*. As any good guest would know, my theme referred to two separate things, the look of the party area being the obvious first meaning. I could not have a white and green party and not have said colors everywhere one looks. The green was a rather easy task: Eden was in bloom year round, with exotic plants and trees that ranged from huge oaks to sad drooping willows (my favorites!) to full, lush evergreens circling the grass-covered party-area. It was the white that was the problem... for an inexperienced mistress of ceremonies. It of course doesn't snow in Eden, but asking the favor of some snow sprites from the nearby mountains made that problem nonexistent. Some are wary of asking favors of sprites, but when you are the presumed 'mother of daemons', they tend not to take advantage.

The chairs around the table follow the green and white theme, as do the linens and the plates and flatware arranged at the start of the buffet table. I of course let my guests serve themselves, as low-class as that may seem. But a buffet gives guests a chance not only to mingle and chitchat, but it also gives them the opportunity to eat what entices their gullet and not be put into the awkward situation of declining what is offered to them.

The food, of course, does not follow any colored pattern; that would just be silly and tacky, although the bar did offer sour apple martinis, grasshoppers, frostbites and white sangrias as our specialty drinks, as well as a variety of other drinks made to order.

The second part of the theme was of course the clothing. A proper guest would contact me after receiving the invitation to find out what was the dress code. For example, if I were planning on wearing a certain color green, they would know not to wear something that would make us match. In this case, I didn't mind if the guests wore green or white or a combination of both. But no other colors would be allowed at my Yuletide event, and those who broke the dress code would not be allowed past the gates.

Sometimes I am a harsh mistress, but if you start letting things slide, eventually your parties turn into something akin to a black light club party in New York City. Tacky, tacky, tacky.

On the day of the tea, I stood at the edge of the clearing and smiled. Everything looked perfect and elegant. There was a slight breeze blowing through the area, rustling the leaves and tablecloth slightly, and making the falling snowflakes do a pretty dance that added a sweet touch to the scene. The caterers had just started arranging the trays for the cocktail hour, and I watched with slight amusement how the 'ladies' teetered on their high heels, but still masterfully carried the full trays with dexterity and grace.

I glanced up at the sky and smiled. It was almost time for the party to start, and if I knew my guests well enough, three of the goddesses were going to arrive right on time, unlike the rest who were always fashionably late like a proper goddess should.

As if on cue the trumpets sounded, and Blodeuwedd entered, her light green dress decorated with real flowers and owl feathers, her wide raptor eyes taking in the scene in one quick glance before hurrying over to me.

"Oh my! I'm not the first one here, am I?" she asked, the same way she did at every affair. "You know, without a man around the house to... delay... me, I always do seem to arrive before the others."

I have heard that same speech so many times, I could recite it word for word, including knowing that she was going to give the huge, knowing wink when she said 'delay'. She always made it sound like it wasn't her fault she was alone, like she didn't try to kill her husband only to have him kill her lover... I made the proper sympathetic sounds as I led her towards the bar. The tender and I exchanged a knowing look and the goddess sat on a stool. Blodeuwedd has unknowingly been drinking non-alcoholic beverages at my events since that dreadful incident at Nu

Kua's large spring gathering, where the nature goddess was aghast to find the drunken Welsher hanging from the pillars singing love songs. From that point forward I wouldn't let alcohol anywhere near her; her problems were not going to ruin one of my events. I left her in the bartender's capable hands and waited for the next guests to arrive.

I was not surprised by the next two guests: Hecate and Trivia went everywhere as one entity, as twins often do. They were both dressed in dark green velvet the color of graveyard mold, and I'm sure they planned it that way. They weren't identical... in fact, most people questioned if they were actually twins. They tried their best to look alike, coiffing their hair and wearing their make-up in the same way and making a point of finishing each other's sentences, even if they were standing at opposite sides of the room. It was rather annoying, but as hostess I didn't have to spend too much time conversing with them. In fact, they usually made a point of not chatting with me; something about me spooked the goddesses of graveyards and witchcraft... I watched them walk to the bar and stand on either side of Blodeuwedd like moldy bookends, ordering identical drinks. It was a comforting sight: it meant that they saw nothing less than expected from my party so far.

I knew I had a good fifteen minutes before the rest of the guests arrived. When the time came I gave a gracious wave to the sprites, who understood my cue and ceased the snowfall just as the rest of the guests arrived, including Baba Yaga and her house.

I stood by the ivy-covered arch and greeted each guest with a slightly secretive smile. There had been whispers around the various parthenons that many of my guests were planning to stay away because of the rumors that had been circulating around the world about the Time. They were worried that in the middle of the *White and Green Gathering* they would be called away because of the Time, like firefighters being summoned to an inferno. It would have been disastrous if more than half of my invited guests declined to come; the mark of a good party-giver is that guests will show up no matter what else is happening... including the presumed "Time".

It had been days before my gathering, and more than half the guest list still hadn't confirmed that they were coming. It was because of the taunting words of Nut, Oya, Nemesis, and Uzume that the rest of the goddesses were coming. They jeered their dark compatriots, calling them cowards and worse (we were never known for having a charming vocabulary) and saying that they were going to my party, the Time be damned... so to speak.

Those four goddesses each received a lovely little hostess gift when they arrived. Each gift was sweet and fresh, bundled up in swaddling and calmed with a drop of brandy on their gums...

I could feel a tension coming from the rest of the guests, even as they went through the motions of having a pleasant experience. It was like they were waiting for the Time to arrive. That would certainly not do! They can be tense on their own time, but certainly not during one of my events!

I stood next to Eris as the goddess filled her plate with caviar and eggs. "I do not like this one bit," I whispered to her.

"The caviar?" she asked, taking a bite. "Seems all right to me."

"No, not the caviar! You know as well as I do that everything Hermafro makes is exquisite." I nodded towards the guests, who were milling around the clearing, having conversations about - I am saddened to say - the weather and the latest fashions in Delphi (which is only a step up from Valhalla...). "Who are these women and what happened to the real dark goddesses?"

Eris nodded. "They are a pretty sad lot this time around. This can't be because of the Time, can it?"

"Do you really think that is going to happen? Today of all days?"

"My dear, I don't think even the Time would be stupid enough to interrupt one of your gatherings!"

"This is very true."

"See?" she said with a grin. "Simple."

"So tell me," I asked, "why are you not tense and boring like the rest of them?"

"Me? The Goddess of Discord?" She laughed. "Why in the world would I be concerned about the Time?"

I nodded as she walked away; that's when I noticed the silence. The goddesses milled around like they were at a funeral instead of a party. Oh no, this would never do. I scanned the crowd for a moment before spotting the Sphinx, in human form, having a quiet conversation with Sekhmet. I called to her across the clearing, causing a few of the goddesses of fear and dread to jump in surprise.

"Sphinx! I think these ladies need their brains worked a little bit!"

"Yes!" Eris replied from the bar. "And none of those four-legged, three-legged puzzles. Tell us some good ones!"

The Sphinx hesitated, but my guests' half-hearted comments of encouragement spurred her on. She walked across the clearing and sat on the garden swing, swaying slowly. "OK now... let me think..."

A slow smile spread across her face as the goddesses sat on the ground around her. "How about this one: The human body holds nine quarts of blood. Suppose you were a human alone in the desert and accidently cut a major artery. If you bleed at one cup a minute, how long will it take you to bleed to death?"

"Oooo, blood!" Sekhmet cooed. "My favorite!"

"Mine too!" Kali agreed, "It's so much fun watching them bleed..."

Arachne hissed at them. "Hush! I'm trying to figure this out!"

"When I killed the boys," Medea said aloud, "it didn't take them long to die..."

Nyx sighed, her white skirt billowing around her as she sat on one of the benches nearby. "This could take a long while..."

"How many quarts was it again?" Pele asked, sipping her brandy.

"Nine," the Sphinx answered.

"Well then," Uzume reasoned, "all we have to do is figure out how many cups are in a quart..."

"That sounds like math!" Morgan said, pointing to the questioner. "And the

Apocalypse 13

Sphinx isn't known for her math skills, she's known to tell riddles."

"Would you all really just sit around waiting to bleed out?" Sheila na Gig cackled, causing the Sphinx to smile. "I don't know about the rest of you, but I'd put a tourniquet on that thing and live to kill the person who hurt me."

The Sphinx started clapping. "Very good Sheila! Very good! Do you want another one?"

This time the response was a more energetic as the women got into the party mood. The riddles got more difficult, the jokes bawdier, and the alcohol flowed more freely (except in Blodeuwedd's glass, of course).

They didn't even realize how much time had passed until the ladies from Hermafro announced that the main course was ready. My guests, seeming to have forgotten that Time may be closing in on them, nearly ran to the buffet. Only Eris was left behind, grinning in a way that I wasn't very happy about.

"What?" I asked her.

She tried to compose her expression into one of seriousness. "What what?"

"That look on your face," I said. "I don't like it."

"Not all of us can be Janus," she replied. "I was born with only one face."

"It's going to happen, isn't it?"

She started chuckling. "Look, no one told you to have your party so close to the oracles' prediction."

"But they weren't *our* oracles. I'm certain they're wrong."

"Whatever gets you through the day, my friend." She put her arm around my waist and pulled me towards the buffet table. "But remember, Chicomeccatl is from the region of the Time, and she is a guest at *all* of your gatherings. You may want to take them a little more seriously..." She saw the expression on my face. "Unless that doesn't go with your party theme, of course."

That was really the problem I was having: I didn't want anything ruining my party. I couldn't understand my guests' reaction to the rumors... so what if the Time was neigh? The Time was a period of darkness, of destruction, of blood. What about this prophesy made them all squeamish? It's not like they did anything else with their lives; this would stir things up...

And that's when it hit me: yes, these were all-powerful dark goddesses, but these bitches were lazy. They only caused destruction and pain when they were angry, jealous, or drunk. But to *have* to do something because of an outside force... they weren't being nervous and concerned. They were sulking like petulant children. This is why the food and jokes and alcohol were appeasing them. They were satisfying their own selfish desires.

Having left paradise because of my insatiable want of sex, it was easy for me to understand that.

A while later I filled my plate with food and sat in between Skadi and Morrigan, feeling the rush that hostesses get from the satisfaction of throwing a successful event. My guests were full and smiling, and the conversation hadn't stopped since the Sphinx told her riddles. All in all, even with the rocky start, this was still a successful event.

And now all that was left was the dancing.

I didn't need to hire a band; no respectable goddess would get to maturity without learning to play at least one instrument, and showing off one's skills was a part of being a deity. Going through the instrument trunk, it didn't take long for the music to start playing and the dance floor to fill up with writhing, gyrating goddesses.

It also didn't take long for the clothing to start coming off. I didn't mind; we were done eating, and with all the alcohol that had been drunk, I was surprised the clothing stayed on as long as it did.

Even with the snow falling, the goddesses were sweating as they pressed against each other as the music grew louder and faster. I didn't dance; I was the hostess. I walked through the crowd with a tray of drinks, making sure that my guests got a balance of hydration and drunken ecstasy, both in drink and pill form (you think you've had hard drugs? Until you get your supply from Tartarus, don't talk to me). Blodeuwedd was given flavored soda and children's aspirin, but no one was dumb enough to tell her...

The music started to pulsate wildly as the motion on the dance floor became less like dancing and more like passionate writhing. Mouths and hands and fangs started to roam as the weather hit blizzard conditions (the sprites had gotten into the pills, I later found out). Just as the dance was about to hit a climax - if not more than one -a phone suddenly started to ring.

Everyone came to a halt as the ringing continued in the frozen silence.

No one was allowed to bring their cellphones to one of my events. It was a rule that didn't even need to be put on the invitation. The gatekeepers removed all electronics from guests before they were allowed into Eden. It wouldn't be Paradise if technology was allowed in it.

I closed my eyes in dread and turned to where I knew it would be. Hanging in the air was an old red rotary phone. With a sigh I picked up the receiver and whispered, "Yeah?"

"It's Time."

"Damn."

I turned to the goddesses, all of whom had sobered up rather quickly. "It's Time."

There was a collective moan as they started picking their clothing out of the snowdrifts. Most of them didn't even bother getting dressed as they ran towards the gate.

I looked at the mess that was left behind and sighed again, knowing it would be here when I got back. Nothing really much affects Eden...

I turned to the ladies of Hermafro and sighed once more, knowing I was breaking a cardinal rule. "Stay here," I said. "Do *not*, under any circumstances, go through that gate."

Hey, it's tough finding a good catering service these days...

I tore off the bottom tiers of my gown as I ran out of Eden and into the barn, passing monster after monster until I got to the last stall, where a huge sloth-like creature looked up at me with three sleepy eyes. At first he looked confused, knowing it wasn't yet time to eat, then I opened his gate and his eyes widened, revealing the single long eyelash that wrapped up and around the right side of each orb. I only opened his gate for one reason.

"Come on Beast," I said, climbing onto his back. "It's Time."

As we flew out of the barn and picked up speed, preparing to break through the Earth's crust, I looked down at the clearing in Eden where my party had been and smiled.

My gathering brought forth the start of the Second Apocalypse. Deities will be talking about this party for millennia to come!

Author Biographies

Keith R.A. DeCandido
Keith R.A. DeCandido's other stories featuring Cassie Zukav can be found in *Tales from the House Band* Volumes 1 & 2, *Urban Nightmares*, *Bad-Ass Faeries 4: It's Elemental*, and her own short-story collection, *Ragnarok and Roll: Tales of Cassie Zukav, Weirdness Magnet*. When he isn't writing about Cassie, Keith writes fantastical cop novels (the fantasy procedurals *Dragon Precinct*, *Unicorn Precinct*, *Goblin Precinct*, *Tales from Dragon Precinct*, and *Gryphon Precinct*; the *SCPD* series of superhero procedurals), media tie-ins (most recently the *Leverage* novel *The Zoo Job*, a *Kung Fu Panda* comic book story, the *Farscape* comic series, more than two dozen pieces of *Star Trek* fiction, and tons more), shared-world stories (contributing novels and short fiction to Jonathan Maberry's *V-Wars*, Steven Savile's *Viral*, and Aaron Rosenberg & David Niall Wilson's *The Scattered Earth*), and the twice-weekly *Star Trek: The Next Generation* Rewatch at Tor.com. Keith is also a musician, currently the percussionist for the parody band Boogie Knights, a black belt in *Kenshikai* karate, a professional editor of almost two decades' standing, a veteran podcaster (*The Chronic Rift*, *Dead Kitchen Radio*, *HG World*, *The Dome*, *Gypsy Cove*), and probably some other stuff that he can't remember due to the lack of sleep. Find out more at Keith's web site at www.DeCandido.net, which is a gateway to pretty much everything he does, like his blog, his Facebook page, his Twitter feed, his editorial services for hire, etc.

Patrick Thomas
With over a million words in print, Patrick Thomas keeps busy writing the popular fantasy humor series Murphy's Lore (which includes 8 books- Tales From Bulfinche's Pub, Fools' Day, Through The Drinking Glass, Shadow Of The Wolf, Redemption Road, Bartender Of The Gods, Nightcaps and Empty Graves) as well as the After Hours spin offs Fairy With A Gun, Fairy Rides The Lightning, Dead To Rites and Lore & Dysorder. His Mystic Investigators series has grown to include the books Bullets & Brimstone and From The Shadows both with John L. French and Once More Upon A Time and the upcoming Partners In Crime both with Diane Raetz. He has co-edited two anthologies - Hear Them Roar and the vampire themed New Blood. Patrick's syndicated humorous advice column Dear Cthulhu has been collected in Have A Dark Day and Good Advice For Bad People. A number of his books are part of the set and props department at the CSI television show. Laurence Fishburne's production company Cinema Gypsy Productions has taken a film and television option on Patrick Thomas' urban fantasy Fairy With A Gun. He was voted Preditors & Editors favorite author of 2010 and first runner up in 2011.As an artist his work has graced covers for Dark Quest, Padwolf and Marietta, interiors and a cover for Space & Time magazine, a cover for Cemetery Moon magazine and comic covers for Ghostman. A mockumentary about him has recently surfaced on Youtube. To learn more, drop by his website at www.patthomas.net.

Apocalypse 13

John L. French

Having worked over thirty years for the Baltimore Police Department as a crime scene investigator John L. French has witnessed more than his share of what horrors one person can inflict on another. Working with patrol officers and detectives, John has been involved in putting many of these people behind bars for very long sentences. In 1992 John began writing crime fiction, basing his stories on his experiences on the streets of what some have called one of the most dangerous cities in the country. His books include *The Devil of Harbor City, Past Sins, Here There Be Monsters* and *Paradise Denied*. He is the editor of *Bad Cop, No Donut*, To Hell in a Fast Car: On the Road to Death and Disaster and Mermaids 13: Tales from the Sea.

Edward J. McFadden III

Edward J. McFadden III juggles a full-time career as a university administrator and teacher, with his writing aspirations. His first published novel, a mysterious-dark-thriller called The Black Death of Babylon, will be released October 2012 from Post Mortem Press. His steampunk fantasy novelette, *Starwisps*, was recently published in the anthology Fantastic Stories of the Imagination, his story *Breaking Down* is forthcoming in the print edition of Abandoned Towers Magazine, and his novella *Anywhere But Here* is scheduled for publication in 2013 by Padwolf Publishing. He is the author/editor of six published books: Jigsaw Nation, Deconstructing Tolkien: A Fundamental Analysis of The Lord of the Rings (to be re-released in eBook format Fall 2012), Time Capsule, The Second Coming, Thoughts of Christmas, and The Best of Pirate Writings. He has had more than 50 short stories published in places like Hear Them Roar, CrimeSpree Magazine, Terminal Fright, Cyber-Psycho's AOD, The And, and The Arizona Literary Review. Over the last seven years he has written six novels, all of which are at various stages of rewriting and submission for publication. He lives on Long Island with his wife Dawn, their daughter Samantha, and their mutt Oli. See for all things Ed, check out www.edwardmcfadden.com

Samantha Mills

Samantha Mills lives in far-too-sunny San Diego with her husband and brat cats. There she splits her time between writing, studying, and working in several museums. You can read more about her at http://vicariousmisadventures.blogspot.com .

Briana Vandenbroek

When she isn't writing about how NASA's moon rocks affect her werewolves, Briana Vandenbroek is either reading to her daughter, trying to keep her doomed flowers alive, or dueling with her husband in World of Warcraft.

Matt Schiariti

Matt Schiariti was born in Trenton New Jersey into an Italian blue collar family. The youngest of four kids, he was the 'happy little accident' that came by eight years after mom and pop thought the house was full enough. As the youngest, if you believe in pop psychology, Matt was predestined to follow more artistic pursuits.

In his younger days, you could most often find him with a pencil in hand on the family room floor, doodling his own comic book creations into surplus computer printout binders from his mother's office. As he entered his teens, despite having won several amateur youth art awards, he lost the ambition to be a famous comic book artist and picked up the guitar. His love for music never wavered, even as he went to college and earned a degree in Civil Engineering. He played lead guitar in two working cover bands for several years in his early thirties until the eminent pitter patter of little feet started to echo through the house.

Fast forward to 2012. Matt has always been a voracious reader. His passion for books eventually planted the idea in his head that he should give writing a try. After having conquered the art and music world (in his own mind) he figured 'how hard could it be?' Turns out, it's harder than he expected but he enjoys the process. When a proposed joint novel writing effort with a friend fell through, Matt started writing his own material in February of 2012.

He currently lives in Southern New Jersey with his wife, six year old daughter, a crazy mutt named Dizzy (aka 'The Furricane') and three hermit crabs. He works as an engineer for the government by day and when he's not reading or chewing his nails to the nub trying to iron out a plot hole or a wrinkle in a story, he can be found spending time with his family or playing guitar in Madison Square Basement or probably drinking a beer. Hollow is his first published short story...but hopefully not the only thing of his to see the light of day.

David Lee Summers

David Lee Summers is the author of seven novels and over sixty published short stories. His writing spans a wide range of the imaginative from science fiction to fantasy to horror. David's novels include the wild west/steampunk adventure *Owl Dance* and *Dragon's Fall: Rise of the Scarlet Order*, which tells the story of a band of vampire mercenaries who fight evil. His short stories and poems have appeared in such magazines and anthologies as *Realms of Fantasy, Cemetery Dance, Human Tales, Six-Guns Straight From Hell,* and *Bad-Ass Faeries 3: In All Their Glory.* In 2010, he was nominated for the Science Fiction Poetry Association's Rhysling Award and he currently serves as the SFPA's vice president. In addition to writing, David edits the quarterly science fiction and fantasy magazine *Tales of the Talisman* and has edited two science fiction anthologies, *Space Pirates* and *Space Horrors*. When not working with the written word, David operates telescopes at Kitt Peak National Observatory. Learn more about David at davidleesummers.com.

Terri Osborne

Terri Osborne has far too many things on her plate, but she wouldn't have it any other way. Her literary life is spent wandering the annals of time, venturing as far back as the First Century CE with *Doctor Who*, and as far into the future as the 24th Century with *Star Trek. A Djinn, A Werewolf, and Grey Walk Into A Bar* continues her original *Realms Next Door* universe, where mermaids, ancient djinn, dark fae, vampires, werewolves, and little grey aliens live and work alongside humanity. She is a regular contributor to syfy.com, and is the owner of Loose Canon, an alternate history publishing venture.

Hildy Silverman

Hildy Silverman is the publisher of Space and Time, a 46-year-old magazine featuring fantasy, horror, and science fiction. She is also the author of several works of short fiction, including "Damned Inspiration" (2009, Bad-Ass Fairies, Ackley-McPhail, ed.), "The Vampire Escalator of the Passaic Promenade" (2010, New Blood, Thomas, ed.), "The Darren" (2009, Witch Way to the Mall?, Friesner, ed.), and "Sappy Meals" (2010, Fangs for the Mammaries, Friesner, ed.). She also contributed an essay on the history of genre magazines to *Sense of Wonder: A Century of Science Fiction* (2011, Leigh Grossman, et al, ed). Hildy is the co-president of the Garden State Speculative Fiction Writers and in the "real" world, she is a Social Media Visibility Content Specialist at LexisNexis.

Robert E Waters

Since 1994, Robert E Waters has worked in the computer and board gaming industry as technical writer, editor, designer, and producer. A member of the Science Fiction and Fantasy Writers of America, his first professional fiction sale came in 2003 with the story "The Assassin's Retirement Party," *Weird Tales*, Issue #332. Since then he has sold stories to Nth Degree, Nth Zine, Black Library Publishing (Games Workshop), Padwolf Publishing, Mundania Press, Marietta Publishing, Dragon Moon Press, and Dark Quest Books. His most recent stories ("The Game of War" , "The Heirloom", and "The Great Grantville Gander Pull") were published in the *Grantville Gazette*, Baen Books' online magazine dedicated to stories set in their best-selling 1632/Ring of Fire Alternate History series. Between the years of 1998 – 2006, he also served as an assistant editor to Weird Tales. Robert currently lives in Baltimore, Maryland, with his wife Beth, their son Jason, and their cat Buzz.

Roy Mauritsen

It was bound to happen, with pictures being worth what they are in words, that a creative, successful award winning artist would eventually entertain the idea of writing a novel. Roy's writing interests and a love of fairy tales started at an early age with a dusty, 1941 hardcover edition of Alice's Adventures in Wonderland. But for this artist-turned-writer, the saying "a picture is worth a thousand words" wasn't enough. He had a story to be told, and it demanded to be written. His first published novel, an epic fantasy fairytale adventure entitled Shards Of The Glass Slipper: Queen Cinder was published in March 2012. Roy has also somehow managed to have a successful career as a digital artist and graphic designer, and also designs book covers and TV commercials. When he's not trying to figure out how that happened, he enjoys photography, volleyball, SCUBA diving, and traveling. But most of the time, he works on 3D artwork, writing short stories for upcoming anthologies, and working on the follow up to Shards Of The Glass Slipper. www.roymauritsen.com

Jordan Pettit

Jordan Pettit has wanted to be a writer since he was a small child when he used to jot down ideas for books and screenplays. He has always enjoyed the freedom and creativity that writing allows. This is his first foray into the world of urban fantasy and he is currently working on a sequel to this story. He plans to continue writing in the future and hopes to one day have his writing transitioned to the movies.

KT Pinto

KT Pinto - awarded 2012's Best Author on Staten Island - writes about vampyres, mutants, witches, merfolk, werebeasts, deities, courtesans, criminals, and pop stars... sometimes all in the same story. For more information, go to www.ktpinto.com

E-BOOK Edition

DECONSTRUCTING TOLKIEN
Edward J. McFadden III

A fundamental analysis of
The Lord of the Rings
& The Hobbit

With Foreword by
Tom Piccirilli

PADWOLF
PUBLISHING

visit padwolf.com

TALES FROM THE SEA
MERMAIDS 13
ANTHOLOGY

Edited by
John L. French

Featuring the talents of:
Danielle Ackley-McPhail, Michael A. Black, James Chambers, John L. French, C. J. Henderson, C. Ellett Logan, Roy A. Mauritsen, Terri Osborne, Darren W. Pearce & Neal Levin, KT Pinto, Hildy Silverman, Patrick Thomas, Robert E. Waters

AVAILABLE NOW!
PADWOLF PUBLISHING

v i s i t p a d w o l f . c o m

Even the things that go *Bump* in the night will learn that you <u>DON'T</u> mess with...
Terrorbelle.

"Thomas certainly brings the goods to the table when it comes to writing urban fiction...I promise, you will love... Terrorbelle: Fairy With a Gun. Who doesn't love a well-stacked, ass-kicking, gun-toting, woman with bullet-proof, razor-sharp wings that investigates all manner of supernatural spookiness? I know I do, and Thomas's humor shows through in every tale. Jim Butcher and Laurell K Hamilton have nothing on Thomas." The Raven's Barrow

From The Murphy's Lore Universe Of
PATRICK THOMAS

Find us on Facebook

www.padwolf.com & www.terrorbelle.com

PADWOLF
PUBLISHING

v i s i t   p a d w o l f . c o m

One Last Chance to Save
Happily Ever After

Can a group of heroes including Goldenhair, Red Riding Hood and Rapunzel help General Snow White and her dwarven resistance fighters defeat the tyrannical Queen Cinderella? And will they succeed before a war with Wonderland destroys everything?

Their only hope to stop Cinderella's quest for power lies with a young girl named Patience Muffet who carries the fabled shards of Cinderella's glass slippers.

Roy Mauritsen's fantasy adventure fairy tale epic begins with *Shards Of The Glass Slipper: Queen Cinder*.

"Fantastic...
A Magnificent Epic!"
-*Sarah Beth Durst* author of
Into The Wild & Drink, Slay, Love

"The Brothers Grimm
meets
Lord Of The Rings!"
-*Patrick Thomas*, author
of the Murphy's Lore series

"....A worthy writer with real talent and a **unique vision**, a combination rare and important."
- Janet Morris, author of Beyond Sanctuary & The Sacred Band

"...**Groundbreaking** twist on fairy tales."
-Edward J. McFadden III, author of Deconstructing Tolkien

PADWOLF
PUBLISHING

Find us on: facebook.

In paperback & e-book
Find out more at:
shardsoftheglassslipper.com
padwolf.com

IT'S A CRIME TO MISS THESE GREAT STORIES!

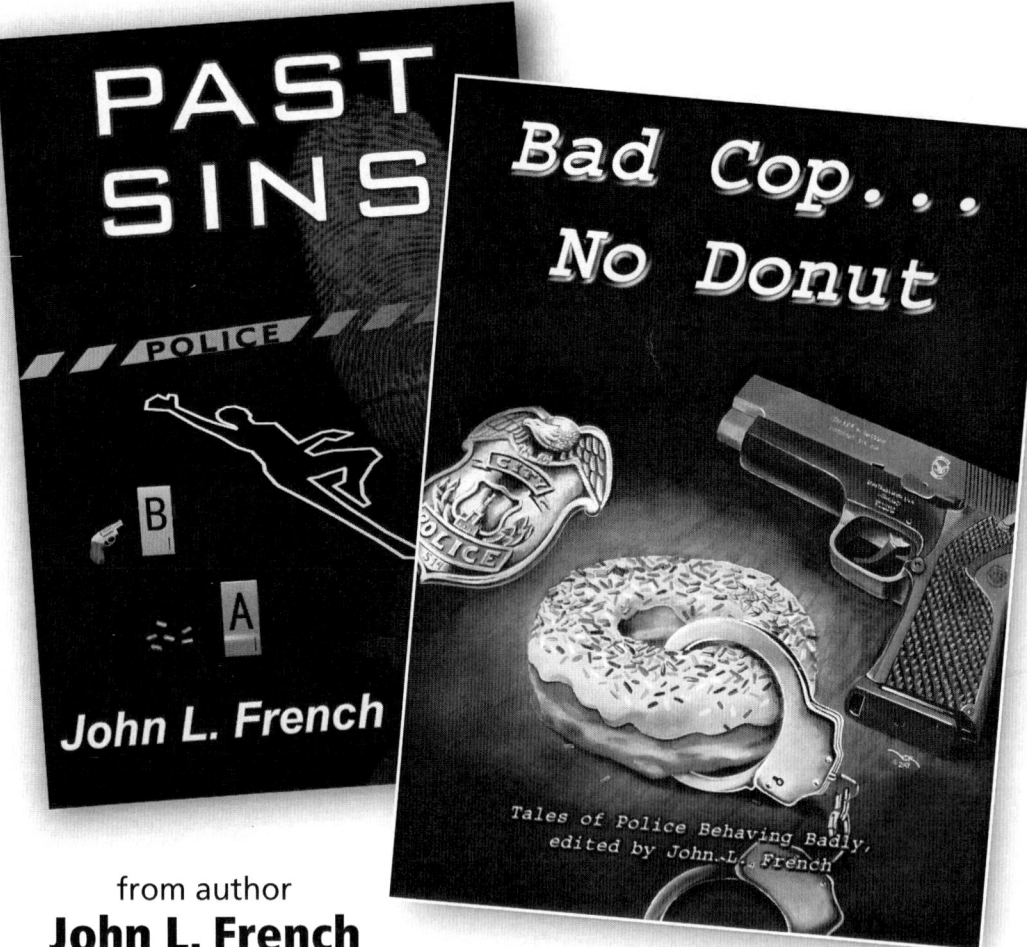

PAST SINS
John L. French

Bad Cop... No Donut
Tales of Police Behaving Badly,
edited by John L. French

from author
John L. French

PADWOLF PUBLISHING

v i s i t   p a d w o l f . c o m

TRY SOMETHING *NEW!*
(Don't worry, she won't bite...much)

NEW BLOOD

Try a taste...
life is short and
undead is not
always forever or
what you expect

Edited by
Diane Raetz and Patrick Thomas

PADWOLF PUBLISHING

v i s i t   p a d w o l f . c o m

YOUR NEXT FAVORITE BOOK
IS JUST A MOUSE CLICK AWAY
AT PADWOLF.COM!

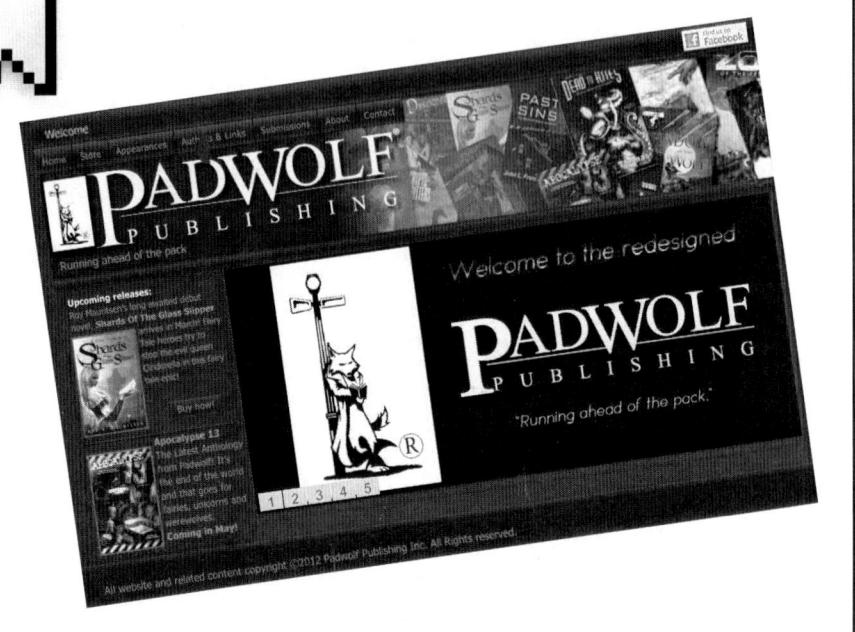

- **Buy books!** Novels, anthologies and more! Urban Fantasy, Horror, Mystery, Science Fiction, Epic Fantasy, Young Adult, just to name a few. From vampires to gun toting fairies, we've got all of your favorites in one place. Check out our newest releases and e-books or browse through our extensive catalog—including the Murphy's Lore series by Patrick Thomas!
- Find out the **latest news** about our authors!
- Location! Location! Location! Get the scoop on upcoming **author appearances** & booth shows!
- **Get social!** Padwolf Publishing is on Facebook! Follow your favorite padwolf authors on Twitter!
- Check out the **Padwolf blog**! Where our authors and editors contribute thoughts, rants, tips and tidbits!

VISIT THE NEWLY RENOVATED
WWW.PADWOLF.COM